# ALL SHE WAS WORTH

# ALL SHE WAS WORTH

## Miyuki Miyabe

Translated by Alfred Birnbaum

KODANSHA INTERNATIONAL
Tokyo • New York • London

Originally published by Futabasha, Tokyo, in 1992 under the title *Kasha*.

Distributed in the United States by Kodansha America, Inc., 114 Fifth Avenue, New York, N.Y. 10011, and in the United Kingdom and continental Europe by Kodansha Europe Ltd., 95 Aldwych, London WC2B 4JF. Published by Kodansha International Ltd., 17-14 Otowa 1-chome, Bunkyo-ku, Tokyo 112, and Kodansha America, Inc. Copyright © 1992 by Miyuki Miyabe. English translation copyright © 1996 by Kodansha International Ltd. All rights reserved. Printed in Japan.
First edition, 1996
ISBN 4–7700–1922–X
96 97 98 99   10 9 8 7 6 5 3 2 1

**Library of Congress Cataloging-in-Publication Data**

Miyabe, Miyuki, 1960–
    [Kasha.   English]
    All she was worth / Miyuki Miyabe ; translated by Alfred Birnbaum.
        p.   cm.
    ISBN 4-7700-1922-X
    I. Birnbaum, Alfred.   II. Title.
PL856.I856K3713  1996
895.6'35–dc20                                                    96-44886
                                                                    CIP

# ALL SHE WAS WORTH

$\diamond$ 1 $\diamond$

The rain started just as the train pulled out of Ayase Station. An icy rain. No wonder his knee had been aching all day. Shunsuke Honma stood by the train door, looking out, one hand on the handrail, the other on his umbrella. He'd wedged the tip of the umbrella against the floor to take the weight off his leg.

At three in the afternoon, any outbound train was likely to be empty. Plenty of seats, if he'd felt like sitting. There were hardly any passengers, only two girls in high school uniforms, a drowsy house-wife slumped over a large handbag, and some kid up by the driver's compartment rocking to the rhythm from his headphones. So few you could get a good look at each face, one by one. No reason to insist on standing.

Obviously, sitting would have been a lot more comfortable. He'd been out since midmorning—first, at his physical therapy session, then visiting the Division. Not once had he gotten a taxi; he'd managed it on his own two feet and public transport. His back felt like an iron plate.

Everybody in Investigation had been out on call, except for the Division Chief, who gave him such an overblown welcome-back it only drove home the unspoken "What are you doing here?" Which made him uneasy, especially since this was only the second time he'd showed up since taking sick leave at the end of last year. But making him feel good wasn't part of the deal, was it? It wasn't a game, where they brought in a replacement if you got sent off the field on a penalty. They could just as easily change all the rules and eliminate your position—what was to stop them? For the first time he felt a pang of regret about leaving.

That's why he had been determined to stay on his feet all the time —his pride was hurt. Even though nobody was looking. Or *because* nobody was looking—nobody saying, "Looks like you're having a rough time."

Honma thought back to when he had been Deputy Chief of Juvenile. There had been this one shoplifter, a real pro. If a friend of hers hadn't turned her in, they would probably never have caught her. She took her special discounts at only the best boutiques, but she never wore any of the clothes in public, and wasn't in a hurry to sell them, either. She'd go back to her own room, lock the door, and try on whole outfits in front of a full-length mirror. Clothes, watches and other accessories—posing like a model in a fashion magazine. Just for the mirror. Out on the street, she'd wear the same old jeans with the knees frayed through.

Was that all really twenty years ago? The girl was probably a mother herself by now, with a kid of her own that age. Would she even remember a rookie detective who tried to lecture his way through her wall of silence, but couldn't even get his words straight?

The rain showed no sign of letting up. Drops streamed down the train windows, leaving fat, wet streaks through which Honma could see buildings that seemed to huddle under a low bank of clouds. Funny, if this all turned to snow and blanketed the dingy streets, it would only look warmer. *That's just what you Tokyo folks think*, Chizuko had once told him. *You don't know real snow.* Still, whenever the gray city streets turned white, Honma couldn't help thinking so.

At Kameari Station a few more passengers got on. As a tight formation of five middle-aged women rammed past, Honma tried to move aside while keeping the weight off his left leg. Without thinking, he let out a groan. The high school girls glanced at him. *That guy's creepy…*

They crossed the river at Nakagawa, where the red-and-white smokestacks of the Mitsubishi Paper Mill belched thick columns of smoke. Even factories looked different at different seasons and temperatures. This sleet was turning to snow, all right.

Getting off at Kanamachi was a struggle. They ought to set aside special train cars for the handicapped, not just those pathetic "silver seats." Let the doors open and close nice and slow, too, so a person didn't need to rush. He still had to fight his way down the station stairs, though. Served him right for doing things the hard way. If he wasn't careful, the umbrella would slip on the wet floor and he'd take a spill.

It was only a five-minute ride to the housing project on the south side of Minamoto Park, but he took a cab after all. As they drove past the canal, he noticed a man bundled up in winter clothes and a down vest, out there in the murk with line and tackle. It made him feel old.

The taxi pulled up at his apartment block. Honma took the elevator to the third floor. Down at the end of the corridor a door opened and there was Makoto. He must have been at the window and seen the cab arrive.

"You're home late," the boy said as he hurried over to lend a hand.

"I'm fine," Honma assured him. His son was just ten years old—too small to lean on. If Honma slipped, they'd both get hurt. But the boy shuffled along sideways, anyway, arms out to catch him if he fell.

Holding the door open was Tsuneo Isaka, a guy who did some of the cooking and cleaning for them. Honma had to smile at the reception he was getting.

"You must be exhausted," said Isaka. "When it started raining, I got worried. Why didn't you use your umbrella?"

"It's got a tear in it," Honma replied, poking his way in amongst the shoes in the entryway. "Beat-up old thing, it's only good for a cane."

"Oh." Isaka's hair had gone mostly gray, but his build was still solid. He leaned in toward him, offering a shoulder as support.

"No sense buying a cane—not for a while yet, anyway."

"You got a point there."

A warm smell drifted through the three-bedroom apartment. Isaka must be heating up some sweet saké. Honma moved toward his room to change his clothes but paused on the way, putting one hand on the wall for balance, looking back over his shoulder at Makoto. "Anything to report?"

The family greeting. That's what Honma used to ask Chizuko

whenever he rang up from outside or finally saw her after several nights out on the job. It was three years since she died, leaving him on his own with Makoto, but he still asked the same thing. *Anything to report?* And the answer was always, *No, not really. Nothing much.*

But not today. "There was one thing."

Honma automatically looked at Isaka, but it was Makoto who had spoken.

"There was a phone call. From Uncle Jun."

Uncle Jun. Who the—?

"You know, he works at a bank," the boy explained.

"Oh—you mean Jun Kurisaka?" Yes, the Kurisakas were on Chizuko's side of the family.

"Yeah, yeah. Big tall guy."

"Hey, good memory there, young man! So you heard his voice and knew right away who it was?"

Makoto shook his head. "I answered like I knew and then I thought some."

Isaka laughed.

"What time did he call?"

"About an hour ago."

"What'd he have to say?"

"Said he couldn't tell me. He asked if you would be home tonight. He said it was real important, so he'd come over."

"Tonight?"

"Uh-huh."

"I wonder what's up. Well, guess there's nothing to do but wait—if he's coming like he says."

Honma went to change, and returned just in time to see Makoto tiptoeing off with a tray and two steaming cups of sweet saké.

The boy answered before his father could ask. "I'm goin' up to Kazzy's place."

That's fine, his father thought. But what he said was, "Does Kazzy drink sweet saké?"

"He says he's never had it."

Kazzy was a classmate who lived on the fifth floor. Both parents worked, so half the time the kid was up there alone.

"Don't use the elevator. If you spill any in there, it'll be a pain to clean up."

"Yeah, I know," he said, heading out the door.

Honma pulled up a chair and let out the deep sigh he'd been holding back.

Isaka set a cup down in front of him. "You should go a bit easier on yourself."

"Tell that to the physical therapist. She thinks just the opposite."

"Tough, is she?"

"Professional sadist is more like it."

"Well, chalk it up to experience." Isaka's round face broke into a smile that was reflected in the polished tabletop. He certainly ran a clean house: no rings where glasses had been set down, no coffee stains. "I'll make supper for three," he added, his thick fingers wrapped around a cup.

"Thanks."

"Two, three—makes no difference. But this Kurisaka—Jun, was it?—he's a relative?"

"A distant one. He's the son of my wife's cousin."

"Which makes him 'Uncle' to Makoto."

"Which makes it too complicated to sort out. We're not that close anyway." So what could be bringing him all the way out here? "I don't think I've seen him in years. He didn't come to Chizuko's funeral."

Honma kept her memorial photograph in the alcove off to one side of the living room, near the window, where it got plenty of sun in the daytime. He glanced over in that direction, and Chizuko stared back from the black frame. She had a puzzled look, her head tilted to one side.

"Don't look now," said Isaka, gazing out the window. "It's snowing."

## ✧ 2 ✧

It was almost nine when Jun Kurisaka arrived.

Meanwhile a good couple of inches of snow had fallen on the roads and rooftops. A north wind had picked up when the sun went down, sending a hail of small white arrows through the frozen air. By six, Honma had already told himself that Jun wasn't coming. There was no phone call, but first the television and then the evening paper, when it finally came, warned of blizzard conditions. And when he saw on the seven o'clock news that not only the outer track of the Yamanote Line commuter loop but also the entire Chuo and Sobu lines were out of commission, he felt sure he was right.

Jun lived in Funabashi, way out in the suburbs east of Tokyo. Honma had been there only once, years ago. The reason for the visit now escaped him, but he seemed to recall riding a bus twenty or thirty minutes from the station. So at night, in this weather, it was hard to imagine anybody traipsing up here north of the city, only to head back later across the bay to Chiba; even on a clear day, the trip was at least an hour and a half each way, what with train transfers and waiting time. If Jun were prepared to go to those lengths on a night like this, something must be wrong.

That's what worried him—call it a premonition.

Honma and Makoto had just finished eating when the doorbell rang. Jun's face looked thinner than Honma remembered. In midwinter, of course, people seem to shrink a bit into themselves, but Jun's drawn features weren't due only to the cold.

Jun had already had dinner, so Makoto just made some coffee for the grown-ups and hurried off to take a bath. Honma had taught him not to stick his nose into adults' conversation without permission;

it was an ironclad rule. And besides, "Uncle" or not, the boy didn't really know Jun. For that matter, neither did Honma. When had the young man gotten so tall?

"So how old are you now?" Honma asked straight out.

"Twenty-nine," said Jun. "It's been seven years. I guess I haven't been in touch since Aunt Chizuko sent me that graduation present, right before I started working."

Ah, yes—Chizuko had agonized over it: *Just what does one give someone who's going off to work in a bank?*

"Still at the Kanda Branch?" Honma said, dredging his memory. But which bank—Daiichi? Sanwa?

"Got transferred all over the place. Kanda, Oshiage, now I'm in Shibuya. But I'm bound to get bumped again this year or so."

"Must be tough."

"Oh, I can't complain. Financial institutions are like that. I don't mind doing the rounds. And I feel I've found my niche workwise. So it's okay with me."

*Doing the rounds*—that must mean drumming up new business. Honma nodded as if he were following this. It was now too late to ask which bank it was.

"But Uncle Shunsuke, you were moved around to different precincts, too, weren't you?" His face clouded over suddenly. "I'm very sorry ..."

Here they come, thought Honma. The formalities.

"I haven't even offered my condolences yet."

*Yet.* It had been three years, but it was all just yesterday to Jun.

The young man peered down at his Dior necktie. "I'm so sorry about Aunt Chizuko. And also about my not being there for the funeral. No excuse, really."

"It was no fun, believe me. I wish I could have invited everyone for something a bit happier."

"At least let me light a stick of incense for her. That's the first thing." Jun shifted anxiously in his seat and went over to sit in front of the memorial photograph. Not another word was said on the subject. Honma wasn't sure if Jun was being considerate or just flustered; either way, he was grateful.

"Well?" he prompted. "What's so important that it brings you out in this kind of weather? The sooner we get to it the better, I imagine."

Jun sat facing Honma again, eyes cast downward. His lips quivered. Finally, he muttered, "It's taken me so long to make up my mind …"

Honma stirred his coffee without comment. Makoto's waterproof radio was playing off in the background. Since when had the boy taken to listening to music in the bath? Jun still hadn't said anything, so Honma broke in again. "About talking to me?"

Jun nodded, then slowly looked up. "I hesitated because I didn't feel I could barge in on you. You're an expert, so I was sure you'd be way too busy. But when my mother told me you were on leave—"

Honma raised his eyebrows. If Jun had come looking for an "expert," a police detective with time on his hands, it had to be one of about three things. "Let's see. You had a run-in with the yakuza. Or a friend gave you a present that turned out to be stolen. Or somebody took your car and later you saw it sitting in a used-car lot with new license plates. Something like that?"

"No, no, that's not it at all."

"Well, what, then?"

Jun cleared his throat. "I, uh, got engaged."

He looked so serious that Honma wanted to laugh. "That's wonderful."

"No, it isn't," Jun countered. "My fiancée is gone, she's disappeared. I need you to find her. Finding people is what you do, isn't it? I'm sure you'd do a lot better than I would just poking around on my own. What do you think?"

Jun leaned across the table, his hands folded, eyes pleading. Honma didn't know what to say; he blinked and looked out the window. It was still snowing. "I don't know the whole story," he began, "and I'm afraid I—"

But Jun only leaned further forward. "I'll explain everything."

Honma raised a hand. "Hold it, hold it right there. I want to make one thing clear right off."

"Yes, sir." Jun settled back.

"Your fiancée has disappeared. Whereabouts unknown."

"Yes, that's correct.'

14

"And you want me to locate her."

"Yes."

"Okay, I don't usually take on new cases without a lot more information than I've got now. You can appreciate that, can't you?"

Jun seemed about to say something, then simply stuck out his jaw and nodded.

"Well, then, for the time being, why don't you fill me in? I'm not saying I'll do it, but if it is something serious, I can't just dismiss it without hearing you out."

Jun couldn't disguise his eagerness to tell someone. "Yes, sir!"

"Okay, open that desk drawer over there and get me something to write with, would you?" Out came one of Makoto's exercise books and a ballpoint pen.

"So, uh … where should I begin?" Jun said.

"How about if I ask you some questions. What's her name?"

Jun seemed to relax a bit. "Shoko Sekine."

Honma handed him the pen and made him write down the characters. "Age?"

"Twenty-eight this year."

"An office affair?"

"No. She works for a client of mine. Or worked, I guess, now that she's disappeared."

"What's the name of the company?"

"Imai Office Machines. They're a wholesaler dealing in cash registers. Lately they've started leasing out office automation equipment too. But it's a small firm, only two employees."

"Two including her? Okay, so when did you first get to know her?"

Jun thought it over. "Um, two years ago, in 1990. Around October. No, before the September holidays. Anyway, that's when we went on our first date."

Today was January 20, 1992, so that meant their relationship was about a year and four months old. Not especially quick for an engagement. Maybe even the standard period.

"And you got engaged?"

"Yes, last Christmas Eve."

Honma couldn't help smiling. Some people might even call it

corny. "And was there a formal exchange of gifts?"

Jun looked uncomfortable. "No, none of that. Just the agreement between the two of us. But I did give her a ring."

Pen in hand, Honma raised his eyes to look at Jun. "Parental opposition?"

Jun nodded cautiously.

"Hers? Yours?"

"Mine. Shoko hasn't got any family left."

"Oh ..." Unusual for someone who was just twenty-eight.

"She was an only child to start with. Her father died when she was still in elementary school. Some sort of illness, she never said exactly what. She lost her mother just two years ago."

"Illness again, I suppose."

"No, an accident."

Under the name "Shoko Sekine" Honma wrote, "Both parents dead."

"So she lives alone."

"Right. Not far from here. In the Suginami district, an apartment in Honancho."

"Where's she from originally? Ever ask?"

"Sure. A few hours north of Tokyo, from Utsunomiya. But like I said, her father died when she was a kid. She doesn't seem to have any happy memories of the place, since they had some trouble making ends meet and the relatives couldn't be bothered. She never wanted to go back, practically refuses to talk about her hometown."

"So as far as family contacts go—?"

"Shoko's all on her own."

*All on her own*—except for him. You could almost tell from the way he said her name that he was her sole confidant and companion. "Know anything about her work background?"

Jun looked uncomfortable again. "After she got out of high school in Utsunomiya, she came straight to Tokyo. That's about all I know ..." Then he added defensively, "But hey, when you go out with a girl, you don't ask her for a record of her schooling and her past employers!"

"Oh, is that right?" Honma said dryly. "But you'd be lying if you said you didn't think about it at all." Gradually it all came back to

16

him. Little things he'd heard from Chizuko. About her cousin—Jun's father—and his family: what snobs they were, with fixed ideas on education and jobs. When Chizuko married Honma, she'd put up with all sorts of grief. *A policeman? No future in that!* Jun's father, on the other hand, had gone straight from one of the best schools in the country to a blue-chip company, where he scored points by marrying the daughter of the number one client's CEO. A bastard, but consistent. No doubt his wife had a similar outlook.

And Jun was their son, after all.

Jun looked away as Honma stared at him. The cup of coffee in his hand was cold. A skin had formed on the surface.

"Listen, don't confuse me with my folks." He set his cup down hard on the table. "All I ask for is a girl who's cheerful and who thinks she can get along with me. Education and all that other nonsense doesn't mean a thing!"

"It's not nonsense," Honma said.

"It is if you make too much of it!"

Makoto had turned off his radio. Honma's voice sounded unnaturally loud in the silent living room. "You mean to say your parents didn't think she was right for you."

"… Right."

"Ever set up a meeting?"

"Just once. Last autumn."

"And?"

"The Cambodian Peace Talks were friendlier by a long shot."

Honma had to laugh.

"So I made up my own mind," Jun continued, "and asked her to marry me. No need for a ceremony, just get it over and done with, that's what I thought. The way a lot of couples do nowadays."

"You weren't afraid that your boss would find that a bit unusual."

Jun smiled, for the first time.

"I'm not so bad I could lose my job just like that."

And it was true, you could see he was capable just by looking at him. You deal with people for twenty years and you get a sense about these things, the same way a chef can tell if a knife is blunt without ever seeing it cut.

If Jun was this far gone on her, Shoko Sekine had to be pretty damn good-looking. Smart, too. Young, on her own, but determined to keep to the straight and narrow. Not drifting toward hostessing like so many girls did these days, even if the nightclub world—the "water trade," as it was known—did mean easy money. No, she had principles.

"Do you think maybe she didn't want to deal with this, since your parents disapproved of her anyway? So she just pulled out?" Honma bit his lip. He'd almost said "gave up."

Darkness welled up in Jun's eyes. They call them "the windows of the soul"; at the moment it was like peering into a warehouse where not a single light had been left on.

"Got any ideas about her disappearance, then?"

For a long time Jun refused to speak. Makoto, a bath towel draped over his shoulder, peeked into the room. Honma shot him a look that said, "Stay out." Makoto nodded and slipped back around the corner.

"Listen … this isn't a cheap novel we're talking about here!" Jun said defensively.

"Fine, then. You know of a definite reason? Did she send you a note?"

Jun shook his head. "She didn't leave anything behind. I only know what I've pieced together. And it's not the whole story, by any means."

"What've you got, then?" Honma's words were more a sigh than a question.

Jun started explaining, his story coming out in a rush. "Over New Year's, we—the two of us—went shopping. The company had offered us some cheap housing and we'd decided to take it, so we'd gone out to buy furniture and curtains and things."

"Right."

"Well, anyway, after buying all that stuff, we decided to look at some clothes, and she bought herself a sweater. She was about to pay in cash, when she discovered she was running a little short." Jun paused and gazed up at the ceiling. "Eventually I ended up paying, as I'd intended to all along. That was when I learned Shoko didn't have even one credit card to her name, which came as a bit of a surprise.

Now, our bank started up a credit service not long ago and of course we have a new accounts quota. But I don't like mixing business with private matters, so I never pulled that how-about-a-credit-card routine with her—or with any of my friends, for that matter."

And yet his boss valued him at the new accounts desk. He must really have a knack for drumming up customers.

"So that same day, we sat down and had a little talk. With all the preparations, we were bound to make a lot of purchases from that point on. But the two of us might not be together each and every time, and it'd be dangerous for Shoko to carry around lots of cash. So I told her, I'll go ahead and get you a card, okay? And anyway, once we got married and she changed her name, we'd been thinking we'd keep the bank account she has now and use it for our daily expenses. Because I'd still need my own account and my own card, of course, for expenses."

Is that how young couples managed their affairs today? Traditionally, the wife was the one who took charge of a couple's joint finances. Jun, it seemed, wanted to be the breadwinner, but had no intention of simply handing over his pay.

"Shoko agreed. So we met again the next day and I brought her the application form for her to fill out, then and there." He had then forwarded the form to the bank's credit card subsidiary. "Usually it takes about a month. But I have this friend there ... You see, banks' subsidiary credit card companies are full of 'outward bound' former employees—retirement-age senior clerks, people who are incompetent but who've been around too long to fire, staffers pulled from bank duty for one reason or another. Well, one of them, a guy named Tanaka, joined the bank at the same time as me." Jun frowned defensively. "He's real bright, only he got sort of wound too tight at one point. Maybe he was too smart. Well, he went a bit off the deep end and found himself temporarily shifted over to the credit card side of things."

Honma nodded. "And he ...?"

"... was the one I asked about rushing Shoko's card through. He said sure. But then last Monday I got a phone call—"

Honma glanced at a calendar out of the corner of his eye. *Last*

*Monday*. That would have been the thirteenth.

"And it was him, saying, 'Sorry, we can't issue Shoko a card.' Not only that, it was, 'Listen, Kurisaka, maybe you ought to have this girl checked out a bit.'"

"Did he give any reason?"

Jun sighed. He rocked back and forth for a few seconds before replying. "The name Shoko Sekine was blacklisted by all the credit rating organizations, the ones associated with banks and the ones used by the credit card companies."

When someone takes out a charge card or makes a purchase on the installment plan, a credit rating organization first runs a thorough check to verify that the person has no past defaults, or at least isn't defaulting on any outstanding debts. Honma understood that much, but there was one detail that was new to him. "You mentioned something about different kinds of credit rating organizations—you mean there's not just one?"

"Oh no, there are quite a few. Related to banks or credit card companies or consumer finance companies. Even Tokyo and Osaka have their different organizations. Data of course does get around, so it's easy enough to find out where a particular customer stands in their payments, even if they've used a card or borrowed money only once."

"Which is why the same data can be used for personal identification."

"Right. Well, I was shocked. Because here Shoko was telling me she'd never owned a credit card in her life. So how could she possibly be blacklisted?"

"Maybe they got the wrong person?"

"That was my first thought, exactly. In fact, I'm afraid I lost my temper with Tanaka—even got a bit nasty. Pretty soon we were arguing, and he was shouting, 'We don't make mistakes like that!'"

Jun was breathing hard; just retelling the story had gotten him all worked up again.

"'No, no,' he told me, 'there's no mistake.' Didn't I think he'd double-checked it already?" Tanaka had suggested angrily that Jun try asking her himself. "I was sure it was a case of mistaken identity. I mean, all the credit union's got on record is a name, date of birth, occupation, maybe an address at most, right? They don't enter your whole family register. And what if you move? Or you could be transferred and then your workplace would change. If it's just a name and date of birth, coincidences do happen."

No argument there. Honma remembered the time a guy on the force had received a call out of the blue from a credit company he'd never heard of. When he'd had them run a search, it turned out that somebody else had the same name and practically the same telephone number—in fact, identical except for the area code. "I'm with you … So then?"

"Well, I didn't want any of this messy stuff getting back to Shoko, especially since it was all a mistake. So I called Tanaka again and apologized, and asked him to trace it back further. Where had the information come from? What was the evidence? If I could just get him to go over it again I was sure he'd find a mistake."

Honma frowned. "Is it really all that easy?"

"Sure thing. That is …" Jun stopped himself short. "Well, actually, no. The only one who's supposed to file an objection about this kind of slipup is the person in question. Normally, Shoko would have had to request that the rating organization call up her data, then they'd have to go through a whole rigmarole to make sure that it was her asking."

"But you were in a hurry, so you skipped that."

He shrugged. "I thought I had the right to file an objection on Shoko's behalf. And in his position, Tanaka had ready access to that kind of information." But the search didn't turn out the way he had expected. "It didn't take much work. Tanaka said there was no doubt about it. It wasn't mistaken identity, there was evidence."

"Which was?"

Jun reached into the inner pocket of his jacket and pulled out a folded piece of fax paper. "This, I'm told, was mailed to the head of customer relations of a major—I don't think I need to say which—credit union. Tanaka accessed it through his credit referral center, then faxed it over to me."

Honma unfolded it. It was a single-spaced document on legal-sized paper, done on a word processor.

MIZOGUCHI & TAKADA
ATTORNEYS-AT-LAW
Sanwa Bldg 8F
Ginza 9-2-6
Chuo Ward, Tokyo

May 20, 1987

To Whom It May Concern:

WHEREUPON, this statement is submitted with the full authorization of Ms. Shoko Sekine, residing at Castle Mansion Kinshicho, Apartment 405, Kotobashi 4-2-2, Sumida Ward, Tokyo.

Ms. Sekine was first issued a credit card in September 1983, whereupon she began to use it for daily shopping and cash loans. However, by the summer of 1984, imprudent credit card use, compounded by insufficient awareness regarding money-lending in general, had led her to accrue sizeable monthly payments. Subsequently, in an effort to correct this situation, she augmented her full-time work with several part-time positions. But this heavier workload proved detrimental to her health, in turn increasing the strain on her finances and forcing her to incur even greater debts. She began to borrow against future wages in order to meet her monthly payments and engaged in serial borrowing to cover yet more loans, inflating her debts to the point where she presently owes a total of thirty creditors some ten million yen. Ms. Sekine has no holdings to speak of. She has no recourse but to plead bankruptcy, on this day, at Tokyo Regional Court.

In consideration of the above, it is with regret that I must humbly request that Ms. Sekine's creditors cooperate and comply fully with these bankruptcy proceedings. Certain money-lending concerns have been known to employ highly irregular means to recover their loans. Please be duly warned that should harassment of this kind be pursued, Ms. Sekine will not hesitate to use every legal remedy available under both the criminal and civil codes against the parties involved.

Yours respectfully,

Goro Mizoguchi
Attorney-at-Law

Honma looked up at Jun.

"Straight-out personal bankruptcy," said Jun.

"What did you do when you saw this?"

He mumbled his reply. "I asked Shoko about it."

"When?"

"The fifteenth."

"At that point, there was still a possibility that there'd been some mistake?"

"I thought so. I sure hoped so." Jun shook his head. "So I, I asked her about it, point-blank."

Honma looked down again at the page. "And that's when she disappeared, is that it?"

Jun nodded.

"When you showed this to her, she didn't deny it?"

"She didn't say anything at first. She just went white as a ghost." His voice began to tremble and he spoke quietly. "You've got to find her for me, there's no one else I can turn to. If I went to a detective agency, my parents might hear something about it, with me still living at home and all. And I can't very well get calls at work, either."

But a relative was a different story, it seemed. And if the relative happened to be a detective on leave of duty, so much the better.

"I want to talk things over with her. When I showed her the letter, she said there were all kinds of complicated circumstances behind it. She couldn't explain right away; she needed a little time. I agreed, of course, because I trusted her. Then the next day she was gone. She wasn't at home and she didn't show up for work." Jun shook his head with each new accusation, as if he were speaking to the girl directly.

"Not a word in her own defense. If she'd put up a fight, it might begin to seem real to me. I've got to hear it directly from her. If I just had some kind of explanation, we could work something out. I'm not trying to blame her—really, that's all I want. But I can't do it by myself. Shoko didn't leave any address book behind, and I know almost nothing about her friends. There's no way I could find her by myself. What do you say?... I'm begging you."

Even after that wave of emotion had passed, Jun's jaw continued to tremble, like a wind-up toy whose wheels keep spinning after it tips over.

Honma stared at him but said nothing. Two separate impulses tugged at his mind. One was simple curiosity, a regular occupational hazard. Shoko Sekine's vanishing act was nothing special in itself. Even so, you didn't often hear of "personal bankruptcy" figuring in a young woman's disappearance. A whole family might skip town in the dead of night, but a single woman? And running not from a man, but from creditors? Not likely, he thought. Shoko Sekine had filed for personal bankruptcy, which meant she had escaped her debts. Or could debts survive intact, right through a bankruptcy?

Mostly, though, Jun's plea left Honma cold. How was it that he hadn't shown up at Chizuko's funeral, sent his condolences or telephoned even once in the three years since? He was just too busy. Yet when it came to asking his own favors, he'd brave a blizzard. Who did he think he was?

Honma's silence must have reached Jun, because next time he spoke his tone was a little more deferential. "Uncle Shunsuke, how's your leg, anyway? You're not straining yourself getting up and around?"

"No," he said, rather curtly.

Jun lowered his head in a show of shame. "My mother says you were shot ..."

"Yeah, that's right."

The incident hadn't made any headlines. It was just a small-time thief who hit on late-night coffee shops and little hole-in-the-wall drinking places. The type who might flash a knife but would never actually hurt someone. But this particular punk also happened to wear a cheap reconditioned pistol under his shirt, more as a good luck charm than anything else—at least until the two officers showed up to arrest him and he'd pointed it at one of them. He didn't mean to shoot, he testified later; he only pulled the trigger by accident. In fact he was so startled when the thing actually fired, he inadvertently fired a second time. Nothing to it. Even Honma, who took that first, "accidental" bullet in the knee, didn't think that much about it at the time (actually finding it funny that the flustered gunman had blown a finger off his own hand with the second blast). It was only later, when they were plastering up the leg, that he had begun to wonder if there might not be permanent damage. Now he knew enough to regret the whole episode, particularly after discovering how grueling physical therapy was. He should have laughed himself silly when he still could.

Jun bit his lip. "I'm sorry, I got so caught up in my own little world. I wasn't thinking ..."

Honma just stared at his nephew and said nothing, but could feel himself growing irritated. He had taken a leave of absence because he would only have been in his colleagues' way. Isn't that what Jun had basically suggested? If a guy couldn't pull his own weight, he shouldn't be on the team at all. Honma knew it and apparently so did everybody else. That's why he'd been so edgy and frustrated on the train today. He felt useless, and blatantly so.

"I don't know how much help I'd be ..." There, he'd gone and said it.

Jun snapped to attention.

"Don't expect too much, now. I'm not saying I'll take the job. There are still too many unknowns. Let's just see what we have to go on."

Jun's features softened a little. "Thanks," he said. "I can't ask any more than that."

## ✧ 3 ✧

Not until the weather cleared up, Honma had told Jun, and not until the snow melted enough for him to walk around outside. Honma had hoped this business of chasing down Shoko Sekine would be put off for at least a day, but the snow had stopped during the night and he woke to a bright sky of alarming clarity. Walkways had already been shoveled clear in the white world down below. The wet concrete glistened in the sun. Slabs of hardened snow slid loose from nearby roofs; ice sweated from the eaves.

Makoto finished his breakfast, grabbed his schoolbag, and started for the front door. Halfway there, he looked back over his shoulder. "Dad, you going out today?"

Honma said "Mm," looking up from his newspaper.

"Uncle Jun ask you to do something?"

"That's right."

"What time are you coming home?"

"I don't know yet. It depends how things go."

The boy stood facing the sunny east window, but the stern look on his face didn't come from the glare. "Everything going to go okay?"

"I'll see that it does."

"So Uncle Jun—what did he want?"

Honma squinted at the digital time on the TV screen. "Hey, you're going to be late."

Makoto hiked his schoolbag further up on his back. "Hanging around here taking it easy isn't good enough for you, huh?" he said.

"Well, it's not like I'm going off to wipe out all the yakuza single-handed."

"Yeah, well, you slip and break the other leg, don't look at me."

"You just watch out for yourself, young man."

"Gee, thanks tons for the thought, Dad. Bye now. *Bye now to you too*," he tacked on as an extra farewell. "That last one is for instant replay when you go out, okay?"

Honma laughed. "Gotcha."

Makoto let the door slam. Honma got up and walked over to the window. Children had clustered in front of each housing block. A group of seven—his son among them—cut into view just beyond the flowerbeds and filed along a walkway toward the school at the south end of the quadrangle.

Honma rattled around the apartment until ten to avoid the commuter rush hour. He spent some time poring over street maps, looking for ways to cut his movements down to a minimum. He also wasn't quite sure he knew what "personal bankruptcy" meant, so he looked it up. He couldn't find it in his standard Japanese dictionary, and the only other reference book he had was last year's *Almanac of Contemporary Usage*. But lo and behold, there it was:

> PERSONAL BANKRUPTCY: A legal process whereby the entire property of a debtor is divided fairly among his creditors in court, and the debtor is thereafter granted a WAIVER exonerating him from liability. PERSONAL BANKRUPTCY refers to cases in which the debtor enters his own plea; in recent years, the number of such cases has spiraled as a result of a marked rise in debt accumulation incurred via credit card abuses and loans. Such individual cases are also termed CONSUMER BANKRUPTCY, as distinct from ordinary corporate bankruptcy. Bankruptcy places limitations upon an individual's financial capacities, which nonetheless may be granted full REINSTATEMENT, also by means of a waiver. Moreover, the fact of bankruptcy is not recorded in a debtor's family register or other identifying documents, nor does it curtail his political suffrage or other civil rights.

The last few lines came as a surprise. Somehow he'd imagined, rather vaguely, that bankruptcy, once declared, lasted forever. If someone like Honma—a professional invader of privacy—was under this impression, there must be a lot of other people out there with the same idea. Otherwise, they wouldn't need to include details like that in the *Almanac of Contemporary Usage*, would they?

As he understood it, hiding a past bankruptcy was incredibly simple. You could just keep quiet about it and no one would ever know! If Shoko hadn't been pressed to get a credit card, she'd have gone undiscovered. But then, maybe she thought it was safe to try again after five years. A simple misjudgment?

He returned the volume to the bookshelf and started getting ready to go out, then phoned for a taxi to the station. He felt a bit guilty doing this first thing in the morning, but, after all, he *had* insisted: *all expenses paid.* And Jun had swallowed his terms unconditionally. It was common practice, wasn't it? Maybe he was stretching it a little in a case like this, but at least it made for good relations between relations. So, as long as he got a receipt, he intended to take taxis whenever he wanted.

He put down the receiver, smoked a cigarette and doused the ashtray before leaving the house. On the way down, he stopped at the Isakas' on the first floor to drop off his key, then limped away, tapping at the mounds of snow on the pavement with his umbrella.

For someone with a healthy pair of legs, Shoko Sekine's office was five minutes' walk from the West Exit of Shinjuku Station. The address proved to be a forlorn five-story building alongside the Koshu Expressway. Five of six narrow glass panels in the foyer window were stenciled with the names of companies. The last panel had no name on it, only a curtain. Design by neglect, perhaps.

Imai Office Machines was on the second floor. It was a small operation laid out on an open floor plan; you could take the place in at a glance. A woman in a dark blue uniform stood up and came over. She looked about twenty-four, at the most. Petite, with a roundish face and big eyes, freckles around her nose.

Honda introduced himself. "I'm a relative of Jun Kurisaka, who is engaged to one of your employees, Shoko Sekine. I'd like to ask a few questions about Ms. Sekine."

"Uh, yes, I see …," said the woman.

"If possible, I'd like to have a word with the manager. Do you think that could be arranged?"

"Sekine? Yes, I know Ms. Sekine," she said, sounding flurried. "Mr. Imai, the boss, he's in the coffee shop across the street."

"In consultation?"

"Consul—? N-no, he's just having some coffee. He's always over there and I mind the shop. I'll go get him." She looked back as she was going out the door. "Um, what should we do if there's a call while I'm out?"

"You tell me what you want me to do."

She had to think for a second. "There won't be any calls," she decided. "Just have a seat. Take off your coat. Put it anywhere." And, like a sparrow, off she went.

The tiny office was a model of tidiness. Three identical desks huddled together, holding an array of files and ledgers, bindings neatly aligned. Everything was so compact and orderly, it reminded Honma of those little kiosks on train platforms selling magazines and candy. But even assuming it had a warehouse somewhere, could this company really be doing much business at all? He could imagine what Shoko Sekine's and this other woman's salaries must be like.

Honma went over to the desk just across from the sparrow's and opened the top drawer. Stowed inside were the usual notepad, ruler, ballpoint pens—and a ready-made signature seal: Sekine. Against the window a big executive desk, its chair fitted with a crocheted cushion, overlooked the other desks. On top were an empty in-tray and a magazine with its cover folded under. Closer inspection showed that the title was *Finance Net*.

"Sorry to keep you waiting," a deep voice boomed out. The woman had returned with her boss, an elderly man with bifocals, wearing a cardigan over a white shirt and string tie. Thick woolen socks bulged from the toes of his brand-new massage sandals.

"A relative of Ms. Sekine's, was it?"

"No, of her fiancé's."

"That so? Of Mr. Kurisaka's, eh?" He motioned toward a sofa and coffee table by the window. "Have a seat."

Honma led the way, dragging his bad leg a little.

"Rheumatism?" the old man asked bluntly.

"No, no," said Honma, a bit taken aback. "An accident."

"Oh? And why the umbrella?"

"I was too stubborn to buy a cane."

"The doctor wouldn't lend you one?"

"They tried to. But if I gave in, I knew I'd feel bad. Like a real invalid."

The boss rubbed his bald head. "Fair enough."

Honma produced Jun's name card, on the back of which he'd had Jun write a short message: "The bearer, Mr. Shunsuke Honma, is a relative of mine conducting an investigation for me. Any assistance you can give him would be appreciated." With this he had an "in"— at least with anybody who knew that Jun was Shoko Sekine's fiancé. Jun had given him a look that said, "You don't really need this." To him, all a detective had to do was flick out his badge for people to start blabbing. That was why he'd come to Honma, right? But Honma had turned in his police ID when he'd submitted his formal request for a leave of absence, which left him empty-handed. And without any identification, to walk into a place and claim to be police was asking for trouble. You'd almost be better off showing a fake ID.

Jun had looked pretty discouraged when Honma told him how things stood, but at least he hadn't decided to go off to a private detective instead. He obviously wanted to keep this from his parents and his co-workers.

Honma pulled out his own private card as well, printed with just his name, home address and telephone number. Imai examined each in turn. Meanwhile, Ms. Sparrow brought them cups of tea.

"You said you're related to Mr. Kurisaka. What exactly is your relationship?" asked Imai. He seemed to want to get that question squared away first.

"He's the son of my wife's cousin."

"Oh."

"Always a problem. I never know just what to call him."

"That's 'cousin once removed,' isn't it? Eh, Mitchie?" he shouted over his shoulder. So the sparrow's name was Mitchie.

"I'll go look it up, sir," she chirped.

"Another thing," he went on. "I notice there's no job title on your name card."

Honma had come prepared with an alibi. "I'm a magazine writer. That's why Jun came to me, since digging around for information is all part of my job."

"Well, what do you know, I do a bit of writing for magazines myself," Imai said.

Honma nodded. "*Finance Net*, am I right?"

"So, you've heard of it?"

Honma played it coy. A smile was not an outright lie. This *Finance Net* was a very small publication, the sort of thing only its own contributors ever read.

"Anyway…" Imai took a sip of the watery green tea and got right to the point. "About Miss Sekine. Hasn't she turned up yet?"

It was four days ago that Jun had called and told him she'd disappeared, Imai explained. January 19, around nine in the morning. Later, at lunchtime, Jun had stopped by on his rounds to ask whether Imai had any clue where she'd gone. "On the sixteenth, when she didn't show up for work, we just figured she'd decided to take some extra time off, it being just after a long holiday weekend. So your Mr. Kurisaka's phone call came as a real shock."

"Prior to that, did Ms. Sekine ever take a day off unannounced?"

"Just once. She was in bed with a fever and didn't call in. Right, Mitchie?" Mitchie tilted her head quizzically, and her boss laughed. "Oh, that's right, that would have been before your time."

"Mr. Imai, would you say you know Jun fairly well?" Honma asked.

"Sure. Only as the rep from our local bank, but still. That's why, when I heard he and Miss Sekine had gotten engaged, I was kind of surprised."

"Did they announce the engagement here, at the office?"

"No, no. We were all out drinking. As you can see, Mr. Honma, we're a tiny firm. Our office parties would be pretty sad affairs if I didn't ask the girls to bring their beaux along. So this past New Year's party, it must have been, the two of them came out with the happy news. Isn't that right, Mitchie, at New Year's?"

31

"Yes, Mr. Imai," she said from her desk, where she was thumbing through a dictionary.

"That's when she showed us the ring. A ruby, I believe it was. Miss Sekine's birthstone."

"A sapphire," corrected Mitchie. It was the first assertion she had made. "You always get things confused, Mr. Imai. It was a sapphire. The stone in the setting was blue."

"That so?" Imai rubbed his head again. "In any case, I guess it must have vanished with her, eh?"

"This is the first I've heard of it." Honma had arranged with Jun to go and look around Shoko's apartment that evening. He'd know more about her belongings then.

"Well, according to Kurisaka, the two of them had a fight the night of the fifteenth. And then when he rang her apartment the following morning, there was no answer. By the time he went there to see her that night, Miss Sekine had apparently packed up and gone."

"Right. It all seems to have hit him pretty hard."

"But if she's kept the ring, it would seem to me that she's thinking of getting back together with him, or maybe just hanging on to it for the resale value, one or the other. But if it was just one little fight they had—don't you suppose she'll come home after a while? If Kurisaka makes too much of it now, it might force her to do something she'll regret later."

There are some older men who automatically side with the woman. Not that they're such sympathetic souls; they've just never had a truly nasty run-in with a female of the species.

"It wasn't a 'little fight,'" Honma said. "It was something pretty bad—I really can't even go into it."

Imai leaned forward. "Serious stuff, eh?"

"Yes. Between the two of them."

The old man seemed to understand that he wasn't meant to pry any further. "Sorry to hear it—but in any case I don't think there's a whole lot more we can do for you. Can't add much to what Mr. Kurisaka's told you already. Right, Mitchie?"

Mitchie nodded without looking up from the dictionary. "I don't think it's 'cousin once removed,' Mr. Imai."

Her boss made no response, so Honma ignored her too. Poor Mitchie.

Imai did ask her, distractedly: "When did Miss Sekine come to work here?" But before he could ask her again, Honma broke in.

"You couldn't possibly show me her résumé, could you? Given the circumstances, I'd like to try talking to her former employers as well."

"Yes, of course," he answered without missing a beat, rising from his chair. Almost effortlessly, he produced a sheet from a file he kept in his bottom desk drawer. It was a standard résumé form, with the usual ID photo attached. For some reason, the night before, Jun hadn't brought along a single photograph of Shoko. This was the first time Honma had actually seen her face.

She was gorgeous.

ID photos tend to make anybody look like a petty criminal, so if she came across this well in a little black-and-white picture, Shoko Sekine was obviously not your average beauty. Her hair was done in a medium short cut—a bob, they'd probably call it. Delicately shaped nose, eyebrows forming soft arcs—penciled or not, he couldn't tell— between a high forehead and a cool pair of eyes. Her lips were pressed together in a hint of a smile.

"Quite a good-looker," Imai observed. "Even more so in person. Especially after she started going out with your Mr. Kurisaka. Got prettier every day, huh, Mitchie?"

Mitchie swiveled around in her chair. "We'd go out shopping together and all these men would come on to her."

Not surprising. "Tall?"

"Oh, then you've never met her?"

"No, Jun kept his engagement secret from the family."

"From what Shoko said," Mitchie spoke up, "his folks were against it. Didn't think she was educated enough."

"That's right." Honma looked at her. "Did it seem to bother her?"

"You bet. For a while there, she was so worried she kept losing weight. Until Mr. Kurisaka said they were getting married no matter what his parents said and gave her that ring, she was moping around all the time."

Nodding, Honma returned to the résumé. Shoko Sekine's birthdate was September 14, 1964. Her education ended with high school in Utsunomiya. Under "Past Employment" she'd listed three companies. The first was an office supply company in Tokyo—Sanko Equipment Leasing, near Shibuya. She started there in June 1983. Assuming she had come to Tokyo right after her March graduation, she probably spent the two months in between job-hunting. She left there in March 1985.

Next was a nondescript Ishii & Company, beside which she had written, "Worked as typist." The company was in Chiyoda, central Tokyo. She started in April 1985 and left in June 1986.

Third was Ariyoshi Certified Public Accountants in the Minato area—even more centrally located. Hired August 1986, worked until January 1, 1990. She'd given the usual "Personal reasons" for leaving in all three cases. The résumé itself was dated April 15, 1990.

"She worked for a CPA before this, I see."

"That sounds right," puffed Imai, craning his neck to get a fresh look.

"You never heard any specific reason why she quit that job?"

"Sure … said she'd been overworked and got sick, I believe it was." Honma looked skeptical. "We're a small outfit, Mr. Honma. Nitpick over past experience and I wouldn't get any employees at all. So I keep an eye out and if I find anyone good, I try not to ask too many questions. Everybody's got some sort of history."

Okay, but what was to prevent him from misreading a person's character? Here he was, president of a little blip of a company barely holding its own in this prime business district. Admittedly, that was no small accomplishment, precisely because of the size of the place. Running a large company, Honma thought to himself, would be like flying a jumbo jet on automatic pilot; there would be no real test of your abilities at every turn. But a one-room enterprise like this was closer to a prop plane. There's no computer navigation system to fall back on. If the pilot slips up, the plane crashes.

"So how do you go about recruiting people?"

"The usual: want ads in the newspapers."

"And when did she start working for you?"

Imai glanced at the résumé. "I offered her the job the day after her interview. Had her start from around the twentieth, I believe."

"And she was doing general office work?"

"That's right. Typing, word processing."

"And her co-workers?" Honma looked over at Mitchie, who gave him a nervous look in return.

Her boss answered for her. "At the time, it was just Miss Sekine. Mitchie here's only been with us six months. Isn't that right?"

Mitchie nodded, visibly relieved.

"Any other—"

"Nope. Just us three. Sometimes we get people passing through, and they might have said hello to her, but I doubt they'd have any idea where she is now."

"No one in particular comes to mind?"

He shook his head apologetically. "Other than your Mr. Kurisaka, I don't even know if—she must have had some close friends, but I'm sorry I can't be of any more help."

"That's fine."

This time when Honma turned toward Mitchie, she was ready for it. "I can't think of anybody, either," she said without hesitation.

"Never heard her mention the names of any friends?"

She shook her head. "Mr. Kurisaka's name came up plenty. Sometimes we'd stop for tea on the way home, once in a while look around a department store or something. Otherwise ..."

"I see."

"Do you suppose she might've gone home to her family?" asked Imai.

"She hasn't got any family left."

Imai slapped the palm of his hand against his forehead. "Ah, of course."

"Naturally, I plan to look into that, though." Honma picked up the résumé. "If you don't mind, I'd like to make a copy of this."

Imai gave a wave of the hand. "Go ahead and take it. I don't mind lending it to Mr. Kurisaka. Ask around at her other employers."

Honma thanked him and accepted the offer.

"Hope you find her."

As Honma rose to go, Mitchie rushed over to get his coat and help him on with it, but the difference in their heights made the procedure difficult. After a few awkward attempts, Honma smiled and slipped the coat on himself. Meanwhile, Mitchie held his umbrella.

"I'm sorry about that son-of-your-wife's-cousin problem," she said solemnly. "All I know is it's not 'cousin once removed.'"

"Well, let me know if you find out." Honma felt he had to say something.

"Yes, sir," she said, "I will."

Shoko Sekine may not have earned much money there, but it wasn't a bad little company, thought Honma as he headed down the stairs.

✧ 4 ✧

There was no need to ring up all three companies on Shoko Sekine's résumé. The last one—Ariyoshi Certified Public Accountants—ought to be enough. She'd been with them for four years. Chances were she still had friends there.

Honma went into the first coffee shop he saw. There was a pay phone just inside the door, but he decided to take a load off his feet for a minute before making the call. Over coffee he looked at Shoko's résumé again. The writing was neat, without being fussy. She probably kept a regular diary and a record of her expenses.

He went over to the phone and dialed directory assistance. When the operator came on, he gave her the company's name and address. Four, then five seconds passed.

"I have no listing for an Ariyoshi Certified Public Accountants at that address, sir."

He couldn't believe it. "Nothing at all? Nothing similar to that?"

"If you'd care to wait, I'll have another look, sir."

Beneath the background noise, he could hear computer keys.

"There's no such listing. Are you sure the address is correct?"

He looked at it again but there was no mistake, so he thanked her and hung up.

Accountants and lawyers, notary publics—businesses that depend on people being able to find them—hardly ever move once they set up shop. That's why they have to be careful picking a location. Of course, somebody young and ambitious might team up with a senior partner, waiting for the right moment to break out on their own. But for a firm registered under a single name to just up and vanish?

Maybe Ariyoshi was an elderly accountant, retired now. No, wait a minute—didn't Imai say Shoko Sekine had quit after getting sick from overwork? A business that works people too hard doesn't just quietly fold. Of course, there was no telling if she'd given Imai her real reasons for leaving.

Maybe he'd have to prowl around a bit, dredge up a few clues from the other offices in that area. What a pain. That could be a day's work in itself.

Honma lifted the receiver again. Ishii & Company. Shoko had worked there only a little over a year. Still, it was worth a shot.

"We have no listing for that party at that address," reported a different woman's voice.

Honma was about to ask about similar company names but, on second thoughts, merely paused and cleared his throat.

"Sir?" the operator said.

"Let me try one more number, if I might." Sanko Equipment Leasing. "I don't suppose you'd have a listing for this company, either?" Just a hunch.

"No such listing, sir," the operator confirmed.

His coffee was lukewarm by the time Honma sat down and looked back over the résumé, feeling a bit foolish. What a trusting guy that Imai was! He'd taken to Shoko on sight and never even bothered to call her past employers or check on any details. But she must have counted on that from the start, otherwise she'd have gone to greater lengths to cover her tracks, or at least used the names of real companies. No, the question of credibility hadn't fazed her a bit. She'd just pasted up a few phony references and walked the paper around, sticking to minor firms, avoiding larger ones where personnel managers were likely to be more thorough. Still, the odds were that someone would catch on. But that was a risk she was willing to take. If the whole thing was going to blow, better sooner than later.

Of course she'd have had to lie on her résumé to hide her bankruptcy. Back in May 1987, though, when her attorney had sent out those letters, she must have been working *somewhere*, surely. And there would have been urgent calls and little reminders to her office from credit unions and loan-sharking operations, maybe even a friendly visit or two. Hardly a pleasant scenario for her company. Honma had heard a few things about these "non-bank" money-lenders; their collection agents weren't exactly known for their polished manners. Even after November 1983, when the Regulation of Moneylending Business Law banned the use of violence or overt threats, they found other methods. They'd buzz a nasty fax straight into your office—"Urgent: Contact Ichiban Credit Company ASAP." What could a person do?

Shoko could never have listed an actual past employer on her résumé. One call and it would have been all over. *Sekine? We weren't too happy about her credit situation ...*

Hot in here, thought Honma, still wearing his coat. Getting in and out of it was awkward, so he hadn't taken it off. He took a sip of water and glanced back over her personal history. God only knows what had led her to the point of bankruptcy. He didn't want to pass judgment, the way any prospective employer was bound to do. Still, he couldn't help feeling that Jun was better off without her. Plausible or not, though, she'd been quite thorough. She must have gone to some trouble to come up with all those names and addresses.

That made him think. At any job she'd held before going to Imai Office Machines, she would have been registered with Public Employment. And Public Employment had computerized its whole operation more than ten years ago. Which meant they updated information on each employee under a certain registration number. Change jobs or retire, you're still on record. Just go in and they give you a card. Shoko Sekine would have *had* to have one. When she went to work for Imai Office Machines, she'd have shown it to Imai. Then he or, more likely, Shoko herself would have taken it down to the New Applicant window at the Shinjuku Public Employment office.

Honma rose again, went back to the phone, and dialed. Mitchie answered. Honma explained the situation, sending her straight into another flap. She had a few quick, muffled exchanges with her boss, then reported back. "Hello? I found her registration form."

"And?"

"Public Employment Registration," Mitchie read off. "Sekine, Shoko (Ms.). Date of Issue: April 20, 1990." The résumé she'd given

Imai was dated April 15 the same year. "She said it was the first time she'd ever signed up for it."

"Really? She'd never registered before?"

"That's what she said. When I got hired, I didn't know how to do the paperwork by myself, and I was afraid the man at the Public Employment office would give me a bad time, so I got Shoko to go along. That's when she said she'd just done it for the first time herself."

The line crackled with static for a minute and Imai came on. "It's just like Mitchie says. But what's this about her résumé being fake?"

"It sounds ridiculous, I know."

"Well, about Public Employment, from what she told me, she was more of a part-timer at the jobs she'd held before, so she didn't sign up."

"Oh? Did she say why she hadn't ever gone full-time?"

There was another brief exchange, then: "The pay's better for part-time, I think is what she said."

"Which means, conceivably, she could have been hostessing nights."

"Hm. Well, I wouldn't know about that," Imai said. "You can't jump to conclusions these days. And anyway, Miss Sekine didn't have that feel about her."

As far as Honma could see, you couldn't tell *what* conclusions to jump to these days. Everywhere now, perfectly ordinary college coeds hostessed on the side. What's more, Shoko Sekine was no ordinary beauty. She'd had no trouble hooking a guy like Jun. Turn that same charm on a wealthy client in a reputable club, she'd be into big money. Maybe that was why she didn't need the security of unemployment benefits … And yet she'd gone bankrupt.

Honma went over to his table and sat down again, ignoring the glare the waitress was giving him. Five years? Plenty of time for a person's life to turn completely around. And judging from Jun's description of the work she was doing at Imai Office Machines, Shoko's had taken a turn for the better.

He sighed as he pulled a handful of change from his pocket, thinking about where to go from there.

What sort of life was Shoko Sekine leading when her lawyer had sent out that letter to her creditors? It seemed like the long way around, but going at it from that angle might actually be faster. The past she'd tried to hide was clearly the point where she'd felt most vulnerable; make straight for it and everything might fall into place. The girl Jun had gotten to know was someone she'd constructed, a person conjured out of thin air.

Shoko had disappeared the minute Jun began to question her. It was like she'd been wearing her getaway clothes all along. Honma felt sure she must have had help from somebody. Not that anyone who could have located her before this vanishing act was going to be much help now. Once her past had come to light, Shoko had dropped everything and run, and no matter where she was headed, she wouldn't want to stop to confide in anybody who didn't know the first thing about her. Nor would she want any flak from the people who *did*. Naturally, that limited her choice of accomplices.

Honma didn't have much choice either. Better go call on that lawyer, Mizoguchi, the one Shoko had hired to do her bankruptcy papers. The office was over in Ginza. That was a straight ride on the Marunouchi Line, no transfers.

✧ 5 ✧

*All kinds of complications … Can't explain right away … Need a little*
*time …* echoed Shoko's parting words to Jun. Honma stood in the hall
on the eighth floor of a small building tucked back two blocks from
central Ginza, just outside a corner office suite. The middle door
bore the name MIZOGUCHI & TAKADA ATTORNEYS-AT-LAW in boldface.

The interior was not quite visible through frosted glass. Nobody
would ever come here unless they had some fairly serious problem,
Honma thought. Presumably the glass doors were meant to seem not
too forbidding.

The door opened at the first knock. "Excuse me just a second," a
young man said breathlessly before racing back to a phone. A hap-
hazard formation of four desks flanked the entrance. On top of a cabinet a digital clock read 3:27—then 3:28.

Now *this* was an office. None of Mitchie's nervous flutter or Imai's
dabbling, the action here was in real time. Everything was in motion,
the sound of voices coming from all sides. The suite was L-shaped,
with the main staff area perpendicular to a corner used for consulta-
tions; but instead of the usual couch-and-coffee-table reception area,
this corner was arranged into three small booths partitioned by
screens like a medical clinic. Two booths for the partners, with a third
for the next client waiting. All three were now occupied.

The young man finished his call and turned to Honma. In the
process he bumped into a computer printer, sending its paper tray
crashing to the floor. "Oh, sorry," he said, more to the machine than
to Honma. "Please have a seat. Mr. Mizoguchi's previous appointment seems to be running overtime."

"No problem. I've got plenty of time," Honma said without thinking. Actually, when Honma had telephoned, Mizoguchi had made it very clear that he could only squeeze in thirty minutes for an unscheduled visitor, from three-thirty to four.

"Here—take a seat." The young man gestured toward an empty swivel chair with one hand while scrawling something with the other. Honma gratefully accepted the offer.

Over at the next desk, a woman of twenty-seven or twenty-eight was also on the phone. Her caller was either very agitated or very insistent, just as Shoko Sekine must have been on her first visit here —a mixture of nerves and desperation.

The young man looked up from his note-taking. Honma seized the opportunity to ask, "Would you know if someone named Shoko Sekine's been in here recently?"

The young man rolled his eyes toward the ceiling as if to say, "Uh-oh, here we go."

"Sekine?"

"That's right. Shoko."

By now the young woman had finished her call. "Like Fujiwara no Michinaga's daughter Shoko," she promptly joined in, "—consort to Emperor Ichijo?"

"Now you've lost me," her colleague said, grinning nervously.

"Wasn't she the one Murasaki Shikibu served as a lady-in-waiting?" Honma answered back.

The woman beamed. "Why, yes, I believe you're right."

Honma himself was no whiz at the classics, but once when Chizuko took one of those adult education courses—"*The Tale of Genji* for Mature Readers"—he'd been given a running account of the whole epic.

"And attending Shoko's rival, Empress Teishi, was Sei Shonagon," he said. "The two great women writers of their time were both at court, attending different wives of the same emperor." How did he remember all this? The passages Chizuko used to read to him always went in one ear and out the other.

"That's right," the woman agreed.

"Here, I've got her photo," he said, forcing an abrupt return to the living Shoko. He pulled her resume out of his pocket and folded it back so that only her picture was visible, then held it out for confirmation.

Showing an interest again, the young man came around in front of his desk to see. "Can't say she looks familiar. And I generally have a pretty good memory for people who come in."

"Can I take a look?" the woman asked, and her colleague immediately brought it over. "No, I don't remember her. You say she was a client of ours?"

"About five years ago, she had Mr. Mizoguchi draw up bankruptcy papers for her."

"Five years ago? I wasn't even here then," said the young man, handing back the résumé and returning to his seat with an air of finality and an expression that said "Sorry, I tried."

The woman, however, planted her elbows on her desk. "Ninety percent of the walk-ins we get are bankruptcies, but I do seem to recall the name …"

With so many people passing through, it would hardly be surprising if she couldn't remember. Shoko obviously wasn't recent history here. Honma put the résumé away in his pocket.

"Wait—Shoko. The name does ring a bell," she exclaimed with a twist of her neck. "Didn't she have crooked teeth?"

Just then someone called his name. "Mr. Honma? Sorry to keep you on hold."

Honma turned, and his gaze met squarely with that of an older man exactly his own height.

Mizoguchi was clearly pushing seventy. Like many executives who hit a fixed retirement ceiling, no doubt he'd opted to stay on a few more years as a consultant. Even so, he seemed to have plenty of energy left in him. The only signs of aging he showed were a slight sag around the neck, a small blemish on his left cheek, and bifocals riding the bridge of his nose.

With only fifteen minutes remaining until four o'clock, Honma explained the situation as succinctly as he could. He withheld only the fact that Jun had come to him because he was a police officer; again, investigative work was merely part of the freelance writer game.

"Tell me," he asked, "do you issue notices to creditors on behalf of your personal bankruptcy clients?"

"Certainly," the attorney replied straightaway. "It's our way of telling them that we've filed for bankruptcy and of seeking their cooperation. Once we do that, they tend to ease off a little. In *most* instances. Of course, some do put on a show of force, but such cases are rare and easily dealt with."

Honma pulled out Shoko's bankruptcy notice. "I believe this is something you sent out."

"Yes, that's one of ours." He nodded, scarcely looking at the fax, tilting his head to one side, trying to recall her. "Ah yes, Shoko Sekine."

"Has she been in to see you lately?"

"No. You say she disappeared on the sixteenth, less than a week ago. Even I wouldn't lose track of something *that* recent." Mizoguchi's voice was hoarse from long hours of discussions. He took a long, slow sip of tea. "But I remember her quite clearly. I'd know her if I saw her again," he asserted, putting his cup down. "Still, your being related to Miss Sekine's fiancé doesn't give me the right to discuss her case with you, as I'm sure you know."

"Yes, I'm aware of that." Attorney-client privilege. "For our part, though, we only want to find her and talk to her. I thought she might have come in to ask your advice."

"I'm sorry I can't be more help. I haven't set eyes on the woman since that time two years ago."

*Two years ago*? But it was already five years since she'd gone bankrupt. He felt a surge of interest. His surprise must have registered, because for a second Mizoguchi's face soured. It was a shot in the dark, but Honma tried it anyway. "Two years ago. You mean when her mother died?"

The attorney's eyes widened behind his bifocals. So Honma knew, did he? "Yes, that's right."

"Then I wonder if you'd also know where she was working at that time. Until a week ago, she was at a small company in Shinjuku called Imai Office Machines. And neither her boss nor the other employee seem to know much at all about her personal affairs."

Honma tried not to sound too critical. "I had them show me the résumé that she submitted when she applied for work there. But it turned out that all the entries were fictitious. Apparently she thought she wouldn't be hired if her past were known. I don't blame her, in any case. It's just that I'm at a dead end."

"What about her fiancé? He doesn't know anything?"

"If he did, he wouldn't have asked me to trace her in the first place. It seems Ms. Sekine didn't let on much about herself."

Mizoguchi's brow furrowed slightly. "Excuse me for a minute," he said, rising from his chair and moving toward the clerical desks with Jun's name card in his hand, presumably to call the bank to check that a Jun Kurisaka actually worked there. Maybe to check Honma's telephone number as well.

Honma settled back in his chair and waited. Three minutes later, Mizoguchi returned. He started firing questions as soon as he sat down.

"This Imai Office Machines, is it a regular company?" He was still frowning but sounded more positive.

"Yes. It's a small business. Deals in cash registers." Then, picturing Mitchie, he added: "A little company where the employees wear office uniforms. Typical, conservative."

Mizoguchi's next volley came low and sharp. "Then I take it Miss Sekine had given up her night work?"

Honma gazed back at the attorney in silence.

Mizoguchi nodded and went on. "Five years ago, when she first came in to discuss bankruptcy, she was working at a 'snack.' In Ginza or Shimbashi, I forget which, but anyway, one of those hole-in-the-wall places where girls sit at your table and pour you drinks."

"So she came to you through an introduction, or—?"

The attorney smiled briefly. "No, no. Back in the early eighties, during the whole 'consumer finance scare,' when everyone started spending beyond their means and a lot of good people were getting eaten alive by loan sharks, I decided to act as a lifeguard. I got into relief efforts directed at individuals facing debt accumulation and bankruptcy—I took part in lecture meetings, spoke with reporters, that sort of thing. Miss Sekine apparently saw something about me—

46

our office—in an article in a women's magazine at a beauty parlor."

Honma nodded casually, opening his memo pad.

"Miss Sekine's hometown was Utsunomiya, wasn't it?" asked Mizoguchi.

"Yes, that's right. She came to Tokyo immediately after high school."

"To begin with, she had a regular office job. She got her first credit card around that time. But she had trouble keeping up with payments, so she started a second job at night, hostessing. It wasn't long, though, before she was having serious problems with bill collectors and had to quit the day job; and after a while, you see, she got used to bar work, so that even after declaring bankruptcy she didn't go back to working in an office. The whole time she was consulting me, she was still working nights. At least that's what she said. It's often the case, they can't just return to—well, a conventional job." Mizoguchi removed his glasses and scratched his nose. "Still, this falsifying past employment, that can't be good," he concluded.

He reached for his teacup, only to find it empty. "Hey, Sawagi, let's have some tea here," he called out. The woman who knew the classics soon appeared with a fresh pot and refilled their cups.

One sip of hot tea got the attorney started again. "And then, two years ago, she came in to discuss her mother's insurance money. I remember that well." Shoko's mother had belonged to the National Insurance scheme and, by the time of her death, had accrued about two million yen. This, naturally, would go to Shoko. "She asked me whether it was hers to take, all of it. A little insecure, I suppose. I told her it was perfectly all right, any income post-bankruptcy can be kept as one's own. She'd lost a little weight, but otherwise she looked well enough. I remember thinking that things would probably sort themselves out."

Only one out of God knows how many clients, but the lawyer remembered her.

"An hour after a meal's over I may have forgotten what I had to eat, but I never forget a client. In Miss Sekine's case, the bankruptcy procedures took a bit of doing—she'd made a pretty thorough mess of things, you see. But two years ago, when she came in again, she seemed more at ease. Happier. I suppose some money had come in."

That would have been in 1990. "In April that same year, she went to work for Imai Office Machines," Honma said. "Do you think her mother's insurance money allowed her to save a bit, gave her a chance to quit the club trade?"

"One look at the records should set that straight. And give us her address and workplace at the time. Let me check."

He got up again and was gone this time for ten minutes. Honma grew edgy. Glancing at his watch, he saw that it was 4:25.

Two minutes later the attorney was back, with a slip of paper in his hand. "Her visit two years ago was right around this time—just a little after the New Year, January 25. These are the contacts she gave us then."

Honma thanked him politely and took the note. Written in large letters was the name of a bar—Lahaina—in Shimbashi, and below that her home address: Minamimachi 2-5-2-401, Kawaguchi City, Saitama. Her former employer was given as a Kasai Trading Company in Edogawa Ward, way over on the east side of the city.

"And this is the company she was forced to leave because of bill collectors?"

Mizoguchi nodded.

"You've been a big help."

As Honma filed away the note, the attorney said: "Could you let us know if you learn anything? Having once discussed this with you, I feel I have a certain responsibility."

"I will."

His next appointment already waiting, Mizoguchi remained standing beside his chair. Honma rose to his feet.

"If all else fails, you might try placing a three-line personal ad in the newspapers."

"You mean, like 'Shoko, let's talk it over. Come back, please'?"

"You'd be surprised, it can be quite effective. Providing you target the papers Miss Sekine reads ... And if there's anything we can do to help explain to your Mr. Kurisaka why Miss Sekine had to file for bankruptcy, we'd be only too glad to cooperate. It isn't as if the blame is entirely hers. This whole debt accumulation thing is a sort of moral pollution."

*Moral pollution.* Interesting choice of words, thought Honma. Too bad Mizoguchi didn't have more time.

"If she does happen to contact us, we'll be sure to tell her that Mr. Kurisaka's looking for her." Only we won't reveal her whereabouts to you, the attorney implied. "That way, she can get in touch if she likes. We'll do our best to convince her. There's nothing to be gained by running away, after all."

"Much obliged."

"If she does happen to contact us, that is," he emphasized with a smile. "These last two years, we haven't heard a word from her. No calls, no letters. She could very well have moved or quit the bar."

"Imai Office Machines is a nice little company," Honma reminded him. "A homey sort of place."

"And your Mr. Kurisaka, he's the serious type?"

"Extremely." If a bit full of himself, Honma thought.

"A banker," the attorney mused. "Well, Miss Sekine must have really changed. Not only her job and her lifestyle, but even her appearance. Because two years ago when we last saw her—her clothes, her makeup, everything still had 'bar' written all over it."

Honma smiled. "If that's the case, she's completely transformed. Or, rather, just gone back to her old self. Admittedly, men used to proposition her all the time. But, from talking to Jun and the people at Imai Office Machines, she comes across as smart but not flashy at all."

"Oh-ho!" Mizoguchi cocked his head to one side. "Sounds like a different person. It just goes to show you about women. Unpredictable creatures."

"Well, flexible, anyway."

"For which we should all be grateful."

It was January 25, 1990, when she had last visited the attorney. She began working at Imai Office Machines three months later, on April 20. Short time for a 180° turn. Could her mother's insurance money have done the trick?

49

Honma and Mizoguchi were halfway to the door. There were two clients already waiting.

"Ms. Sekine was—how shall I put it?—prone to entanglements with men," Mizoguchi said. "I didn't think she could extricate herself easily from the bar world ... Incidentally, I think she said she was going to save up some money and get her teeth fixed. She had these crooked front teeth, you see. I tried to convince her they had character, but no, she wanted to get them straightened."

Their pace was already slow, but this revelation stopped Honma in his tracks.

*Crooked teeth*? That Sawagi woman had said the same thing ... *Wait—didn't she have crooked teeth?* Must have been a prominent feature if they made more of a lasting impression than that bookish name of hers. There was no way of telling: in her résumé photo, her mouth was closed. Of course, Jun wouldn't have mentioned anything about her teeth. Or else maybe she'd had them fixed before she met him. It was possible she'd used her mother's insurance money for just that.

*A 180° turn ... between January 25 and April 20, 1990.*

No, impossible. What was he thinking? This wasn't a case—it was just a favor for a relative.

"Is anything the matter?" Mizoguchi asked, sounding slightly impatient.

*Like a different person ... in a very short time.*

Honma felt like whacking himself on the forehead. Two months away from the job and already he was losing it. In any investigation, what was the first thing you absolutely had to do? Get a positive ID. Find out who you were looking for, so you didn't waste time questioning people only to find that you'd run down the wrong person. Do the name and the face match up? The crooked teeth might not add up to much, but they were still worth following up. His police training was so ingrained, he could still hardly believe Jun hadn't brought a photo of Shoko along with him, and that he himself hadn't asked for one.

"Sorry, one last question." He pulled out the résumé and held it up in front of him. "The woman in this photo *is* Shoko Sekine, right?"

50

Mizoguchi looked at it. And kept looking, much too long. Honma counted to ten. His intuition had been right.

*Like a different person ... in a very short time.*

"No," said the attorney, shaking his head slowly. He pushed the thing away, scowling in displeasure. "This is not the Shoko Sekine I know. I've never seen this woman before. I don't know who it is, but it's *not* Shoko Sekine. It's someone else entirely."

# ✧ 6 ✧

It was after eight at night when Honma got out of the car in front of
the apartment house. Jun, meanwhile, went looking for a parking
space further down the street. The place was a good fifteen-minute
hike from Honancho Station on a suburban branch of the Marunouchi Line subway: an informal modern building block with stylish
bay windows. Shoko lived in 103—ground floor, southeast corner.
The other residents all kept their bikes locked up right outside her
window.

Jun had agreed to pick him up at home, but then had clearly been
displeased when Honma didn't fill him in en route about every detail
of the day's investigations. He'd driven badly.

"You know, I was supposed to work late today, but I took off
around six just for this. You ought to at least tell me something," he
said irritably, thrusting a hand into his pocket for the apartment key.

"I doubt missing a few hours of overtime will blot your record
much," Honma answered calmly, leaning up against a column in the
entrance.

Jun kept Shoko's key in his wallet instead of on his own key ring,
so his mother wouldn't see it. He sighed heavily as he turned it in the
lock. "Don't you think I feel just a little put out?"

Honma ignored him and went in first. "Where's the light?"

Behind him Jun flicked the switch that turned on the ceiling lamp.
Both men took off their shoes and stepped up into a short hallway.

After leaving the lawyer, Honma had called Jun's office and asked
them to ring his beeper. Jun then phoned him at a coffee shop.

"Look, do you know where Shoko is registered to vote?"

The abrupt opening had left Jun speechless. "What do you want to know *that* for?"

"Do you know?"

"Do I know?... Yes, I know. At her Honancho address, is where. She's been there a while already."

"Really?"

"Yes, really. During the Tokyo City elections, a card came to her there."

"Okay, then, I want you to get a copy of her residence certificate. You think you can do that for me while you're out on your rounds?"

"And why is that necessary?"

"I can't explain. But if you tell them you're her fiancé and that she asked you to get it for her, I don't imagine the Ward Office is going to refuse. Take some form of personal ID. If they say no, well, that's that. But see what you can do."

"Uh, okay. I'll give it a try."

Honma gave only those instructions, then headed home. He'd had a bad headache the whole way back on the train. His head was still throbbing with the last of it now.

Around seven, when Jun came by to pick him up, Honma had a crisis on his hands—a small bomb in the form of his son. The boy knew his father was planning to go out again that night. Honma, of course, understood that Makoto was worried or, more precisely, scared. Ever since his mother's car accident he'd been like this. His father was all he had left and if anything happened to him—the thought sent him into a panic. He couldn't have Honma take any risks or face the least danger. Honma managed to calm him down whenever possible, but tonight it was no good: the boy shut himself in his room as he was leaving.

"Sorry," Jun said as soon as Honma got in the car. "The residence certificate—I couldn't get it." For a second, he looked almost smug.

"Then you were wrong, about her having applied for a new residence certificate at Honancho?

"No. They turned me down flat. Said that being her fiancé wasn't enough, I needed to have a letter giving me power of attorney."

So much for that idea. Probably got himself a real "public servant" type at the window, knowing his luck. "She didn't have a roommate?"

Hands on the wheel, Jun turned and gave Honma an incredulous look. "You mean, someone who lived with her? You must be joking."

"Then did you ever meet her landlord?"

"Just to say hello. She lives in the neighborhood. Shoko sometimes stopped and chatted with her."

There went any possibility of a switch. Jun's "Shoko Sekine" had lived in the Honancho apartment under that name right from the beginning, was friendly with the owner, and was registered to vote there.

But what if the real owner of the name had sold her family register? Right after her bankruptcy, when she couldn't get back on her feet. What if she'd sold it to a woman her own age who needed a "background"?

A grimmer possibility, though, was that the real Shoko Sekine was already dead. Honma certainly didn't want to bring up either scenario, but he couldn't help considering them. So for the remainder of the journey he kept quiet. And Jun kept his foot on the accelerator.

The Honancho apartment was cold inside. Cold as Honma's mood.

On the left-hand side of the hallway was a bath-toilet unit; on the right, a tiny kitchenette. A refrigerator, a cupboard and a microwave oven on a cart stood flush against the wall, with just enough space for one person to move around. Everything was neat and tidy. The stainless steel sink was scrubbed to a dull gleam. One empty beer can had been tossed into the corner of the sink—left over from Jun's last visit, no doubt. Otherwise there was not a thing out of place. The ventilator fan gave two spins from an outside breeze and stopped. The blades shone. Honma left the kitchen.

The living area was equally spotless. Rectangular in shape, the room was wide enough to double as a bedroom. A simple bedframe was set back along the right-hand side. The bedcover was drawn up over the pillow. On a shelf above the headboard sat a lamp and two paperbacks, *Traveling Alone in America* and *European Shopping Tips*. Two compass points, opposite directions. The cover of *America* showed more wear and tear. Right beside the bed, beneath a window, was a wastebasket, empty.

There was one built-in closet, as well as a sizable wardrobe and an assembly-kit bookcase. On top of a small chest of drawers on casters was a cordless phone. Two chairs and a round table of unfinished wood stood on a carpet. Next to the table, a large wicker hamper held an unfinished sweater and various balls of wool skewered with knitting needles.

"She was making it for me. We were supposed to go skiing next month."

"Did she have skis?"

Jun nodded. "Out in the locker on the veranda."

Honma slid the door open. Up against the partition between her veranda and the next apartment's—space that in theory was to be kept clear in case of fire—stood one of those storage lockers you see advertised in mail-order catalogs. Inside were a brand new pair of skis and an oversized carryall for ski boots. Both were sealed neatly in plastic bags.

"When did the two of you take up skiing?" asked Honma.

"Shoko, the year before last, after we met. Me, I've been skiing since high school."

"And when did she buy all the gear?"

"Also over the last couple of years. First she bought skiwear. Then with last year's summer and winter bonuses, she got herself some skis and boots. We went together to buy them, I remember." He added, somberly, "She always paid in cash. Even when the store was pushing revolving credit."

Honma refrained from comment. He could have told him that his "Shoko Sekine" wasn't the one who had gone bankrupt—and wasn't for that matter named Shoko—but now was not the time.

The skis were Rossignols, the boots Salomons—both leading import brands.

"Aren't these kind of expensive, as ski equipment goes?"

Jun bent over to touch the boot bag. "Not that bad. Not if they're slightly older models. New models'll break you if you lay in the lot all at once. But one item at a time … These brands aren't too fancy for a beginner. Her skiwear was Cresson, I think."

Honma moved the boot bag aside and found an upended toolbox.

55

Next to it was a small capped bottle wrapped in a dustrag. The bottle gave off a strong smell.

"What's that?" asked Jun, peering into the locker.

"Gasoline," said Honma, putting it down again. After five minutes outside in the night air, his fingers were numb. The veranda backed onto another condominium. That and an extra screen fixed above the railing for privacy obviously blocked out any sunlight. No clothesline in sight. "What did she do for laundry?"

"She used the laundromat," said Jun. "There's no place to put a washing machine in the apartment. No place to dry clothes, either. Anyway, this being the ground floor, she wouldn't hang up her underwear in full view."

Stepping back inside, Honma pulled up a chair and sat down. He took another look around. Neither the curtains nor any of the interior furnishings were of particularly high quality—except for the wardrobe, which looked like good hardwood and must have cost a fair bit. Something to last a lifetime, so she probably talked herself into splurging just that once.

"What's the rent here? Did she say?"

Jun looked up blankly from the unfinished sweater he'd spread out before him—a body with no sleeves. Honma repeated his question.

"Ah … a little over sixty thousand yen."

"Cheap." And small and dark. And, chances were, poorly insulated. But, anyway, it was in town and fairly new.

"Apparently the landlady built it as an inheritance tax dodge. Can't make a profit or she gets in trouble. Shoko was rather proud of finding a property like this." Then, casting a suspicious eye at Honma, he asked, "What makes you want to know?"

Honma, meanwhile, was occupied with the wardrobe. On closer inspection from the side there was a large discoloration or blotch by one of the handles. They had probably knocked down the price for that. The occupant of this room seemed to be quite a practiced bargain hunter. "Any idea what she took with her?"

Jun sat on the bed, looking at the closet. "A few clothes and the

Boston bag she always uses on trips. That and her bankbook and seal."

"That's all? Are you sure?"

"Positive. Shoko kept her valuables in a cookie tin under her bed." Jun crouched down and brought out a square box from a famous confectioner's in Ginza. It was practically empty. All that remained was a small seal that read "Sekine."

There, she's rid of that name, thought Honma. "I'd like you to find three things. First, her photo album."

"That'll be on the bookcase."

"Next, her high school yearbook."

Jun blinked. "What for?"

"Did she ever show it to you?"

He winced.

"Did she?"

He slowly shook his head. "No. She said she never wanted to think about her past, where she came from."

"But usually that's something you would keep. Or do you think she's renting some storage space somewhere else?"

"I'm sure she isn't. To begin with, she doesn't need it. She lives by herself and doesn't have that much money. You saw Imai Office Machines, right? She's living on that salary. She isn't in any position to spend on extras."

"Okay. Anyway, a high school yearbook or something like it."

"And the third thing?" Jun seemed to have no idea what to expect. He reached out and put a hand on the wall for balance, like somebody walking with his eyes closed. He didn't know what Honma was after, where this was all leading.

"When she declared bankruptcy, she must have received various papers from her attorney or from the court. Could you look around to see what became of them?"

Jun's mouth twitched at the corners as he thought better of whatever he'd been about to say. For the next half hour, the two of them worked in silence, searching the well-ordered room. There were gaps in the closet where items of clothing had been removed.

Ultimately Jun managed to locate only her photo album, in precisely the place where he knew he'd find it all along. Honma discovered a small bottle of perfume pushed to the back of her bookcase. He uncapped it and was shocked by the heady smell it gave off. If she'd worn this to Imai Office Machines, old man Imai would have had a seizure.

"Is this the perfume she used?" asked Honma, holding out the bottle.

Jun wrinkled his nose. "No, she never wore anything this strong. It was a lighter cologne. A little atomizer spray she kept in her handbag."

Honma returned the bottle to the bookcase. A clean and comfortable place, all in all. You could easily rent it out as is, without rearranging a thing.

But *she* was gone, Honma reflected. Like a spider, gone without a trace, leaving a perfect web behind. "Let's call it quits," he said. "Mind if borrow her photo album? I'll return it as soon as I'm finished with it."

"What do you need it for?"

"Do I have to explain my methods at each and every step?"

Jun looked away, the album clasped under his arm. "They're my fiancée's pictures."

"Your rather secretive fiancée's. I'm trying to help you find her, aren't I?"

Jun gave an angry-sounding snort, but handed over the album just the same.

"By the way," said Honma, "I heard about a ring you gave her. It looks like she took it with her, huh?"

When he spoke next, Jun's voice was slow and gloomy. "What's going on? You haven't used Shoko's name once tonight. You've just been saying 'she' or 'her.'"

"Have I?"

"Why did you want to search her apartment?"

Honma didn't answer. He pulled the door shut, leaving Jun's questions to the dark apartment along with his own, bigger question: just who had been living there?

## ✧ 7 ✧

It was ten by the time Honma got home, photo album in hand. He was exhausted. He stopped to rest once in the lobby of his building and once again halfway along the third-floor corridor to his apartment. Oddly enough, the front door was unlocked, which he only realized when he turned the key to find he'd just locked the door. On the second try, he heard footsteps as Isaka came and opened it from inside.

"You came over to mind the house?"

"Hisae was late getting back from her New Year's party and I was bored all alone, so your boy and me, we watched some TV." Isaka looked embarrassed. The truth was probably that Makoto had thrown a tantrum, and he hadn't wanted to leave him on his own.

"Sorry." Honma lowered his voice. "Was he a lot of trouble?"

Isaka shook his head and glanced toward Makoto's room. "He's asleep. Told me absolutely not to wake him up if his father came home."

"Oh boy, he *is* mad." Honma smiled wearily.

Isaka suppressed a laugh. Then the two of them started toward the living room, where the television was still on. By the time Honma got there, Isaka had switched it off and turned on the lights. Isaka now looked Honma over, almost like a tailor sizing up a customer. "Hard day?"

"Ran around too much in one go. Things got kind of out of control."

Honma put the photo album down on the table. Isaka gave it a curious glance, then asked, "How about a beer?"

Trust Isaka to tempt him. Honma had been on a no-drinking, no-smoking regimen since he left the hospital, though recently he'd gotten a bit lax. When he couldn't sleep, a little alcohol in the system was better than sleeping pills. But tonight, on top of all this? He'd end up sleeping the whole day tomorrow. He shook his head.

"Okay, shall I make some coffee?" Isaka suggested, heading into the kitchen. Give him an apron and put him in front of a stove or a dish rack and he was right in his element. Isaka lived with his wife Hisae in a two-bedroom apartment at the east end of the ground floor. They had no children. He'd turned fifty this year, but seemed older. Hisae, at forty-three, was a year older than Honma, but she looked ten years younger. She ran an interior design office together with a friend in a fashionable part of town. Their services were in such demand that she only got time off at the New Year holidays.

Isaka had been working at an architectural firm that had dealings with her office, till the recession set in and construction work slowed. Hisae was still going strong, though, and both of them had savings, so they decided he'd stay at home until things picked up again. Initially, that was how Isaka became a househusband. They'd always divided up the housework, so there was no fuss over the new arrangements. And after several months, he discovered a "calling" for housework and decided to make it a full-time job.

By now, he'd contracted out to do cleaning and washing for two households in the apartment block besides Honma's. This didn't mean, though, that he and his wife stopped sharing their own housework evenly between them. Hisae was always saying she wouldn't have it any other way.

"Makoto says he's angry because Uncle Jun came and asked you to do him some 'dumb favor,' " Isaka said, pouring the coffee.

Honma laughed, digging his elbows into the armrests of his chair and rubbing his face. "A 'dumb favor' is right. It's doing a real number on my head."

When Chizuko was killed and Honma wasn't able to take an extended leave from work, Makoto had been left on his own. It was the Isakas who came forward and offered to help look after him. They began to see him off to school in the morning and pick him up in the afternoon. They did everything for him. Thanks to them, Honma and Makoto were able to get a new lease on life. So whenever something came up—whether in his work or at home—Honma would usually find himself talking it over with them. In fact, since his hospitalization, Honma had been leaning more and more on them.

"What is it this time? Missing person?" asked Isaka, stirring two teaspoons of sugar into his coffee.

Honma nodded. "Jun's fiancée ran out on him ... or I guess you could say that."

"You mean she ... whoa, better put some sugar in that," Isaka said before Honma could drink his cup. "When you're run-down, you should have some sugar. I always tell Hisae, too. Cut out the sugar because you're on a diet, drink those vitamin drinks because you're tired—you're going to burn yourself out. Nothing more unnatural than that. If you're tired, sugar's the best thing."

Okay. Following this wise advice, Honma drank his coffee sweet. And it worked like a charm. Maybe he wasn't feeling any less exhausted, but it did take the edge off his nerves.

"So, about Jun's fiancée ...?" Isaka backtracked.

"Or whoever she is," Honma replied. "I'm still not sure of anything. Other than it doesn't feel right."

Honma spoke slowly, sorting out his own thoughts. He retold the events of the day, explaining how things had gone from strange to stranger—the false résumé, the unidentifiable ID photo. Isaka nodded at every turn.

"This going around using someone else's name ..." Honma rubbed the back of his neck. "And not just the name. She's borrowed the person's whole life, in a way. Though it's not unprecedented. Way back around 1955 there was this guy who took someone else's identity, using a borrowed family register. He was sued for infringing that person's rights."

The case made news because it was a first for Japan, the first time the legal standing of personal identity was tested in a country that based everything on the family. Until the American Occupation in the late 1940s, the individual had had no rights in Japan; in fact, the whole notion of "rights" was a Western import. Instead, the family had always been the legal unit. The family was actually responsible and liable for the actions of its members. All that talk about not doing anything to make your family lose face was more than just Confucian morals.

Even now, if you get down to it, you aren't your own person, you're just one new line entered in the record of an entire family. The record is registered in the family's hometown, and it goes back for generations. Everything that happens in the family is recorded in detail: births, deaths, marriages. When a daughter is married off, she is removed from her parents' family register and put in a new one with the husband as the head. These documents are officially confidential, but in fact anyone in the family has access to them. Each time legal identification is required—say, when you get married or receive an inheritance—you have to go to the local government office in person and get an official copy of your family register. They'll ask you to sign for it with a certified seal bearing the family name. All very proper and correct.

Then the Americans came in and "democratized" the system. Sort of. With the introduction of voting and local taxation, it became necessary to keep closer track of people, so another layer of documentation came into being: the residence certificate. Individual but temporary. This is valid only as long as you stay at a specific current address, but it doesn't affect your permanent address, where your "real self" is considered to reside. For less official purposes like taking out a library card, all you need is the residence certificate and not the family register. For most legal purposes, though, you need both. And if you live far away, getting the family register through the proper channels can take forever.

So the man who borrowed that family register in 1955 kept his distance. He didn't make any changes, because if he had, he was bound to be discovered at some point. If the actual person saw that his residence certificate or anything had changed, he'd have known something was up right away. So the guy just held his breath and altered nothing on paper. He just borrowed the name.

That's where he and Jun's "Shoko Sekine" parted company.

"Nowadays, though, I wouldn't be surprised if folks bought and sold family registers," Isaka said. "I mean, like those women from Southeast Asia who get married on paper to a Japanese man just for the work permit." Isaka was obviously pleased with himself for coming up with this angle. "Hey—when you really think about it, what's the whole point of the family register?"

"They don't have it in the West."

"There you are! Only in Japan."

"Still, that's not to say it's totally useless. It helps prevent certain crimes."

Isaka blinked. "Like, for instance?"

"Bigamy," chuckled Honma. "You see it all the time in foreign movies and novels. Over there in America, all they've got are birth certificates and marriage certificates. Nothing's centralized. Let's say you're born, get married, and die in three different cities—then your records are scattered across the country, without any cross-referencing. And the country's huge anyway, so bigamy's not that uncommon. Here, we can just look up your family register and find out your marital status."

"A guy can't fool around."

"No. The best you could do would be to move your register around, to make it harder for people to find out you'd been married before."

"Okay, but if that's really all it's good for, the whole system is dead weight and we'd do better to scrap it."

Yes, like Isaka said, there had to be an easier way. A more streamlined legal apparatus to protect people's privacy without all the rigmarole.

"It has its problems, I agree. Not to mention all the complications of adoption. Remember, they only introduced that Special Ruling on Adoption about five years ago." Honma noted that Isaka acknowledged this digression with a nod and no particular expression on his face. Trying hard to act nonchalant, out of consideration.

Makoto wasn't Honma and Chizuko's natural child. They had adopted him when he was still a baby. That was before the Special Ruling on Adoption allowed the biological parents' names to go unlisted on the adoptive parents' family register.

People are cruel by nature. As soon as they see a person being a little different they have to get their jabs in. When Makoto was in nursery school, somehow the word had gotten out—some teacher who saw the register must have whispered something to a friend— because soon enough everyone knew he was adopted. The kids were only four years old at the time, so they didn't really care one way or the other. But the mothers carried on so much that it had Chizuko alternately angry and depressed for quite some time.

That's when the two of them talked it over and decided that since Makoto was bound to find out eventually, rather than let him hear it from someone else, they'd tell him themselves as soon as he turned twelve. Then just three years later Honma had lost Chizuko. So now he would have to tell the boy himself. But there were still another two years to go.

Isaka broke into Honma's thoughts. "Jun's girlfriend, the one he was engaged to, I suppose she didn't know that this Shoko Sekine had gone bankrupt?"

"Probably she was more startled than anyone." No wonder she'd gone white as a sheet. It was a huge miscalculation.

"But then she realized that if people started poking into that bankruptcy, they'd find out she wasn't who she said she was. Which is why she ran."

"In one hell of a hurry."

"And maybe it's not heaven she's heading for," said Isaka, slow and serious.

"I get this awful feeling. But I still don't know about that residence certificate of hers."

"Jun's pretty straight, I'm afraid," Isaka observed. "He probably lost his nerve when he got to the window at the Ward Office." But since Honma hadn't let him in on the whole story, he hadn't known how important this mission was. "Why not have someone down at the Division run a requisition on it? The Division Chief doesn't look over every single application like that, does he? Nobody needs to know. What could be simpler?… But you probably don't want to pull those strings."

"No. Because, well, this is a private investigation. And it's still within Greater Metropolitan Tokyo. If things spread further afield, I couldn't handle it myself. I'd ask for regional assistance."

"What if you went to the authorities yourself and explained the situation. Wouldn't they give you a hand?"

"Not a chance. Bureaucrats are real sticklers about that sort of thing. They have to be."

Isaka thought it over, chin propped on his hand. "What if you got a girl roughly the same age as Shoko Sekine to go in and say, 'That's me.' Do you think they'd check her ID?"

Honma shook his head. "I doubt it … but no, it's hard to say."

"Well, then, it's settled," said Isaka with a sly smile. "We'll get Hisae to send one of the girls from her office."

"No, we can't do that. That's going too far."

"It's an emergency, so who's to say what's too far? I'll talk to Hisae."

Isaka shambled off around eleven, but Honma wasn't in the mood for sleep, not yet. He began leafing through the photo album. Jun and his fiancée apparently weren't shutterbugs. They ought to have had a good year-and-a-half's worth of snapshots since they started going out together, but the album wasn't half full. Either that, or …

Honma stopped flipping the pages. Here was someone living on the edge, inhabiting someone else's identity. That meant constant vigilance: take no photos, leave no evidence. Her small circle of acquaintances made sense, too. This was someone stripped for battle. She'd been ready to move out at a moment's notice. Honma remembered the bottle of gasoline in the locker at the Honancho apartment. A spoiled kid like Jun would have no idea what it was for—he'd never done any housework—but Honma clicked immediately. He'd seen Chizuko do it once: wipe the grease from the kitchen fan with gasoline. Hence the shiny blades. Not that Jun's fiancée would have stopped to clean the fan before her getaway; she must have routinely put the dustcloth to everything, every single day. Take no prisoners, leave no traces.

What if things had gone normally and they'd gotten married?

What if she'd been discovered after they had put down roots, what then? Would she still have run?

The last photo in the album was a large close-up of her face. She was standing just in front of the brightly lit spires of Cinderella's castle at Tokyo Disneyland. Probably their last outing. Maybe last Christmas or New Year's Eve. She was smiling. A beautiful straight set of teeth.

Honma saw a young woman as particular about cleanliness as about her personal appearance. He saw her vacuuming the floor, using a screwdriver from the toolbox to assemble the bookcase, wiping the kitchen fan blades with a gasoline-soaked rag.

*Detergent will do, but to get them whistle-clean, there's nothing like gasoline.* Or so Chizuko used to say. But since it made her skin go red, she'd apply gobs of hand cream afterward. It was hard to believe that any woman familiar with the same tricks of housekeeping that Chizuko had known would have a murky past. Honma wasn't in the habit of digging up nice girls' sordid histories.

Suddenly a sound came from behind him and Honma swung around. "What are you doing out of bed?"

Makoto stood there as only ten-year-olds can do, half-smoldering, half-shivering, pouting at the floor.

"If you're going to walk around, put on some clothes. You need to go to the toilet?"

Still no answer.

Honma lowered his voice. "Out with it. I can't tell what's the matter if you just make a face." For a while all he could hear was Makoto's breathing. Uh-oh, he's caught a cold again, thought Honma. "Your nose is all stopped up, isn't it?"

Makoto gave him a not-on-your-life look. "Is not."

"Stand around like that in your bare feet for ten minutes and you *will* be sniffling."

"Can I?" Makoto gestured toward a chair by jutting out his chin. He then scowled at his father and asked again: "Can I sit down?"

"Yes, you *may*."

Makoto climbed onto the chair and turned to face him, edgy and squirrel-eyed. "Where you been?"

"Here and there."

"What's that?" He pointed at the photo album.

"Something I borrowed from Uncle Jun."

"What'd Uncle Jun ask you to do? Something so important you got to go out when you're not in shape? Didn't you promise you'd stay home till you got better?" His words got faster and faster, ending in a splutter. Makoto must have been thinking his little head off in bed. Planning on this and that to say. But almost the minute he opened his mouth, he'd forgotten everything. All that came out was anger.

"Sorry," Honma said straightaway. "I did break my promise. I shouldn't have." Makoto blinked impassively. "But listen, Uncle Jun's in a real bind right now. He needs somebody to lend him a hand."

"Uncle Jun's never done anything to help us out. So why do you have to? Seems kind of funny to me."

Makoto was right about that.

"You really think so?"

"Uh-huh."

"Well, if that's so, we'd never help anybody who's in trouble."

Makoto went quiet, then, after a couple of feigned sniffles, resumed his protest. "Yeah, but why's it gotta be us? Couldn't Uncle Jun ask somebody else?"

"Like who?"

Makoto gave it some thought. "How about going to the police?"

"At this stage, the police wouldn't lift a finger. I should know, right?"

Makoto swung his legs impatiently. "Is he looking for somebody?"

"Uh-huh."

"Somebody in the photo album?"

Honma nodded.

"Can I see?"

Makoto wanted to have a look at the person who had made his father break his promise. Honma showed him the last photo in the album and said, "This woman here."

The boy stared intently at the photograph. "That's Disneyland, isn't it?"

"Probably."

"This lady's nice-looking, huh?"

"You think so too?"

"What about you, Dad?"

"Well, sure."

"I bet Uncle Jun thinks she's pretty."

"Definitely."

"Did she run out on him?"

Honma paused a second, then said, "Well, that's not a very nice way to put it."

Makoto lowered his eyes and swung his feet, his bad mood slipping away. "You know, today …," came a small voice.

"What?"

"Blockhead got lost."

Honma's mental stapler had run out of clips. Incoming reports wouldn't hold together and just shot straight through his skull. "Sorry?"

"Blockhead's lost. Didn't come home to Kazzy's last night. What if he's been taken away?"

Blockhead was Kazzy's family dog, a mutt. Three months back, Kazzy and Makoto had found him in the park. Makoto wanted to keep him, but Honma wouldn't let him; pets weren't allowed in the housing project. And, besides, it would have placed an extra burden on Isaka. Somehow, though, Kazzy managed to talk his parents into letting Blockhead—as the dog came to be called—stay with them, and Makoto took him out for walks now and then.

"Blockhead is a big dog now," Honma offered. "Sometimes he's going to stay out for two or three nights at a time."

Blockhead was, in fact, an adult dog, but still on the small side. You could pick him up with one arm. Probably had some terrier blood in him. That would also explain his temperament—so friendly that he'd run up even to total strangers. Yet try teaching him the simplest tricks—shake hands or roll over—and he just couldn't or wouldn't learn. That was how he got his name. A dog like that would have let anyone passing by lead him away.

"Don't worry, give him a little time. He'll probably turn up tomorrow morning, bright and early."

So *that's* what was eating Makoto. Okay, he probably was keyed up about his father walking around on his bad knee, but he also just wanted some sympathy over the dog thing.

"If he doesn't come back, can I go look for him?"

"I don't see why not."

After a moment, Makoto spoke up again. "Dad, you worried 'bout Uncle Jun's girlfriend, too?"

"Of course I am."

"Like me and Blockhead," said Makoto with a little nod. "Just don't overdo it and wear yourself out so much that that therapy lady calls you again, okay?"

Honma's physical therapy regime was so intensive he'd once skipped a session, which had prompted a call from the therapist to lecture him about it. The sort of thing that ruined a father's image.

"It's a promise."

Makoto chuckled as he slid down from his chair. "Oops, sorry!" he said when his elbow hit the album and bumped it off the table. He scrambled to pick it up, and a photograph fell out. Honma retrieved it. A Polaroid of a house, taken straight-on and filling the entire frame.

"What's that?" the boy asked, craning his neck.

It was a fancy Western-style suburban house. The walls were chocolate brown, and the windows and door were edged with white trim. Flowerboxes stood on either side of the porch. A pitched roof, tilted just so, like a lady's hat, sported a tiny skylight. In the foreground, crossing the picture from right to left, were two women. Both seemed to be aware of the camera as they passed in front of the house. One of them was facing straight ahead; the other had her head turned toward the camera and her hand raised slightly as if to wave. Both women wore bright blue skirts and matching vests, with long-sleeved white blouses and maroon ribbon bow ties. Uniforms, probably.

A house and two women. Other than that, a patch of blue sky in the upper left-hand corner. And some kind of metal tower. Only a small part of the tower was visible, but after a moment Honma thought he recognized it: a baseball stadium's lights?

Opening the album again, Honma saw that the snapshot had

come from a pocket on the inside cover. A pocket for holding negatives, made of opaque paper. That would explain why he hadn't noticed it before.

After Makoto had gone back to bed, Honma sat staring at the Polaroid. A full frontal view of a house, that's all. Suddenly two women had happened to walk into the frame. It must have been that way; otherwise, they'd have been better posed. No, definitely, the house was the subject of the picture. Then why would she have kept it? Was it her house? If so, it might be a lead. And what about the bank of lights just out of the picture? A house by a stadium? Precious little to pinpoint the location. How many stadiums were there, anyway, in Japan?

Deciding to keep the Polaroid, along with the close-up of Jun's fiancée, he slipped them into his notebook just as the cuckoo clock in Makoto's room was striking midnight.

✧ 8 ✧

At ten o'clock the next morning Hisae Isaka showed up with copies of the family register and residence certificate. Her cheeks were flushed from the biting cold. Her breath hung in the air, as white as the brand-new sneakers she was wearing. For someone who drove a bright red Audi and generated enough income to support a secretary and three designers, her dress was pretty casual.

"Rie at the office went and got it. It's true, you just go and say 'That's me.' Couldn't be simpler," she said, peeling off her mustard-yellow jacket.

The minute she got a good look at Honma in the kitchen, she exclaimed, "My God! You look like a prisoner of war they've just rescued from somewhere."

Okay, maybe he could have shaved a bit better, Honma thought, rubbing his chin. But he wasn't feeling at all bad today. "Do I look that tired?" he asked.

"No, that's not it—quite the opposite," she assured him. "You look years younger. You must have had enough of being cooped up in here."

"Especially once he got a taste of life on the outside," added Isaka, stepping into the entryway with a whisk broom in his hand.

"True enough. The only outside life I had for a while there was the Nautilus."

"The what?"

"You know, weight-lifting machines. They make you use them in rehab."

"Oh," said Hisae flatly. "They name them after monsters?" And from her oversized bag she pulled a residence certificate in an official envelope and laid it, together with a transcript of the family register, on the table. She gave a nod of confirmation. "Here, check for yourself. Everything you asked for."

The Honancho residence certificate, naturally enough, listed Shoko Sekine as the sole occupant.

| | |
|---|---|
| HEAD OF HOUSEHOLD | Shoko Sekine |
| ADDRESS | Honancho 3-4-5, Suginami Ward, Tokyo |

And in the "Resident (1)" column:

| | |
|---|---|
| NAME (Given Name, Surname) | Shoko Sekine |
| DATE OF BIRTH | The 14th day of September, 1964 |
| SEX | Female |
| RELATIONSHIP | Head of household |
| FAMILY REGISTER | Honancho 3-4-5, Suginami Ward, Tokyo Moved April 1, 1990, from Minamimachi 2-5-2, Kawaguchi City, Saitama Prefecture |

This meant that the move from Kawaguchi came soon after Shoko's visit to Mizoguchi's law office on January 25, two years ago. The new job at Imai Office Machines also started around then. So it was a safe bet that the switch in identity had happened before April 1990.

"Her family register says that she was born in Utsunomiya," Honma pointed out. "But she wrote 'Tokyo' as her permanent address on her résumé ... by which you'd think she meant the new address she registered when she moved. But look, that's not the reason. She started her *own* family register."

| | |
|---|---|
| HOUSEHOLD | Honancho 3-4-5, Suginami Ward, Tokyo |
| PRINCIPLE REGISTRANT | Shoko Sekine, Ms. |
| REGISTER DETAILS | Established on the 1st day of April, 1992 (seal) |

| PERSONAL DETAILS | Born on the 14th day of September, 1964, in Ichozakacho, Utsunomiya City, Tochigi Prefecture, as registered by her father on the 20th day of September, 1964 (seal) |
| | Removed from the family register of Shoji Sekine, Ichozakacho 2001, Utsunomiya City, Tochigi Prefecture, on the 1st day of April, 1992 (seal) |

| PARENTS | Father | Shoji Sekine, Mr., deceased |
| | Mother | Yoshiko Sekine, Mrs., deceased |
| | Relationship | Daughter |
| | Name | Shoko |
| DATE OF BIRTH | | The 14th day of September, 1964 |

And for good measure, since this involved establishing a new register, not just transferring the old one to a different government office, the attached official list of addresses included only this latest address:

| ADDRESS | Honancho 3-4-5, Suginami Ward, Tokyo |
| RESIDENCE ESTABLISHED | The 1st day of April, 1990 |
| NAME | Shoko |

That was all. The list was meant to verify the residential history of just the head of the household listed, so the Utsunomiya record headed by her father was not attached. Look up the file kept under his name, however, and it would show everything, including the new addresses where the real Shoko had applied, each time she moved, for a new residence certificate, before her impersonator came along and established an individual family register. And the last of those addresses should read Minamimachi 2-5-2, Kawaguchi City, Saitama Prefecture—where the real Shoko Sekine lived when she was working at the bar Lahaina and went to ask Mizoguchi whether it would be all right for her to collect her mother's insurance money.

Poring over the columns of words, Honma could feel goosebumps rising on his arms.

"Maybe I'm reading too much into it, but …," Hisae said quietly.

"What?"

"It seems strange. She wasn't satisfied with borrowing Shoko Sekine's register, she had to make everything her own, from scratch."

"You mean taking the extra step of creating a new family register?" Honma had the same sense of foreboding.

"And then there's this 'deceased' entry in the columns for her father and mother. Actually, you have to *ask* for that to be put in."

"Really?" said Isaka.

"Yes, I know because when my mother died, they asked me if I wanted the word 'deceased' by the name or not."

Honma scowled at the documents.

"But why would she go to all that trouble?" she went on. "Some kind of personal statement? She's already the only person listed on the register. Maybe she didn't want any connection with someone else's parents, or … Oh, I probably *am* reading too much into it, don't you think, dear?" This was said to her husband.

Honma glanced at the "deceased" entries again. What Hisae was saying didn't seem far-fetched at all. Someone else's family register and parents. Bought or taken over. However she'd managed it, she'd as good as become the real thing.

"Think about it, though. It's not so easy for a person to change places with a total stranger," said Isaka, his hunched shoulders suggesting that he too was worried.

"It's not easy at all. But it's not impossible if you push the right buttons," said Honma.

"Still, family register aside … If you're working, you're entered on health insurance and pension schemes, right?"

"And they're all organized on a local ward basis. Now, health insurance—or at least the kind provided by an employer—is made out in the name and address you list on your résumé when you apply for the job. As long as those check out, that's all there is to it. Then, if you quit, you're automatically withdrawn from the scheme and have to rejoin at the next job. On your last day at work, you even have to turn in your insurance card. So it'd be hard to get away with using somebody else's card, which means there's usually no need for elaborate checks."

Hisae noticed her husband looking at her questioningly and nodded at him. "Rie does all the paperwork at our office," she said. "We don't look into it very closely."

Honma continued: "If you sign up for National Health Insurance instead of a plan offered by an employer, it's based on the residence certificate. So when you move and sign up at a new address, you just have to show proof that you've withdrawn from your previous scheme —whether National Health or any other sort. The same goes for pension funds too. Again, the checks are very loose. And even though everyone's supposed to sign up for the National Pension Fund, lots of people don't."

Isaka peered down at the documents as Honma went on speaking.

"When the real Shoko Sekine was living in Kawaguchi, she was working at a bar. So most likely she had National Health, not the other kind. The fake Shoko would have got a new insurance card through Imai Office Machines when she began working for them. All she then had to do was take the card to the Ward Office in Kawaguchi and say, 'I got a job, I want to quit National Health.' They would probably make some minor calculations to balance the books as they closed out the policy. A few polite words and she'd be done."

"Hmm ... "

"The main thing, in any case, is that when the woman showed up at the Ward Office and said, 'I want to quit National Health,' they wouldn't check the person standing there against some photo on file. Who's going to suspect anything? You just take along your own snapshots, together with a health insurance card, and you're in. So long as there's no obvious discrepancy in age or sex, pretty much anybody could walk in—assuming they had the proper papers—and say 'That's me' and they'd be in and out in a matter of minutes. National Health; establishing a new family register, say, when you get married; applying for a new residence certificate when you move—it's all the same."

They might look at your papers, but they'd never give your face a second glance. You were home and dry, on one condition: that the real person didn't make trouble.

Isaka was deep in thought. He seemed to be searching for a flaw in the woman's planning. "What if a person had private life insurance? Wouldn't they check and then see that it wasn't the same policyholder? Anyhow, agents in those places have a good memory for faces, don't they?"

Honma gave it some thought, then shook his head. "These days most insurance premiums are automatically deducted from bank accounts. All you'd need to do would be to get hold of the bankbook and make sure your payments went out regularly. Even when the policy expired, you could just have it renewed. There'd never be any need to meet your insurance agent. And anyway, what agent's going to remember a customer's face ten or fifteen years down the road?"

Hisae was nodding emphatically. "If you got cold feet, you could cancel your policy. Sure, the agent isn't going to like it, and he might try to talk you out of it, but as long as you have the proper documents he's not going to check your story at all."

Honma looked at her. "But there is one possible catch. Public Employment." According to the girl at Imai Office Machines, "Shoko Sekine" had said she'd only been a part-timer until she registered with Public Employment in April 1990. But that didn't tally with what the attorney had told Honma. "Mizoguchi said the real Shoko Sekine went to work full-time for Kasai Trading in 1983. Seven years later, when the woman posing as Shoko started work at Imai Office Machines and went to the New Applicant desk at the Public Employment office, they can't have checked or there would have been trouble."

"I can get one of our people to call and find out," Hisae said, "... though I doubt it'll go beyond a name and an enrollment number. Still, I wonder if a person could get away with it—with saying that this was their first job?"

But if you could get the Public Employment office to confirm that they had duplicate records for one Shoko Sekine, born September 14, 1962, it would certainly suggest there'd been a switch. No matter how forgetful people might be, nobody forgets whether they've ever held a job before.

"When did the real Shoko quit Kasai Trading?" asked Hisae.

"Probably right before she declared bankruptcy. The creditors must have been putting so much pressure on her that it was hard to stay on."

"That would make it sometime in 1986, at the earliest," she said. "Should be okay. Public Employment holds on to all its data for seven years, an accountant friend once told me."

While Honma was jotting this down, Isaka suddenly clapped his hands and broke into a smile. "Hey, what about a passport or driver's license? Those have ID photos, right? They should show if there'd been a swap, right?"

Honma was quiet, so Hisae echoed her husband's question. "Did your Jun Kurisaka check into that?"

"No, not yet."

Isaka had a point. But if the real Shoko Sekine had a driver's license, Jun's fiancée would have said she didn't drive. A license was the last thing she'd have wanted. Same with a passport. Jun's "Shoko" would never have made plans for a honeymoon abroad. One tiny photograph and the game would have been up.

"I'm going to poke around Kawaguchi, the last place we know the real woman was living in," announced Honma, tapping the address on the residence certificate. "It won't hurt to find out more about her life back at that time."

Hisae glanced at her husband. "Last night, when I heard all this, I had an awful thought ...," she confessed.

Isaka studied her face. "Awful?"

"You mean about what happened two years ago?" asked Honma.

Hisae scowled slightly, nodding. "Shoko Sekine's mother died, right? And so her insurance money came in."

"And if Shoko had her eye on that money—" Isaka continued.

"No, it wouldn't be just that," Honma said, pushing his chair back from the table and getting to his feet. "Money's not the only issue. The Sekine family was down to just a mother and a daughter. Once the mother died, there wouldn't have been a soul around to keep tabs on Shoko."

A girl whose most remarkable characteristic was her lack of connections. A girl who could disappear without anybody trying hard to find her.

It was too perfect a coincidence, Hisae seemed to be suggesting. Just what Honma himself had been thinking the whole night before. First the family around her, then the target herself.

As Hisae stood up, she told her husband: "Maybe you'd better finish the cleaning and then we can have lunch together, okay? Meantime, I'll give him a ride to the station." The color that had brightened her face when she'd first come in had long since drained away.

## ✧ 9 ✧

Kawaguchi Co-op was an aging four-story apartment building with two small businesses on the ground floor, their names on boards propped out in front. One was a sparkling clean convenience store that had obviously just been remodeled, and the other a coffee shop called Bacchus that looked out on the world through dingy tinted windows.

A quick search failed to turn up a resident superintendent. The kid behind the cash register at the convenience store looked sharp enough, but Honma decided to start at Bacchus. Convenience store staff tends to turn over fast. Often employees are night owls or loners and aren't particularly good sources of information, especially about local goings-on. Once, on an armed robbery case, Honma had dropped into a few of the stores in the area, but the clerks could hardly remember any of the customers' faces, let alone what went on down the street.

A CLOSED sign still hung over the door of Bacchus, but the door itself was standing open. Honma called out as he entered. A young girl and a middle-aged man standing behind the counter, sharing a laugh, looked up. Their arms were covered up to the elbow in suds.

"Sorry, we're not open yet," said the man in a reedy voice, swiping at his face with one wrist and trailing a line of white foam across his neatly trimmed moustache.

Honma stopped just inside the door and explained: he was looking for someone who might know a woman who used to live in the building. Could they tell him where to find the landlord or realtor?

"I'm the landlord," said the man, drying his hands on a towel as he came out in front, leaving the rest of the dishes to the girl. "When you say 'used to live here,' how long ago would that be?"

"1990. Year before last. I'm pretty certain she was living here that April. She was in Number 401. Her name was Shoko Sekine. She worked at a bar."

"Hm." The man narrowed his eyes and looked Honma over carefully. "You know a lot about her. You a relative of this Ms. Sekine's, mister?"

Honma went into his usual routine. The man nodded along, then turned and spoke to the girl washing the dishes. "Akemi, go get your mother, will you? Tell her to bring the apartment files. Make it snappy, now."

"Oh, all right," the girl said, coming out from behind the counter. An amazingly micro miniskirt revealed a pair of legs that were equally amazing. Honma had already gathered that these two were father and daughter; if he hadn't, he might have gotten the wrong idea.

"Have a seat." The man sat down, gesturing toward a nearby chair. He searched his pockets for cigarettes and lit up. Honma presented his name card. The man patted his pockets all over again, but failed to find his card case. "Guess I'm out. The name's Konno," he said, cigarette wagging at his lips.

"Sorry to bother you. You must be getting ready to open." It was almost 11:00 A.M.

Konno grinned and shook his head. "We're more your happy hour place. Got a karaoke set and everything." The smallish coffee shop did look a little like a bar. Glass shelves were junked up with souvenirs, and the countertop was jet-black. One corner was curtained off. That was probably where they stored the stereo equipment.

"You have any recollection of this woman, Shoko Sekine?"

"Well, see ... I don't get involved much with the apartments. I leave that to the wife. She'll be here in a second."

His daughter Akemi returned just then, as if on cue. Leaning in through the door at the back of the coffee shop, she called out, "Da-a-ad! She said to bring him along. Mom practically jumped when I told her he was a relative of Miss Sekine's."

Nobuko Konno sat in a tiny office space, surrounded by ledgers.

The family owned two other rental properties besides this one, and Mrs. Konno managed all of them by herself.

Konno dutifully passed Honma over to his wife, then withdrew. An easygoing guy, if a little bit mousy.

Soon after they started talking, Nobuko pulled out a cardboard box about the size of an orange carton. It was printed with the company name Roseline and a rose-shaped emblem, both in pink. "I've been keeping this in storage all this time. I didn't know what to do with it." She tapped the top of the box. "Ms. Sekine left all this behind when she moved out. I couldn't just throw away someone else's things."

"What sort of things are they?"

Nobuko raised both eyebrows—nice-looking ones, not penciled in. "Actually she left all her belongings behind when she took off. Everything."

Honma leaned forward. "She go without saying anything?"

Nobuko gave a firm nod. "She left a note. Said she'd had nothing but bad luck, so she was leaving Tokyo to make a new start. Asked me to just go ahead and dispose of her things. Well, I tell you—we've been in this business a long time, but that's the first time I had a tenant do *that*."

"She just took the one suitcase?"

"I suppose. I don't know."

"So you didn't see her."

"No. We don't live here in the building. But in the morning there was an envelope shoved into the shop's letterbox. Together with the room key."

"When was that?"

Nobuko pulled out her files: a binder bulging with papers, and "Kawaguchi Co-op Rentals" in pencil on the spine. "That was 1990, two years ago. Boy, hard to believe it's been that long already."

Shoko Sekine had gone to see the attorney that January 25. Her "replacement" had shown up at Imai Office Machines and rented the Honancho apartment in April. The new family register was drawn up on April 1. So the two of them must have changed places—or the real woman must have disappeared—"Sometime in March, was it?"

Nobuko skimmed through the files and nodded. "That's right. March 18. A Sunday. That morning, like I said, was when I found her letter."

She had left here on Saturday. Abandoned all her furniture and belongings and headed out alone, without a word to her landlady …

"Could I take a look at the note?"

"Sorry, I didn't think to save it."

Well, not too surprising, Honma thought. "Was she the kind of tenant you'd expect that from? A bit messy, or …"

Nobuko tilted her head as if to sift through her recollections. "No, not especially. That's why I was surprised. I mean, sometimes she put her garbage out at night or tramped up the stairs too loud when she came home late. But just little things."

"Did she pay her rent on time?"

"Yes. Each and every month. Without fail."

"She worked in a bar, I believe. Did that make for any trouble when she moved in?"

Nobuko smiled. The laugh lines around her eyes only made her face that much prettier. "If I made a fuss about things like that, I wouldn't get any tenants. We take three months' deposit and write a tight contract here. So, within limits, we don't mind what the tenants do at home or at work."

Mrs. Konno was a businesswoman. She wore no makeup, and seemed unaware of her own appeal. "No, she was fine. An ideal tenant, really, I thought. Whenever we met, she'd say hello."

But without warning she'd cleared out, leaving her possessions behind. That couldn't be a good sign, thought Honma. If the real Shoko had sold her family register off, then why the vanishing act? At the very least, she could have had a word with her landlady.

March 17 two years ago was the last this place had seen of Shoko. Then, first thing the next month, a different woman started life at Honancho under the same name. Honma was starting to feel queasy. He noticed Nobuko's eyes on him and decided to ask about the cardboard box. "Can I take a look?"

"Yes, of course." She set the carton down on a table and pulled it open. "The furniture I either sold or put out for them to take away. But these things, well …"

There wasn't much. Three cassette tapes, five cheap pairs of earrings. A pearl brooch in a case. A yellowed household accounts book—with just one page of entries. An old National Health Insurance card, expiration date March 31, 1990, giving this apartment as the address. A rumpled beauty parlor customer card. Two paperbacks, both historical novels. Altogether, a slim inventory.

"The cassettes?"

"Music, I think. My daughter tried them out once. They seemed to be recorded off the radio, is what she said."

Other than that, there were only a few odd papers. A pamphlet with the title "To Our Patients" from a Tokyo hospital. Folded inside it was a bill dated July 7, 1988, made out to Shoko Sekine: for an outpatient consultation. Unremarkable except for a telephone number scribbled in the margin with a ballpoint pen.

"This number," he said, pointing at it. "Did you try it?"

Nobuko nodded. "As a matter of fact, yes. I thought it might turn up a friend of hers."

"And?"

She rapped lightly on the box. "This is what I reached."

"Huh?"

"Roseline. It's a mail-order company. I suppose Ms. Sekine came across an ad in the hospital waiting room and copied it down. Then maybe had them send her a catalog."

Honma took another look at the top of the carton. "It's the name of a mail-order company?"

"Yes, but I doubt it would be of much interest to men. They deal in 'intimates' and socks and all that sort of thing."

"Intimates?"

"Also known as underwear," she said with a laugh.

Under the hospital pamphlet was a full-color flier advertising a cemetery. Green Grove Mortuary in Utsunomiya.

"Perhaps she was planning to buy a plot for her mother?" Nobuko said, echoing Honma's thoughts.

"Then you knew about her mother's death?"

"Sure. Her mother had co-signed, as guarantor, when she moved in. So Ms. Sekine felt she should tell me when her mother passed on."

"An accident, if I remember right?"

She looked slightly distressed. "Fell down some stairs near her house, apparently."

"In Utsunomiya?"

"Yes. Her mother lived all alone out there. Still working. Her health was quite good, that was my impression."

"And Ms. Sekine, did she seem upset about her mother's death?"

"Well, it seemed to come as a big shock. Even more perhaps because they hadn't been on especially good terms."

That didn't make sense, thought Honma. If the real Shoko Sekine weren't close to her mother and had no intention of ever returning home, why choose to live here in Kawaguchi, with only one change of trains between? Jun had said she didn't like to talk about her hometown, but that was the other Shoko, the false one, who wouldn't have wanted to go near Utsunomiya.

Honma put the stuff back in the box and asked, "Could you hold on to this for a little while?"

"Certainly. But I hope you'll let me know when you find her."

"Of course."

"Is that everything?" Nobuko did a quick one-finger check of the contents.

On second thoughts, Honma asked, "Actually, could I borrow the cassettes?"

"Go ahead. Might be worth a listen."

It occurred to Honma to ask, just in case: "Did you happen to find any old photos in her apartment? Or anything like a school yearbook?"

Nobuko shook her head. "No. If I had, I would have kept them. But I should think photos are just the kind of thing a person would take with them if they were leaving in a hurry, no matter what the circumstances. Don't you think?"

"I suppose so." He then asked her to let him copy down the

address that she had in her files for Shoko's mother.

"By the way, you wouldn't happen to have any pictures of Ms. Sekine?"

"Afraid not. We don't have much contact with individual tenants."

"Would you know if there were any other residents she was particularly close to?"

"Hmm …" Nobuko thought it over. "But none of the people here now would have been here then. We get a pretty good turnover." A credit to her managerial abilities, no doubt; the more tenants, the more deposit money.

"When she disappeared, did you try calling the place she worked at? Lahaina, a bar in Shimbashi, I think it was."

Nobuko frowned and nodded. "Yes, I did. They were just as surprised as me. 'What? She's quitting?' they said."

"And in fact she didn't show."

"Right. Come Monday and still no sign of her, they rang me up. She still had wages coming to her, they said—should they just write them off?"

Honma's queasiness was back. There could be no mistake now. The real Shoko Sekine didn't disappear for her own reasons. She'd been removed.

"Any men friends ever drop over to see her?" Honma stumbled over his phrasing. A boyfriend would be sure to know something.

Nobuko shook her head. "We certainly didn't keep track. Wouldn't you stand a better chance asking at the bar?"

She rose easily and moved over to the door, which she held open. As they made their way out, she remarked, "That looks painful. Arthritis?"

"No, an accident."

"And yet you're going out of your way to find her yourself? Why not just report it to the police? Surely Missing Persons would take it on?"

Honma smiled wearily. "I'm sure they would, if I wanted them to … We'll be okay."

Going into the shop, they found her husband still behind the counter, brewing up some coffee. The daughter was cleaning the windows. Now that he had all three family members together, Honma decided to try one last question. He pulled out the photo. "Any of you ever see this woman before? Around the time Ms. Sekine was living here?"

First Nobuko, then Akemi, and finally Mr. Konno looked at Jun's "Shoko." Each gave the same little shake of the head in turn; their mannerisms were so similar it was plain to see they were a family.

"Okay. Thank you anyway."

That afternoon on his way home, Honma stopped in front of the station to order an enlargement of the Polaroid. The young man at the photo shop took one look at the chocolate-brown house and drawled, "What's this supposed to be?"

"That's why I'm having it enlarged. To find out."

"Yeah? So, like, do you want the original back right away? I can get it back to you in, um, thirty minutes. The enlargement will be done the day after tomorrow."

"Fine. I can wait half an hour."

The chair in the store was small and its legs were wobbly. Not one other customer came in while he waited. It was too drafty and cold just to sit there. On the spur of the moment, he stepped outside and went to a public phone down the street where he dialed Mizoguchi's number. A woman answered. Must have been that literary Ms. Sawagi.

The attorney wasn't in; he was away on business for a few days. "He'll be back the day after tomorrow."

"I'd like to see him if I could. Any chance of an appointment?"

A brief pause. "I'm sorry, but his schedule seems to be full."

"I see." Honma sighed but gave no sign of being ready to give up.

Ms. Sawagi gave a familiar laugh. "Mr. Mizoguchi always has lunch at the same place. It's a noodle shop near the office here. Why don't you try to catch him there? You'd have a good thirty minutes to talk."

The place was called Nagase. Honma took down the directions, thanked her and hung up, just as he saw the young man from the photo studio come out looking for him.

It was past three when Honma got home. No sign of Isaka. He must have been at another apartment or out shopping. Honma put some water on to boil for a cup of coffee, then sat down on a kitchen stool and thought about his next move.

He tried calling Investigation. He didn't imagine he'd get through right away, and sure enough the person he wanted wasn't in. A detective from another squad answered. Honma caught up a bit on recent news, then hung up and sat there drinking his coffee.

The return call came twenty minutes later. Honma didn't let the phone finish ringing once. When he picked it up, a gruff voice said, "Hey, that was quick! Calling from the grave, are you?"

It was Sadao Funaki. He'd been in the same class at the police academy with Honma, but their careers had taken very different paths until two years ago when Funaki had been transferred to Enforcement, the division next door to Honma's at headquarters. *Well, how do you like that? We both get kicked upstairs anyway.*

"I heard you called, so I stepped back out again. Can't talk with those ears pricked up all around me. So what's up?" Funaki was a short guy but built solidly enough to take his knocks without much damage, and he talked a mean patter in a voice as loud as it was deep. His family had been shopkeepers in Tokyo for generations, selling Buddhist altars in an east-side trading district.

"Sorry to bother you when I know how busy you are, but I've got a favor to ask."

Funaki chuckled hoarsely. "I'll just put it on your tab. I can make you work it off when you're back on the job."

"Yeah, well, just be sure to give it to me first. Think you'll be able to run it under the Chief's nose?"

"No problem there. The old bastard doesn't notice anything going on around him. So what's it to be? A bank?"

"Nope, Public Employment. That and the residence certificate window at the Ward Office." Honma read off the birthdate and address for Shoko Sekine. "What I need is her employment listings. If I'm not mistaken, you'll find that the same person has signed up twice with Public Employment as a first-time worker, with two different companies."

"Gotcha. And the company names?"

Imai Office Machines and Kasai Trading, he told him. Funaki took down the addresses without his needing to repeat a thing. Funaki had always been pretty quick.

"The second thing, from the Ward Office?"

"That's a family register cancellation. The same person. I'd like an extra copy of the cancellation form too." Honma read off Shoko Sekine's pre-cancellation permanent address in Utsunomiya.

"Bit of a tall order ..." Funaki lowered his voice slightly. "What are you up to? I would have thought that physical therapist of yours would be keeping you off the streets."

"This is a favor. For a relative. I've been asked to trace someone. I wouldn't come to you otherwise, but there seems to be something weird going on here."

"Meaning?" He could hear Funaki take a deep breath. "It looks like case material?"

"Uh-huh."

"Well, then, get back here, why don't you? Turn it over and save yourself the effort. Why kill yourself going it alone?"

"It's just that, well, I don't have much to go on yet. I just want to play it close to my chest for now."

"Anybody ever say you were stubborn?"

"Anyway, sorry. Just do this one for me."

There was a rustling sound, which Honma took to be Funaki scratching his head. A sure sign that he'd given in. "Okay, okay. I just hope that when you say 'relative,' this doesn't have anything to do with Makoto." Funaki was like a doting uncle to the boy.

"No, no, not him. It's a distant relative, actually. Chizuko's cousin's son. Got any idea what they call that?"

"You asking me?" he said. He was about to hang up, but Honma sprang another question on him.

"Been to see that matchmaker lately?" At forty-two Funaki was still single and still trying, in fits and starts, to find somebody.

He burst out laughing. "I did, I did. Just last Sunday. Set me up with this widow, right? One with a twenty-one-year-old son, no less."

"And you thought she had possibilities?"

"How did you guess?"

"The lilt in your voice."

"Liar. My voice is the same old croak as before." His tone suddenly turned serious. "Hey, you said you're trying to trace someone."

"Check."

"A woman?"

Was it so obvious? "Yes, but …"

"She alive?"

Honma paused. Like he said, Funaki was sharp. Eight, nine chances out of ten, the real Shoko was already dead. It was way too early to say whether she'd been murdered or not. One thing was for sure, though, and that was that a woman who went by her name was alive somewhere.

Honma spoke slowly, to himself. "She's alive, very much so, and I'm going to find her."

The line was quiet till finally Funaki said, "Be careful now," and hung up.

Honma put the phone down. He sat there for a little while, leaning on the table. Then he struggled to his feet and went to Makoto's room to borrow the boy's portable tape recorder. He popped in one of Shoko Sekine's cassettes.

It was Top 40 music; love songs mostly. Completely forgettable melodies. As he listened, eyes closed, it was Nobuko Konno's face that flickered behind his eyelids.

## ✦ 10 ✦

Again, Jun didn't show up until after nine and, as usual, he was look-ing pretty irritable. Was he that snowed under with work, or had he simply not been free to leave till his boss went home? In any case, he hadn't even taken off his coat when he said abruptly: "What is it you need to touch base about?"

Honma hesitated. He'd been planning to build up to what he had to say. Shove the facts at Jun cold and he simply wouldn't listen. "Have a seat. This is going to take a while."

"Is it Shoko? Did you find her?"

Honma shook his head. "Things don't look so good. I think you should sit down."

Jun still didn't get it. "Being a bit overdramatic, aren't we?"

"I wouldn't say that."

"Okay, okay. But let's get on with it. I don't see any point in drag-ging it out."

Makoto was playing a computer game; every so often an elec-tronic *bleep* or *brrp* came from his room. Meanwhile, in the kitchen, the refrigerator hummed steadily. The two machines provided a dou-ble accompaniment as Honma laid out the whole story, step by step: "Shoko Sekine's" fake résumé; her family register; her residence cer-tificate. By the time the papers were spread on the table, Jun's face was wiped clean of any expression, becoming just a mask, with only the eyes alive at all. Yet when he started to speak, Honma was still a bit surprised at the young man's bitterness.

"This has got to be some kind of joke," he said in a ragged voice that sounded as if he'd been holding his breath the whole time.

"Unfortunately, it's the truth."

Jun started laughing, waggling his half-closed hands about. "You expect me to believe this? About Shoko not being Shoko—it's ridiculous!"

Honma realized that nothing he could say right now would get through.

"We're talking about the woman I'm going to marry," Jun said hotly.

"Maybe so, but she isn't Shoko Sekine." Honma spoke slowly, in measured tones. "She's someone else entirely. That's why she didn't know about going bankrupt less than five years ago." If she *had* known, she would never have let Jun get her a card, however insistent he was. "I visited the condo in Kawaguchi today. There were no papers there, no evidence of it. For her, the bankruptcy never happened. Your fiancée never saw anything relating to it, she never had a clue." The real Shoko had probably gotten rid of the documents, as just so many bad memories. "This must all come as quite a shock, I know. But now that I've come this far, I may as well keep going and see where it leads." Honma broke off and focused on Jun. The young man's eyes were glazed over, guarded. "What do you want to do? Are you with me on this? I'd really like to have your help. You know her best and I'll need all kinds of details, no matter how small."

Nearly a minute went by before Jun responded. "I ... I don't know a thing."

Makoto's computer game chirped and chittered in the silence.

Then Jun raised his head and looked straight at Honma for the first time. "Oh, I get it—"

"Get what?"

"This was Shoko's idea!" Jun's eyes finally came to life, and his smoldering anger burst out. "I get it. You found Shoko, and she asked you specifically not to tell me, is that it? Shoko wants to break up with me, so she got you to go through all this song-and-dance. She's found somebody else. That's why you're giving me this story. I'm not a complete idiot, you know!" He lurched forward, slamming into the table, knocking an ashtray to the floor. "Well? Admit it!"

The computer noises stopped. Makoto's door opened and a small head peered out. Honma maneuvered himself to his feet and placed a restraining hand on Jun's arm. "Is that what you honestly think?"

Jun fell heavily back into his chair and sat there, slumped over, holding his head in his hands. Makoto crept out into the hall. The boy hesitated a minute, then bolted for the front door.

Jun almost seemed to be crying ... till he raised his face. "I've had enough of this!" he exploded. "I should never have trusted you. You expect me to sit here and take this crap?... I'm not *that* stupid!" He grabbed his coat from the peg.

Honma remained seated. He knew Jun wasn't going home, not like that. Not without one last effort to restore his pride.

Sure enough, Jun stopped just short of the door to the living room. His shoulders were shaking. He fished his wallet out of his jacket pocket, pulled out some bills, and saying "Here's your expenses—this ought to be enough!" tossed them at Honma. A few ten-thousand-yen notes fluttered to the floor. No dignity, no thanks.

Oh—thought Honma—he remembered the money. He might curse and swear and blow his top, but when all was said and done, for him the bottom line was money. A true banker.

"Fine. But did she ever show you a Polaroid?"

Jun was breathing hard.

"A photo of a house. Fancy, Western-style, chocolate-brown color? She show you anything like that?"

"Come *on*—" Jun's voice broke. "You're going to have to do better than that!" And that was the last of him. The front door banged open and shut. Footsteps clattered away.

Makoto came running in with Isaka, both of them wide-eyed. "You okay, Dad?"

Honma was picking the bills up off the floor. "I'm fine."

"Honest? You're not hurt?"

Isaka looked pale. "I was worried for a minute there. All Makoto said was that you were in trouble. Then just when we're getting off the elevator, this young guy comes hurtling out of your door like a bat out of hell and ... what's that?" His eyes fell on the money.

"My fee and expenses."

"He threw them at you!" Makoto was indignant.

Isaka burst out laughing. "But it's only thirty thousand yen. What a cheapskate."

"No," Honma said, laughing too. "It's too much, actually."

"What a creep!" cried Makoto, the only one still worked up.

Honma patted his son on the head. "There's no reason to get mad. He just got a big shock and he's kind of confused right now." Raising one eyebrow, he added: "More to the point, young man, you seem pretty hooked on those computer games. You keeping track of how much time that leaves you this week?" Makoto was strictly limited to seven hours' play each week. Even ten minutes over that and the software got impounded for the whole of the next week.

"I got two hours left," Makoto protested. "I'm keeping track, don't worry."

"Good."

Makoto shuffled off to put the game away, leaving the adults alone.

"Looks like you're no longer on the case," said Isaka. "What are you going to do now?"

"Investigate. I was never officially on the case anyway, so why should I stop now?"

"You're going to keep on looking?"

"Sure." His eye lingered on the window. The whole housing complex was shrouded in darkness. Somewhere out in that darkness was the missing woman.

"What's your plan?" Isaka asked, looking at Honma's reflection.

"I'll trace the real Shoko Sekine. How she lived, the trouble she ran up against. If I can get a handle on that, maybe I'll have a better idea of just what caught the eye of this woman who was out shopping for a new identity."

"Shopping for trouble is more like it," Isaka muttered to himself. "Out for a little spin in that old car—the one they mention in the sutras—that flaming wagon that takes sinners off to hell."

"Flaming wagon?"

Isaka recited:

> On wheels of fire
> Are sorrows borne,
> I hear them creaking past my gate.
> Where to, I wonder?
> Where to?

He grinned. "Last night, when I was talking to Hisae about the bankruptcy and everything, it popped into my head. It's a poem from that old anthology, *The Jewel of Attainment*, if I remember right."

Yes, the wheels of karma, spinning around.

Shoko Sekine had tried to stop them. She'd gotten off the wagon at one point. Then, without even realizing, the woman who became her had climbed back in.

But now where was she? More important, Honma thought darkly, who was she?

✧ 11 ✧

As Mizoguchi ducked under the curtain hanging over the door of the noodle shop Nagase, he was enveloped in steam. The owner, standing behind a counter of unvarnished wood, dressed in a clean white chef's apron, had just taken the lid off a cauldron. Mizoguchi headed for a small table right in the back and eased himself in. His glasses had fogged up, but when Honma worked his way down the aisle a few minutes later, he saw him and waved.

"So you were able to find the place all right?" the lawyer said, gesturing to the chair across the table.

"Sorry to bother you when you're about to eat."

"That's quite all right. My assistant said you'd be stopping by." He removed his glasses to clean them and added, "I can recommend the tempura noodles."

Honma placed his order when the waitress came by with a glass of water. The lunch hour peak had passed, but the place was still crowded. Even so, it was not so loud that conversation was difficult; in fact, the level of background noise was about right for what they had to discuss.

"Making any headway?" asked Mizoguchi, settling his glasses back onto the bridge of his nose. He'd looked younger with them off.

"I'm not sure I'd call it 'headway.' Things keep getting more and more complicated."

Mizoguchi's eyes widened slightly behind the lenses. "So you *were* onto something after all?"

Honma nodded. "It's a long story," he began. Having gone over everything with Jun just the night before, there was a certain economy now to his delivery. Practice makes perfect, he guessed—at anything.

The food arrived. Mizoguchi raised his chopsticks and motioned for Honma to start eating. Then he just listened, impassively, never looking startled or surprised. But, then again, no attorney who let every reaction show on his face was likely to get anywhere in a hurry.

By the time Honma finished his story, Mizoguchi had finished his noodles. He gave a single nod. "I see," he said. "Now you eat, and I'll talk."

Honma glanced at the clock.

Mizoguchi shook his head. "If it's my time you're concerned about, don't be. I've got as long as it takes." He took off his glasses for another rub with the handkerchief, while he sorted out his thoughts. Then he spoke—calmly, collectedly. "You've told me that you want to find out about Shoko Sekine and the sort of life she led. Well, I'm willing to tell you what I know. I think perhaps I can dispel several misconceptions you may have."

"Misconceptions?"

"Yes. Correct me if I'm wrong, but I suspect your thinking runs along these lines. Shoko Sekine drove herself to bankruptcy. What's worse, she was a bar hostess, for who knows how long. So she was bad about money and generally a loose woman. Etcetera, etcetera. And since that was the sort of life she led, tracing her personal relations will take some doing. Or am I completely off track?"

Honma lifted his chopsticks to indicate "no contest" on any of the charges. Mizoguchi's summary was just what Isaka had suggested. Most people encountering the words "personal bankruptcy" would probably have drawn the same conclusions.

The attorney smiled, flashing a full set of teeth. Small, but remarkably good for someone his age. "That's one misconception. The truth is that, in today's world, it's people who are quite sincere, cautious— timid even—who are driven to the brink of bankruptcy. That's because of the way the credit industry works."

Reaching into his breast pocket, he produced a dog-eared black leather notebook, which he placed in front of him. "What year were you born in, Mr. Honma?"

"1950."

"So you're forty-two. Hm, I would have said that you were younger," he said with a smile. "But that means you were about ten when it all started. It was Marui Department Store that set the ball rolling back in 1960. Of course their little Red Card is one of the most famous retailer credit cards now, but things were very different then. All they actually did was decide to use the English word 'credit' in place of the familiar *kappu*, or 'payment by installment.' They didn't in fact offer any new services at all but just introduced the word, which they liked for its exotic, foreign-sounding appeal. Don't forget, 1960 was the year of the U.S.–Japan Security Pact. That same year, the Diner's Club card was established. It was known even at that time for its rigorous screening and select membership, and is still regarded as one of the most reliable cards used in this country."

That would put it in its thirty-second year.

"1960 was also the first year of the so-called era of rapid growth, when we began to work our way up toward the status of an economic superpower. As the economy took off, a credit industry became necessary." Mizoguchi spoke easily, as if he'd been over this many times before. "Indeed, without such retail financing, I doubt whether the Japanese economy or our standard of living would ever really have gotten off the ground. But there's been no turning back since then.

"Well, let's see. I used the term 'retail financing' just now. It would be more exact to say 'consumer lending.' This can be divided roughly into two parts. First, there's 'credit sales,' which is basically your credit card industry. The other type is 'consumer loans'—loans against fixed deposits or with postal savings as collateral—your bank overdrafts and the like. This term, 'consumer loans,' encompasses borrowing against credit cards and even the so-called consumer finance companies—you know, the places that people refer to as 'loan sharks.' Do you follow me?"

Honma had finished eating and was taking notes.

"The first category, 'credit sales,' further divides into 'installment'

97

and 'non-installment' schemes. This simply refers to whether a card allows the holder to choose to pay over several months. Typically, with bank-issued credit cards, you don't have the choice of payment over time, but with non-bank cards you do. That's all that means. Then there are simple periodic payments contracted for a particular product, where you don't even have to own a card. Thus we have 'installment' and 'non-installment' subcategories, each of which can be further divided into 'single-item' and 'cardholder.' "

He shifted in his seat and leaned forward, as if for emphasis, then checked some sort of crib sheet he pulled out of his notebook. "Now, according to our data for 1990, if we look at credit sales, and first at the installment type, the amount of newly extended credit came to eleven and a half trillion yen. For the non-installment type it was almost twelve trillion. In the other large category, consumer loans, the data for the same year comes to three times that, or nearly thirty-four trillion yen. Adding the two together brings the total to—" He obviously had it all worked out and didn't need to make any calculations, but he paused anyway for effect. "Well over fifty-seven trillion yen in consumer lending in 1990. An industry on the scale of the national budget, is what it is."

"Big money," said Honma.

"Call it fifty-seven trillion. That's fourteen percent of Japan's gross national product for that year. Or twenty percent of our per capita disposable income. In America the figures are about the same. There's no doubt about it, consumer financing has become a major pillar of our economic life."

What was more, the industry showed no sign of leveling off. Here Mizoguchi referred to his notes again. "The growth in the volume of consumer lending is nothing short of astounding. In 1980, the total was approaching 21.5 trillion. Let's make an index where this figure equals one hundred. Well, five years later, in 1985, that index stood at 165, for a grand total of 34.75 trillion. By 1990, the index climbs to 272. It's almost tripled in just ten years."

He traced a line along the tabletop with his finger. "Suppose we make a graph linking it with the rise in the gross national product. All right, the GNP looks something like this …" A thirty-degree gradient. "And here's consumer lending …" He drew a gradient of forty degrees. "Looks like a ski slope, doesn't it? Maybe even a trifle steep for that. Is there any other sector with that kind of growth?"

"It's like a giant bubble."

Mizoguchi reflected for a moment, then shook his head. "But what people call 'the bubble'—the economic bubble that burst last year—that's something different. The money-lending market, now there's a *ghost* if ever there was one. Nothing tangible about it. Never was, not since people first started using currency. Slips of paper and metal disks, that's all it ever was. Am I wrong?

"But, for a fact"—the attorney was just getting warmed up—"a ten-thousand-yen bill does have that much value. And unlike some token that's useless as soon as you set foot outside the door of a game center, any vending machine will accept your hundred-yen coin. That's because we've all agreed on it. Every schoolboy knows what a monetary system is, about how it's a ghost, about the 'real unreality' of money as a social contract. Thanks to which, we don't have to drag a boar carcass down from the hills to barter for clothes and vegetables and rice for the family. We're free from all that. Because our society is founded on monetary economics, I can earn a living trying to help other people with their problems. Not a bad deal, eh?"

Honma nodded.

"Right. So, by definition, the money market is a ghost," he repeated. "But it's a ghost that casts a disproportionate shadow beside our social reality. Our social reality, of course, has its set limits—only what society will allow. Consumer financing, on the other hand, has swollen out of all proportion. It was never meant to be inflated this way, it was pumped up artificially. Just as an analogy: Mr. Honma, you're fairly tall, but you're not over six feet, are you? Now suppose your shadow were to grow to sixty feet long, that wouldn't make much sense, would it?" The question was clearly rhetorical, the practiced locution of a lawyer arguing a case.

"Just for fun, let's look at the number of credit cards issued. According to data for the fiscal year ending in March 1983, it was 57.5 million cards. By 1985, nearly 87 million cards. By 1990, it's up over 166 million cards. That's a 16.5% growth rate. Year in, year out, the number issued means that there's *that* many in consumers' wallets out there."

Did Chizuko ever have a credit card, Honma wondered. Not in her own name, at least.

"Incidentally, I've been talking about credit cards as if they were all the same, but in fact these too can be divided into several groups. Actually there are three main types. First, there's bank-issued cards: the UC Group, the DC Group, the JCB Group, VISA Japan—ten companies, all told. These claim the lion's share and have the highest figures both for number of cards and frequency of use." Mizoguchi checked the data. "Here we see a 20.2% increase in the growth rate between 1983 and 1990. Next come the non-bank cards: Nihon Shimpan, Oriental Finance, Greater Mercantile—about eight companies, counting only the major players. Their growth rate is 16.1%, which again is huge. Next there's what we call retailer-affiliated cards. Marui, of course, falls into this category, but these days every department store and even all the major supermarkets issue their own cards, right? Each card is valid only in the store chain, which is a disadvantage as far as that goes, but that's offset by special discounts on purchases and waived application fees. Anyway, the stores aren't so strict about screening and can even issue a card right over the counter, which gives the other two groups a run for their money. Why, nowadays, even some shopping arcades at train stations are issuing their own cards. This group has shown a growth rate recently of 19.2%. Really taking off. It's getting so you can't walk the streets without running into some card campaign or other. Tell me, do you have any credit cards?"

"I, uh ..." The question was unexpected and Honma stumbled for a reply. "I have one. Union Credit, I think it is."

"It's convenient, isn't it? Especially for someone like you, on call at all hours, never knowing when you'll have to rush out in the middle of the night. Me, I have two daughters. The younger one had her purse snatched once. And they never caught the thief. Ever since then, she's been afraid to carry cash around with her and relies on credit cards almost exclusively. With a card, even if you do have the bad luck to get robbed, you can at least keep your losses to a minimum."

"Like when you're traveling."

"That's right. What's more, it serves as a form of identification. That's definitely one of its strong points. Just because I specialize in bankruptcies and am always rescuing the victims, you might suppose that I'd consider credit cards the root of all evil and want to see them abolished altogether. But actually that's not the case at all."

"No, I guess not."

Mizoguchi went on. "All right, then. Here's consumer financing, casting a sixty-foot shadow from something only six feet tall. The main reasons for this are indiscriminate overextension of credit, and exorbitant interest and commission fees. Now we come to the real heart of the matter." Pausing to choose an example, he said: "About a year ago, I handled a personal bankruptcy case. An office worker, twenty-eight years old. He had thirty-three different credit cards. His total debt ran to more than thirty million yen, and he had no property to speak of. What do you make of that?"

Thirty million yen—that was more than a lowly public servant like Honma could ever hope to see, even as severance pay.

"Now, how do you suppose a person who pulls in a mere two hundred thousand a month could ever manage to borrow thirty million yen? Who's going to lend him that much? Why would they? This is what I mean by overextended credit."

He reached for his glass of water, but found it empty and set it back down.

"The typical scenario for getting deep into debt goes like this. First a person gets himself a credit card. He finds it handy for shopping, for taking trips. It's nice and simple, and one card does the trick quite well. Then pretty soon, without thinking about it much, he gets himself a couple more. Assuming that he's a regular company employee, he shouldn't have any problem with the screening procedures. The department stores, banks and supermarkets will all encourage him to take out cards. 'Become a cardholder and you'll get all these discounts and member benefits,' they'll say. 'Special deals galore.' So he adds a few more cards to his hand.

"Soon enough, he's using them not just for shopping but for cash as well, again because they're so convenient. Now he's made that imperceptible shift from *using* credit cards to *borrowing* against them. This happens almost before a person realizes it. With bank-issued cards, cash machines will deduct money straight from depositors' accounts. But with non-bank and retailer-affiliated cards, somewhere in or around the store you'll find one of those cheerful-looking machines that look like bank cash machines. You just stick the card in, punch in your PIN number, and it's as easy as taking money out of your own bank account. A very simple way to run up debts."

The waitress came to clear away the dishes and refill their glasses. Mizoguchi thanked her with a wave of his hand.

"That's what you might call an archetypal example. You wouldn't believe how many clients tell me they got started borrowing cash by mistake."

"By mistake?"

"Yes. The client wants just to withdraw money from his bank account, but somehow sticks his credit card into the cash machine instead of his bank card. Since he's chosen the same PIN number for all his cards, money comes out anyway. He may think it a bit odd that the transaction slip doesn't show any balance, only the amount withdrawn, or he may not really notice. Often it's not until the end of the month, when his credit card bill comes, that he realizes his mistake."

"Must be a jolt. Especially being charged interest on top of that."

"Probably. But it may also get him thinking,'Hey, borrowing cash is easy.' The interest, at that point, doesn't strike him as particularly high—a mere three thousand yen per hundred thousand borrowed. So every now and then, he dips in." Mizoguchi gulped down half his water and continued. "He uses his card habitually, for shopping, for cash, for sheer convenience. He doesn't draw out huge chunks all at once, but just a little at a time, so he never feels he's doing anything risky. Still, loans are loans. When they come due, you have to pay up.

"Imagine a young businessman just starting out. Suppose his take-home pay is, say, a hundred and fifty thousand yen. He can afford to pay maybe twenty or thirty thousand a month in purchases on the card. Forty to fifty thousand would be tight. If he's not careful, though, pretty soon he's up there anyway. So that's when he starts borrowing cash with the card. In order to meet his payments to com-

102

pany A, he draws cash on company B's card. And once he does that, the whole thing snowballs to the point where he can't keep up by borrowing on the card any more. So what do you think he does?"

"Goes to a loan shark?"

"Exactly," the attorney said, nodding. "And with the loan sharks he repeats the same cycle. Before long, he's borrowing from company B to make payments on money from company A. Then it's gone and he goes on to C, D and E. Some unscrupulous consumer finance companies even introduce clients to other companies. Only to lower-profile firms, of course, the ones with less capital clout, who are especially lax in their screening. They need whatever business they can get, so they don't set a ceiling on total debt. That's what drives up the interest. And that's how the system works.

"The customers, all they can think about is when their next payment is going to come due. If there's another loan to be had, they'll go for it—that's just part of the vicious circle."

"So what you're saying is it's the honest, hard-working types?"

Mizoguchi nodded emphatically. "Yes, exactly. The timid guys who would never dream of simply taking off in the middle of the night. One way or another, they've got to pay their debts. That's the only thing they can see themselves doing. And that's how they dig themselves in deeper and deeper. They just stay on the treadmill and work themselves sick. Or worse."

"And Shoko Sekine?"

"—was your classic case."

At first, he explained, she'd worked part-time at night in addition to a full-time day job, but things went from bad to worse, until finally there was nowhere else to go but the worst place of all—the partial buy-back outfits. "I'm sure in your line of work, Mr. Honma, you've heard of these wonderful institutions. You get a credit card and you buy whatever goods they ask you to, from a third party. In return, they pay out some quick cash—typically less than seventy percent of the items' face value. But then you get stuck with the full bill. It's a quick losing proposition. Often it's bullet train tickets in bulk. They're traded through credit jobbers and resurface as super-discount fares. I buy them myself for business trips. It's perfectly legal. And ridiculously cheap." The attorney's lips curled in a wry smile.

"Once you're part of the game, it's structured so that it's really difficult to pull out. The more honest, the more serious you are, the deeper you sink. You thrash about as long as you can, but pretty soon you can hardly move at all. Finally, you look for any way out possible—which often is something criminal.

"By any common-sense standard, the idea of a company loaning ten or twenty million yen to a kid barely out of his teens is crazy. But it happens. These companies just lend and lend all over the place— so long as they're not the ones left holding the bag in the end, and meanwhile they're collecting all that interest. Usually it's the individual anyway, not the bank or the loan shark, who loses out. It's a sort of upside-down pyramid, with the debtor at the bottom supporting the lenders. All it takes is one slip and down you go. Heavier and heavier debts piling up above you, till in the end you're crushed flat."

He continued, "Things were different in the old days, when your only option was the good old-fashioned pawnshop. Back then, you couldn't borrow unlimited amounts. Nobody wanted to lend money without some collateral, not to the average person, anyway. Still, I can't really say I prefer things that way. We live much better lives today."

The restaurant was starting to empty. Another blast of white steam came from behind the counter.

"And, anyway, how *could* we go back to the days before consumer lending? I mean, this is fifty-seven trillion yen a year we're talking about. How are you going to get that genie back in the bottle? It's impossible. All I'm saying is, surely there's no need to sacrifice tens of thousands of people every year. To drive them to suicide or some family tragedy, or force them to skip town or commit some kind of crime."

"So we should change the structure of things?"

"Yes. And clamp down on unreasonably high interest rates. The bigger loan sharks charge anywhere from twenty-five to thirty-five percent interest. Yet they fall into the cracks between the Interest Rate Control Act and the Revised Financing Statutes. It's a gray zone where the authorities tend to say, 'Yeah, there are bad things going on, but let's not be too quick to point any fingers.' Meanwhile, for the individual debtor, it's a major crisis. Look at it this way ..." Mizoguchi drew another line on the table: starting off at about a twenty-degree incline, it rose steadily to forty-five degrees. "Getting cash with your card, struggling to keep up the payments, resorting to loan sharks. Following this pattern, two million yen borrowed at thirty percent interest annually mounts up to sixteen million yen over seven years. That's this curve," he said, tracing the upsweep again.

"Once I had a client, a guy in his thirties, saddled with a twelve-million-yen debt, of which nine million was interest. It kept ballooning out of control. He didn't have a clue when he first borrowed the money how frightening this whole business is. And cash machines certainly don't bother to explain how interest works." His mouth crinkled in a silent laugh. "Yes, and this relates to the third thing I'd say we need—more thorough education. Wider dissemination of information. Remember I mentioned that when people first start taking out cash loans, often they don't feel that the interest is so high?"

"Yeah, I remember that."

"Right. Well, at first this guy hardly noticed. But I tell you, interest is like a woman's makeup: it gets thicker and thicker as the day wears on. Even the phrase 'cash loan' sounds like magic. Going to a loan shark—everybody knows that's bad, especially young people. But borrowing cash with your credit card—nothing wrong with that. The fact is, though, that the interest rates come out to twenty-five to thirty-five percent on an annual basis—almost exactly the same as the major loan sharks. Maybe because the collection methods are fairly low-key, it's easy to get the impression that borrowing on a credit card is nice and safe. That's the first mistake."

Mizoguchi's glass was empty again.

"Young people are particularly susceptible. And consumer financing businesses are really pushing nowadays to expand into the youth market. They'll say anything to get a new customer. So it's up to us to get smart. As things stand, we have a gaping hole here. This year marks exactly the twentieth since the major city banks first started to issue credit cards to students. But in all those years has any school or university offered instruction on how to use cards properly? This is something we could start doing immediately. In Tokyo public high schools, I hear they assemble the girl students before graduation for lessons in using cosmetics. Well, if they've got the time and inclination for that sort of thing, they can darn well teach them the basics for surviving when it comes to money matters!" He slammed his fist down on the table. "I'm not one to blame everything on the people upstairs, but this one really gets my goat. The whole problem falls between the cracks in the bureaucracy. There ought to be one agency in charge of keeping track of the whole consumer credit industry."

"There isn't?"

"Credit sales is the responsibility of the Ministry of Trade and Industry. Consumer loans comes under the Treasury. The authorities that ought to be clamping down on the industry are scattered around, and they don't necessarily communicate very well. And this even though many banks, for instance, do both credit sales and cash loans. Sometimes even with the same card."

Mizoguchi edged forward in his seat. Honma noticed the owner of the shop glancing in their direction, smiling slightly. He'd apparently witnessed this scene more than once before.

"You say you want to know what kind of a woman Shoko Sekine was. Well, consider everything I've told you so far as an extended prologue."

"About the industry that made it possible for her to do all this."

"Right. So you're probably thinking, okay, I understand there're all kinds of problems in the world of consumer credit—structural problems, interest problems, administrative incompetence, lack of education. True enough, but when it comes to borrowing money through the nose, that's an individual's problem. Either they've got some character flaw or they're just plain fuzzy about the way things work in this world. Witness: not everybody in Japan is running up massive debts. Regular people who've got it pretty much together are safe. The bottom line is, debt accumulation is a reflection of some personal failure or shortcoming. Am I wrong?"

Touché. Honma glanced at the guy behind the counter, who was grinning now and watching them openly.

"Did I hit the mark?"

"Dead center."

Mizoguchi coughed, then paused before asking, "Do you drive, Mr. Honma?"

"Sorry?"

"A car. Do you have a driver's license?"

"Yes, I do. Only I don't drive."

"Is that because you're too busy with work? No time?"

"No, it's ..." He had to say something. "Actually, three years ago, my wife had an accident. It was a rainy day and a truck came plowing into her from the opposite lane."

Mizoguchi's eyes widened for a moment. "And she ..."

"Almost instantaneous. Not since then, I haven't driven. Don't even own a car, it got to me so bad. Although I do still hang on to my license."

Silenced, the attorney drew back, then bowed, a quick, puppet-like bob of the head. "I'm sorry ... I didn't know."

"No, of course. Don't worry." Quite a decent guy, thought Honma. "Anyway, what's this about driving?"

"That was inexcusable of me." The attorney sat up straight, thinking, then resumed his argument. "And yet from what you just told me, I'm sure you'll understand."

"How's that?"

"Your wife was a safe driver, wasn't she?"

"Yes. She often had our son with her. If anything, she was too careful."

"And the driver of the truck?"

"Asleep at the wheel. Overwork, he said. They were running understaffed, and he hadn't had a minute's sleep the whole two days before. He'd been on a long haul—the entire length of Japan. South to north and back again. When I heard that, I honestly couldn't press charges."

The attorney nodded understandingly. "Was there an island between the lanes of traffic? How wide was the road? When the truck came at her, was there room for your wife to veer out of the way?"

Honma shook his head in reply to all the questions.

"So who was in the wrong?" asked Mizoguchi. "Granted it was a mess-up on the part of the sleepy trucker. But surely some of the blame must lie with the employer who made the man work under those conditions. And with the administration that didn't bother to provide safety islands on highways that are shared by cars and huge trucks. That and the fact that the road was too narrow, which means that the local authorities who planned the roads had some part in it too. But that was all because the price of land went sky-high." He looked up. "There's a long string of factors in that accident. Any number of things that might have helped prevent it. But suppose I just toss all that aside and say, 'Ultimately it was the fault of the two drivers. Some personal shortcoming, I suppose.' Would that be fair?"

Honma didn't feel much like answering, and he knew there was no particular need to.

Mizoguchi nodded and went on. "It's easy to lump everyone who gets deeply into debt together and pass sentence on them. 'Shortcomings.' But that's no better than writing off all drivers who get into accidents, saying, 'They're bad drivers. That's why they wreck their cars. They should never have been given licenses in the first place.' With no consideration of the circumstances before and after. 'And the proof of it is,' you say, 'some people don't get into accidents.'"

Honma remembered the trucker; he remembered the time the man had come to his place with a detective from the Traffic Division. He could picture him in a vague way, but couldn't recall his face. The trucker, too, had been unable to look Honma in the eye. The man's hands had trembled when he offered incense in front of Chizuko's memorial photo, scattering some of the ash about. Afterward, when Honma went to clean this up, the spot where the trucker had knelt felt extraordinarily warm. Alive. That's when Honma started shaking with rage. Knowing it wasn't only the man's fault didn't help, it just made it worse.

Honma stared blankly at the attorney for a few seconds before the sound of his own voice brought him back. "I know what you mean, Mr. Mizoguchi."

Mizoguchi continued, slowly at first. "With traffic accidents, you can go on about the responsibility of the driver. But what about our so-called auto safety commission? Or the car makers themselves, who play up fuel economy over safety features? Yes, part of the blame must go to the drivers, but merely to say 'Anybody who has a smash-up is a lousy driver' is ludicrous. The same holds true for consumer lending and spiraling debts."

His tone brightened. "The existing bankruptcy laws need amending on various points, as the press, with its usual hyperbole, has been telling us. You know the sort of headline: 'Make a Killing through Personal Bankruptcy.' Are you familiar with the procedures for filing bankruptcy?"

"Roughly."

"The actual steps are pretty simple," he explained. "First you declare bankruptcy to whatever regional court has jurisdiction over you. You submit a completed declaration form, together with a copy of your family register and residence certificate, a record of your holdings, a list of creditors and a detailed written description of the circumstances in which you incurred the debts. After that, you receive a summons and appear in court, and the judge goes over the facts with you. This is known as the 'surety inquest.' The actual court investigation and this inquest don't take that long. In individual cases, most bankruptcies are completed within a month or two of filing.

"In cases where a person has a house or other visible holdings, a court-appointed executor will screen the creditors, liquidate property, and distribute the proceeds fairly. During that time, the bankrupt party cannot move or travel without the court's permission. In many cases, mail is even forwarded straight to the executor. However, when a bankrupt is under twenty, the procedures obviously differ. After all, what does a young person own that's worth enough to liquidate? Clothes, a bit of furniture, stereo equipment—little things they're usually allowed to keep.

"Naturally, if the holdings are not worth repossessing, there's not much reason to perpetuate the state of bankruptcy. So a 'cancellation' is issued, with the bankruptcy halted at the moment the order is signed. Since this procedure terminates the bankruptcy, the restraining order preventing a person from traveling is lifted.

"Even so, we haven't seen the last of the debts. Within a month of the cancellation, you also have to file for a 'debt exemption.' Only after that comes through are you finally free from paying. That ruling can take six or seven months. By and large, individual cases do get exonerated. But there are a few conditions that have to be met. First, a bankrupt must have no history of a bankruptcy or debt exemption during the previous ten years. In other words, the statutes set a maximum of one bankruptcy per person per decade.

"The discovery of any fraud, though, can nullify an exemption. There can't be any holdings kept hidden, or any lying to creditors so as to borrow as much as possible while preparing to file. But, otherwise, it doesn't matter how you frittered your money away, or how long you took to do it—except in cases where sudden short-term borrowing is construed as willful bankruptcy. The bankrupt party simply has to want to 'turn over a new leaf.'

"The aim is always to save the debtor," he said, "although the procedure has come under fire recently as being just a convenient way of wiping the slate clean." He sighed, looking suddenly old. "It does raise moral questions. Even I tend to think that we'd be better off with a system that forced people to work off their debts. Not these outrageous interest charges, perhaps, but just the principal. Little by little, in installments."

Then he grinned. "But, you know, most of the time people don't come looking for help until they're looking straight into the flames. Which of course gives me very little leeway to counsel them about prevention or policy. The first thing is to save lives."

Honma nodded. "That's understandable."

"Debts drive people to suicide. They break up homes, force people to skip town … It sounds unbelievable in this day and age, but tragedies occur all the time, for sheer lack of knowledge about the ins and outs of personal bankruptcy."

"Will that ever change?"

"Lately—and I like to think it's partly due to our efforts—we've seen an increase in the number of clients coming in for counseling before things get too far out of hand. The number of people filing for personal bankruptcy is spiraling too. The bankruptcy courts are all backed up." Mizoguchi flipped through his notebook. "In 1984 alone, over twenty thousand cases were filed nationwide. That was the year of the so-called 'consumer finance scare.' Since then it's gone up and down, but these past few years it seems to be on the rise again. In 1990, there were twelve thousand cases, but last year it was up to twenty-three thousand. This year it's certainly even higher than that. Why, the other week, for two whole days the six 'credit hotlines' in our office never stopped ringing. Most of the calls were from young people. We even had a call from the parents of a child who'd run away from home to escape his debts."

They were the only customers left by now. Mizoguchi grunted as he rose to his feet. "See you tomorrow!" he called out to the man running the place as they made their way outside.

They stepped out into the sleepy back streets of a Ginza that was unrecognizable at that time of day: bicycles were leaned casually against storefronts, bags of garbage lay strewn about here and there. No tinsel, no neon. Bars might suck the town dry by night, but that money slept peacefully in the bank during the day. Ginza was at rest, from sheer exhaustion probably.

As they started walking, Mizoguchi dug his hands deep into his coat pockets and said: "Five years ago, when I started doing Ms. Sekine's papers, I had her write out a statement listing her outstanding debts. She said to me, 'I don't know how I ever got so far into the hole. I just wanted to be happy.'"

"'Happy,'" said Honma.

"Not much of a revelation, I'm afraid." He walked a few steps further and added, "If you need her work addresses and that sort of thing, I'll give you whatever I can. I'll have a word with Sawagi, to get out the files for you."

"Thanks. That would be a big help."

"In return, let me know how you're coming along, would you?"

"Yes, certainly."

"By the way, do you think Ms. Sekine's all right?" he asked quite casually.

Honma didn't answer, and the attorney didn't press.

At the main intersection in Ginza, they stopped before heading off in different directions. They'd already said goodbye when Mizoguchi put in a final word. "Don't forget what I told you. There was nothing fundamentally wrong with her. She was doing her darnedest to make a life for herself. There but for the grace of God ... Remember that. Otherwise you won't recognize her, or the woman who took her place."

"Okay. Thanks very much for your time."

With a wave of the hand, the lawyer turned away. The light changed and he moved off into the sea of people.

Further off, swept along in the tide, how many others had drowned?

✧ 12 ✧

The sun was rust red, low in the sky. A bunch of kids had gathered in the playground and were climbing the fence, squatting in the dirt, scratching their backs, stamping their feet. Right in the middle of them stood a short, barrel-chested man, hands on his hips, barking out commands. He was too far off for Honma to make out his words clearly.

The kids were only half listening. Two young mothers sat side by side on a pair of swings, each with an infant on her lap, watching the man and smiling guardedly.

"… We have to do it properly, you agree?" the little man called out. He was almost shouting.

A boy who had been crouching off to one side got up and asked, "Sure, anything you say, mister. But who the heck are you, anyway?"

"Me? Why, I'm Sherlock Holmes, of course!"

Several of the kids glanced at one another, eyebrows raised.

Honma already had a hunch who this character might be, but when he got closer, the voice clinched it. He came to a stop by the playground fence.

"Oh, su-u-ure. You're Sherlock Holmes," one kid muttered.

"Just the most famous detective of all time. Can't believe you didn't know me! Kids these days! No respect."

"Except you're not him, mister." Some of the other children sniggered. Even the two young mothers put their hands up to their mouths.

The little man raised his voice again. "Anyhow, we haven't time for arguing. We've got a search to make—a dragnet search, like I said.

All right? So split up and get to it, then!" The kids wandered off in every direction.

Honma was just turning the corner toward his building when that voice rang out behind him. "He-e-e-y!"

Honma didn't turn around or even slow down, though admittedly his speed was hampered by his leg.

The little man was gaining on him. "Hey, what is this? You can't just breeze on past like you don't know me!"

Honma waved his hand behind him. "I don't. Never saw you before in my life."

"Liar!" said Sadao Funaki loudly, catching up and then slowing to match Honma's pace. "Having a tough time of it, eh?"

"Thanks, I hadn't noticed."

"I'd trade places if I could."

"Hey, could we change the subject?" By now he was laughing. "So what do you think you're doing, anyway?"

Funaki puffed out his chest. "Organizing a search. I'm turning these boys into a team of crack detectives."

"And what are they searching for?"

"A dog. A lost dog."

Honma stopped in his tracks. "Not Blockhead?"

Funaki looked surprised that he knew about it. "Yeah, that's the one. Stupid name for a dog. That's probably why it decided to run away."

So Blockhead still hadn't come home. "He's a friendly dog, but not too clever. It wouldn't be hard for someone to walk off with him."

"Well, I just hope he didn't get hit by a car," Funaki said, lowering his voice slightly.

They paused in the elevator lobby for a minute to catch their breath.

"Who'd you hear about Blockhead from?" Honma asked.

"Makoto," he replied. Makoto was fond of "Uncle Sadao," even if the boy did say he was always yelling.

"While you were out traipsing around, Makoto got his pals together for a search operation. I lent them a little expertise, is all."

"But Makoto wasn't there just now."

"He's on special leave," he reported proudly. "Him and Isaka and that Kazzy kid, the three of them went off to check the pound."

Funaki always seemed to be wearing the same suit, though actually he rotated three suits of the same fabric and cut. This made him look as if he were careful with his clothes. His smoky-brown jacket was unbuttoned. And as if by magic, he pulled out a large manila envelope from an inner pocket, saying: "Here you are, as ordered."

The heater in the living room was still warm. Funaki gave himself the run of the place, cutting across the hall to light some incense in front of Chizuko's photo. Honma, meanwhile, pulled the documents out of the envelope: Shoko Sekine's canceled register from Utsunomiya and her employment listings.

"Thanks. I owe you one," he said.

Funaki raised a hand in acknowledgment and then, turning to the photo, said in a stage whisper, "Hey, Chizuko, your husband's up to something again."

Funaki and Chizuko had been friends since childhood. They'd gone to the same elementary school. In fact, it was Funaki who had introduced Chizuko to Honma when the two men were at the police academy. *She was like my little sister*, Funaki had said. *I didn't want to see her hooked up with anybody who didn't deserve her.*

But when Honma had asked, *So why didn't you marry her yourself?* Funaki had had to think.

*She was too close*, he'd said finally, *too close to be in range.*

Funaki hardly ever came around any more; he was too busy. But when he did, he always spent a while with her photograph. Honma let him take as long as he liked.

Honma spread the contents of the envelope out on the table and sat down. The canceled family register was perfectly straightforward. The real Shoko Sekine never once altered her permanent address until the fake Shoko established the Honancho family register. The address, written by the head of the household—her father—read Ichozakacho 2001, Utsunomiya.

An additional entry duly noted that she had set up "current residence" elsewhere—South Kasai 4-10-5, Edogawa Ward, Tokyo—as of April 1, 1983. This no doubt was where she had lived when she had gone to work at Kasai Trading. He reached for the phone, flipped back through his address book to the number for the company, and dialed.

A woman answered. Explaining that he had something to mail and needed to verify the address, Honma read off the address from the register. Ah, the woman told him, that wasn't the company but its employees' dormitory.

Honma put the phone down and looked up to see Funaki watching him. "Tea would be nice," Funaki said offhandedly.

"Bottom compartment," Honma answered.

Funaki went over to the cupboard, pulled open the doors at the bottom, and took out a little canister. Then he went to fill the kettle and put it on the gas. "Changed over to self-service, huh?"

"Correct."

"If you stop moving around altogether, you'll be an old man in no time."

"I feel pretty ancient already, thank you."

The next residence on record was the Castle Mansion Kinshicho where Shoko Sekine had lived when she filed for bankruptcy. Very likely, when she left the Kasai Trading dormitory and moved into the apartment, she was beginning to be pressured for payments. Her first misstep. When young employees move into a company dorm, they start to long for the freedom of living by themselves, with no curfews, prudish house mothers or bitchy people down the hall. They tend to gloss over the amount of cash that freedom actually costs. The hard fact that the most basic things—electricity, gas, flush toilets—cost money in the outside world just doesn't seem to get through.

The final entry was where she moved after her bankruptcy came through—where she vanished into thin air on March 17, 1990: Kawa-guchi Co-op.

After her mother died, Shoko Sekine had called on the attorney to ask about the insurance money. She hadn't mentioned any property, which probably meant that her mother had lived in a rented place. It figured. Her father died early on, which wouldn't have left Shoko and her mother much in the way of support. According to the listings in the canceled register, her mother had moved three times—all within the city of Utsunomiya—before her death on November 25, 1989. When she died, she was registered at Ichozakacho 2005, and had lived there almost ten years. Not far from the family's permanent address.

Had her mother stayed in Utsunomiya simply out of attachment to her hometown? Or had she been guarding the "nest" for her daughter's eventual return?

Funaki deposited himself in the chair across from Honma. He reached for the register as soon as Honma had finished and thumbed through it briefly, without a word.

The employment listings supplied by the Public Employment office likewise confirmed Honma's suspicions. There were two registration numbers for Shoko Sekine. One was the one issued when the real Shoko went to work for Kasai Trading. The other was issued in April 1990, when the fake Shoko was hired by Imai Office Machines —the first time she had ever signed up for Public Employment, supposedly.

"After I got hold of the papers, I rang up Public Employment," Funaki began. "And they were surprised at the duplication. Not that some people don't try to hide a record of past employment. People like that, they told me, will just come in and say, 'It's the first time.' Sometimes they run a spot check, but for your ordinary secretarial type, they generally let it pass. They can't be bothered. Anyway, they only hang on to records for seven years, so there wouldn't have been any from when Kasai Trading hired her, only from the time she quit. After that, she was on unemployment for a while."

Honma thought it over. When Imai Office Machines hired the fake Shoko Sekine, she wouldn't have been able to get hold of the real Shoko's employment listings or Public Employment papers. She'd have had no choice but to go the "first time" route. Or maybe she just hadn't given it much thought.

No, she didn't seem the short-sighted type, not from what he knew of her. Without the proper Public Employment ID, she'd just been forced to lie through her teeth. After the real Shoko had quit Kasai Trading, then tried to escape debts and bill collectors by running to Kawaguchi and skidding into bar hostessing—through all the

117

troubles of her life at the time—one thin piece of ID could easily get lost. The woman who came along behind her could have turned the Kawaguchi apartment upside down and not found a thing.

The kettle started to whistle. Funaki jumped up and made a quick pot of tea. He poured it into two cups and carried them over to the table. "Got what you needed?" he asked, blowing lightly at the steam.

"Uh-huh. Thanks," Honma said, straightening the papers. He paused.

Funaki was looking at him. "There's something else?"

"Actually, it'd be helpful if you could find out whether this woman had a passport or driver's license."

"Hm." Funaki eyed the telephone. "I could try calling, but the passport part's a bit tricky. I might get some joker who wants to make things difficult. Let me get back to you. Is tonight okay?"

"Tonight would be great."

Funaki didn't ask what this all was about. He knew as much as he needed to know. For now this was strictly a Honma family affair. He was merely lending a hand—and that only went so far. Honma would tell him if the search was more than he could handle.

"That makes a great big one I owe you. I'll pay you back, I promise."

"Pay up now," Funaki said abruptly. When Honma just looked blankly at him, he continued, "I'm stumped. How about lending me a little insight?"

It turned out he was working on a homicide. "It was in Nakano. The house is ten minutes by bus from Nakano Station, and it was just past two in the afternoon. Forced entry, armed robbery. The house belongs to a couple. The husband gets stabbed—killed—and the wife is tied up. The robber gets away, but the neighbors catch a glimpse of him as he's taking off."

"Okay."

"The couple was rich. The husband was fifty-three, the wife thirty. His second wife."

"Any kids?"

"Not by this wife. But moneywise, they're loaded. They run two coffee shops, a video shop and two convenience stores."

"That's rich."

"And—the husband's got a life insurance policy worth a hundred million yen. They've been married a year and a half. His family can't think of a single good thing to say about her. They think she was after his money all along."

Honma grinned mischievously. "And?"

"The way I see it, the whole thing is staged. The wife masterminded the whole show, for her husband's money. She's got somebody else. Anyway, that's what the rumors say. That the guy helped her."

"Believable."

"Right?" Funaki thumped the table. "But—and here's the problem—there isn't anybody. No suspects."

"Huh?"

"She hasn't got anybody. Run her private life through an X-ray machine and you won't find any trace of another man. Nothing. She's squeaky clean."

"How is she for looks?"

"Let's just say you wouldn't throw her out of bed for eating crackers. That's what attracted the husband in the first place."

Honma remembered Nobuko Konno, the woman who ran Kawaguchi Co-op while her husband tended bar. Now there was a good-looker. Smart, too—although she probably wouldn't have appreciated Honma's interest in her at all.

"I don't get it," Funaki moaned. "Any way you size it up, there's got to be a man somewhere. But nothing turns up. Ever hear such a crazy story? A nice-looking woman, and twenty years younger than the husband …"

Honma wandered off in his thoughts. Nobuko. File under her arm, giving clear answers to Honma's questions. While her husband and daughter were busy washing the dishes … *Akemi, go get your mother.*

"Yeah …," Honma said suddenly out loud, breaking right into Funaki's monologue.

"What?"

"About those shops you were saying they had. Was it the husband who actually ran them? Or the wife?"

Funaki looked puzzled. As if he'd sat down at a noodle counter and been served French food.

"Well?" Honma asked again.

"… Why, the husband, I guess."

"You guess? Is that an educated guess?"

"No, the husband definitely kept his hands on the money. In fact, the tax office had their eye on him. Suspicion of tax evasion."

"So the husband kept his hands on the money," Honma repeated slowly. "But that, in itself, isn't running the business. There's the interior decoration to consider, and deciding what videos to stock—all kinds of planning goes into it. Who did all that?"

Funaki answered immediately. "Yeah, yeah, that was the husband too. The wife didn't have much say in that. He spoiled her, told her not to worry her pretty little head about that sort of thing."

"No sign of hard feelings or arguments on the subject?"

Funaki shook his head. "As far as I can tell, no. The wife didn't seem to take much of an interest, anyway. She'd known just what she was after and she'd gotten it. So she was set to coast through the rest of her life."

"You so sure?"

"Seems that way," he said with a shrug. "But it's true, the employees were kind of taken with her. The manager of one of the coffee shops even told me she'd made some decent suggestions about background music. Said she had a good idea what kind of music a younger clientele might go for. I guess it wasn't so long ago that she used to hang out in cafés herself."

Honma gave a big nod. "Two more questions."

"Okay."

"What did the wife do before they got married?"

"Your regular secretary. Did the odd paperwork, nothing fancy. Plus some accounting, so she must have had something on the ball."

Once again, Nobuko Konno came to mind. "Second question. You said there were rumors the wife had a lover. Anything besides rumors?"

"Nope, just talk. Some days the neighbors or the staff would see her get dolled up and then go out by herself."

"But no specific man, nobody you could put your finger on."

"Which is why I'm going crazy."

"What did she look like on those days?"

"You mean her clothes?"

"Yes. A suit? A kimono? A frilly dress? Did she wear perfume? Heavier makeup than usual? What sort of handbag was she carrying? That's important. Something small, compact, the size of about a handkerchief? Or more functional, big enough to hold a notebook and an appointment book? The shoes make a difference, too. Glitzy? Or more practical?"

Funaki pulled out a memo pad and jotted down some notes. "What does this all add up to?"

Honma clasped his hands behind his head and leaned back in his chair. "You're telling me that there's no particular evidence of a man on the sly. So I'm going on the assumption that there isn't one. So the wife slips out? Well, if she's in ordinary good clothes, goes light on the perfume and makeup, carries a practical bag and wears simple shoes—that narrows down who she's going to see."

Funaki nodded, to prod him along. "Yeah?"

"The most likely suspect is ..."

"... is?"

"A bank. Not the one where her husband keeps the money. A different one. Someplace that deals directly with her. There would be all kinds of explaining to do if the husband found out, right?"

Funaki shrugged, spreading his small, squarish hands. "Of all the stupid ... What's she got to talk to a bank about?"

"Business. Financing."

"For what?"

"Maybe she wants to run her own shop? She's got her own ideas about management. A coffee shop or a video rental place." Honma laughed. "You and me, we've been in this business a long time. Long enough to pick up some preconceptions. When a woman commits a crime, there must be a man mixed up in it somewhere. Left to their own devices, women don't have much of a criminal impulse. They do it for the man, right? Women's crimes are crimes of passion. Even infanticide, if you want to look at it that way."

"... True enough."

"Well, it's true that that's what we expect. But lately things have changed. No, not even lately. Things probably started changing a good while back. Sometimes a woman's motives might not be to get a man—it may be just as common nowadays to want to get *rid* of a man. A woman wants to start being more enterprising, so she gets rid of the person who's holding her back. There seems to be more of that now than there used to be."

Funaki was about to argue, but decided to keep his mouth shut.

"What if," Honma went on, "what if, from the very beginning, she didn't marry her husband for his money but for his businesses? Say she thought, 'That'll give me an easy in. After we're married, maybe I'll try my own hand at it.' Secretaries reach their late twenties and find they're still cleaning up the office and making the tea. They get frustrated. Used to be, the only way out was marriage. But not any more. Now it's independence—study abroad, business—all sorts of things have opened up. But those take money, and lots of it. As a first step, maybe she thought she'd try marriage to an older, successful businessman."

Funaki blinked cautiously. "But then things didn't go the way she'd planned."

"Right. The husband gave her money and spoiled her rotten. But he wouldn't let her touch the businesses. It was always, 'Don't worry your pretty little head over that.' So nothing had changed from her days as a secretary."

"A lot of people seem satisfied with exactly that kind of life," Funaki protested.

"Well, sure. But there are women who aren't."

"I suppose so."

"To a woman with a certain independent streak in her, having some man tell her, 'Now don't go troubling yourself over things that are too hard for you,' that must be hard to take."

"But they say she never argued with her husband."

"Maybe she couldn't. Maybe he never took her seriously enough to actually fight with her. Who knows, maybe that was an even bigger blow to her pride. She was probably stewing inside—and scheming away." Honma searched for the words. "What's more, she had to prove herself no less capable or decisive than him. Eliminating him was one surefire way. So maybe she caught him off guard and let all that rage in her come out."

Funaki now looked like he'd just been handed the bill for that full-course French meal at the noodle shop. "But the accomplice. There had to be an accomplice," he said as a last resort. "That must have been the lover, right? A guy. Had to be. She must have gotten him to help. I mean, it was probably him who actually did it."

"But there's no sign of a man, right?"

"Maybe I just haven't been looking in the right places."

"I doubt it," Honma remarked dryly. "If no trace of a man shows up, you've got to consider the possibility of a woman accomplice. Somebody from her office days. Someone she could approach about going into business together once they'd dealt with this overbearing husband of hers. Think about it. Two women getting together and talking: who's going to bat an eye? And if they worked as a team, they could stab a man to death, no problem. How about running an MO on that?"

Funaki looked dazed. He cleared his throat. "It just happens that the wife's got a really close woman friend. Helped with all the funeral arrangements."

"Well, there you are. Could be her."

A slow grin spread over Funaki's face. "I'll check it out."

That's the spirit, Honma was about to say encouragingly, but instead he fell silent. All this had only occurred to him thanks to "Shoko Sekine": women don't always commit crimes of passion.

She'd stolen someone else's family register, assumed that person's identity. When she was about to be exposed, she ditched a marriage-in-the-making and ran. What was she after? What had led up to all this? He didn't know, but one thing was for certain—it wasn't love or a man or anything emotional that was driving her.

Her assumed identity had nothing to do with wanting to marry Jun. The affair with Jun came later, as part of the false life she'd built on that false name. And when a flaw revealed itself in that life, she left the people at Imai Office Machines and Jun too, apparently without a twinge of regret.

She's on the run, thought Honma. He couldn't put his finger on it,

123

but something had her running. And yet, deep down, this woman is a loner anyway. She's going to carry this through alone. No emotional attachments, no orders from anybody.

She's like a wall covered with paper in a bright floral pattern: underneath it, reinforced concrete. Impenetrable, as solid as they come. An iron will to survive.

For herself and no one else. That was her. A woman who ten years ago scarcely existed in Japan.

Isaka and Makoto came home just as Funaki was on his way out.

"Couldn't find Blockhead," the boy whimpered. "You think maybe he got killed? Uncle Sadao said if he was hurt, the pound would have found him right away."

"Blockhead is an easygoing dog. Anybody driving past could have said 'Here, boy,' and he would have jumped right in."

Makoto leaned against the wall and moped. Honma and Isaka looked at each other.

"Dad ..."

"Yes?"

"At the pound, there were so many dogs."

Uh-oh, thought Honma. He could see what was coming.

"Those dogs, are they gonna kill them all? Why do people want to get rid of dogs like that? Why don't people want to keep them?"

Isaka rubbed his forehead and stared at the floor.

"I don't know," said Honma. "I can't understand what makes people do things like that. But I do know we don't like it, and we don't do it, in this family. If we see someone doing something like that, we think about what we can do to stop it. Anyhow, we try to do what we can, right?"

Bending over a little to look Makoto in the face, Isaka added, "It's like Aunt Hisae said. There are all kinds of idiots out there. People who get a pet and then dump it when it gets to be too much trouble, they're just idiots." He nudged him and said, "You better wash those hands. I'll go run a bath for you. You must be pretty tired out."

Giving Isaka a look that said he wasn't convinced, Makoto obediently trundled off to the kitchen. The adults looked relieved.

"Places like that pound really get to me, too," confessed Isaka. "It's pretty grim."

"Sorry to put you through it."

"No, no, it's all right. But still, there really are a lot of dogs in that place." He took a step toward the kitchen, then stopped and reached inside his jacket. "When we were just leaving, there was a phone call saying that your enlargement was ready. The photo shop was on the way to the pound, so I thought I'd save you the trip."

Enlargement? Honma had forgotten all about it. The Polaroid. He'd practically given up on it, since it hadn't seemed very promising.

"Oh, thanks. It completely slipped my mind."

Isaka took it out of the envelope. "From what the man at the store said, the original is slightly out of focus. So the bigger you blow it up, the less you'll be able to tell what's what. This is about the limit." It was a little smaller than a letter-sized piece of paper. The chocolate-brown house looked large and flat, but there were no dramatic changes. As the man said, blowing it up had only made the image even grainier. All Honma could make out was the house, the two women and those floodlights …

That's when he noticed.

At first he thought his eyes were playing tricks on him. He hurried over to the desk to find a magnifying glass. No, he wasn't seeing things.

"What is it?"

Honma looked up and handed Isaka the photograph. "You follow baseball, don't you?"

"Mm?"

"Go to any games?"

"Yeah, I go. Generally to games at the big ballparks around Tokyo."

Honma got excited. "Well, you must know, then. Are there any kind of stadiums where they can reverse the floodlights? Where the lights can be pointed outside the field?"

Isaka blinked. "Huh? What do you mean?"

Honma pointed at the lights in the photo. "These sure look like stadium lights, wouldn't you say?"

Isaka put on his reading glasses. "Yes, but …"

"So we know this house must be near a stadium somewhere, don't we?"

"I guess that's a safe bet."

"All right, then, what do you make of these?" He tapped his finger on each light unit in turn. A bit higher and they would have been off the upper left-hand corner of the picture. "Look at these lamps. They're facing the house. They must have been rotated outward. There's no stadium with a house built inside it, is there?"

Sure enough, the lights were turned toward the chocolate-brown house.

Isaka brought the photograph up to his nose. "Well, I'll be …"

"Any stadiums like that? That you're aware of?"

Isaka stared at the photo in his hand. Slowly he replied: "I take it you're not a baseball fan."

"Can't say I ever have been."

Isaka nodded. "Well, if you ever saw those lights at the ballpark, the real ones, you'd know what a hell of a job it'd be to turn them around."

"They're huge, I know."

"Floodlights are for lighting the ballfield. That's their one purpose. So realigning them to face outward …"

"What if each whole unit swiveled, pole and all? Automatically. Like turning its neck." Honma had to admit it sounded rather ridiculous.

Isaka laughed. "It'd make the news if they introduced something like that. It's awfully dark outside Meiji Park, for instance; if they could turn the lights around after a game, it would sure help the spectators see their way home."

Honma set the photograph aside and scratched his head.

## ✧ 13 ✧

When Honma called from home to check the address of Lahaina, a woman gave him directions, starting at the old locomotive out in front of Shimbashi Station, one of the most popular rendezvous points in central Tokyo. The bar was still in business, she was proud to say. Same owner, same Mama-san since the day it opened ten years back.

Lucky, thought Honma. In a business as fickle as the "water trade," odds were the management and the bar's name would have changed even in the last two years.

Mizoguchi had put in a word with his assistant by the time he made his next phone call, and she had the information at her fingertips. Honma then quickly drafted a chronology of Shoko Sekine's "missing years."

| | |
|---|---|
| March 1983 | Arrives Tokyo. Employed by Kasai Trading. |
| Summer 1984 | Begins incurring debts. Moves from company dormitory to small apartment in Castle Mansion Kinshicho. |
| April 1985 | Begins part-timing at the bar Gold (Shinjuku). |
| Spring 1986 | Hospitalized 10 days due to exhaustion from overwork. Debts worsen. |
| January 1987 | Bill collectors put pressure on. Quits Kasai Trading. |
| May 1987 | Files for bankruptcy. Leaves the apartment at Castle Mansion Kinshicho, |

|                    | moves in with Gold co-worker Tomie Miyagi. |
|--------------------|--------------------------------------------|
| February 1988      | Bankruptcy finalized. Quits Gold, goes to work at bar Lahaina (Shimbashi). Moves from Miyagi's apartment to Kawaguchi Co-op. |
| November 25, 1989  | Mother dies in accident in Utsunomiya. |
| January 25, 1990   | Visits attorney Mizoguchi to discuss insurance money. |

Then on March 17 she'd disappeared.

Honma planned to work backward for the time being. He'd already been to Mizoguchi's office, so the next stop was Lahaina. After that he would head for Utsunomiya. Or Gold. Or try to locate her old roommate, this Tomie Miyagi. It all depended on what he found out at Lahaina.

Makoto had hardly touched his supper. The search operation for Blockhead had failed and he was feeling down. When Honma peeked into his room on the way out, the boy was engrossed in a long phone call. Honma couldn't very well complain. He'd as good as abandoned his son lately.

Another taxi ride to the station, and from there the train. He decided not to take his umbrella, now that he was starting to hobble along without support. Must just be willpower, as his injured knee showed no dramatic signs of recovery. It was only four days, in fact, since Jun had first come to him—last Monday.

His therapy involved two sessions a week. As a rule he went on Mondays and Fridays, but skipping it today wouldn't be such a crime. Especially as he was getting out and about on this leg of his. He might actually get well faster this way—or so he argued to himself.

You couldn't really call it "rehabilitation," anyway; it wasn't even an outpatient clinic. After he'd been discharged from the police hospital, he had gone to a sports club recommended by a friend. The idea of exercise sounded good. And the place was affiliated with a number of private hospitals, so he could ask a doctor to set up a special training program.

Honma's therapist was a woman from Osaka, in her mid-thirties. Likable enough, he supposed, but no-nonsense. He'd work himself into a sweat and she'd just egg him on, telling him that *Tokyo men have got no balls!*

Even here in Tokyo, a city that neuters everything, Osaka people managed to keep their own coloring. They might modify their drawl to a "standard textbook" Japanese, but their accent remained Osaka. It wasn't without its appeal, he had to admit. Honma himself didn't have a "hometown" to give his speech any particular flavor.

His father was from Tohoku in the far north. The third son of a poor farmer, he'd made his way to Tokyo soon after the war, looking for work. And had wound up as a cop. He'd had his reasons, but "seeing justice done" wasn't one of them. Back then, the Japanese had not only been stripped of their honor, with no new cause to fight for, but their rice bowls were empty. Also, there were quotas on how many people could move in to Tokyo from the countryside. But joining the police force automatically gave you the right to live there.

Becoming a cop had just been a way of surviving for him. So Honma's mother had never been able to work out why her son should want to follow in his footsteps. *Don't tell me it's in the blood,* she'd moan. The old man, too, had felt sorry for Honma's wife right from the beginning. *If ever you want to leave him,* he used to tell her, *just say so. I'll shake him down for the money to raise Makoto.* He meant it, too. Usually, Chizuko just smiled.

All three of them—his parents and his wife—were from the north. And all three of them now gone. His mother from his father's village; Chizuko from Niigata, with its heavy snows. Whenever he and Chizuko visited his folks, Honma had been the odd man out, as if he had no roots, nowhere he could call "home."

*But you're a Tokyo boy*, she used to tease. Honma, however, had never considered himself a native son. There was an indefinable gap between being born in Tokyo and being a "Tokyoite." They say that "three generations makes Tokyo home," but could a person ever feel a bloodline connection to the place? That was the real question. How could you really speak of "hometown Tokyo" or being "Tokyo born and bred"? Today's city was no place to put down roots. It was a barren field, soil that gave off no smell, unplowed and unwatered. Nothing grew in the big city. People there were tumbleweeds, living on the memory of roots put down somewhere else by their parents or their parents' parents. And those roots dry up and wither.

That must be why, he thought. Why he always felt a bit sad whenever, in the course of his job, running around the city listening to all these people's stories, he came across someone whose accent or phrasing identified them immediately as having a "hometown." Like a child out playing at dusk. One friend, then another gets called in to supper, till finally he's on his own.

That evening, at eight-thirty, Honma pushed though the door to Lahaina. A girl who couldn't have been much more than twenty called out a greeting, and here again he heard an accent—a southern one, from Hakata, too strong to ever let go. Maybe Shoko Sekine had had an Utsunomiya twang when she came to work here?

After a few minutes, Honma was approached by the Mama-san. "Excuse me," she said quietly, "but you're with the police, aren't you?"

"Bingo," he replied. "How did you know?"

The woman shrugged her bare shoulder. She was wearing one of those single-strap dresses that exposed the swell of one shoulder and the crest of her collarbone. A slipped piece of underpinning showed at the base of her neck.

The modest floor space was taken up by two seating booths and a horseshoe-shaped counter. The decor as such was minimal, consisting of a single poster of a gigantic tree on one wall. Minimal staff, too—one male helper and two hostesses. All part-timers, probably. The girl with the Hakata accent was a bit younger than the other one.

Honma sat at the very end of the counter. Behind it stood the Mama-san and a bartender, whose profile reminded Honma a little of Isaka. A large vase occupied the opposite end of the counter, but the flowers were artificial.

These small bars tended to be on the quiet side. No karaoke system like Bacchus had. Not much money spent on fixtures and fittings like there would be in a bigger place. Not likely to attract walk-in customers, more of a roost for mid-level white-collar workers—and not the better-paid ones at that. A place to keep a bottle of Scotch on the sly. Even now, when there were four customers in the bar, all four of them were drinking alone. Still, it was comfortable enough. Probably that was why it had managed to stay in business for ten years.

When Honma tried saying, "I used to know someone who worked here," she cut him short.

"You're on a case, are you?"

"First maybe you could tell me how you knew I was a cop," he pressed. "Couldn't a guy come into the place where his girlfriend used to work, for old times' sake?"

That made her laugh. "We don't get the sensitive type in here. And I generally got a finger on who my girls' men friends are, anyway, so it wouldn't wash with me."

"A finger?" He scratched his forehead. "More like both hands, maybe?"

"Come on, mister. Only a cop would make a dumb joke like that." She swept a hand over the counter. "So you're not going to flip out the badge?"

"And risk upsetting your other customers?"

"Yes, it might spoil things a little." She bit one shiny lip as she gave it a moment's thought. "You from Sakuradamon? Or around here … say, Marunouchi Precinct?"

"Would the guys from Marunouchi come in here for a drink?"

"Outside their territory—might be kind of relaxing for them. Of course, they'd never say they're cops. But I can tell."

"What gives them away?"

"It's written all over their faces. They've all got hawk eyes. Not you so much, mind you," she said, leaning forward to get a closer look.

"Thanks."

"So, you're Sakuradamon?"

"Mm."

"Homicide? What's the big secret? You look a lot straighter than most of the boys from there, though."

"Yeah, Homicide." Why not? He pulled out a name card with no official title on it and laid it on the counter.

The woman picked it up with both hands. "Mr. Honma, is it? Well, then, what's your business? And what's it got to do with my girls?"

He shifted on his barstool. "Maybe you remember one called Shoko Sekine. Worked here till March two years ago?"

The Mama-san first blinked at Honma, then turned to the bartender. "Hear that, Kikuchi? It's Shoko."

Kikuchi, who was drying some glasses, gave a nod. "Yeah, I heard."

"So it's a name you've some reason to remember?" said Honma, turning toward him.

"She just up and vanished—*poof!*—never even collected her pay."

"Like he said." The woman leaned closer, pressing so hard against the counter that her dress strap dug into her left shoulder. "That's just never happened, before or since. And I've got an eye for people, I like to think." She patted her right hand over her heart, as if the memory were still lodged in there. Then she looked up, her eyes bright. "So you're looking for Shoko?"

"That's the one."

"Did she ... was she ...?"

"No, nothing that bad. Which is why I don't want to pull the badge." It was time for Jun's sob story. "She was engaged to my nephew. But apparently got cold feet and ran. Knowing my nephew, I can't really say I blame her. So I certainly don't mean to pressure her. What takes precedence for me is, he borrowed some money through her. And I think he ought to pay it back. My nephew's saying, forget about it, but these things can get messy. I don't want to get caught in the middle later on."

The Mama-san and the bartender looked at each other. Seen front-on, the bartender was better-looking than Isaka.

"Shoko got engaged?" She practically choked on her words. "Is your nephew a cop, too?"

"No, a banker."

"Our Shoko was going to become a banker's wife?"

"Didn't she seem the type?"

"No, it's not that. But ... how shall I put it? She wasn't really the domestic type."

"Not your born homemaker?"

"Not exactly," she said with a smile. "She wasn't too keen on cleaning and washing up."

A far cry from the "Shoko Sekine" who fled the Honancho apartment.

The Mama-san was fast approaching forty, Honma decided. Running a bit on the heavy side, with the makings of a double chin. But she could still turn the heat up with her eyes. "Sorry," she said, "but I really don't know where she could be. Since she quit on us like that two years ago, we haven't had a word from her—not even a New Year's card." Take her words at face value or read deeper: Okay, we accept your credentials, but we don't necessarily buy your story. Even if we did know where she was, what makes you think we'd tell you?

Honma smiled. "Naturally I didn't come here expecting any real leads. I was just hoping you could fill me on what she was like when she worked here, maybe give me the name of a friend or two." Before the Mama-san could reply, he added, "My nephew knows she worked in a bar. A lot of secretaries work part-time these days, right? It didn't bother him. So that's not what went wrong between them. But he's a bit spoiled, and he'd built up his share of illusions about the girl."

"Lot of that lately, too," the Mama-san said coyly.

"Shoko wasn't one to waste money, was she?" he asked, going out on a limb. "She seems to have been a lot more practical about it than my nephew." After the bankruptcy, that is. She'd had to pull way back within her means.

The Mama-san took the bait. "Maybe even a little too tight, the way she scrimped."

"Anybody still working here who would have been here when she was?"

"Let's see. There's Maki," she said, looking over at one of the hostesses. Honma followed her eyes, glancing over his shoulder toward the older girl—all smiles and whispers, getting an earful from a placidly aging company man.

"Did Ms. Sekine get on okay with the other staff?"

The Mama-san raised her arched eyebrows. "She was a good girl." An evasive answer. She reached for a new glass and, filling it with ice, said, "My, your Scotch is getting watery."

"Since you keep such close tabs on your girls' private lives ..." Honma brought out the close-up picture of the fake Shoko Sekine and showed it to her. "Was this girl among her friends? Apparently she's staying with her now."

The woman stared hard at the photo. Then, with a slight turn of the head, she motioned for the bartender to come take a look. Scarcely pausing, she grabbed a glass filled with chocolate-coated pretzel sticks and called out, "Maki, you want to put these out?" Passing them to the older girl, she whispered, "You remember Shoko Sekine?"

Maki was wearing alarmingly heavy mascara. "Remember who?"

"You know, that gloomy girl."

"Ah, yeah, I remember," Maki said, the sweet smell of orange pop on her breath. She gave Honma a flicker of a smile.

"Did Shoko have a friend who looked like this?"

"Ever see this face?" Honma added. "Did she ever mention anything about any of her girlfriends?"

Maki looked at the photo and shrugged. "Got me. It was a long time ago, anyway."

"You don't remember any girlfriends?"

Maki shook her head, releasing a wave of perfume from her hair. "No, sorry. She never really talked much."

"Do you remember her living in an apartment in Kawaguchi?"

"Kawaguchi? Maybe. Anyway, somewhere in Saitama. She always had to finish up while the trains were still running, because the taxi fare was so high. Right, Mama?"

The Mama-san nodded in agreement. Honma pressed on. "Did she ever talk about where she worked before coming here?"

"She said it was a regular company."

"Yes. It was called Kasai Trading."

"Oh yeah? The name doesn't mean much to me. All she said was it was somewhere out in Edogawa."

Interesting. She'd obviously glossed over the years she'd spent hostessing at Gold. The place had bad memories for her; it was where she was working when she went bust. So even the real Shoko lied and omitted details about her past when she took on a new job. Naturally,

134

she wouldn't have said a word to anyone here about the bankruptcy.

"Did she have any boyfriends?"

The Mama-san laughed, but her answer was unequivocal. "None that I knew about, and I knew about those things."

"She was a bit weird, that kid," Maki volunteered. "She lived in her own little world. A guy'd ask her out and you'd have to beg her to go. Even with good customers who you'd swear up and down only wanted to take a girl out for a nice meal."

Unexpectedly, the bartender now spoke up. "Hey, it's just my opinion, but there was something about her eyes that said she was hurting for money."

Honma took a good look at him as he stood staring at the snapshot on the counter. "What makes you say that?" he asked.

Kikuchi turned toward him. "Sixth sense, I guess."

"No special reason, then?"

"No."

"Think some man could have cheated her out of her savings?"

The question pricked Maki's interest. "Not her," she said.

"Oh yes?"

Maki picked up the chocolate sticks and walked away, feigning a bored look.

"I take it Ms. Sekine wasn't what you'd call very sociable?"

"Not really. She never did anything with the rest of us, anyway. We never went on any trips together or anything."

Just before Honma had left the house, Funaki had called in to report that Shoko had had a driver's license but no passport. Honma now remembered to ask them about this. "She ever travel abroad?"

The Mama-san answered immediately. "No. But not because she wasn't a team player. She was terrified of airplanes. She never even flew domestic."

"Never?"

"Absolutely. You see that picture of a tree there? Know what it is?" She pointed at the framed poster on the wall. "That's in Hawaii, in a town called Lahaina on the island of Maui. Big old tree that's like the symbol of the town. My sister married an American and lives on Maui. Well, every year she comes to visit and each time she invites the girls along back with her ... But Shoko, she never went. An open invitation, but she couldn't stand the thought of getting on a plane."

Hence no passport. Had the fake Shoko Sekine not known that? If the real one didn't have a passport, there would have been nothing to stop the fake Shoko from going abroad with Jun. Which figured into a more fundamental issue. Before she took on the other woman's identity, she must have done her homework. A person that cunning, that cautious, wouldn't overlook something like a driver's license or passport, would she? No, she'd have had all her data in hand before judging that the coast was clear. You'd imagine the woman would have been close enough to Shoko Sekine to pick up all the information she needed.

So how about a colleague from Gold or from Kasai Trading? Yet neither was a real possibility. Why? Because any woman from either place who could easily have learned whether Shoko had a passport or a driver's license, and maybe even gotten her permanent family register address, would probably also know about her bankruptcy. True, the people at Kasai Trading may not have been in a position to know all the details—unlike the girls she met afterward at Gold—since she quit the company before filing for bankruptcy, but they would have seen how hard up she was; and anybody clever enough to plan this whole switch could have gotten her to talk about her debts. How would Shoko have responded? Maybe by saying she'd borrowed money from her mother. Or found a "patron" to bail her out. But even then, the fake Shoko would have checked the facts. Very likely, with a little effort, she could have found out about the secret bankruptcy. Ask the right questions and Shoko herself would have owned up. So Jun's woman shouldn't have been caught unawares, by agreeing to apply for a credit card.

Close enough to obtain her personal data, but not enough to know that she'd gone bankrupt a few years before—what kind of woman friend was that?

Once again, Honma showed the snapshot of the fake Shoko to the Mama-san. "You don't know this woman at all? Not even as a customer?"

She shook her head, without the slightest hesitation. "No, and I never forget a face." Neither, apparently, did the bartender.

"I don't suppose you'd have a photo of Ms. Sekine here, would you?"

The Mama-san shrugged. "We don't have much call to take any pictures."

"When she was working here and her mother died, did it seem to come as a big shock?"

This time the Mama-san sat up straight. "God, that was a horrible story! Falling down the steps drunk like that."

"Steps where? I never did get all the details."

"A shrine, maybe? Maybe in a park?"

"Don't ask me," said Maki, after seeing a customer to the door. Then, as she set about clearing the glasses away from the far table, she suddenly said loudly, "No, wait!" Her mascara-heavy eyes widened. "Shoko did mention one thing. Remember, Mama?"

No, Mama didn't. Neither did the bartender.

"What?" asked Honma.

Maki came over and latched onto his arm. Her nails were sharp. "When Shoko's mother died, the person who found her and called the ambulance was a young woman. Shoko told me she'd spoken to her. To thank her and all."

"Did she mention a name?"

Maki lowered her head coquettishly. "She didn't say. Or maybe she did, but I don't remember."

It looked like it was time to give Utsunomiya a try.

# ✧ 14 ✧

The New Tohoku Line bullet train from Tokyo Station gets to Utsunomiya in under an hour—just about the same amount of time it took to get to the center of Tokyo from the suburb where Honma lived, during the off hours when connections were slowest. It wasn't hard to understand why more people were moving out to the country and coming in by bullet train these days.

It was a few minutes after noon. Honma found an empty seat in a non-reserved no-smoking car and put his briefcase down on the floor by his feet. Right on schedule, he felt the train begin to move. Most of the other passengers looked like middle and senior management types, around Honma's age: the lifeblood of this artery running to and from the business capital of Tokyo.

A young man seated diagonally across the aisle was shouting instructions into a cellular phone. So maybe he was in a position of authority, but did he have to throw his voice around like that?

The train went underground soon after leaving Tokyo Station. The reception must have been bad, because Junior Executive switched off his phone with an irritated click of the tongue.

Cellular phones were expensive, Honma thought, wondering if the man had bought it on credit. And what about him? How much of what he owned had he gotten on "easy terms"? Probably half the larger furniture and appliances. Each was contracted for separately, to be paid off in a slow trickle. That had been Chizuko's department. Everything in the house had the colors and features she liked. Honma was only consulted on the cost.

Most men were probably that way. In fact he'd never run across any man who was picky about furniture or who had an eye for carpet patterns. Only the most discriminating types would pay much attention to interior decoration. But there was the age factor, too. Today's twenty-year-olds in their studio condos probably spent hours deciding on the placement of furniture and the selection of knickknacks. But since there was no rookie detective in the Division to ask about these things, he could only speculate.

Judging from the photos in newspaper inserts, mail-order catalogs, and TV commercials for the big department stores, there seemed to be no end of nice things on the market these days. And to look was to want, preferably right there, on the spot. Producing a card at the cash register and signing the little receipt would be an easy habit to fall into. Who wouldn't take "one of these and a couple of those"? It was only human nature.

There was nothing to tell a person when to put on the brakes. "Nice, isn't it? You like it, don't you? Well, go ahead, it's yours!" Desire was easy enough to arouse, but where was the clerk who'd remind you of the spiraling monthly payments, or who'd say "Better leave it at that for today."

From the retailers' point of view, of course, all that was beside the point. "Who has the time?" they'd say. "Who could be bothered to look out for customers who can't control themselves?"

The first stop, at Ueno, was brief. Soon the train was moving again. They emerged above ground and raced between the buildings. The loudspeaker announced the upcoming stops, adding a reminder about the dining car.

Outside the window, Tokyo sped past.

Honma recalled the telephone conversation he'd had with that Sawagi woman at the Mizoguchi law office. She mentioned that she'd been working for Mizoguchi for ten years now, right through the "consumer finance scare" of the early eighties.

"That was before the Regulation of Moneylending Business Law, back when it was a really rough business. They passed the law only because people were demanding that they do something. Mr. Mizoguchi himself would get threatened sometimes by these guys when he asked them to forgo collecting. The fellow who was Mr. Mizoguchi's partner at the time was even shot at with a pistol at the door to his own house. It was only sheer luck he wasn't hurt." Plenty of debtors were roughed up, too. But it was hard for them to go public. Most just cried themselves to sleep.

"Say somebody threatens you, you dial 110 for help, right? Well, okay, a policeman comes around. But just mention debts and suddenly he doesn't want to know. The gangsters aren't dumb, either. They don't do anything that can be used as evidence against them. They're just trying to collect what's owed them—or so they make it seem. Which leaves the police with nothing much to do."

Honma was very familiar with police reluctance to get involved. " 'Non-intervention in private affairs,' isn't that the phrase?"

Ms. Sawagi laughed. "Exactly. Though Lord knows, intervention is just what some people need. I remember one person who came in shouting, 'How about if I just go ahead and get myself killed, then maybe you'll get them to look into it?' "

"The only improvement I've noticed is that nowadays the overwhelming majority of people who get into debt and file for personal bankruptcy are in their teens and twenties. At that age, people can start all over again if they have to. And at least their insolvency doesn't break up families. What you saw during the 'consumer finance scare' was husbands who would get millions of yen behind, and let the wife and kids absorb a lot of the shock waves."

"But what caused it? And why then, in the early eighties? What was different then?" Honma asked.

She thought for a minute, then said: "It seems to me housing loans were at the root of it; the desire for a house of your own, regardless of whether interest rates were reasonable or not. People would be unable to make the payments, and pretty soon they'd have to borrow from the loan sharks—that whole pattern."

"Which bankrupted entire families."

"Exactly. We used to see more cases out in the suburbs than in the cities themselves. But today the problem's centered on young people, right? And all the cities are feeling it, not just Tokyo. This time I'd say it's the fault of our throwaway lifestyle. Our consumerism has run away with us. And nobody's being taught any more how to manage their money."

It was ironic to think that the recent decline in housing loan bankruptcies was the direct result of skyrocketing land prices.

"Real estate has just gotten so expensive now," she said, "that no matter how hard you try, you'll never be able to own your home. It's just impossible. So most ordinary would-be homeowners make do without because they can see that the loans would bury them.

"Nowadays the overwhelming majority of bankruptcies involving real estate start with people borrowing a lot of money to buy investment properties. They think they're going to turn a profit on a studio condo and they borrow massively to buy it. Only the bottom falls out of the condo market. Sell at that point and you're not even making back what you paid. So it's the less experienced, younger buyers especially. Not teenagers, granted, but people in their twenties and thirties. Then there's also the opposite end of the scale, your pensioners and older people drawing retirement pay. Lots of windfall stock market players, too."

She gave it a little more thought. "It seems to me that what was behind the panic of the early eighties was the gotta-have syndrome: gotta have a bigger house, gotta have more fancy things, gotta have a better lifestyle—it was mostly pure greed, but some of it too was peer pressure, keeping up with the Tanakas. That's what kept this incredible boom in consumer financing going. But today I'd call it something more like 'hype bankruptcy.'"

"Hype bankruptcy?"

"Uh-huh. 'Here's how you make big money—it's stocks'; or 'it's condos'; or 'it's country club membership shares.' With younger people, it's where to live, what part of town's cool to live in, how to set up a beautiful apartment. Designer clothes, a sports car … it's all hype, right? Everyone's chasing mirages. Enter consumer financing, still as loosely regulated as ever, each lender only concerned with the bottom line … Want to hear something really stupid? Nowadays, banks have formed separate companies to provide unsecured financing, just like the loan sharks, right? Well, the thing is, as long as it's a bank running the business, it's not considered an infraction of the Regulation of Moneylending Business Law."

The whole time she was speaking, the background was buzzing: people talking, phones ringing. It reminded Honma of a train full of people struggling to shift a lever and move onto the other track, the one not headed straight down the side of a cliff.

"Last time you came in, Mr. Honma, remember, we talked about Emperor Ichijo's consort? Well, that got me going, so recently I started rereading *The Tale of Genji*. I'm enjoying it immensely," she said, ending the conversation on an upbeat note, though how she could work like she did and still find time to read one of the longest sagas in world literature was a mystery to him.

Honma hadn't been able to get Shoko out of his mind since the beginning of that day. At breakfast, he'd had the morning paper open but hadn't actually read a word, just managed to dip a corner of the front page in his coffee cup. Snap out of it, he'd told himself, giving his forehead a whack.

"Got a headache?" Makoto had asked. He obviously remembered that his mother had been prone to migraines. Chizuko used to tap her temples sometimes. There were other things like that. Lots of Chizuko's little quirks were still alive in Makoto. In extremely cold weather, at about this time of year, she'd change into her nightgown by stripping off everything, from her sweater and blouse to her underwear, all in one go. Next morning she'd slip the lot back over her head as is. A brilliant, if lazy performance.

*But it's cold*, she'd say with a laugh, not seeing anything wrong with it. *You should give it a try yourself. It's nice and warm.*

Try as he might, though, Honma could never get the hang of it. One layer, a shirt or a T-shirt sleeve, would invariably go wrong. Even if he did manage to pull everything over his head, it wouldn't feel right. He'd only have to take it all off and put it on again.

*You're just too set in your ways*, was Chizuko's verdict.

The odd thing was, last autumn he'd caught Makoto doing it too. Odd because when his mother was still around, she had always taken his clothes off for him carefully, layer by layer. Yet now, all these years after her death, he was suddenly doing it her way, without ever having known about it. When Honma pointed it out, Makoto's eyes had gone wide with surprise. *My mother?*

And so the dead leave their traces in the living, much as shed clothes retain someone's body heat.

The same was no doubt true of Shoko Sekine, Honma thought as he rode along the same New Tohoku Line she'd used, on his way to Utsunomiya, just as the woman who stole her name had done. And for the same reason—to find out more about Shoko. A bullet train to her home ground, moving past the same roads and rooftops.

When Shoko's mother fell down those steps, the person who found her and called the ambulance was a young woman, Maki had said.

Mustn't get ahead of myself, Honma thought. But he couldn't help wondering: had the fake Shoko taken this same train here to kill the real one's mother?

# ✧ 15 ✧

Everything was new in Utsunomiya. Even the train station.

There were exits east and west. Honma wandered back and forth along the corridor connecting them, trying to decide which looked more promising, and peering, as he went, into the shops on either side. He could easily have been in Shinjuku or Ginza. The selection, colors and styles of the clothes on the racks seemed, at least to his untrained eye, as cosmopolitan as any in the major Tokyo department stores. Utsunomiya had already become a bedroom community for bullet train commuters—one more satellite town drawn into the greater metropolitan gravitational field.

Ten years ago, when Shoko Sekine was eighteen, none of this would have existed. Was that why she'd set her sights on Tokyo? If she'd gone there to go to school, he would have understood. But nine years ago she had simply gone to work for a company in Edogawa, which by Tokyo standards was out in the sticks.

The station was clean and lively, and busier than he might have expected. The only difference from Tokyo was that he didn't see any foreigners. Most foreign workers—women, especially—stayed in Tokyo or Osaka, or else headed all the way out to the hot springs or the other resort areas. Utsunomiya was too close and, at the same time, too far.

Honma took the larger of the two exits. The first thing he saw as he went through the turnstile was a large pedestrian bridge: a solid passageway built over an open plaza, an architectural feature common to many stations along the New Tohoku and New Joetsu Lines. He looked down over the concrete handrail at the bus terminal below.

The destination signs were so confusing he couldn't tell which bus went to Ichozakacho. He decided to take a taxi.

When Honma gave the address, the driver cocked his head to one side. "Might be a while getting there. Weekends, you know how it is. Slow because of the races."

They turned right on the main street in front of the station and drove for five minutes, then left onto another large street, which meant they were heading west. Honma glanced at the pocket street map he'd picked up at the station kiosk. Up ahead should be Utsunomiya's central area, the prefectural government offices and police headquarters.

He hadn't completely decided against giving the local police a visit. If Shoko's mother's death was an accident, it should be on record. No doubt his old friend Funaki would have introduced him, if Honma had asked—it would have been quicker and easier—but he wanted to take a fresh look at things. It had been two years and two months since Shoko's mother died. During that time, no suspicions had arisen about the circumstances of her death. Her daughter had collected the insurance money in full. The police had closed the files. What was the hurry? He'd check things out for himself, get the story from people in the neighborhood. If there were any need for the police, he'd do that last.

It was a full twenty minutes before the driver pulled to a stop and said, "It's around here someplace." A lamppost at the entrance to a narrow one-way street had "Ichozakacho 2010" on it.

"Number 2005's at the end of the street," said the driver. The automatic door pulled slowly shut and the taxi sped off. Honma was totally disoriented. From the moment he'd left the station, he had been struck by how flat Utsunomiya was. No big surprise—the city was at the heart of the Kanto plain which spread all the way down to Tokyo Bay. Yet the name Ichozaka—"Gingko Hill"—had led him to expect some kind of elevation. Where in this flat town would there be any steps high enough for a person to fall to their death?

Ichozakacho was a quiet residential area. In that way it was a lot like his own neighborhood. But here there were hardly any apartment complexes. Most houses were old, sprawling, single-family dwellings. Real homes rooted in this soil.

A young couple came strolling past, hand in hand. The girl's eyes went to Honma's leg, then looked away. The boy kept up his banter, oblivious. A beauty parlor had a sign hung out reading L'Oréal Salon. Across from it was a small school that taught kids how to use an abacus. Next door, a long three-story building with a repair shop on the ground floor and a riot of laundry spilling from the windows. Set back one car's length from the street was a two-story stucco apartment house. Over the metal sliding door at the entrance hung an old-fashioned plaque with hand-drawn lettering: Akane Villa.

Number 2005.

Honma shoved his hands into his coat pockets and got ready to make a move. Just then the door slid open and a couple of grade-school kids came out. A girl and a boy; the girl a few years older. She had some trouble shutting the door again, although it didn't look so heavy. Perhaps it was sticking in its tracks. When it finally closed she took the boy by the hand and started leading him along the road. There was nobody else around.

"Hello," Honma said.

The children stopped and Honma noticed their matching, cartoon-patterned sneakers. The girl had a large pendant hanging around her neck. She said hello and waited.

Honma bent over, hands on his knees, and smiled. "You kids from this apartment house?" The girl nodded. The little boy just looked up at his sister questioningly.

"Yeah? Well, you know what? I know somebody who used to live here. And I'm looking for them. I came all the way from Tokyo to look for them. Maybe I'd better ask the landlord. Do you know where the landlord is?"

The girl was decisive. "Don't know."

"Maybe he lives in the neighborhood somewhere?"

"Don't know. Never met any landlord."

"Oh …" Okay. Just to keep her talking, Honma asked her about the pendant she kept running along its string with her free hand. "That's nice. What is it?"

"It's a rape whistle."

Oh.

"It's dangerous around here," the girl said matter-of-factly. "But this whistle, it's really loud. That's why Mommy bought it for me. Want to hear it?"

Not unless he wanted to talk to the police sooner rather than later. "No thanks. But is your mother home?"

"Nope." She shifted her weight from one leg to the other and her little brother followed suit, like a sidecar coupled to a motorcycle. "She's right over there." The girl pointed behind Honma.

Honma turned quickly, half expecting to see a woman glaring at him. But there was no one, just the L'Oréal Salon sign.

"Mommy's got her own rape whistle," the girl added.

It was almost thirty minutes from the time Honma pushed through the squeaking door and rang the little bell announcing the arrival of a customer before hairstylist Kanae Miyata emerged from inside. For somebody in the service sector and a young mother as well, she could have been more attentive.

Honma got straight to the point: there were a few things he'd like to ask about Shoko Sekine, his nephew's fiancée. He presented his name card.

"If she's gotten herself in some kind of trouble, count me out."

"No, no, it's nothing like that. It's just that she disappeared without leaving any word. He only wants to make sure she's all right." He hoped he sounded serious enough.

She nodded. "A real shame about how old Mrs. Sekine passed on." It seemed Mrs. Miyata had known "old Mrs. Sekine" better than the daughter, whom she knew only just well enough to offer her condolences to at the funeral.

Mrs. Miyata had no trouble filling him in on the details of the mother's death. Yoshiko Sekine fell down the staircase of an old building a few miles away, near Hachiman Park. "It's a three-story building, with a bank that takes up the first and second floors. Mrs. Sekine was a regular at a bar on the third floor called Tagawa. She used to stop in there once a week or so for a drink. On the outside of the building, see, there's this concrete emergency staircase. But not one of those things—you know—that zigzags like a fire escape; this one goes straight down from the third floor. It's really steep, too. With a little landing on the second floor."

Yoshiko Sekine was found at the bottom.

"She probably fell the whole three floors. Didn't stand a chance. Broke her neck, they say. Everybody knows it's an old building and all, but still it's got to be against the Building Code. The newspaper even wrote an article about it—not a long one, though."

The tiny beauty parlor didn't do a lot of business. There was one other beautician, plus the owner, who was out shopping at the time. There was only one customer, an elderly woman sitting in a crimson leatherette chair, dozing off while Mrs. Miyata finished putting curlers in her hair.

Honma found the bench he was sitting on uncomfortable and moved to one of the plush recliners that had an attached hair drier you could pull down over your head. He didn't ask if it was okay, nor did Mrs. Miyata complain. She seemed tired, probably from having to cope with her two kids.

"It must have caused quite a stir."

"Oh sure. But those stairs—it isn't like anybody was actually surprised. People had been saying they're dangerous for the longest time, and just look what happens."

"Did the police look into it?"

"I think so. But they could see it was an accident, so there wasn't all that much for them to do."

Get somebody drunk and unsteady on her feet, then push her down the stairs. Do it right and nobody would have any reason to suspect a thing.

"Anybody see what happened?"

She tilted her head quizzically. "I wouldn't know."

Honma decided to take a different tack. "Were you and your family close to Mrs. Sekine?"

"Sort of," she said, explaining that she lived with her husband and the two kids in Akane Villa 201, and Mrs. Sekine had been directly

148

below them, in 101. "And she must have been in there, what, close to ten years."

"But the rent must have gone up every time she renewed the contract. Surprising she didn't move."

"Oh, it's obvious you're from Tokyo. I hear it's highway robbery, what they charge there. It's not like that around here. If you're talking about a big modern high-rise near the station, well, sure, that's expensive. But something simple like the Akane, rents never get up that high, I assure you."

"Is it common for people to stay in one place for ten years?" Rent a place long enough and you lose all inclination to move, presumably.

"Moving can be a real pain. You have to do everything yourself … in our case, my husband didn't lift a finger." Her expression darkened and her lids narrowed. Her fingertips kept up their precise movements, even though she barely glanced at the curlers she was setting.

"And you all moved to Akane Villa in—?"

"Let's see … this is our fifth year."

"Did you get to know Mrs. Sekine right away?"

She nodded. "Because of our kids. They're always jumping down off the chairs or making some sort of racket. So I went around straight off and introduced myself. Figured that was better than waiting for them to come and complain."

"And was Shoko still in and out of the house at that time?"

"The daughter?… I must have met her twice. I guess she came home for the summer break and for New Year's." Kanae Miyata clicked the last curler in, gave the old woman a quick once-over in the mirror, then went to get a dry towel.

"Was she pretty?"

"Sure, she's a good-looking girl."

Honma still hadn't seen the real Shoko Sekine's face. It was a shot in the dark. "Though maybe a little flashy?

Mrs. Miyata was busy wrapping the customer's head in a towel. Her only response was a slight twitch of one eye.

"Seems she was working in a bar," Honma added.

The hairdresser secured the towel with a large rubber band. "I don't know whether I should say this, but the girl was having all kinds of trouble with loan sharks. Or didn't you know?"

"Yes, I did."

She looked disappointed. She had obviously been hoping to surprise him. "It was just awful the way those bill collectors came around to Mrs. Sekine's. She even had to call the police at one point."

"When was this?"

Mrs. Miyata paused, a bottle of perm-setting lotion in her hand. "Well, let's see. It must have been the eighties, anyway."

No question about that.

"Incidentally, speaking of debts, I heard that the parents don't have to pay a cent if one of their children runs up a pile of bills." Her eyes were beady.

What was so strange about that? "That's right. And vice-versa too. So long as there's no joint guarantor. Unless they're debts both parties shared, the same goes for husband and wife."

"So, say my husband ran up some debts at the races, I wouldn't have to pay?"

"Of course not."

She squeezed some lotion on, and the dozing customer's eyes flipped open; it must have been cold. "What's this? Don't tell me your husband's still hanging around at the track?" the old lady snapped.

Mrs. Miyata laughed. "Says he'll build me a house."

The customer turned to look at Honma, but addressed Mrs. Miyata. "That him?"

"No, no. He's a visitor come up from Tokyo."

"My, my. There I go, jumping to conclusions. So what brings this nice-looking man all the way here from Tokyo?" Again, not a word to Honma himself. Mrs. Miyata, meanwhile, had pushed the woman slightly forward and was squeezing her head into a rubber cap.

"He says he came to see me—let me know if it gets too hot, okay?" she warned, lowering the apparatus over the woman's head. She flicked a switch and the drier began to rumble and glow infrared. Then, setting a timer on a machine nearby, she came over to where Honma was sitting, and sprawled out on the waiting area bench. She pulled a pack of Caster Mild cigarettes from her apron pocket and lit

150

up. The long, slow drag said it all—this was the longed-for break from work. "If what you want is a character reference on the daughter," she said, lowering her voice, "you'd be better off going to the school than asking a neighbor like me."

"The school?"

"Yes. Old Mrs. Sekine used to work in the cafeteria of the elementary school. The same school the daughter used to go to."

"Can't say I see much point tracing her back that far."

"You never know. Don't you think the old lady might have sounded off to her co-workers?" A malicious gleam returned to her eyes. With a girl like that, making her mother ashamed of her by working in a shady job and getting deep in debt to loan sharks, there must have been signs of going bad even back in elementary school.

"And one more thing," she went on. "I bet there are still lots of Shoko's classmates from junior high and high school around here. What about getting in touch with them?"

"Would you know of any close friends she had?"

"Hm …" Kanae Miyata tipped her head to one side. "Some of her friends from when she was little must live right around here. Who knows, maybe they even come in for perms." Then, leaning close in to the woman under the drier, she said loudly, "You remember old Mrs. Sekine who lived right under us?"

"The one who fell down the stairs?" the woman shouted back, her head held in place.

"Yeah, right. And she had a daughter. Twenty-five, maybe twenty-six?"

"She's twenty-eight this year," Honma corrected.

Mrs. Miyata was surprised. "No! Already? Twenty-eight, he says. Know anybody around that age who might have been in her class at school?"

The old lady yawned. Her eyes watered. Probably nice and warm under that thing. This is going nowhere, Honma thought.

"At the funeral. That Honda boy—was his first name Tamotsu?— he came, didn't he?" the customer said.

"Tamotsu?"

"Sure. Remember? You set his wife's hair for the ceremony."

Mrs. Miyata laughed. "I did?"

Tamotsu Honda. Honma took down the name and the address of his family's auto repair shop and got up to leave. "One more thing."

"What's that?"

He brought out the photo of the fake Shoko. "Ever see this woman before? Perhaps she came in here at some point with Shoko."

She took the photo, then passed it over to the woman under the drier.

"No, don't recognize her," Mrs. Miyata said.

"What's this girl got to do with it?" the other woman asked.

"Oh, nothing really."

Mrs. Miyata took another look at the photo. "I wonder if I could borrow this for a while," she asked. "I'd like to show it around to a few people. I'll be sure to return it. If I find out anything, I'll give you a call."

Good thing Honma had had the foresight to have extra copies made. "Yes, of course. Please do." He grabbed his coat and turned to go.

She stopped him. "So what kind of fellow is she marrying, this Sekine girl?"

"My own good-for-nothing nephew."

"No, I mean, what sort of work is he in?"

Honma hesitated. "He works in a bank."

Kanae Miyata and her customer looked at one another in the mirror and nodded. Then Mrs. Miyata came out with some unsolicited advice. "I expect it'd be just as well if he called the whole thing off."

As the mother of small children and the wife of a gambler, she was used to carrying a lot of responsibility. It was only natural that she'd cast a cold eye on the likes of Shoko Sekine—someone who had left home for the big city, only to slip into the dark underworld of Tokyo's clubland.

"I'll be sure to tell him to think it over," said Honma. Mrs. Miyata smiled, satisfied.

This time the door to the L'Oréal Salon hardly made a sound. Honma gave a sigh of relief as he emerged.

"Tamotsu, you've got a customer!" a middle-aged mechanic in

greasy overalls shouted into the garage. A young man stood up way in the back and came forward. He was short and solidly built, with a thick neck and strong jaw that gave him an obstinate look. He wore his hair in a crewcut. As he got closer, Honma could see he was sweating at the temples.

A ten-minute walk from the L'Oréal Salon, the repair shop was on a main thoroughfare leading from the station. A quick look around showed about twenty cars and a few motorcycles. There was even a small truck parked over to one side. Five mechanics—that he could see—were working here and there. A boy of high school age huddled over a 50cc bike. Everybody wore white overalls with Honda Motors embroidered on the breast pocket.

"Tamotsu Honda, is it?"

He nodded his head quickly, without looking away.

"Sorry for dropping in like this."

As Honma explained the reasons for his visit, Tamotsu's eyes widened. "Shoko's okay, right? Whereabouts in Tokyo is she?"

"You mean …?"

"I lost track of her after she left that place in Kawaguchi. I've been worried about her."

"You visited her at the Kawaguchi apartment?"

"Sure, I tried. But they said she wasn't there any more."

"Did you see the landlady?"

"Yeah, and was she pissed off. Said Shoko had left without a word, that same week."

"So you must have gone there at the end of March, the year before last, is that right?"

Tamotsu wiped his hands on his overalls and thought. "Yeah, I guess."

"Were you and her close?"

"Well, sure, but …" Tamotsu's eyes narrowed in a look of growing distrust. "Hey, I don't like this. You want to poke around in Shoko's private life, go ahead, but don't ask me for help." He squared his shoulders. "I don't like gossiping about my friends."

"Listen, it's not like that. I don't mean her any harm." This was the first breakthrough Honma had had. No way was he going to let Tamo-

153

tsu go. "Why don't you let me explain. Could you spare me a little time? I could come back later, if you want. Shoko is missing, actually, and I'm looking for her."

Honma spent the next thirty minutes waiting in the reception room there. A phone kept ringing and somebody in an unseen office kept answering the calls. Other than that, all was quiet. They trained their employees well.

Tamotsu Honda brought in two paper cups of coffee on a tray. There was more light here than in the garage and Honma could see a diagonal scar running the length of his jaw. Had he been in an accident? His left eye strayed slightly too. But on the whole, he was a nice-looking guy—handsome, even.

As Honma had said, things were complicated. Tamotsu had to stop him and ask questions from time to time. Otherwise, he kept his comments to himself and listened. The next time the phone rang, he reached over and switched off the bell.

"Right now," Honma said, "I can't show you any proof that I'm with the police. I'm on leave and I've turned in my ID for the time being. I can only ask you to believe me."

Tamotsu looked down at the coffee table. "That's okay," he said after a moment. "All I have to do is ask Sakai. He'll check for me."

"Sakai?"

"He's a detective with the Utsunomiya Police. When Shoko's old lady died, he was real helpful and I got to know him."

"Could I meet him?"

"I'll ask. I'm sure it'd be okay. But if things have gone this far, shouldn't you be doing a regular investigation? The sooner you find Shoko and catch this woman who's been passing herself off as her ..."

Honma spread his hands. "Supposing we searched and found that both of them were perfectly okay, except they'd made a friendly agreement to sell or trade their family registers? That's probably about the best we can hope for, but as long as the possibility exists, it makes it harder to call in the police."

Tamotsu licked his lips. He didn't want to say it. "And what if ... what if Shoko's been murdered? Do they need a body to go on?"

"It would make it easier, to build a case."

Tamotsu sighed.

Honma looked at the young man's sweaty forehead. Finally, a real friend of Shoko Sekine's.

"You know …," Tamotsu said in a sudden rush, "when her old lady died and I went to Kawaguchi and found she'd moved out, I couldn't help thinking the worst." He looked at Honma with haunted eyes. "I actually figured Shoko might have killed her and run off."

This sent the ball flying into another court. "You mean … because you knew she was in trouble with loan sharks?"

He nodded, reluctantly. "Especially after what Ikumi said. That when Shoko's old lady fell down the stairs, there was this strange woman in the crowd who'd come just to watch. Wearing dark glasses so you couldn't see her face. Ikumi thought it might have been Shoko herself."

Honma leaned forward. "Ikumi?"

"My wife."

"Was she a friend of Shoko's as well?"

He shook his head. "No. See, Ikumi, she's the one who found Mrs. Sekine and called the ambulance. She just happened to be passing by at the time. She wound up going to the funeral. That was the first time we met, at Shoko's mother's funeral."

✧ 16 ✧

Tamotsu couldn't go anywhere till he had closed the shop, so Honma arranged to meet him after nine that night. Tamotsu knew a nice little drinking place near the station, and promised to phone ahead to reserve a private room. "That'll be warmer," he said.

At ten past nine Honma understood what he'd meant. When Tamotsu ducked through the entranceway, he had a young woman with him. She wore a turtleneck sweater over a loose woolen skirt, but even that didn't hide her figure. She must have been at least six months pregnant.

"This is my wife, Ikumi." After introducing her, he set out two thin cushions next to the heater so that she could lean back against the wall.

"Pleased to meet you," said Ikumi as she slowly lowered herself down. She seemed cautious, yet self-assured.

"Is this your first child?" asked Honma.

She beamed at him, the corners of her eyes crinkling. "It's the second. Though you'd never know it to look at Tamotsu, the way he fusses over me."

"Yeah, but Taro came a bit earlier than we thought," he countered.

"And how old is Taro?"

"He's just past his first birthday. Things have been pretty busy with us."

A waiter arrived. The place was warm enough to make him sweat as he dashed about. "Sorry about all the cigarette smoke," he said before he went out, sliding the door shut behind him.

"Is this your first time in Utsunomiya, Mr. Honma?" asked Tamotsu.

"Yup. With a job and everything, I never had the chance."

"And it's not so far that you'd make a trip of it. Not from Tokyo," Ikumi suggested.

"I was surprised what a big city it is."

"Thanks to the bullet train."

Tamotsu, it turned out, had gone to work for his father straight out of high school. He had known Shoko Sekine for years, from kindergarten all the way through middle school. In high school the classmates had split up, with Tamotsu opting for vocational school, but they had still lived in the same neighborhood and attended the same cram school in the afternoons. "Of all the girls, she was always my closest friend," he said, glancing quickly at his wife.

Ikumi was born and raised in Utsunomiya too, but she and Tamotsu hadn't been classmates. She had graduated from a Tokyo junior college and then stayed, putting in five years as a secretary in the Marunouchi business district. Her return to Utsunomiya came when her older brother, who had always lived at home, was transferred elsewhere, leaving their parents alone. "I was getting tired of living by myself anyway, and everything in Tokyo was so expensive."

"Not to mention that when women hit twenty-five and still aren't married, companies can get pretty hard on them," Tamotsu said lightly.

Apparently this was a touchy subject. "You can laugh, but it's true," she declared. "I hated it."

If she were still a single woman working in Tokyo, she would never have spoken so frankly; she'd just have teased Tamotsu right back, or remarked how "lonely" it gets, taking care all the while not to look the least bit lonely.

"Even though it was in Marunouchi, it wasn't a big company. The salary and bonuses were only so-so. All the overtime went straight to taxes. We didn't get any fancy company trips, and you practically had to bang your head against the wall to get a raise. It didn't take me long to see why everybody is so keen to make it into the major companies. And then to top it all off, people were just basically unfriendly. I didn't like it one bit."

Common complaints, Honma knew. To show his sympathy, he said: "Salary aside, the big companies are no better than smaller ones when it comes to the way they treat women who've been there a few years. Not unless you're very lucky."

Still, being made to feel redundant at twenty-five was terrible.

"Women cops or teachers or anyone with special skills and training, that's probably a different story," she went on. "But for ordinary office work, they want people as young as they can get them. Twenty-five's about the limit. Sure, you hear on the news all the time, 'Times have changed. Nowadays women are still young at thirty'—but it's a lie. Even a girl of twenty-one, as soon as a junior staffer of twenty signs on, she feels like she's getting old."

"How about the work itself, was it interesting?"

Ikumi thought it over, sipping at her oolong tea. "It was okay. When I think back on it now." From the perspective of someone with a husband and a child and a home.

"Want to hear a funny story?" she asked. "About six months ago, a girl who was in my section back in Marunouchi—even though we were never very close, she suddenly calls me up. At my folks' place. I only happened to be there because I'd brought Taro over to spend the night with his grandparents."

Tamotsu was hanging on every word, as if he hadn't heard any of this before.

"So as soon as I get on the line, this super cheerful voice is asking, 'How's everything?' And I'm thinking, 'What's the deal?' But I just say, 'Oh, fine.' So we catch up on the company gossip since I quit. She did practically all the talking, actually. How she'd been to Hong Kong, how this year's company trip was to a hot spring resort. Then finally she started winding down and got around to asking what I'd been up to lately. And I say, 'Raising a kid is about all I've been able to manage.'"

"And?"

Ikumi gave a wry smile. "She was speechless. All she could say was, 'You got married?' And I said, 'Well, sure. I didn't want to be a single mother.' Well, she didn't have anything else to say. The conversation just petered out, and finally she hung up."

A brief silence settled over the table. Ikumi ran a finger around a bottle of local saké that was sitting beside her. "I guess maybe she was looking for someone worse off than her."

"Worse off?"

"Yeah. I bet she was depressed. Feeling left out and at the bottom of the heap. So she thought I'd left the company, not to get married or study abroad or anything, but only to go crawling back to the sticks. I *had* to be more miserable than her. At least she was still living in the big city. So she called."

Tamotsu looked like he'd bitten into something and couldn't figure out what it was. "I don't get it."

"Of course, *you* don't. *You* wouldn't."

"Maybe it's more of a woman thing," Honma said.

Ikumi shook her head. "Hm, I wonder. Men, they've got promotion and raises and what not. But Tamotsu here, he doesn't get all that."

Tamotsu glared. "What about it?"

Ikumi smiled and put a hand affectionately on his arm. "Don't get mad. I'm not saying you're stupid or anything."

"Like hell you're not!"

"I'm not. You've got something that probably a lot of them will never have."

Honma asked her to explain.

"I mean, he's always liked cars, since he was little. Liked them so much that he chose auto repair training at school. Then his dad's got a workshop where he's already proven himself as the top mechanic."

"Wasn't always so good at it," Tamotsu said in a show of modesty.

"That's right. You worked hard at it. But working hard to get so good at it means you've got talent. A deadbeat might like fixing cars, too, but he's still no good. But Tamo's been at it since he was a boy and really learned. Now that's what I call happy." Ikumi wasn't the most eloquent speaker, but there was truth in what she said.

"Yeah, but it's not like I was satisfied. I wanted to be a technician at a bigger place."

"Like working for Mazda and racing at Le Mans?" Ikumi said with a smile.

"Damn right. But Dad's workshop was here. So I gave up that idea."

Ikumi kept quiet and just smiled. Tamotsu still had his illusions, fundamental ones. But Ikumi was smart enough not to poke holes in them. Honma admired her for that. She was thoroughly ordinary, nothing special to look at, probably hadn't gotten particularly high grades in school, but she was one smart woman. She kept her eyes open.

Honma saw the opportunity, and took it. "Why do you think Shoko Sekine went to Tokyo?"

The young couple's eyes met briefly. Then Ikumi looked down and picked up her chopsticks, as if to say that it was Tamotsu's business, not hers.

"Let's eat before the food gets cold," she suggested. "I'm starving."

"But I thought you already had supper."

"I'm eating for two, remember? That was for the baby," she said demurely.

Honma looked over at Tamotsu. "You wouldn't have any idea what was going on with her around the time she graduated from high school and started looking for a job, would you?"

Tamotsu bit his lower lip, then said gruffly: "What's that got to do with anything? That's ancient history. And personal, too."

"Well, I'll I tell you. I'd like to get to know Shoko as a person, how she decided things. If I know that, it might give me an angle on what happened to her later."

"And that'll help you find the woman who's passing herself off as her?" Tamotsu gave Ikumi a look out of the corner of his eye. "I told my wife everything you told me before. She's a lot smarter than me." He reached for her handbag. "Brought this. It's from high school, something my dad took." Out came a photograph. At long last, Honma's first glimpse of the real Shoko Sekine.

Dressed in her sailor-suit schoolgirl uniform, holding a black cardboard tube under one arm, she was looking straight into the camera. She was the picture of earnest youth. Long, slender eyes, tiny pinch of a nose. Hair hanging down below her shoulders, matchstick knees jutting out below a pleated navy skirt. A slip of a girl with average looks—the kind of face that cried out for a little makeup. It was an old photo, but still it was clear she wasn't nearly as good-looking as her impostor was.

160

"I saw her two or three times after she left for Tokyo, when she came back to visit. Then there was the funeral. Her hair was about the same length as always, but she'd had it permed and dyed red. Said she hadn't had time to get it back to normal. She talked louder, looked louder. It was like the real Shoko was locked up somewhere inside her."

Honma said, "You know that at one point Shoko was in trouble with loan sharks, right?"

They both nodded. Ikumi told him: "I heard about it after Tamotsu and I started going out."

"I knew about it all along. My mom used to go to the same hairdresser as Shoko's mom, and she heard the whole story there. I guess things got so bad her mother even had to call the police. So I told her just to call me next time one of those goons came around."

"You told Mrs. Sekine that?"

"Yeah. I knew her real well."

"Did Shoko always come home during her summer vacations and at New Year's, after she'd gone to work in Tokyo?"

Tamotsu paused to think. "Hm. Seems like she didn't one year, but the rest of the time ..."

"Did you ever have a class reunion?"

"Why, sure. Our junior high class did. But she didn't come."

"No?"

"People were talking about her, though. That's how I heard she was hostessing in Tokyo." Tamotsu wet his lips. "Another guy from our class who was working in Tokyo, he went to some cheap joint in Shibuya and Shoko was there in fishnet stockings."

"Shibuya? She never worked in Shibuya."

"Where was she working?"

"At a place called Gold in Shinjuku and another called Lahaina in Shimbashi. I still haven't been to Gold yet, but Lahaina wasn't such a bad place. And the girls weren't in fishnet stockings."

"Maybe the guy said it to get a reaction," said Ikumi.

"Your friends, the people from school, did they all know Shoko was having money problems?"

"Sure, they knew. Rumors like that get around."

"Then, what about the way she cleared up her debts?"

Tamotsu shook his head. "No, not the real story. Not about that ... What'd you call it again?"

"Personal bankruptcy."

"That's right. Even I didn't know till you told me. Her old lady said Shoko had gone around borrowing from relatives to get back on her feet. All this time, that's what I thought."

Interesting, thought Honma. Apparently, Shoko hadn't even told her mother how bad things had gotten.

"So around here, that's what everyone thinks?"

Tamotsu nodded. "Yeah. Except that it was odd she had all these relatives to lend her money, because nobody knew them. At least not up here."

"Knowing all that," Honma ventured, "did anybody ever think there was anything suspicious about Mrs. Sekine's death? Ever wonder about Shoko?"

Tamotsu looked straight at Ikumi, as if for support. "Yes, I did."

"That Shoko might have been tempted by her mother's insurance money?"

Tamotsu nodded again, and Ikumi spoke up. "Yes. After all, word was that it came to around twenty million yen."

Honma smiled knowingly. "Well, actually, it was only two million."

"Really?"

"Right. All she had was National Health."

"How'd it get so blown out of scale?"

"Rumors."

Ikumi asked Tamotsu, "Where exactly did you hear it was twenty million?"

He hung his head. "I don't know." There was a pause.

Honma said, "At the funeral, did you ask Shoko if she'd got her debts sorted out?"

"Come on, I couldn't ask her that."

"Yeah, I guess not."

"In any case, Shoko seemed so shocked by what'd happened that money was the last thing a person ..."

"But it did occur to you?"

He looked ashamed. "Yeah."

"Your detective friend—Sakai, wasn't it?—did he ask her? Did she have an alibi?"

"But there was a full investigation and they didn't come up with anything."

Okay, thought Honma, putting the matter on hold for the time being. He knew just how "full" police investigations could be. "After the funeral, when you went to see her in Kawaguchi, was that because of your suspicions?"

"That's right. That's why I went all the way down there."

"And when you got there, she was already missing. So you figured she'd run away."

"Right."

Honma brought out his photo of the fake Shoko and showed it to Ikumi. "Ever see this woman before?"

Ikumi grabbed the photograph.

"When Mrs. Sekine fell down those stairs, I understand you happened to be going by and called the ambulance. And one of the people there watching was a woman you'd never seen before, who was wearing sunglasses. Right?"

Ikumi nodded, without taking her eyes off the picture.

"Did she look anything like the woman in that photo?"

Ikumi studied it at length. The other two kept quiet. Loud voices cut through the paper sliding doors, customers shouting out orders. Ikumi shook her head, though clearly she was still trying to remember. "She doesn't look familiar. But it was two years ago, and anyway I only saw the woman for a second."

"Can't you remember anything about what she looked like?" Tamotsu said, leaning forward.

"Not really. Nothing specific."

Honma felt they should back down. "Okay, don't force it." He didn't think Ikumi was easily influenced, anyway. "The night she fell down the stairs, you remember that fairly well, don't you?"

Ikumi drew her arms in tight across her chest. "Sure, I think so. I was on my way home from work. I was working part-time at a coffee shop in the station, and sometimes I got to take home the leftovers— a piece of cake or something. Well, that night, I was carrying some cake, but when I got home, what with all the commotion, it was all squashed. I must have swung the bag around when I screamed."

"Sorry to make you go over this again, but when she fell, did Mrs. Sekine cry out?"

Ikumi shook her head. "The policemen asked me that too, but I didn't hear anything. All of a sudden, this body just came tumbling down in front of me, out of nowhere."

Tamotsu broke in. "That's why the police, the first thing they said was 'probable suicide.' Even now it's a toss-up. Sakai—the detective I mentioned—he went with suicide. Said that unless you had a death wish, you wouldn't even think about going down those stairs drunk. There was an elevator, after all."

"Oh yes?"

"But according to the folks in that bar of hers, Tagawa, she never liked the elevator. Especially not after drinking. Said it made her feel sick. She always took the stairs."

"Uh-huh."

"Still, Sakai thought it was suicide. He said if it was an accident or someone had pushed her, she'd have screamed, for sure."

Not necessarily, thought Honma. Not if she was knocked out cold or somehow caught unawares ... "Sometimes, they say a victim will barely make a sound. Is it quiet around there?"

Tamotsu laughed. "Well, Tagawa has got karaoke, and the club next door's got a dance floor. I've gone dancing there before, and it's so loud you can't hear a word anybody says."

Ikumi agreed. "Right. I mean, when I screamed, the only people who came running out at first were from the other buildings and shops around there. Nobody from Tagawa even noticed until there was a pretty big crowd."

"And Mrs. Sekine was in Tagawa that night?"

"Seems she went there a lot."

"Regularly?"

"I guess. At least that's what Shoko told me. For years, from back when Shoko was still living at home. She said that was the only fun her mom had."

"She have any particular day?"

164

"Saturday nights. She worked in the school cafeteria, remember. Sunday she didn't need to get up early."

Every Saturday night. The only other thing you would need to know was where to wait. All you had to do then was wait for Mrs. Sekine to totter out of Tagawa and give her a whack from behind. It sounded simple enough; but still, the person planning to kill her would have had to keep tabs on her for quite a while beforehand. There had to be an easier way, surely. Maybe the woman had gone door to door, posing as a saleslady. Or perhaps she'd been tipped off about the Saturday routine and come up to Utsunomiya for that specific thing. But where would she have gotten information like that?

"Instead of sitting here talking, maybe we should go to Tagawa," said Tamotsu.

"I'll come too," Ikumi said.

"No, you'll catch cold."

"I'll be fine. I dressed warmly," she told him, thrusting her chin forward.

Some kind of hidden message passed between them, prompting Tamotsu to put his glass down and say: "Mr. Honma, I want to help you out."

"Help me?"

"Help you find Shoko. I'm offering to work full-time on this."

Honma looked at Ikumi. She pressed her lips together and gave a quick, firm nod.

"But what about your job?"

"I'll take time off. No problem. So it's decided, okay? Ikumi's agreed, too." He spoke quickly, then sprang to his feet. "Be right back."

His wife patted him on the back of the legs as he left the room. "He's a good guy," she said, sitting up and straightening her skirt.

"Mm," Honma agreed. "I'm sorry to drag you into this mess."

"It's all right. We'll get through it fine," she reassured him quickly. She refolded the handkerchief on her lap. "He told me you're a detective from Tokyo."

"Well, I'm on leave just now."

"I heard. Tamotsu's pretty organized, actually. This evening, right after you left the garage, he rang up his friend in the police and had him check whether there was a Shunsuke Honma on the force in Tokyo."

"Oh?"

"And now he's revved up and raring to go. He's excited about working on a case with a real detective. He really wants to do it."

"You're sure you don't mind? He'd have to take time off from work, maybe leave you on your own up here."

"Honest. Please take him on."

Honma paused for a couple of breaths. "I don't think I can."

Ikumi looked up abruptly. "Why not?"

"Because I can't believe *you* really want it, and I don't want to cause problems. I'll keep your husband informed, but I think he should stay at home."

"That won't work. It'd be better if he gave you a hand."

"You honestly don't mind?"

"Of course I mind! I mind like crazy," she burst out, her face looking tense. "But I'd hate even more to have him sitting at home thinking about Shoko."

"Hang on. I think you're letting your imagination run away with you."

"What makes you so sure?" she said curtly.

"Well, even if they *were* childhood sweethearts, you and his family are much more important to him now than this Shoko woman. That much I can tell."

"Yes. We're important. And he takes good care of us. But that's not the point." Her voice grew thinner, less energetic. "Mr. Honma, do you have any friends you've known since childhood?"

"Yes, but I'm not close to them any more."

"Well, then, you wouldn't understand."

"Were Tamotsu and Shoko close even after they grew up?"

"Tamotsu still cared about her, anyway. When she went off to Tokyo and got into a mess there, I could see that he wasn't just concerned—he loved her."

"But not the same love he feels for you."

"No, it's different. That's why it's all right. I can forgive him for getting so worked up about her. But it's not something I want to let drag on forever and ever." Ikumi looked down. A single tear slipped onto the back of her hand.

"You shouldn't get so upset, it's not good for the baby." Honma smiled and tried to catch her eye.

But Ikumi wasn't smiling. She hunched her shoulders. "He's always loved her and he's always thinking about her. They share memories from way back when they were kids. There's no way I can compete with that."

Honma thought of his friend Funaki and the heart-to-hearts he had with Chizuko's framed photo back at home. "If he loved her that much, why didn't he marry her?"

Ikumi gave just a trace of a smile. "Shoko didn't seem to take him as a serious prospect. They were too close for that."

*Too close*—that had been Funaki's line, too.

"Besides ..." Ikumi dabbed at her eyes with the back of her index finger, not trying to hide the tears any more. "He feels he let her down—by suspecting her of killing her mother. And he's felt guilty ever since."

"So he wants to make up for it?"

"That's right. Three hours, we argued about this. Believe me, he's made up his mind to help you. So I just hope you'll let him get it out of his system." Ikumi wanted none of this business, but wanted even less to have to compete with a memory.

She kept saying how determined Tamotsu was, but Honma was struck mainly by her own resolve. He sighed and said, "When all this is over, I hope you'll make him buy you something really expensive."

Ikumi smiled. "He's going to build us a house. We've already got the land. I want to live in one of those split-level homes."

"That's wonderful."

The door slid open and Tamotsu returned. He'd probably been waiting outside the door. His eyes were downcast.

"Shall we go?" Ikumi said, starting to get up. Half crouching, she turned to Honma. "Hey, if Tamotsu makes out okay, could he get an official testimonial or something from the police?"

Tamotsu was embarrassed. "Come on, lay off it."

"What's wrong with asking? I'd love to have a fancy certificate framed on the wall, wouldn't you? All we have now is that commendation you got in second-grade gym class."

For the first time in a long while, Honma felt warm inside. "I'll see what I can do."

## 17

They went by taxi to the foot of the staircase where Mrs. Sekine had died.

"With that leg, you'd never make it up there," Tamotsu said, stating the obvious.

One look said everything. Two long concrete flights of steps came sweeping down like a fairground slide. So steep, so poorly lit that each stair was deep in shadow. There was a handrail, but the angle was so treacherous and every step so shallow that, even sober, the slightest loss of balance would send you crashing straight down—nothing would stop you.

"Well, if I had to pick a staircase to use as a murder weapon," Ikumi said, and coughed, huddling down as far as she could inside her coat. "Even before it happened, every time I walked past these stairs I used to think it was like something from *The Exorcist*."

"Exorcist?"

Ikumi looked incredulous. "Don't you go to the movies?"

An elevator was tacked onto the side of the building. It was carpeted in cheap red acrylic, the walls covered with scratches and graffiti. The thing barely managed to creak and wheeze its way up to the third floor. If my leg were in better shape, Honma thought, it would be faster to walk.

There was just one customer in Tagawa, an older man who got up from the window booth where he was sitting as soon as he saw Tamotsu. It turned out to be Sakai, the detective from the local police station. Again, Tamotsu was one step ahead of Honma.

Honma had met cops who got self-conscious working with somebody from the metropolitan police. They'd either grovel or start talking big and dropping names. Fortunately, Sakai did neither. He was at the end of his career—"Just another two months to go till retirement"—and beyond impressing.

"I got the lowdown—the bare bones, anyway—from Honda here. Seems you got yourself a complicated case."

There are two kinds of detectives: those who absolutely never let down their guard in public, and those who carefully choose the right circumstances. Sakai was the last sort, and Tagawa was one of those places. A heated carafe of local saké stood before him.

"About Yoshiko Sekine's death, then," he said without any preamble. "Whether there was anything suspicious—that's the first order of business, I take it?"

"Yes. Can you definitely rule out foul play?"

Sakai gave a calm, reassuring smile. Honma imagined it must be a very effective weapon: never give a suspect cause for alarm, soften him up so he'd do what you wanted at the tap of a finger. "No one could have killed her. I guarantee it."

"But ..."

Tamotsu edged forward, his voice insistent. "Like I told you, more than once. Nobody could've pushed her down the stairs. It's impossible."

"Impossible?" said Honma. "Because no one heard a cry? Or is it something else?"

"What do you say we go out and look around? That'll be faster."

Leaving Ikumi inside—it was cold out there and "not very safe"—the three men went out onto the third-floor walkway: a bare concrete passage no more than a yard wide running along the back of the building, only partly covered by concrete eaves. If you stood with your back to Tagawa, the elevator was to your right, the staircase to your left. Tagawa was the middle of three small establishments; on the right was another bar, and, on the left, the place with the dance floor that Tamotsu had mentioned. There was no other door in sight. No storage room, no toilet, nothing.

"Get the picture?" Sakai said confidently as he wandered toward the staircase. "No place to run and hide. Suppose somebody did do it.

170

Afterward, they'd have only two choices. One, go down in the elevator. Two, duck into one of the bars—whichever—and make like nothing had happened."

"Either way, you'd need guts and some acting ability," acknowledged Honma, drawing another smile from Sakai.

"More than most people can come up with."

The three men stood at the top of the stairs, Sakai furthest forward, Tamotsu in the rear.

The second-story landing was less than a yard square. It was the only stop. Beyond that, a flurry of small concrete steps slipped straight down to the gray cement pavement at the bottom. It was enough to make your head reel.

"After Yoshiko Sekine fell, absolutely no one else went down these stairs. Your wife swears by that, right, Tamotsu? And there was no one at the top of the stairs, either," the detective said, looking back over his shoulder. "Of course, there is one other possibility. The person goes down to the second-floor landing and escapes through the bank. But you'd have to be awfully quick on your feet. Plus the whole place is locked up after hours, and it would be a heck of a job getting in, for anyone other than a bank employee."

Tamotsu scratched his neck and said nothing.

"What about the elevator?" Honma asked, trying not to grin.

"That pile of scrap metal?" Sakai was grinning too. "Let's get this straight. Mrs. Sekine goes down the stairs, Ikumi finds her and starts yelling, people come running. Meanwhile, the murderer goes down in the elevator and runs off before anyone notices? Any acrobats on our list of suspects? Because we're talking about a matter of seconds. Other people were around by then."

"Well, then, what about popping into one of bars and acting like a customer?" Tamotsu asked, keeping the questions going.

Sakai shook his head. "Like I said before, it doesn't work. We questioned the people in all the bars that day." He rapped on the door of the noisiest establishment. "They all said nobody stepped out and returned around that time, and that no new customers walked in, either. Each place has a toilet and a telephone on the premises, so there's no need to go outside."

Tamotsu gestured toward the heavy door. "But in a place this loud, you think they actually keep tabs on everybody? Don't you think they could have said whatever came to mind?"

"Well, sure, maybe," Sakai said, just to humor him. "But let's say the guy who pushed Mrs. Sekine down the stairs was waiting in one of the bars, how would he keep watch on her and know when she'd stepped out of Tagawa? All right, he could hang around outside the whole time. That'd be a sure thing, but it would seem kind of strange to the other customers passing through. If he had done that, somebody would remember. Okay. So put him inside, and he'd never hear Mrs. Sekine leave over all the singing. Which is it to be?"

Tamotsu was stumped. He suddenly looked cold, and jammed his hands in his pockets.

"What about the daughter's alibi?" asked Honma.

"It checks out. The time of death was about 11:00 P.M. The daughter was working in her bar all evening. We have her co-workers' testimony on that. It was a Saturday night. The place wasn't closed."

"Sure. Co-workers." Tamotsu was dismissive.

Honma and Sakai exchanged a look. "This isn't TV, you know," Sakai said.

Detectives actually place more weight on alibis than people imagine. If an alibi is solid, an investigator has no choice but to remove the person from the list of suspects and look elsewhere. Amateurs are often more stubborn, willing to overlook alibis and evidence alike. They get stuck on motive and can't see beyond it.

Typically, Tamotsu, from the minute he got it into his head that Shoko might have done it, couldn't seriously consider anything else. To him, Shoko's debts carried more weight than any alibi. Honma, however, never even entertained the notion that Shoko might have killed her mother. He was looking for Jun's "Shoko."

At Sakai's insistence, Tamotsu went back inside Tagawa to check on his wife, leaving the two detectives alone.

Honma's ears were getting numb. "I can understand why you rule out murder," he said.

"But you've still got reservations, I take it." Sakai saw right through him.

"Just my opinion. I could be wrong."

"Fair enough. That's all I'm saying too."

"According to young Honda, you consider Mrs. Sekine's death a suicide?"

Sakai pulled up his coat collar against the cold and nodded. His eyes watered in the sharp wind.

"I assume you checked with the other women at her job and regulars at Tagawa who knew her well."

Sakai stared straight down the gray steps. "She took a spill from here once before. I mean, right before her death, only a month or so. That time she fell backward, four or five steps down."

"Anybody see it?'

"Yes. It seems she managed to give a yell this time. Somebody who'd just gone into Tagawa heard and came running." He gave Honma a penetrating look. "The person who helped her up says she told her, 'Careful, Yoshiko, you want to kill yourself?' "

Honma could feel the wind chapping his lips.

"I figure it was worry, about the future. Her daughter gets tangled up in debt, she's nearly thirty and still showing no sign of finding her way in the world. Working in some cheap dive, doing God knows what there. And Yoshiko herself, it wasn't as if she were going to be around forever to bail her daughter out. One of the people working at the cafeteria was telling me, 'Yoshiko used to get so depressed she'd say she wondered if there was any reason to keep going.' "

"When she died, Mrs. Sekine was ..."

"Fifty-nine. Not that old. But she'd had her share of hard knocks. I can sympathize in that department." Sakai wound one hand around to massage the small of his back. " 'What's going to happen to me?... No savings, no security for the years when I can't work any more.' That's what she faced, and she brooded about it, till finally she couldn't take it any longer. At least, that's how I figure it."

"But there was no will." Not that that was so uncommon among suicides.

Sakai lowered his voice to a whisper. "If you ask me, there's more than one kind of suicide. Swallowing bug spray or jumping off a tall building is dramatic, sure, but there's also the let-fate-take-its-course approach." With that, he did an about-face, walking back to the stairs. Honma started to reach for his sleeve, but stopped himself when he saw the detective grab the handrail.

Sakai went down just one step. Below him spread the gray pavement.

"Every time she came to Tagawa, Mrs. Sekine would get drunk and take the stairs. Maybe she knew that sooner or later she'd slip or lose her balance, and hoped she'd tumble all the way to the bottom. Anyway, that's my best guess."

"The old lady was that …" Honma's mouth was open, but a cold lump stuck in his throat. "… lonely?"

"From what I can gather." Sakai had his back to him, but he now turned around and climbed back up. "Up until she died, she kept coming out here, week after week. Everybody at Tagawa, the staff and the customers too, knew she used these stairs, even when she was blind drunk. And they warned her, sure, they warned her all right. But none of her drinking buddies ever offered to see her out safely."

Sakai's graying eyebrows drooped. His lips formed a smile, but the rest of his face wasn't smiling at all. "I'm a fine one to talk. I've sat in that bar myself, acting friendly and concerned, when she was there a couple of times."

They headed back to rejoin Ikumi.


Honma had taken a room in a hotel by the station. When he went to pick up the key at the front desk, they said he had a message.

It was from Makoto, received at 7:25 P.M. He was planning to spend the night with the Isakas, much to Honma's relief. When he called their place, Makoto answered right away. "Dad? I've been waiting for you."

What time was it, anyway? The bedside clock read close to midnight.

"Sorry, I got back really late … What's up?"

"Well, uh, there was a call from Dr. Machiko."

"Who?"

"You know, Dr. Machiko."

Of course, the physical therapist from Osaka. Dr. Machiko Kitamura. She even had Makoto using that Osaka drawl now. Not Doctor but Doctah.

"She call because I missed my therapy session?"

"Uh-huh."

"You stayed up this late to tell me that?"

Makoto sounded angry. "Don't yell at me long-distance, okay? It's a waste of money. This is the Isakas' phone, you know!"

"Don't you worry about that, silly—I did the calling, so I pay."

Another voice could be heard in the background, saying, "Here. Let me do some ground control." Hisae came on.

"Hello?"

"Shunsuke? Hey, listen. It's about that photo with those crazy ball-park lights."

"The ones facing out?"

"Right, right. Well, we kept thinking about it, even asked a few people about it—we figured you wouldn't mind. Anyway it's more effective, getting information from more people, right?

"And ...?"

"Let me finish, will you? So anyway, Makoto, being a good boy, he kept it in mind too. He even forgot to do his homework, thinking about those lights so much."

"Don't tell him that," Makoto groaned in the background.

"We can let the homework slide this once. Go on."

"So today, when the phone call came from Dr. Machiko and she told Makoto his father was a deserter and that if he didn't report back within three days the MPs would come arrest him, even then he was thinking about it. So Makoto asked her. A doctor for a sports club and all, right? Maybe she'd know."

Honma got a better grip on the receiver. "And? Did she?"

"Well, she said, 'Why didn't you ask me right away?' I may not have the accent quite right, but ... "

"So she knew?"

"Well, why do think I'm telling you?" Hisae said, exasperated. "Ready, Shunsuke? Those crazy lights, they're not crazy at all. We were looking at them wrong."

"Hmm?"

"The lights in the photo, they're ordinary stadium lights. The same as in any ballpark anywhere in the country. They're not pointing the wrong way. In fact they don't even turn."

"But in the photo ..."

Hisae cut him off. "Like I said, we were looking at it wrong. You said it was a house by a ballpark, right?"

"Yes."

"Which seemed more than likely. But here's the good part. You said that since the floodlights were facing the house, they must have been lighting the area outside the ballpark."

"And?"

"That's where you went wrong."

Makoto came back on, the excitement in his voice contagious. "Dad, listen. Dr. Machiko told me there's only one place in the whole country where they got houses built inside a ballpark. Get it, Dad? The lights are facing the right way! There's houses inside the stadium!"

Honma was thrown for a minute. He managed to ask, "And Dr. Machiko knew where it was?"

"Uh-huh. She's a sports doctor from Osaka, and a super baseball fan, too."

"So it's in Osaka?"

"Yup," said Makoto, "Osaka. It's a stadium they never use, see? In 1988, the Nankai Hawks were bought by Daei, and moved out of town. So it's empty now, the Osaka Field. But they didn't tear it down. They just use it for big events, car shows and stuff. And one time they did this 'Housing Festa.'"

"'Housing ...'?"

"They did it again, not so long ago, she said. You know—a show of a whole bunch of model houses. Get it? The house in the picture's a fake, it's a model!"

✧ 18 ✧

Take the New Tokaido bullet train to Osaka. A five-minute walk from
New Osaka Station puts you on the Midosuji subway line, which cuts
straight across the heart of the city, north to south. Twenty minutes of
jostling brings you to Namba Station. Navigate the underground shopping arcade which is so big it would take a devoted shopper a couple
of days to explore properly, then emerge into a jumble of small-time
retailers and rental office buildings jammed up one against the other.
Wedged in among them is a baseball stadium.

The old Osaka Field. The outside wall is all but obliterated by a
random collage of signs and billboards. Hardly your usual home-run
hall of fame. You could be looking broadside at a derelict warehouse
somewhere. But as a string of newer team franchises came up with
the very latest, fully equipped venues—Seibu Stadium, Tokyo Dome,
Kobe Green Stadium—there had to be teams like the Nankai Hawks
that just didn't make it and played in run-down ballparks like these.

The entrance was thoroughly unremarkable: a carport built to the
maximum allowable six feet and, next to it, a sliding door set into a
metal wall. A yellow banner tacked over the door read "Osaka Field
—Housing Expo Information."

Honma headed inside. The plain white plaster walls of a corridor-
cum-office space bore cheerful color panels showing houses of various architectural styles, each with a number at the bottom. To his
eyes, which had grown accustomed to the bright morning light outside, the interior looked a bit dim and gloomy. The hallway ended in
another sliding door, which led out onto the field itself. Out there
Honma could see a fleet of model homes framed against the tiers of

faded red and yellow seats. Just on this side of the door, several long desks were placed together in an L-shape. A prim, thirtyish receptionist was ensconced there.

Sunday afternoons drew big crowds, and there were plenty of visitors nosing about. Luckily Honma didn't have to beat anyone else to the receptionist's desk, nor was the lady fazed at all when he pulled out the Polaroid. "I wonder if you could tell me when you might have had this model on display?"

"Oh dear," she exclaimed. "I'm afraid this one's no longer up. Are you looking for a house like this?" Her drawl wasn't as pronounced as Dr. Machiko's—she had a prettier voice—but her intonation still said Osaka. "If you're interested in another Western-style home of this type, we do have a newer model."

"No, sorry, I'm only interested in this one."

"Oh, too bad," she said, touching the corner of her mouth with the long nail of her little finger—the only polished fingernail on her hand.

"How long have you been holding Expos here?"

"This one has been on since last autumn. Since September."

"And you've had the same models up the whole time?"

"That's right."

"And this model isn't one of them? You didn't change the models midway through or anything like that?"

"No, sir, they're the same ones. Here's a copy of our pamphlet. You can also go out and look around for yourself."

Honma ran his eye over the stack of "Osaka Field—Housing Expo" pamphlets on the desktop. "It would be a long time ago now, but did you ever hold an event called 'Housing Festa' here?"

"Yes, I believe so."

"When would that have been?"

"Well, now …" She paused and began flipping back through a large desk calendar. Honma laid both hands on the desk and waited. "Housing Festa ran for four months, July through October, 1987," she said. She looked up from her handwritten notes. "The number of builders taking part was much smaller than in the current Expo, maybe not even half."

"Are all the companies from that show represented this time around?"

"Yes, but ..."

Honma picked up a pamphlet and spread it open on the desk. "Sorry to bother you, but could you mark the companies that are showing now and were also in the earlier show? That would help me find my way around. I assume the reps for each company are inside the houses?"

"Yes, they're all there." The receptionist checked the pamphlet against her records, and promptly ticked off a total of five companies.

Stepping out onto the field, Honma could hardly believe that this little arena was a regulation-size major-league stadium. And the day seemed too warm for last week's snowstorm to have been anything but a mistake. Whole families were out shopping for houses. Young couples with dreams of building someday darted about, calling to each other and making plans. Then, as if to snap them out of their illusions, a herd of middle-aged housewives would pass through, grumbling "This here doesn't work" or "Impossible to clean." One could see them ganging up on some salesman and asking questions, and hear his smooth response: "In this line, we also have a deluxe model with even sharper design features. And of course, all the rooms have radiant floor heating ..."

Whenever Honma cornered a salesman, though, he started by saying, "Ever see this uniform before? Or this girl?" Rather than going into a long explanation about the Polaroid, he simply said he was looking for his runaway daughter, which proved far more effective than he ever hoped. People wanted to help. Did he look more like the father of a grown daughter than of a ten-year-old boy?

But all the answers came back negative. One company, two, three— the longer he circled the stadium, the more convinced he became that pinpointing the house wouldn't help him get any real bearing on his "Shoko." The mystery of the stadium lights had suddenly cleared up and he had hauled himself down to Osaka on the sheer momentum of it, but how could he put so much stock in one blurry little image? Supposing he did track down the builder, "Shoko" could still only have been someone who had happened to pass a model home she apparently liked. It would be almost impossible to trace her through a snapshot.

The last of the five companies, however, took the bait: New City Housing, whose "Grand Japanesque" boasted an entrance the size of Honma's entire kitchen. The saleswoman was small but pretty in her gray skirt-and-vest uniform and a pair of two-inch heels that gave her a stiff, straight back. Her name tag said "Hi! I'm E. Yamaguchi."

"Yes, that's one of ours, I'm sure. Type 2 Chalet 1990 from the Housing Festa collection." Textbook-perfect phrasing and pure Osaka intonation, a treat for the ears. "Just like a real Swiss chalet, and it comes with a working fireplace option. Let me go check with our main office whether we still have any brochures available." She had turned toward a room on the right that served as a temporary on-site office, when Honma stopped her.

"No, that's all right. I just wanted to confirm that the house had actually been here."

"Pardon?"

"Actually, there are a couple more things I'd like to ask, if you wouldn't mind." Moving away from the flow of visitors, over to a window in the tastefully appointed living room, Honma tried his usual questions. But she knew nothing about "Shoko." Honma apologized and was about to go when Ms. Yamaguchi asked him to wait a second.

"The uniform in the photo looks familiar, but I can't quite place it," she said, touching her cheek with one finger as if she had toothache.

"Are you sure?"

"Pretty sure. But there's someone else on the staff who was here during the Housing Festa. Let me just run and get her. Could I borrow the photo?"

"Certainly, here you are."

"I'll be right back." While she was in the office, people passing through the living room cast curious looks in Honma's direction. Was he a buyer waiting for his contract papers?

E. Yamaguchi returned with a taller, slightly older woman in tow. The latter wore an identical gray uniform and a tag saying, "Hi! I'm

K. Komachi." She gave a little bow as soon as she saw Honma. The Polaroid was in her hands.

"I believe this is a Mitomo Agency uniform," she said, without waiting for an introduction.

"Agency?"

"Travel agents." She handed the photo back to Honma.

"I remember from our regular trainee orientations. There's no mistake," Ms. Yamaguchi confirmed. "We're all, New City Housing included, under the Mitomo Construction Group umbrella. And this Mitomo Agency is another of the subsidiaries."

"So they're a sister company."

"That's right. Once or twice a year employees from all the companies meet at the Mitomo Group's headquarters to hold training sessions and exchange know-how."

"The session I attended was for first- and second-year staff," Ms. Komachi added. "There were women there from all the affiliated companies. We all had to practice office etiquette. Oh yes, and we had to compete. For instance, there was a telephone-answering contest. First prize was a big silver cup."

They both smiled, then Ms. Yamaguchi said: "The Mitomo Agency woman in the picture waving at the camera? I'd guess that whoever took the picture was probably also an employee, here for the same orientation."

"Definitely," her colleague agreed, nodding enthusiastically.

"Is there any way to check? A list of participants or anything?"

"Not really, but you could try the Research Center."

"Where's that?"

"It's near the Mitomo Group's headquarters. All the staff records are kept there. If you explain what you need, I'm sure they'll help. The place is right by Umeda Station."

The receptionist behind the counter on the ground floor of the seven-story Mitomo Group Research Center wasn't quite as helpful as he had been led to believe. She hadn't even heard him out when she told him abruptly: "We do not give out information about our employees."

No further questions. Now that he had grown accustomed to the Osaka drawl, this woman's standard accent sounded flat and peremptory. Admittedly, he had prepared himself for that sort of response. He wasn't on official business, so his hands were tied. No one was obliged to speak to him. And it was true that a company releasing information about its employees to any and all comers would be guilty of a serious breach of privacy.

"Fine, but I would like to ask a favor. Could you possibly take a look at this photo and confirm whether or not this woman might have come here for orientation between July and October 1989?"

"No, I am afraid not."

"I'm looking for someone who's been reported missing. I'd really appreciate your help."

"And what evidence do you have that the woman was in fact at some point employed by us?"

"As I was trying to say, this photo ..." He pulled the Polaroid out and proceeded to explain.

The receptionist, an otherwise smooth-faced PR lady, scowled. "I am sorry. I can't help you."

"And you alone have the authority to decide that?"

"I do."

"I can't get you to cooperate even a little?"

"Sir, I am simply not authorized to respond to this kind of question. You might want to try submitting a proper written request."

"I see. I have to put it in writing, is that it? Then I can be sure of a response?"

That finally put a dent in her self-confidence. Her gaze faltered. "Wait here a minute, please." She came out from behind the counter, moved across the lobby, and disappeared through a door in the far wall.

Honma leaned against the counter and gave a sigh. Good going, he told himself. With a pang of regret, he reminded himself how much clout that little leather case with his ID in it used to have. How powerless he was as a mere civilian! The lobby was completely still and he was alone. His own breathing sounded unnaturally loud. He rested his elbows on the counter to take the load off his leg, knowing he'd have to straighten up as soon as the woman came back.

Just then, he noticed stacks of brochures in different colors and sizes inside the counter. The largest, thickest one, embossed with the title "Moving Ahead with Mitomo," listed all the subsidiaries. Honma wasn't sure, for a minute, what had caught his attention; at first, all he saw were the lines of characters. Four columns of fine print under the name Mitomo Construction, a vast and varied portfolio of interests. Many companies had nothing to do with housing or real estate at all. Mitomo International, Mitomo Trading, Mitomo Sports Center, Terra Bionics, Mitomo Engineering, Mitomo Systems Center, Minami Green Garden—he read the long litany of companies twice and still it didn't come together. What had caught his eye? Was there a name he knew from somewhere?

That's when he saw it. That company.

He was leaning halfway over the counter when he heard footsteps. He promptly straightened up as the woman came trotting back, a hostile look on her face. "I checked with my superiors," she said quickly. "I'm sorry but, as I suspected, we can't comply with your request."

"No?"

"Moreover, the records that the Research Center keeps on participants in our orientation programs do not include photographs. So, in any case, there would be no way to match an employee with a photograph from our files."

"I see."

"So, even if you were to inquire in writing, we wouldn't be able to provide an answer."

"Very well," was all Honma could say.

"Mm?"

"I see. I'm very sorry to have bothered you."

The woman glared at him. His sudden meekness had come as a surprise.

Honma reached out and pointed at the large brochure. "Just one last request. Could I take one of those?"

The woman, her face stiff with hostility, extracted a single copy and slid it across to him with mechanical precision.

"Thanks." Honma pointed to one of the companies listed on the cover. "Is this firm under the Mitomo umbrella, too?"

"Yes, it is."

"So its employees would also come here for orientation?"

"That's right."

"And this company is also in Osaka?"

More suspicious than ever now, the woman opened up the brochure and said, "Yes, it's got an office in the main building of Mitomo Construction."

"Any other branches?"

"No, sir. Only the warehouse and distribution center, which are in Kobe." She showed him the appropriate page in the brochure. "This should give you all the details you need."

The company's name was written in boldface across the top of the page. Underneath, a pink rose-shaped logo and the catchphrase "Fine imported intimate wear at affordable prices." Honma hardly needed to read the copy. It was the same logo he'd seen on the box that Nobuko Konno had shown him at the Kawaguchi Co-op.

It was a box from the mail-order underwear company that Shoko Sekine had patronized.

Roseline.

# ✧ 19 ✧

Umeda, the heart of the great commercial city of Osaka.

The Mitomo Group's headquarters wasn't hard to find. It looked a bit run-down compared with the gleaming new Research Center, though its gray color scheme made it somehow more dignified. The directory showed a Roseline, Inc. on the fourth floor. Minami Green Garden was on the same floor, suggesting that both were probably among the smaller companies in the Mitomo empire.

The Roseline receptionist wore a pale pink uniform, the same color as the logo emblazoned on the suite's glass door. The carpeting, though, was a deep burgundy which shaded almost to black at a certain angle.

Honma began by asking to see the personnel director.

"Do you have an appointment?"

"No, sorry. But it's quite urgent." He put on his most serious face and pulled out his photo of "Shoko." "Perhaps you could tell me whether this woman worked for you at some point. She's missing, and I'm trying to trace her."

The receptionist studied the photograph. Then, perhaps alarmed by Honma's grim manner—she didn't even ask his name—she told him to wait. The photo fluttered between her fingertips as she trotted off to a back room.

Honma wandered over toward the elevator, where he noticed a display cabinet filled with Roseline catalogs. He opened one up, glanced at the table of contents, and flipped through it at random. He'd never seen anything quite like it.

"How to Place Your Order" was the only section not strewn with photos of lingerie-clad models in various challenging stages of undress. At the bottom of a carefully worded explanation written in contractual form was a tear-out mail-order postcard.

> When placing your first order, please be sure to include your name, address and workplace. We are happy to take your order by phone—just dial our toll-free number. Orders also accepted by fax 24 hours a day. Convenient payment by credit card or postal transfer. Specified-date delivery and gift wrapping services available on request.
>
> Do you have a friend who might like to receive our catalog? For every new customer you introduce, you receive a Special Friendship Club 5% discount toward your next purchase, as well as a chance to receive a handsome bonus gift in our Lucky Prize Drawing.

Honma was interested to see, a few lines further down, an appeal for consumer feedback.

> Care to participate in our Customer Survey? Are there any other products that you would like to see Roseline carry, in addition to our line of fine intimate apparel? Help us provide you with the ultimate in beauty and gracious living as we expand into a Creative Lifestyle Company. You can help us anticipate the needs of the Twenty-First Century Woman by taking just five minutes to complete this simple questionnaire and posting it to us before the deadline listed below. All respondents will receive a Special Roseline Travel Kit.

It was worth coming just to get a load of this questionnaire. Let's see now. First the standard stuff:

> List family members
> Homeowner or tenant
> Number of years' continuous employment at present job

But then came some more unusual items:

> Have you ever changed jobs? If so, when and how often?

Special qualifications—word processing, driver's license, abacus certificate, etc.
Approximate amount of personal savings
Types of insurance held, name of company/companies
Credit cards held

Then under the heading "Unmarried Respondents":

Where would you most like to hold your wedding? At a hotel, a wedding hall, a Buddhist temple, a Shinto shrine, other?
Where would you like to go on your honeymoon?
Have you ever traveled abroad? If so, list date of first overseas trip

And under "Respondents Living Alone":

Do you plan to own a house in the future?

Honma raised his eyes and stared at the pink wallpaper.

Roseline was a mail-order retailer of imported underwear. They offered fancy goods at affordable prices. That was all they did. But if they got customers to reply to this questionnaire, they would have themselves an instant, rather extensive database. Anyone who worked here, who knew how to punch the right keys, would have immediate access to all that data.

"Sorry to keep you waiting." The receptionist reemerged from the back room. "If you'd care to come this way," she said, nodding.

Close behind her, however, stood a woman in her mid-thirties, chic in a pale green suit. Before Honma could open his mouth, Green Suit was laying down company policy. "We regret to say that we can't assist you with the inquiry that brings you here." Firm, even a little pompous, she seemed intent on fending him off, no questions asked.

Honma made his tone conciliatory. "I'm afraid I didn't explain myself very well, so it's not surprising that you should find my question a little irregular. If you give me five minutes, I can sort it out." But the woman showed no sign of budging.

"I'm very sorry, sir. That's out of the question. Our regulations expressly forbid company staff from receiving visitors who don't have an appointment." Honma had clearly hit on the wrong person. Or was there something else behind her reaction? Honma was searching for something else to say when, behind the two women, a young man peered out around a door. Sensing that Honma had spotted him, if just for a moment, he quickly withdrew.

"Very well, then. I'll come back another time," Honma said dryly. Green Suit didn't even bother to smile politely. "Could I get my photograph back, though?"

The woman glared at the rose-pink receptionist, who wilted slightly and then scurried off behind the scenes. Honma glanced down the corridor after her, but there was now no sign of anyone there.

The photo was soon returned to him. Honma noticed the look of satisfaction on Green Suit's face as she showed him the door, sending him away without a shred of information. Little did she know how relieved *he* was to be getting out of there.

He headed back to the elevator and pushed the DOWN button. A red light flashed, showing that one was on its way. On an impulse, he looked around and slipped into a side stairwell. The elevator came up to the fourth floor, opened its doors, and slid shut again. No one got on or off.

Maybe he'd been mistaken, he was thinking … when he heard footsteps approaching. A young man skimmed across the carpet and rang for the elevator. It was the same person he'd glimpsed in the rear corridor of the office. The man tapped again and again at the CALL button. No elevator came. He glanced at the emergency-exit floor plan posted nearby, gave a sharp click of the tongue, and turned toward the stairwell. Seconds before he collided with him, Honma stepped out of the shadows. "Looking for me, by any chance?"

Startled, the young man blurted out an introduction: Roseline Management Section, Chief Assistant, Hideki Wada. "The lady in the suit, she's one of my bosses. She's in Sales, though, which has got nothing to do with this. I handle staff affairs."

Honma figured he was about thirty-four or thirty-five. Just this side of a playboy in looks, he had a perfectly even, if fairly discreet, artificial tan. His shirtsleeves gave him a casual look, but his shoes were no-nonsense business wingtips. It was the first time Honma had heard such a trendy yuppie type speak in an everyday Osaka drawl. The two didn't go together somehow.

"How did you know I'd come chasing after you?" he asked as they started down the stairs.

"I couldn't be sure," Honma answered with a grin. "You just seemed to know something."

Wada stopped on the second-floor landing. The air in the narrow stairwell was perfectly still.

"Mr. Wada, you saw the photo I brought in. You knew the woman, didn't you?" Honma asked, standing one step below the young man. He took out the photo again and held it out. "Take a good look."

Wada reached around and wiped a sweaty palm on the back of his thigh. He was still a little jumpy.

"Yes," he said under his breath.

"Did this person work for Roseline?"

This time he only nodded. The simplest of gestures. Not quite a satisfying answer, but a start.

"Why is it you're asking about her?" Wada wanted to know.

"It's a long story."

"Give me an idea what it's about."

There was something about the young man—an urgency—that touched a nerve. What if "Shoko Sekine" had been more than a former colleague to him? Honma decided to come right out with the truth, or at least as much of it as he knew.

"The fact is, this woman has assumed somebody else's identity. There is a possibility that the other woman was a Roseline customer, someone by the name of Shoko Sekine."

"Shoko Sekine ..." Wada repeated the name to himself.

"There you have it. I've come here to look into those two things."

Wada responded immediately. "Turn right as you leave the building, walk straight for four lights, look diagonally across to the right: you'll see a coffee shop called Kanteki. Wait for me there. I'll be over in just a few minutes."

Honma did as he was told and found himself waiting for more

than an hour. It wouldn't have seemed so long if he hadn't had an awful cramp in his neck. He felt as jittery as he did the first time he ever got a suspect to confess.

When Wada finally showed up, he was wearing a jacket. A nice cut, matching the full shape of the trousers—an expensive suit by some designer whose name Honma wouldn't have been able to pronounce. Wada apologized profusely for keeping him waiting and sat down in the chair opposite, then transferred a large company envelope from under his arm to the chair next to him.

"I gave them a good story at the office, so we don't have to worry about time. Now maybe you can tell me the whole story, from the beginning."

Wada didn't interrupt even once. Nor did he touch his coffee. When it was over he sighed, looking at the photo of "Shoko" that Honma had laid on the table. When Honma stopped, he asked, "Is that it?"

"That's everything," Honma said with a nod, his throat a little dry.

"Well, then." Wada reached for the envelope. "I expect it'll save time if you just look at these." He pulled out three stapled legal-sized photocopies and a fan-fold computer printout, which he laid to one side. "This here is a former employees file. We don't clear out our employees' résumés or our payroll documentation right away, you understand." He held them out to Honma. "Look these over. I don't believe there's any mistake."

The first sheet was a résumé. At the top of the page was the same face he'd seen for the first time ten days before on the Imai Office Machines résumé. The hairstyle was different, but there could be no doubt. And there, in the same hand, was the name.

"Kyoko Shinjo," Honma read out aloud.

Wada nodded. "I remember Ms. Shinjo very well. Only she had her hair permed when she was working for us."

Born May 10, 1966. That would make her twenty-six, two years younger than Shoko Sekine. The place where her family register was kept was given as Fukushima, up in the north.

"We hired her in April 1988," said Wada. "The second page is from her personnel file, and lists her exact dates with the company."

Just as he said, the entry read "Began April 20, 1988—Terminated December 31, 1989." This meant Kyoko Shinjo was twenty-two when she started work, a good four years after she got out of high school. There was no mention of any previous employment; the space for that was blank.

"Would you have any idea what she was doing before coming to work here?"

Wada scratched under his nose, thinking. "Something the matter?"

"No ... nothing's the matter," Honma hedged.

"She said she was married."

"Married ..."

"Yeah. Got married too young and it didn't work out, is what she said."

"It must have been awfully young."

"She had a few jobs right out of high school, but she didn't bother to write them down, she said. Anyway, we don't care so much about those details ..."

Fair enough, thought Honma. But what if the "facts" here were just more fabrications? Under "Awards and Citations" she'd written "None." "Qualifications: Abacus, 2nd Rank." Beneath that, "Driver's License."

But the real Shoko Sekine had had a driver's license too. And driver's licenses carried photos, which meant that Kyoko would never have been able to renew Shoko's. Kyoko must simply have tossed it out and pretended "Shoko Sekine" couldn't drive.

The entry for "Family" was likewise blank.

"Didn't she have any folks?"

"Both her parents died early, is what she said."

"Then I take it she lived alone."

"That's right. In a condo near the center of Senri in Osaka. She had a roommate, though. The rent was too high for one person, she said."

*A roommate?* "Would you happen to know the roommate's name?"

"Well, not here ..."

"Any way to find out?"

"I'll give it a try. I think I can probably dig it up."

Honma nodded and looked up from the résumé. He watched Wada's face. The young man was looking down, eyes fixed on the snapshot on the table. A picture of Kyoko Shinjo as "Shoko" with the Tokyo Disneyland castle in the background.

"You knew her pretty well, did you?"

Wada blinked, as if somebody had flicked water in his face. "Ms. Shinjo?" he stuttered. "Why, sure … she was my junior. I was the one who interviewed her for the job."

That's not what I meant, thought Honma. And you know it. Who gets this concerned about a junior staffer?

"I don't mean to seem nosy, but how about on a personal level?"

Forcing a smile, Wada replied, "At work, I guess we were closer than most. We sometimes ate lunch together. Yes, and when she said she was quitting I remember being real surprised."

"Did she give any reason?"

Wada shook his head. "She didn't say."

"And you didn't probe any further?"

"What right did I have?" He smiled. A real smile, if a rueful one.

"Is that what she said? That you had no right to question her?"

Wada didn't answer, but there was no need. His forlorn look said it all.

Honma thumbed through the rest of the pages in silence. Kyoko Shinjo was a real beauty. She must have had scores of men running after her. Wada would have been just one more. His smile had faded, but he was still looking at the photo.

"What was Ms. Shinjo's job description?" Honma asked.

It was hardly the most difficult question, but Wada didn't reply to it right away. "Let's see if this fits. You're thinking that when she worked here, she got hold of this Shoko Sekine's data and took it into her head to impersonate her, right?"

The question caught Honma by surprise. If Wada was this far ahead of the game, the rest would be easy. Honma nodded. "That's the way it looks to me."

Wada, however, was shaking his head. "It's impossible. Couldn't have happened."

"Why not? The customer data is just sitting there in the computer, ripe for the picking. It'd be simple to hit a few keys and access the information."

There was certainly enough there for Kyoko Shinjo to have decided to take over Shoko's identity. How else, if she hadn't been close enough to her to know about something as important as her bankruptcy, could she have found out all about her register and family background?

"What about your customer questionnaire? You've got to admit, it does include a lot of private information ..."

Actually, it may have been just a few key things she was looking for. Honma tried to put himself in her position. First, she'd look for a woman about her own age. The woman couldn't have any family, or live with anyone else. That was essential—her not having any ties. Anything else Kyoko would be able to deal with when the time came. It might be inconvenient if the woman had ever had a passport; ditto a driver's license or other form of photo ID; but those would probably be details to think about afterward. A good income and savings would be nice, but only once the two main requirements were met. Oh yes, and one last thing. The woman would have to live as far as possible from where Kyoko was, in Osaka. That would be important, very important.

Shoko Sekine fit the bill on all counts ...

"But there'd be no way of telling, simply by looking at the questionnaire, that Shoko Sekine had ever filed for bankruptcy, would there?" Honma said. "Ms. Shinjo wouldn't have known that, not just from this."

Wada nodded and picked up the fan-fold paper he'd laid to one side. "Here, take a look at this. It's something I just printed out."

The name Shoko Sekine jumped out at Honma from the top of the page. So she *had* been a customer.

Wada reached over and pointed. "The top page is basic customer data. See that '205' at the bottom? That's your basic data reference code. Gives you all the tabulated data on any one person. It's perfectly straightforward."

"So it would seem," Honma agreed.

Shoko Sekine, distilled down to a data file, but still there, all right.

The connection between the two women *had* been lying hidden in the Mitomo Group mainframe.

"The second page is a record of which products Ms. Sekine ordered, when the order was received, processed and shipped. The code is '201.' And the last page is a running account of her billing status. The date after each figure shows when payment was received. 'P' means postal transfer."

Honma nodded. "She couldn't use any credit cards."

"But she did meet all her payments. Never once missed a due date. She never bought that much, but to us *that's* a good, faithful customer."

The page prickled with small figures. ¥5,120, ¥4,800 ... ¥10,000 at the very most.

Wada flipped back through the printout. "Looking at the basic data, you can see the questionnaire item 'Credit cards held' marked 'No reply.' That alone wouldn't lead anyone to guess she was bankrupt. So as far as that goes, Mr. Honma, your thinking's right on the money ..."

"As far as that goes ...?"

"Don't get the idea that I'm sticking up for Ms. Shinjo," he said, turning stubborn. "Our system's foolproof. There's no way customer data could ever leak out."

Honma was about to object, but Wada waved his comment aside. "If you want, I'll show you around the office and you can see for yourself. In the evening ... After 7:00 P.M., when all the staff's gone home except for the guard on duty, should be okay."

"I'd appreciate that."

"You'll see, it's airtight. It's what we call a 'closed system.' Doesn't need to communicate with anywhere except the distribution center and the warehouse."

"But in a mail-order company, there has to be a telephone receptionist on at all times."

"Sure, we've got our 'telephone ladies.' "

"And these 'ladies,' they deal with their share of information, right? You call up and they can check on stock by using their computers. So what's to stop them typing in one of those codes of yours and extracting all the customer information they like?"

Wada let him finish, but then shook his head, looking adamant. "It can't be done."

"Why not?"

"Well, for one thing, our operators are so busy on the phones, they hardly ever get time to catch their breath. If they did try some fancy computer commands, they'd get a warning right off the bat. They can't download or print a thing without the proper authorization. All they do is input the orders." He leaned forward. "But you're set on thinking Kyoko Shinjo worked here with the one aim of looking for an identity to take over, is that it?"

"Basically, but I can't tell whether that was her purpose right from the start or whether she only realized later how easy it would be for her to access information."

"Yes, but you know how much work that would actually involve? Assuming she did have her own agenda here, imagine how many files she'd have to go through to single out one person?"

"I suppose so." Honma felt a bit deflated. Could Kyoko Shinjo really have found her target by the time-consuming process Wada had described? The reverse was impossible: there was no way she could have targeted her from the outset. Which meant the whole process of learning how to use the computer, call up data, and select an appropriate candidate would have taken incredible patience. No telephone receptionist would have that kind of time on the job.

Wada smiled knowingly. "It's just more than any TL could ever handle."

"I don't think you can rule it out completely." Honma didn't want to give up.

"It just doesn't work like that," Wada said, shaking his head.

"What makes you so sure?"

He pulled out Kyoko Shinjo's personnel file one more time. "Take a look at her job description."

Honma's eyes went straight to the words "General Clerical." "Then she wasn't a ..."

"A TL? No, she was a regular office worker. Paperwork mostly. She was in Accounting, as I recall, calculating paychecks. Of course, she did use a computer, but the system was completely different from the one used for customer data processing. The codes are different. In fact, you can't even access the customer side of things from the office workstations."

Wada looked pleased. But was he proud of the company's computer system, or did he have his own reasons for vindicating Kyoko? Honma couldn't tell.

"Okay," he went on, "let's just say for the sake of argument that Ms. Shinjo knew the name of this Shoko Sekine. Even then, all that other stuff was beyond her scope. That much I can swear to."

They locked eyes. "You sure you didn't help her?" Honma said, shooting to kill.

Wada showed no reaction—except for a twitch of his left eyebrow.

"You sure she didn't get you—for whatever reason—to pull data for her? Or else to show her how to access it for herself?" He aimed to hit square-on, but was a hair too quick on the draw.

"Absolutely not!" Wada replied. "I never did anything of the kind!"

Kyoko Shinjo's smile shone out from between his long, thin fingers.

## ✧ 20 ✧

"And so what happened? Did you get a tour of the office?"

"Sure did," Honma replied.

He hadn't gotten back from Osaka till very late, and his left knee had throbbed the whole night. First thing the next day, he had called Funaki to fill him in. Funaki had dropped everything and come straight over, arriving early in the afternoon and depositing himself at the coffee table, where he ground out one cigarette butt after another in a glass ashtray that Isaka had carefully wiped clean.

"So did their operation look as tight as he would like you to think?"

"Roseline employs thirty-eight of these 'telephone ladies' full-time. They're there from ten in the morning till eight at night. All of them at their phones, lined up at their little desks." The scene was straight out of a TV commercial: a bevy of young women in their twenties and early thirties, all in uniform, all quite attractive, all facing Honma's way. "I say phones, but actually they were like the old switchboards, but more compact. Pushbutton, of course, and a headset with a tiny mike sticking out, the kind singers wear so they can play keyboards at the same time. And everyone who places an order gets their own customer code for reference."

"Everything's coded?"

"Yup. Cuts down on response time. Not a bad little system. Said they introduced it on New Year's Day, 1988."

"January 1988, huh?" Funaki scratched his thick neck. "And Kyoko Shinjo started in April that year, wasn't it?"

"That's right. April 20, 1988, their records said. So before she came on the job, the new system would have been up and running."

"And Shoko Sekine was registered as a Roseline customer on—?"

The hospital receipt he'd found at Nobuko Konno's place, which had had Roseline's toll-free number scribbled on it, was dated July 7, 1988. According to the Roseline records Wada had shown him, it was July 10 when Shoko called in and asked them to send her a catalog, and the fifteenth when she returned the questionnaire, placed her first order, and was assigned a customer code.

"Not much lead time, is it?" Funaki sounded disappointed.

"No, unfortunately. That's what this Wada fellow said when he was going on about how his Kyoko couldn't have stolen Shoko Sekine's data." *Imagine how many files she'd have to go through to single out one person.* "In any case, his point was that the system for in-house accounting, calculating paychecks—the sort of office work Kyoko Shinjo did—was on a completely different loop from the customer processing system. There's no way to browse around from one to the other. The only people who can do that, he said, are the guys in the 'system management class.'"

"Whatever that means," Funaki said, frowning slightly. "But in any case, people in that class can get their hands on whatever information they happen to want, right? What if Kyoko managed to pick up those skills?"

Honma laughed and shook his head. "Let's not get ahead of ourselves. Wada says she was a complete beginner when it came to computers. She hadn't even played a computer game before."

"You believe that?"

"He had some sort of thing going with her. He says it never amounted to much, but I'm going to look into it."

"You'll be talking to him again?"

"So far, he seems about my best source of information about her. Places like Roseline see a quick employee turnover. There can't be a whole lot of people left there now who worked with Kyoko and knew her at all. I'm having Wada ask around."

"You trust this guy?" said Funaki. "He seems awfully cooperative to me. Wonder why."

Honma thought for a minute and then said, "It may be he knows more than he's letting on. But what exactly? I mean, if the guy had been in on it with her, would he have come chasing after me and shown me all those documents?"

Funaki grunted noncommittally.

"The way I see it, he and Kyoko Shinjo were close. He probably had a hand in seeing that she got that data. At the time, he wouldn't have thought much about what she was planning to do with it. Now it's come back at him and caught him off guard."

"You think so?" Funaki wasn't satisfied. "I don't know. I like this Wada as an accomplice. I'd say there's a possibility he's in as deep as murder."

"Whose? Shoko Sekine's?"

"Or her old lady's."

"I don't know about that ... but he certainly reacted when he saw Kyoko's photo."

"Never can tell."

"Okay, okay. But to look at things fairly. He is personnel manager there, after all. He can't just let this pass. Think about it—it's scary. One woman disappears and the person who's taken over her identity suddenly throws up a secure office job. Even a kid could smell a crime there somewhere. Remember, he hired her himself. And it hasn't been two, three years since she quit."

Funaki still looked unconvinced.

"Not to mention that leaking customer data is completely taboo for a mail-order company. It's sure to reflect badly on the parent Mitomo Group. Wada had to help me out. There'd be all sorts of strange talk floating around the company if he let me go poking around on my own.

"But back to the computers. Suppose one of the TLs sitting at her console wants to make off with a sizable chunk of information without anybody finding out about it. She'd need expertise. Say she smuggles in her own floppy disks to download the data. As soon as she attempts any operation that's not in the manual, the person sitting next to her or behind her is going to know."

Funaki made a face. He wasn't familiar with even the basics of word processing, and had little patience with the subject.

"It wouldn't be any easier for her to try to hack her way into the right system either. That's got to be risky. The computer links with the outside—back and forth between the warehouse and distribution center—they have their own reserved phone lines, with unlisted numbers. Now even assuming that, as an insider, Kyoko Shinjo might have been able to get the phone numbers, that alone wouldn't be enough. You can't withdraw money with just a PIN number and no cash card. According to Wada, it's the same thing."

Funaki scowled. "So that deep-sixes this angle for the time being?"

"Seems so. But only the part about Kyoko using the computers herself to get the data."

"What about her roommate? Did you meet her?"

Honma shook his head. "She was on vacation. Girl by the name of Orie Chino, also in General Clerical. She's gone sightseeing in Australia for two weeks, on a trip she's been planning for a while. I did get a phone number, though."

"Wada gave you all that? How do you know he wasn't just making it up?"

"Because I had him get online and call up her address and time sheet, just to be sure."

"They even got everyone's working hours on computer?" Funaki winced. "Then how about Kyoko Shinjo's …"

"Her alibi?" Honma grinned, then assumed a serious expression. "You mean whether she was on the job November 25, 1989, when Shoko Sekine's mother died? Sure, I checked that, all right."

Naturally, Wada had been suspicious about why Honma should be interested in Kyoko's whereabouts that day, but he'd obliged. "I even got a printout," said Honma, sliding the paper under Funaki's nose. "From November 18 through November 26, 1989, Kyoko Shinjo was off on sick leave."

Funaki whistled quietly.

Honma went on. " 'And seeing as you seem to have been on pretty good terms with her,' I told him, I had him call up his own time sheet as well."

"And?"

"November 25 was a Saturday, but he was on the job. At the office until 9:00 P.M."

"So that lets him off the hook?" Funaki said skeptically. "I don't know, I still think he's got something going on that he may not want us to know about."

"Well, let's just keep an eye on him for a while and see if he does anything interesting."

The tangle was starting to look like something now. The knots were beginning to loosen, so there was no need to rush things.

"After my talk with Wada I took a stroll through Osaka."

"Your leg all right?" asked Funaki with undisguised concern, which seemed somehow out of place in a detective.

"I managed to hobble around a bit," Honma smiled. "You know what? Osaka's a great city. There's a whole different dimension to it compared to Tokyo. It's a no-frills kind of town."

"No frills?"

"Yeah. In Tokyo, downtown around Nihombashi, you've got these ultramodern offices and 'intelligent buildings' right up against the old two-story shops. Osaka's got none of that. Where it's a trade district, it's one hundred percent shops and nothing else. Cross over one street and suddenly you're in a red-light district, the sort of area where you wouldn't be too surprised to see a mob shootout."

"Me, I could never live in Osaka. Can't stomach the food or the Hanshin Tigers," Funaki mumbled.

Honma let it drop. "Say, I was wondering if I could ask you another favor."

"Let me guess. A copy of Kyoko Shinjo's family register," Funaki said with a smile.

"You got it."

"Working backward from the address in her Roseline papers, it's not such a tall order."

"Only …"

"You still want me to keep it hush-hush, right? No problem." He clamped his jaw shut, for emphasis. "In actual fact, it *is* a difficult case. If we go official with it at this stage, they might just bump us off it. Who knows, they might not even treat it as a missing persons case."

This time Honma beat him to the punch. "Because they've got another, more pressing case to get on with, huh?"

"How'd you guess?"

"Which is precisely why I'd like to keep it under wraps a while longer," said Honma, looking down. "I mean, we haven't even got a corpse. They could say we weren't sure that Shoko Sekine was really dead, and that'd be that."

"You think she could be alive?"

"I'm almost positive she's not."

"I'm with you there."

"But how would you have disposed of the corpse?"

Funaki suddenly sat bolt upright. "Right! It'd take a lot of muscle for one woman. So maybe she did have some friendly help."

Honma nodded absentmindedly. "Me, I think she was working alone from start to finish. I've got no particular reason for saying that, just a gut feeling." The sheer strength of her will, her deadeye aim. The total lack of emotion she showed in dropping out of Jun Kurisaka's life, and probably Wada's before that. The way she just threw out any excess baggage. Everything about her said "alone."

It was because she was so alone, Honma thought, that she had tried to become someone else. If a close friend had been there to understand, she wouldn't have done it; she'd have accepted some help and skipped out as Kyoko Shinjo. A name only exists because another person calls you by it. If someone had cared for her, she'd never have tossed her name away like an old tire. There's love in a name.

"No accomplice? Then that would mean ..." Funaki followed Honma's eyes. There in the kitchen, fixed to a corner of the counter, was a knife rack. Vegetable, fish, paring knives. Five different blades, housed neatly in a sheath block. Isaka had brought it over. He was particular about his cooking implements.

Funaki said nothing.

"I'll look into that angle," said Honma. "Check newpapers in the library, and have a magazine reporter I know get onto it, too. Not everything's police work."

"Easy enough to spot. Makes a big splash," agreed Funaki, rubbing his chin. "Unidentified body parts."

The next afternoon, Tamotsu Honda came by.

He was wearing jeans that had been washed over and over again to a warm light-blue shade, and a hand-knit sweater over a white cotton shirt. When he took off his heavy wool jacket and reached up to hang it on one of the hooks just inside the door, Honma noticed that the spare buttons had been snipped off the lining. Ikumi was obviously a sharp housewife. Chizuko used to do the same. Whenever she bought new clothes, she'd cut the spare buttons off and put them away in her sewing basket, saying they would rub and damage the fabric. All the clothes Honma had bought since her death still had the spare buttons attached. Somehow he couldn't bring himself to clip them off.

Tamotsu lingered awkwardly in the entryway. Honma needed to urge him repeatedly before he would even sit down. After a brief silence, he placed a bag from a well-known bakery on the table. "This is for, um, your son."

His wife's idea, no doubt, Honma thought as he thanked him.

They were just about to start talking when Isaka showed up after having his lunch at home. "Young Tamotsu here is soon to be a second-time father," Honma said after introducing them.

"Hey, I'm twenty-eight."

Isaka smiled in evident pleasure, before saying abruptly: "Shoko Sekine was twenty-eight, too, wasn't she? Couldn't have been more different, though, your lives."

Tamotsu looked shocked to hear her spoken of in the past tense.

"So when did you arrive in Tokyo?" Honma said quickly.

"Hm? Oh, yesterday."

Before he left Utsunomiya, Honma had taken Tamotsu aside and asked him to collect as much information locally as he could about Shoko's life before her disappearance. Where they would go from there was anybody's guess.

"I came up with all sorts of stuff," Tamotsu said, pulling open his knapsack.

Isaka put on a pot of coffee and drew up a chair.

Tamotsu took out a small notebook and placed it open on the table. "Ikumi said I should write down everything I found out."

"Mm, good idea."

He cleared his throat. "One girl from our class in school said she'd run into Shoko once, two or three years ago. Said she was wearing such a loud getup, she didn't know what'd come over her."

"Must have been when she was working at Lahaina."

"She couldn't remember the exact date. Two or three years ago was the best she could come up with. She did say Shoko was carrying half a watermelon, so that would make it summer."

In Honma's experience, this was about as good as most people's memory was.

"Shoko seemed happy enough, but she was wearing real heavy makeup. This classmate had heard some of the usual rumors, so she just said, 'Tough breaks, huh?' And Shoko had answered, 'Yup. Guess so.'"

"About all she could say," Isaka said, as if speaking from experience, "—meeting up with an old classmate when you're down on your luck."

Tamotsu went on: "I figured my best chance would be to ask around about what had happened when Shoko's old lady died, so I went and found everybody who'd come to the wake or the funeral. Thought it was going to take a lot of doing, but it wasn't so bad. There were only a few who had anything to say—old women, mostly."

Tamotsu asked first about Shoko, then if any of them had ever seen the woman in the photograph. "They didn't hold the wake at Akane Villa. The landlord's wife wouldn't let them. They rented a place that was about five minutes away by car. The neighbors handled a lot of the arrangements for Shoko."

He took a sip of coffee as he flipped back through the earlier pages of the notebook.

"Most people just thought the same as me. That Shoko looked really shocked. Some of them had comments to make about her red hair, how it wasn't the time or place, stuff like that."

"People are conservative when it comes to weddings and funerals," offered Isaka.

"That's for sure. But anyway, nobody had ever seen the woman in the photo, the one who's passing herself off as Shoko. They all said that if some young woman they didn't know had shown up to offer her condolences, they'd have been asking all about her."

Honma nodded. People at funerals are either vultures or hawks.

"But ..." Tamotsu rubbed his nose. "There was one person who recognized her."

Honma and Isaka leaned forward.

"And the funny thing is," he said with a hint of a grin, "it was my old lady."

Honma's eyes widened. "Your mother?"

"Yeah, and I never even asked. It was her who brought it up. Said she'd heard at the beauty parlor that somebody was in town asking about Shoko."

She must have had her hair done by Kanae Miyata, the beautician Honma had loaned the picture of Kyoko Shinjo to, back when he'd still known her only as "the fake Shoko." He was glad to see it had been put to good use.

"At the L'Oréal Salon?"

"Huh? You mean you knew?" Tamotsu was impressed. "Mrs. Miyata, the hairdresser, showed her this photo."

And his mother had recognized the woman?

"Usually she's got a terrible memory. But the minute she smells something a bit fishy, it's amazing what she can remember. When my grandfather died, the priest who did the last rites couldn't sit still, apparently. She says she can remember the mole on his neck. Then later that same priest embezzled some money from the parish and ran off with this woman and it was a big scandal—sorry, I don't know why I'm telling you this."

"No, that's fine. I get your point: it's like your mother's memory comes with a sort of a sixth sense."

Tamotsu bobbed his head in agreement. "Well, she says she saw that woman one time as she was leaving the beauty parlor."

"When? Or about when?"

"Well, she was a bit hazy about the date at first," he said. "But she'd been getting ready for the memorial service for Mrs. Sekine—

the forty-ninth day of mourning. So she checked a calendar and saw that it was a Sunday. January 14, 1990."

"Wait, run that by me again ..."

"See, Shoko didn't have any relatives. So all the neighbors arranged the forty-ninth day service. I had this urgent job I couldn't shake, so my old lady went instead. And, well, she had to look presentable, so she went to have her hair done.

"When she comes out of the place, she sees this young woman standing there across the street, in front of Akane Villa. She calls out to her, 'Hello there. Can I help you with something?' But the woman takes off. Which must have really gotten to my mom, because she actually ran after her a little ways, shouting 'Hey, wait—you—wait a minute!' But the woman was too fast. She still remembers her face, though—says she was as pretty as a movie star."

Honma sketched out a rough timetable in his head. The forty-ninth day service was held on January 14, 1990. Not exactly forty-nine days after Mrs. Sekine's death on November 25, 1989, but they probably chose the first Sunday after the New Year's holidays. Ten days later, Shoko Sekine goes off to see the attorney to ask about the insurance money; the cost of the funeral was probably weighing on her mind. Kyoko Shinjo quits Roseline on December 31, 1989, and gets busy preparing for the big switch. Maybe comes up to Utsunomiya once, to check things out.

"Where was the service held?" asked Isaka.

"At the temple where Mrs. Sekine's ashes are being kept for the time being."

Isaka rubbed his eyebrows. "But when a wife dies, don't they usually put her together with the husband, in the same grave?"

"That's right."

After a short pause, Honma said: "You mean her husband didn't have a grave, either? Couldn't he afford one?"

Tamotsu shook his head. "Nope. He was the third son in a large family, so he never had much to begin with. And he died when Shoko was still just a baby. Things were always tight, and yet ..."

"And yet," Isaka read his mind, "when Mrs. Sekine went to her husband's family to ask them to help her buy a plot for him, they gave her the brushoff. One of those old families: everything for the first son, nothing for the rest. Is that it?"

"Pretty much. That's why she had to leave her husband's ashes at a temple, which is where they've stayed all this time. Every five or ten years, she'd make a small offering to the temple, but not nearly enough for a plot."

"So Mrs. Sekine's remains finally went there as well."

"Right. It broke Shoko's heart. She swore that someday she'd see her folks laid to rest in a proper grave. Even though she herself was pretty deep in debt at the time."

"And aside from your mother," Honma said, steering the conversation back to the photo, "no one else saw the woman?"

Tamotsu shrugged. "Afraid not. Mrs. Miyata says she's sorry she couldn't do any better."

Nothing to apologize for, thought Honma. Witnesses to the most shocking crimes sometimes only have sketchy memories of them, but here he'd asked about something perfectly normal—had anybody seen a pretty but otherwise unremarkable young woman?—and the L'Oréal Salon had come through.

Shoko Sekine and Kyoko Shinjo. Two individuals connected only through the Roseline database. Together again in another, completely different place—in Shoko's hometown, for her mother's memorial service.

"Actually, we've identified the woman we're looking for," Honma said.

Tamotsu seemed to shrink. What had been only a notion was suddenly real. Shoko's stand-in was no phantom now but flesh and blood. He'd been afraid of this moment.

"So who is she? How did she know Shoko?" If she turned out to be a friend of Shoko's, someone Shoko had trusted, he wasn't sure what he would do.

"A total stranger."

Tamotsu listened intently. He bit his lip now and again, and kept his eyes cast down. When Honma finished, all three men fell silent. Then Isaka got up to clear away the coffee cups, just to be doing something.

After a time, Tamotsu said, "But Shoko was only minding her own business."

"Exactly."

"She wanted something nice, so she bought herself some fancy underwear. Even I can understand that. Ikumi hardly ever gets to buy any new clothes, but she says she doesn't mind as long as she feels pretty underneath."

"Shoko was punctual about her Roseline payments. She paid by postal transfer. They said she was a good customer."

*A good customer.* Tamotsu mouthed the words to himself, clenching his fists under the table.

Bit late to try and protect her now, thought Honma. But then what was *he* doing looking for Kyoko Shinjo himself instead of turning the case over? Just force of habit? Morbid curiosity? Whatever the reason, he wanted to meet this Kyoko Shinjo. To hear her voice. To hear what she had to say when he asked, "Why did you do it?"

Honma wouldn't even consider letting Tamotsu stay in a hotel; he insisted on putting him up, starting that night. So they went to collect his things. Then, after taking a short rest, Honma began sorting though his notes, which reminded him to give that magazine stringer who owed him one a call.

The reporter was curious and asked all kinds of questions, but was unable to pry anything out of Honma. Nevertheless, he agreed to help. "Whenever I work with you, Honma, I usually turn up something I can use. So give me two or three days, I'll see what I can find. Tokyo-Kanto area, right?"

"Uh-huh," he answered automatically, then corrected himself. "No, make that Kofu-Shinetsu, too." No particular reason. Just a hunch about Kyoko Shinjo: knowing her, she might well head up into the mountains to dispose of a body.

Next, Honma went to the library to look for articles on Mrs. Sekine's death. Two of the three major national papers had carried the story—tiny filler pieces, but all the facts were there. He made copies and left. He now felt in a position to try to work out Kyoko Shinjo's *modus operandi*.

For some reason—probably because somebody or other was after her—Kyoko needed a new identity. She goes to work at Roseline specifically as a means to that end—this seemed more likely than imagining that she'd simply stumbled onto the idea once she'd started the job. Just how she gets around the checkpoints in the computer system is still a question mark, though she probably used Wada in some way. That would explain why he was so nervous. But obtain the data she does, and Shoko Sekine becomes her prime target. For Shoko's family register and residence certificate, all she has to do is go to the Ward Office in Shoko's neighborhood and get them "in person."

Her next step, then, is to get rid of Shoko's one living relative, her mother. So many questions remained about how she might have pulled this off that even to Detective Sakai's trained eyes the whole thing had to be an accident or a suicide. But what if ...

What if on that night—November 25—she manages to lure Mrs. Sekine out on some kind of pretext. Say she arranges to meet her somewhere not far from Tagawa. If she sets a time, then naturally she has a good idea when Mrs. Sekine should be leaving.

*How would anyone waiting in that noisy bar know when Mrs. Sekine stepped out of Tagawa?* Make an appointment, that's how.

As a pretext, Kyoko comes up with something minor, nothing big enough to make Mrs. Sekine give up going to Tagawa altogether and stay at home waiting. Suppose she says she's a friend of Shoko's from Tokyo, and that Shoko asked her to pass something over. That she'll be arriving late at night, with a friend, and can't stay long—could she just see her for maybe five minutes? That would be enough.

So Kyoko waits in the bar next door. She steps out just in time to catch Mrs. Sekine leaving Tagawa, pushes the old woman down the stairs, then hurries back to her bar. The dance floor is crowded. Nobody notices one customer more or less.

Still, Kyoko would need to have known in advance about Mrs. Sekine's drinking habits, not to mention the dangerous staircase at the bar. None of that was there in the Roseline files. At some stage, she must have met up with Shoko—that seemed obvious. Evidence of that contact was the next thing Honma planned to find.

Okay, then, jumping forward in time a bit: Kyoko kills Shoko, disposes of the body, and assumes her identity. She moves out of Kawaguchi Co-op, takes an unannounced permanent leave from Lahaina, and disappears. Suddenly she's working for Imai Office Machines. She's set herself up in the Honancho apartment and registered herself as the head of her own family, listing the new apartment as her permanent address. She also uses it as her current local address and on her applications for National Health, National Pension Fund, private insurance and so on. Public Employment proves tricky because she can't get her hands on Shoko's Public Employment card, so she goes to the window and tells them, *It's my first real job.*

Then she gets to know Jun Kurisaka, gets engaged ...

The credit card, that was another unanswered question. Up until the time Kyoko-as-Shoko started planning for the wedding and Jun put pressure on her to get a card, she had never taken out *any* plastic. If she had, she'd have known right away about Shoko's bankruptcy. Did she simply dislike credit cards? Some people are just against them on principle.

Then there was the Polaroid, the only real clue he had to Kyoko's identity. Why had it been taken? And why on earth had she held on to it? Was there some special memory attached to it? But why cling to a memory connected with a person she was desperate to disown? It didn't figure. Honma closed his notebook.

Soon after four, Makoto came home just long enough to announce that he'd "made plans" with Kazzy. Isaka was starting to cook dinner, steaming up the kitchen, when in walked Tamotsu, Boston bag in hand. Just then the phone started ringing.

"Is that the Honma residence?" It was Imai of Imai Office Machines, calling from the office. He wanted to know if Honma had found Miss Sekine yet.

"Well, not so far," Honma told him.

He sighed. "Mitchie here is worried, too. Oh yes, there's something else she's been meaning to tell you. Here, let me put her on."

"Mr. Honma, remember that question you asked, about what to call the son of your wife's cousin?"

"Did you find out?"

"No, I didn't." She sounded apologetic.

"Well, I thought it might be tough. You haven't been checking all this time?"

"I'm not too good at this kind of thing."

"Nobody's good at this kind of thing."

Mitchie changed her tone of voice. "Ms. Sekine hasn't shown up yet?"

"Maybe it's hard for her to come back."

"It must be hard on Mr. Kurisaka, too."

"Could be just what he needs, though."

"You know, I happened to remember something. They had a fight once, the two of them."

"A fight?"

"That's right. Over the engagement ring. Ms. Sekine, see, she said that a person's birthstone had nothing to do with it, you could buy any ring you liked. But Mr. Kurisaka said it had to be either your birthstone or a diamond; otherwise it wasn't a real engagement ring."

Just the sort of pigheaded thing Jun would say, Honma thought. "Mitchie," he asked, "did Ms. Sekine have a favorite stone? One that wasn't her birthstone but that she wanted him to buy anyway?"

"Uh-huh, that's what it was all about."

Covering the mouthpiece with his palm, Honma gestured to Isaka in the kitchen. "Know anything about birthstones?" he asked him.

Isaka stood there, blinking, a ladle in his hand. "Ah ... no more than average."

Honma shot him a question. Isaka answered in the same breath. Honma then uncovered the receiver. "Mitchie, Ms. Sekine's birthstone was a sapphire, I believe. And that's what they ended up buying, wasn't it?"

"Yes. The stone for September."

"Now, let me guess what she wanted Jun to buy."

"Uh—so, you know?"

"My guess would be an emerald."

Mitchie squealed. "Amazing! How did you know?"

That Kyoko was a sly one, Honma thought. Emerald was the stone for May, the month of her birth. She'd wanted her own birthstone—a *real* engagement ring.

Mitchie's voice came through again. "If Ms. Sekine comes back, please tell her that Mr. Imai and I have been worried about her. Tell her we really want to see her."

He would, he promised, and just for one brief moment, as he hung up the phone, he almost felt a little sympathy for their "Shoko," the one he knew as Kyoko.

*We really want to see her.*

Suddenly his thoughts were interrupted by a commotion in the hallway as the front door slammed open and shut. It was Makoto. He was digging into the closet, trampling on fallen stacks of newspapers, kicking a stray ball out of the way, tugging at a metal softball bat with both hands.

"Makoto! What's gotten into you?" Honma shouted. "Where do you think you're going with that?" But the kid wasn't listening. His face was a tearful, muddy mess.

"I'll stop him," Tamotsu said, going over to the boy. "Hey! Don't go swinging that thing around! Give it to me." Makoto kicked and cried, but Tamotsu wrestled the bat away from him. Makoto sank to his knees.

"Did you get into a fight?" Honma asked, crouching down beside him. His knees and elbows were covered in scrapes. One shin had a fresh bruise that was growing bluer by the minute. "If you did, that bat's not playing fair. You ought to know better! You could hurt someone with that."

Choking with tears, panting, Makoto struggled to get out a few words in his own defense. "Block ... Blockhead ..."

"Blockhead?" Honma and Isaka both prompted.

"*Blockhead*?" Tamotsu asked.

"Dog's name," Honma explained. "What happened? Did you find him?"

"He's dead," Makoto said between clenched teeth.

"Dead?"

"That bully, Tazaki, from school. He killed him—killed Blockhead, then threw his body away."

"What?" Isaka's voice broke. "Are you sure?"

"Sure, I'm sure. I just ... just found out."

212

"And that's why you were fighting?"

"Uh-huh," came a different voice from above. They all looked up to see Kazzy standing in the doorway, a pudgy little guy, no less scuffed up than Makoto, his face also streaked with mud and tears. There was a gash in his cheek. "Tazaki, that bum, he killed Blockhead and put him in the trash. We knew he did it, but at first he wouldn't admit it. But then all of us ganged up, so finally he admitted—"

"No, it wasn't like that," Makoto wailed. "He'd have come out and told about it anyway. He was bragging about it at school."

"But why would he want to kill Blockhead?" asked Isaka, anger burning in his cheeks.

"He said you're not supposed to have pets here in the apartment project. Said it was against the rules."

"Still, is that any reason to kill a dog?"

"B-b-but …," Makoto said, "it was against the rules, he said, so it was okay to kill him. To teach us a lesson."

"That's horrible," said Tamotsu. "That's what you were fighting about? Well, next time count me in, too."

But by then both boys seemed to have cooled to the idea of going another round with Tazaki. Kazzy just muttered, " 'If you don't like it,' he says, 'go buy yourself a real house.' "

" 'A real house'—"

"Like his family lives in, I suppose."

"Which is why he can have a dog. But let a poorer family keep a pet, never. Must be some complex he's got." No sooner had Honma spoken than both boys burst into tears again. Honma and Isaka looked at each other over the heads of the sobbing children.

"What the heck's going on?" Tamotsu said, glancing at the metal bat lying at his feet.

## ✧ 21 ✧

The next day, Honma found himself face-to-face with the woman Shoko Sekine had begun rooming with when she filed for personal bankruptcy and could no longer pay the rent on the Castle Mansion Kinshicho apartment. Her name was Tomie Miyagi. Honma had been give the name and phone number by the girl in Mizoguchi's office.

Shoko's former co-worker at Gold had the long fingernails, gold-dusted sandals, frizzy auburn perm and indelible perfume of a bar girl. Twenty-five, maybe twenty-six, though Honma would have sworn, from talking to her on the phone, that she was over forty. Her sand-and-gravel voice had silted up heavily for her age.

"I can't take bright light, this time of day. Hope you don't mind sitting in the back."

They'd arranged to meet in a coffee shop that had just opened near her condo in Shibuya. Tamotsu had come, too. It was well past noon, and the place was deserted.

"I was worried about Shoko when she cut off all contact like that. But I told myself, who knows? Maybe Mr. Right's come along. Who am I to go sticking my nose in?" Tomie puffed on a Seven Stars and gave a little shrug, her shoulders enveloped in a huge, loose sweater. "So you've got no idea what's happened to her?"

"No, she just disappeared without a trace. When was the last time you saw her?"

Tomie shook her head. "I've been trying to remember, ever since you called. The year before last—around New Year's, I think it was."

Honma showed her the photo of Kyoko Shinjo. Tomie examined it long enough for her cigarette to burn down in the ashtray. Then she said slowly, "I don't know her. Never seen her before in my life."

"Not even at the club?"

"No, she's a real knockout, so I'd remember her. There's five girls at Gold. That's kind of a lot for one bar, maybe, but we're only a step up from those feelie cabarets."

"How about as a customer?"

Tomie lit a new cigarette and let out a smoky puff of a laugh. "No girl would come in by herself. Or in a group, for that matter. It's not that kind of place. We don't get write-ups in the women's magazines."

Tamotsu swiftly looked away. Tomie was staring at him with great interest.

"What was Shoko like at work?"

She didn't have to think long. "Desperate."

"For money?"

"What else? Those bill collectors were practically beating down the door of the club. Luckily, they weren't your hard-core yakuza types. She managed to steer clear of *them*, which is something to be thankful for, I suppose. It's a wonder, though, she didn't get herself sold into one of those soap-and-sex joints. For a while there, I tried to convince her just to drop everything and run."

"Counting both credit card companies and loan-sharking operations, she'd racked up debts of over ten million yen. Were you aware of that?"

Tomie shrugged. "Crazy. I knew it was a lot."

Tamotsu looked up sharply. "Easy for you to say 'crazy.' Happens to a lot of people, though."

"Oh, you must be the old friend from back home," she said with an acid edge. "So I guess you'd know, then, Shoko always used to say she came to Tokyo only because she couldn't stand it out there in the boondocks any more."

Honma glanced at Tamotsu, who was holding himself very straight, with no expression on his face.

Tomie looked at Honma. "Not a single good memory, that's what she said. It seemed like she always wanted to get away from her hometown and lead a totally different life. Guess she found out, though, it's not so easy. Can't change your life just like that."

215

"At least not for the better," Honma added.

"Right, not for the better." She smiled knowingly. "Any dreams Shoko might have had about the life of a glamorous working girl went out the window with her first office job. The salary was next to nothing and the dorm was a dump."

"Kasai Trading," said Honma. "I stopped in this morning, actually." A complete waste of time. The personnel manager was remarkably unfriendly. He claimed that staff turnover was so brisk there would be little point in checking personnel files. Naturally, he didn't bother to look at the photo of Kyoko Shinjo. Not that it mattered much. If Honma was right in thinking that it was after she went to work for Roseline that Kyoko had picked out Shoko—in other words, sometime after July 1988—then the visit to Kasai Trading was only double-checking. Still, it was never pleasant to get that kind of reception.

"I didn't catch the name of the company, but that's probably it. Anyway, the dorm was bad enough, but things got even worse when she left there. She really hit bottom then. Not surprising, considering. The rent at Mansion Kinshicho was *ridiculous*."

"Which is probably why she started borrowing."

Tomie looked into her pack of cigarettes and counted the number left, then took another out and lit up. "She started living on credit and, next thing she knows, she's in cuckooland."

"Cuckooland?"

"I don't know what else to call it," she said, throwing up her hands. "No money, no education. No special skills. Her face is nothing to make a banker go open up the vault. Working for a third-rate company. For her, the good life isn't anything she's going to get by plugging away at it. She wants it, she's just going to have to go after it, *some* way. Back in the old days, used to be you either worked your way up or put up with what you had. Right?"

Tamotsu looked like he had something to say, but Honma nodded for her to continue.

"Not any more, though. Now nobody wants to work at their dreams. But nobody's willing to give them up, either. For Shoko, it was money for shopping, courtesy of the credit card companies. No limits, no questions asked. With other people, it's something else.

"It's not just women, either, you know. There are so many men knocking themselves out to get into a good school, to land that perfect job, right? Same thing, same kind of fantasy, although *that* one's considered respectable."

Honma thought back to what Ms. Sawagi had said about the "consumer finance scare" of the late 1980s. How people *had* to have their dream houses, even if it meant putting their souls in hock. As if owning a piece of land would mean instant happiness.

"Used to be not every young couple could lay their hands on the kind of cash to back up their fantasies. Also there weren't so many different places to pour money into. No expensive makeovers, no cosmetic surgery, no fancy prep schools, no glossy magazines showing every product ever made." Tomie was so wound up she forgot to light her cigarette. "Everything's easy now. All the dreams that money can buy. Those that have, spend it, and those that don't, borrow their pocket money and wind up like Shoko."

"By the way, how long have you been at Gold?"

"Seven, eight years. Before that I buried one club myself. My husband and I owned it together till it went bust and he ran off. Didn't file for bankruptcy, though. It wasn't so hard to settle up decently. I talked things over with my creditors. Actually, I'm still paying off the debt."

Another puff of smoke curled from her lips. "Something my husband said one time? I had to admit it was a good one. So why does a snake shed its skin, he says?"

"A snake?"

"Yeah. It takes a lot of effort to do that. So why does it do it?"

Tamotsu jumped in ahead of Honma. "So it can grow another."

Tomie cackled. "Wrong. So it can grow *legs*. The thing is, snakes get on okay without legs, but they look around and see everybody else has them. So they get the idea they've got to have them too. Score one for my husband there. The world's full of snakes who'd slither right into debt for some legs."

*I just wanted to be happy ...*

"Me, I'd seen it all before. So when Shoko didn't have anywhere else to turn, I let her stay with me," said Tomie. "Then she filed for bankruptcy and went to work at some new club—"

"Lahaina."

"I guess. Even after she started there and moved out to Kawaguchi, she'd call up every once in a while. We'd have lunch. That would have been up through the spring of the year before last, maybe earlier. When her mother died, see, she got really depressed. So I said, let's go stay at a hot spring. Lighten up a bit ..."

"And that was the last time you heard from her?"

"Right." Tomie frowned vacantly. "I'm not one for chasing after people. If someone stops calling me, I usually just let it go. That's how things ended with Shoko. Afraid I'm not much help."

"About the time Shoko was living in Kawaguchi—say, around the time her mother died—do you remember hearing anything else in particular?"

"What do you mean?"

"Some change, something new. Maybe she made some new friend, started going to a new beauty parlor, anything."

Tomie ran a hand through her hair. "Ever since you called, I've been trying to come up with some details about her you might be interested in. But I keep drawing a blank. Hey, what do you expect?— I can hardly remember a phone call the minute I put the receiver down." She sat frowning, with her hands pressed together at the tip of her nose. Honma and Tamotsu looked on in silence.

"It's no good," she sighed. "Trying to force it doesn't help. Let's see, for a while there, she was getting dirty phone calls and it had her spooked ... but that's not so unusual." Her eyes brightened. "Wait a minute, now I remember. She called me, all paranoid on account of those phone calls, and said somebody had been opening her mail."

"Her mail? At Kawaguchi Co-op?"

"I forget the name of the apartments, but yeah, in Kawaguchi. She said the envelopes had been cut open. I told her she was making too much of it, that it was probably just a prank, or maybe some mistake at the post office. This was right around the time her mother's insurance money came in, which was the first real money she'd seen since she went bankrupt. I had to laugh because she said she was planning to buy a grave for her mother. That's a good million or two right there."

Honma just looked at her. He was thinking back to the box of things Shoko had left behind, which the landlady had pulled out to show him. One was a brochure from a Green Grove Mortuary, if he remembered right. "Was she seriously thinking of buying a plot?"

This, too, provoked a laugh. "Seriously? I'd say it was serious. She even went on a guided tour. Took one of their private buses. I told her I bet she was popular with the company, somebody so young going to a place like that. But I remember she said no, there was another girl there, even younger than her. And the two of them had gotten to talking about how strange it was, having to buy graves at their age ..."

Honma called Shoko's landlady first to check on the name of the cemetery, then phoned Green Grove Mortuary itself.

The head office was on the ground floor of a tidy little building in north central Tokyo. The walls were covered with photos of gravesites for sale and of different hills and wooded areas in the cemetery. A huge scale model in the lobby showed a second, soon-to-be-completed site nestled in the hills of outlying Gumma prefecture.

The middle-aged funeral director who greeted Honma and Tamotsu was polite and soft-spoken. When Honma asked about Shoko and the brochure she'd had, the man said she probably would have toured the grounds near Imaichi which they'd been promoting for some time.

"She's been having some trouble over an inheritance. I just wanted to check whether my niece did in fact come here."

He didn't miss a beat. "Everyone who participates in our tours receives a handsome group photograph as a memento. We also keep copies for our records. Would you care to have a look?"

Honma and Tamotsu hung around in the lobby until the man returned with a large photo album.

"This covers the period January to April 1990." He opened it, then left them to their own devices. Tamotsu and Honma raced through the pages—January 18—January 29—February 4—February 12—

"Here!" Tamotsu was tapping his finger on one page.

Sunday, February 18, 1990. Green Grove Mortuary Visitors—Tour Group 13.

Two employees, a man and a woman, crouched on either side, holding out the ends of an official-looking green banner. The tour group consisted of no more than eight people. Front and center was Shoko Sekine. They must have put her there specially. So young, poor girl.

With so few people, the group shot was fairly close-up. All the faces were in sharp focus. Shoko's was the face he'd seen in Tamotsu's high school snapshot, but under a new hairstyle. Long tight curls dyed chestnut brown had started to grow out, showing the dark roots. Dressed in a loose cotton jacket and jeans, she was squinting into the light and looking altogether too casual for someone on a cemetery tour. Smiling, even. You could see her teeth. Framed by crescent lips, a jumble of crooked teeth.

And there, right alongside her, showing a perfect set of white teeth, was a smiling Kyoko Shinjo. Two women, too young to be alone in the world or to be out shopping for family plots. They were shoulder-to-shoulder, arm-in-arm.

"Shoko," murmured Tamotsu.

## ✧ 22 ✧

An hour and a half from Nagoya by Kintetsu Line special express lies the quiet provincial city of Ise, famous for Ise Shrine, the most sacred site in the Shinto religion. This was the home of Kyoko Shinjo's ex-husband, Yasuji Kurata, who was now thirty years old. Honma had tracked him down via the records Funaki had gotten for him.

A cursory look at the Ise phone book in Honma's local library yielded a surprisingly large number of companies under the name Kurata. Among the biggest was a real estate agency near the station. Their quarter-page ad listed the company president, Sojiro Kurata, and, right below him, Yasuji Kurata, as licensed agents.

Divorced from Kyoko over four years earlier, he had married again and was now the father of a two-year-old daughter.

When Honma called from Tokyo, Kurata's mother answered. No sooner had he mentioned the name Kyoko Shinjo, however, than the conversation died. There was a full ten seconds of silence, during which he didn't dare speak.

Okay, so let her hang up, Honma thought—he'd just call back again. But no, the mother's voice finally rasped through the line: "What do you plan to ask him?"

Honma sketched the situation between Kyoko and her new fiancé as simply as possible. "I thought perhaps he might be able to put me in touch with friends of Kyoko's, who would know where she is. That's all I want to ask." He tacked on various apologies, saying he knew it was an imposition, and bound to be unpleasant …

Quite unexpectedly, the old woman said, "Things *were* unpleasant, but that's all past now." Then, after a moment, as if to herself, "Poor Kyoko."

"Could I possibly speak to him?"

Another silence, followed by another thrust. "We all have things to regret about the way we treated Kyoko. But you're looking for information about her present situation and I'm afraid that, frankly, we don't have any idea where she is. And speaking to my son would only open up old wounds." This was clearly meant to be the last word on the subject. Before he knew it, the dial tone was buzzing in his ear.

Honma had never imagined that the Kurata household would be an easy nut to crack, but being dismissed out-of-hand this way only got him more fired up. He told Makoto and Isaka that he'd be away for a couple of days.

"Call to say you're still alive, okay?" was all Makoto could say.

As the bullet train pulled out of Tokyo Station, he caught a glimpse of Isaka and Makoto trudging down the stairs from the platform. Out to do some shopping; that was their excuse for coming all the way into town to see him off. By now *they* looked like father and son, he thought.

Honma changed to a special express at Nagoya. Settling into the plush seat, he started leafing through the material on "unidentified body parts" that his magazine contact had found and downloaded for him. It was the off season, and the train was virtually empty. Honma took advantage of the extra space to stretch out his legs.

The journalist had been efficient. He'd even drawn up a detailed chart: Site, Part(s) Found, Approx. Age, Sex, Personal Articles Found, plus a Remarks column for progress reports. It didn't take Honma long to find what he was looking for.

On "Children's Day," 1990—May 5—the remains of the left arm, torso, calves and feet of a young female had been found at the edge of a cemetery in Nirazaki, in the mountains of Yamanashi prefecture. The flesh was in an advanced stage of decomposition. The bones were partly exposed, yet the fingers showed traces of red nail polish. The only "Personal Article" was an anklet on the right foot.

That's her, his instincts told him.

The time frame matched. Shoko Sekine had disappeared from Kawaguchi Co-op on March 17, 1990. Assuming that she'd been killed within a week, the body would easily have been in that condition by May 5.

The various parts had been wrapped in separate plastic sheets and buried in a pile of rubbish in one corner of the cemetery. Crows and stray dogs must have found them first. A protruding arm had caught the eye of someone come to spruce up a family grave.

The plastic sheets were from a take-out sushi chain franchised throughout the Tokyo-Kanto region, and used as wrapping paper. They were so common they were no help at all. The same went for the anklet. A cheap gold-plated thing set with rhinestones, worth two or three thousand yen at most. Hardly worth checking into.

The Yamanashi police had launched an intensive search for the missing head, right arm and thighs, but found nothing. Testimony collected in the vicinity of the crime failed to point to any suspicious characters or mysterious vehicles. Business—regular funeral business—was as usual. The graveyard in question, though small and inconspicuous, was within walking distance of the Nirazaki Kannon, a Buddhist statue of some interest to tourists. The local history museum was nearby, too. Visitors came into town on holidays and weekends, Nirazaki being not far from the vineyards of Kofu or the Sekiwa hot springs. The stray outsider had ceased to attract any attention.

A cemetery in Nirazaki? Would that have been within Kyoko's radius of movement? He'd have to ask her former husband.

So what had happened to the rest of the corpse? Particularly the head.

The whole purpose of dismemberment—cases of ghoulish behavior excluded—was limited to one of two things: to make a victim unidentifiable, or to make a body easier to hide. Often it's women who will cut a body up in order to hide it. Take the case of the dismembered policeman found some years back in a canal on the east side of Tokyo: the culprits turned out to be the dead man's wife and her mother. Ordinarily, carving up a corpse requires tremendous strength, but criminals, like people defending themselves against some physical threat, can sometimes get surges of adrenaline that give them superhuman strength. Or, if a woman set her mind to it, she could shut herself up at home and go about the process at her own pace in the bath.

So Kyoko cuts up Shoko's corpse, dumps half in Nirazaki Cemetery and the rest—where? Technically it might be too early to say that Kyoko did it, but Honma no longer had any doubts. He felt the dark pull of certainty: her signature was on this one.

It was like a game of connect-the-dots, with him tearing all over the country to fill in the blanks. And he wasn't even on official duty. Honma felt his day go gray; the clouds that had loomed overhead as he left Nagoya now pressed in low enough to touch, and just as the loudspeaker announced their imminent arrival in Ise, raindrops beaded on the window. The gloom matched the depressing facts: how short, in retrospect, Kyoko Shinjo's days as a housewife in this quiet town had been, how unhappily they had ended.

Passing through the ticket gate he looked up at the sky, straining his eyes against the cold curtains of mist. Over Kyoko's head, it had always been raining.

Kurata Realty was smaller than he'd expected. It was a narrow, four-story, gray-tiled building with a couple of businesses on the ground floor and office space above. The tiles by the automatic door glistened. Honma had stood to one side, to spy discreetly on the office, when right behind him up popped what looked like a bright yellow squid. It was a schoolkid wearing a long, hooded rainslicker. A pair of oversized rain boots skipped and flapped, then stamped down hard in front of the automatic door. The glass panel slid open.

"What do you think you're doing, silly!" A mother appeared out of nowhere to give the child a slap on the behind, then tugged him sharply by the hand. The boots now gave a stamp of seeming protest and the closing door slid open again.

Honma couldn't help smiling. Even without seeing the face, he knew it was a boy. Left alone again, the kid was now attacking the revolving WE CUT KEYS sign out in front of the shop next door. The mother had to go over and grab the back of his slicker, and drag him away. Makoto was never that impossible, though there were times when he'd cut up a bit with Chizuko.

Honma turned back just as the door was beginning to close. His eyes met those of a young man standing behind the counter in the brightly lit office, about five or six yards away. The automatic door must have caught his attention. The young man seemed to be waiting for Honma to look away first, though doing so meant ignoring the other agents and customers.

That had to be Yasuji Kurata.

Obviously his mother had already warned him.

As Honma took a step forward, a colleague tapped the young man on the shoulder. A telephone call. He took the call, but still seemed distracted.

Muzak wafted through the interior. Several customers sat at the counter, each talking with an agent. A woman arranging resort villa brochures on a display rack stepped over. "May I help you, sir?"

He'd come to see Yasuji Kurata, he told her.

The woman looked surprised. "Mr. Kurata? Do you have an appointment?"

"Yes, I called earlier." Kurata was still on the phone, facing the other way, but he suddenly looked back, as if he'd been listening.

"It's all right, Ms. Kato, I'll be right with him," he said loudly, one hand over the mouthpiece. The woman turned away and went back to her brochures.

As Honma waited for him to hang up, he thought of Kyoko Shinjo, how familiar she must have been with the place: her father-in-law owned it, her husband worked there. She'd probably dropped in from time to time, chatted with the women employees.

Kurata came around the counter and hurried over. "Let's step outside," he muttered, grabbing an umbrella. He followed close on Honma's heels and steered him just out of view of the others inside. "I take it you're the one who called?"

"I figured your mother would have said something."

Kurata licked his lips nervously. "I believe she also told you we had nothing to discuss."

"Does that go for you too?"

"Listen, about what Kyoko is up to—"

Honma cut him short. "Kyoko might be dead."

"What? Why do you say that?" he asked, a bit shaken.

"Any evidence to the contrary?" Get him rattled, then we'll see, thought Honma.

Kurata's nervous laugh broke off. "No … nothing, really."

Standing under the shelter only of a thin umbrella, Honma explained everything again, as he had for Kurata's mother. Kurata hardly looked at him; he seemed to be counting the raindrops dripping from the taut nylon.

"She doesn't mean a thing to me now."

"Is that right? Funny, because she means a lot to me."

Kurata looked up sharply. "Because she dumped your nephew? Is that why you're looking for her?"

"Let's just say I'm concerned."

"Oh, you are, are you?"

"I'm concerned that Kyoko has run out on my nephew for no reason that anybody can name. I'm worried she might be in some kind of serious trouble that she isn't able to handle alone."

"Well, she's no concern of mine any more," he said, spitting out the words.

Honma sighed and got ready to leave. "That's up to you, obviously." He looked down and added, "I'm sorry. I didn't know Kyoko had caused you so much pain."

Kurata glanced at him. "Have you been to Ise Shrine?" he asked suddenly.

"No, never."

He was wavering. The story had hooked him, though any love he'd once felt for Kyoko had long since vanished. At least, he would never use that word to describe it now. But clearly the woman still aroused some feeling in him.

A rotten business, thought Honma, digging up the memories people have worked hard to forget. But dig he must.

Kurata switched the umbrella to his other hand. "Take a taxi to the station and tell the driver to let you off at a place called Akafuku. Everybody knows it. Go into the teashop in the back, not the part where they sell the little sweets. Wait for me there."

"Not that I mind, but won't there be a lot of tourists? You think we can talk there?" Akafuku was famous for its traditional confectionery. It was in all the guidebooks.

"This is the off season. It won't be so crowded. Plus it's a weekday. Anyway, it'll be better for me if you act like a tourist." Kurata lowered his voice. "If I tell everybody you're a Tokyo acquaintance here on business and I'm just showing you around Ise, there won't be any talk. My father's pretty well known around here and people tend to notice me too. If I really wanted to meet someone on the sly, I'd have to go all the way to Nagoya."

"So if word got around that someone was asking about Kyoko, it wouldn't look so good?"

"I wouldn't want word to get around."

His divorce four years earlier must have been a scandal.

"There's my wife to consider, too."

Arranging to meet at four o'clock, they went their separate ways. Honma heard the door slide shut behind him.

It was a set from a made-for-TV samurai drama. A country inn made of dark timber with a large, raised seating area, covered with tatami, at the back. The shop at the entrance was busy, but only a few customers had removed their shoes to step up for tea—in fact, only a group of four middle-aged women in kimono, who were cackling away at the table furthest from Honma's.

Hibachi braziers were set out here and there, their coals giving off a warm glow. Honma had just taken off his wet coat, laid it to one side, and settled back when, right on cue from the samurai drama, a young woman in a farm girl's old-fashioned kimono brought over a teapot and a plate of bean-cakes. Honma wasn't much for sweets. More to Makoto or Isaka's taste, he thought, as he sipped the peaty-tasting green tea. Maybe it was the antique atmosphere—a big iron kettle suspended from a chain was boiling away over a wood fire at the entrance—but the tea tasted quite different here from what he drank at home. He looked up from his cup and saw Kurata pausing to step up into the tatami-matted area.

Kurata settled in at the table and the waitress hurried over with another tray of tea and cakes, which he accepted with a weak smile, then set aside. He looked drained. In the short span of time since they'd met, the knot of his necktie had wilted. He stared vacantly at the coals in the brazier and said nothing. Abruptly he threw out an awkward "It's famous, this place."

Once he got started, though, small talk came easily to him. "Did you notice the number of new wooden buildings around here? We're seeing a lot of local businesses going back to traditional construction instead of concrete. It's something of a trend; people seem to want a return to tradition. It makes a difference with the tourist trade. Next year will be the ritual rebuilding of the shrine that they do every twenty years, so the town will be jammed." Almost in a whisper, he added: "My father's got a hand in these construction projects. Which is why I have to be careful."

"I see. Well, I don't want to stir up any old grudges."

"I have to take your word for it. I could just try getting rid of you, but if that backfired it would only be more trouble in the long run." Reaching for his teacup, he said, looking Honma in the eye: "I warn you, though. If you're one of those media types aiming to dig around in our personal affairs and then go printing a string of lies, you'll be sorry." A brave last effort. And who could blame him? He was only sitting here at all because of some old score between him and Kyoko.

Honma forced a smile and said, "You've got nothing to worry about from me." He then proceeded to fill him in on Kyoko's recent past, the way she'd posed as Shoko Sekine, the way both of them had disappeared—everything except his suspicions of murder. That would just have shut him up completely.

Kurata showed almost no reaction till Honma mentioned that Kyoko had disappeared when her fiancé learned of Shoko's bankruptcy. Half rising from his seat, he said, "I never heard anything so stupid!"

"Stupid?"

"Kyoko would never try passing herself off as someone who'd gone bankrupt."

"She didn't know it had happened."

"You think she assumed someone else's identity without finding out something *that* basic?"

"That's how it would seem." Honma put a hand to his forehead, then suddenly asked: "Are you saying it's impossible because Kyoko had some kind of hangup about credit and loans and all that?"

Kurata nodded. "She *hated* the whole thing, detested it. She always steered clear of it."

That made sense, Honma thought. It fitted in with the puzzling fact that Kyoko-as-Shoko hadn't possessed a single credit card. "Yes, there are lots of people who don't trust plastic."

"That isn't it at all," Kurata said heatedly.

"What, then?"

"There's a lot more to it than that."

A large group of older men—all retired from the same company, apparently—swarmed onto the tatami, taking up several tables near the middle-aged women. They called the waitress over and started barking out their orders like schoolboys. Honma turned away from them and looked Kurata full in the face. "What is it, then?"

"Kyoko's family broke up, a long time ago, over problems with debts." His voice caught slightly, as if the subject called for a different tuning, a scale long disused and unfamiliar. "They couldn't make the payments on their house and had to leave town in a hurry. That was also the reason why Kyoko and I got divorced."

His hand twitched on his lap. He loosened his tie. "When she married me, they took her off her family register back in Mureyama— her hometown—it's in Fukushima prefecture. But they added the usual line to it, saying who she'd married and where my family register was kept. Even after she was living with me and shouldn't really have been involved at all, the bill collectors were still pestering her. They'd dug out her address here, and they came pounding on our door. Kyoko's family had done their flit in the spring of 1983—which was four years before we got married. And the creditors kept their meters running the whole time, so by then the interest was astronomical. They used every trick in the book to get her to pay up. Till finally we decided that the best thing we could do, for everybody concerned, was split up."

## ✧ 23 ✧

Kyoko Shinjo and Shoko Sekine: two of a kind. Shackled to the same past, chased by the same shadow.

"So that's how it was?" Honma murmured. He wiped a hand across his forehead and was surprised to find that it came away damp with sweat. He looked at Kurata and saw a similar surprise in his expression.

"You didn't know?"

"No, this is absolutely the first I've heard of it."

But it figured. It explained why Kyoko Shinjo desperately needed a new identity, and why she was willing to go to such lengths to get one. Kurata was right. If a bill collector were somehow to get access to a person's family register and residence certificate—both supposedly secure and inaccessible—he could keep track of them and hunt them down. This was another reason why debtors were always moving from place to place, unable to hold down a solid job.

That was Kyoko Shinjo's world. She'd been on the run with her parents since—"Let's see, spring of 1983? She'd have been seventeen, still in high school."

"Right. Which is why she dropped out. And she'd really wanted to graduate."

Then four years later, as Kurata had said, they got married. Since she had stayed out of sight for all that time, Kyoko must have thought the bill collectors had given up. But she'd left a paper trail. For under Japanese law, when a couple is married, the bride is automatically removed from her father's family register, with the line "Deleted due to establishment of new household" appearing together with the couple's new address.

230

"It was a housing loan they were running out on?" Honma asked.

Kurata nodded. "Kyoko's father worked for a small firm in Mureyama. An ordinary mid-level office worker. He couldn't keep up the payments, not on what he was making, but he couldn't shake the idea of owning his own home, either. Kyoko told me all about it."

Honma could well imagine the vicious circle the Shinjo family had been caught up in. A small down payment and a large loan. Then, when things got tight, a second loan, for a smaller amount, this time from a loan shark. That set the pinball rolling, picking up speed, then going too fast for anybody to stop.

"Finally, they came up against one of those operations that charge ten percent interest every ten days, a front for the yakuza—all the debts had fallen into their hands, apparently."

The ball had rolled into the worst possible hole. Game over.

"Gangsters would bang on the door in the middle of the night, lean on their relatives, threaten all hell unless somebody paid up. Her mother had a nervous breakdown. The family was thinking about a suicide pact. Kyoko was scared out of her wits." The corners of his mouth twitched. "In fact, the family decision to skip town was made in order to save Kyoko."

A pretty seventeen-year-old schoolgirl was a salable commodity. "They were trying to force her into the skin trade?"

Kurata ducked the question. "She never told me the details. But I know her parents were scared enough to drop everything and run."

The Shinjos had gone first to some cousins in Tokyo, although they knew they couldn't stay; even distant relations would eventually be traced. "That's when they decided they had better split up. Kyoko's father took to the streets. Again, she never said whereabouts, but in Tokyo that probably meant Sanya, where all the day laborers live. The women headed for Nagoya and stayed in a cheap rooming house there, her mother working in a bar and Kyoko waitressing part-time."

They lived like that for maybe a year, keeping in touch with her father by telephone and letters. Then her father had a minor traffic accident and Kyoko's mother went to Tokyo to visit. "It had been a whole year without any hassle, so they let down their guard. The father's whiplash wasn't very serious, and they'd managed to scrape together some savings, so they began making plans to reunite the family in Nagoya. The coast was clear, they thought. And the two of them began visiting those cousins of theirs again. But these harmless visits had repercussions. The mob back in Mureyama had relations in Tokyo too—mob relations—and, sure enough, somebody had been keeping an eye on the place. One day they were leaving the house when they were suddenly grabbed and shoved into the back of a car. I only got all this secondhand from Kyoko, so I don't know the details but … Her father was forced to sign a new interest-bearing repayment contract that required him to work under their surveillance. Her mother was sent back to Mureyama, where she spent the next year in a 'companion service'—more or less a prostitution ring. She was virtually a prisoner. Of course, they put the screws on both parents to try to find out where Kyoko was, but neither of them would say."

When her mother had failed to show up, Kyoko knew they were in trouble. She immediately quit her part-time job in Nagoya and ran, something they had always told her to be ready to do at any time. She then kept sending letters general delivery to a certain post office in Tokyo till eventually—a year later—her mother escaped and managed to get in touch. But her mother had changed, Kyoko said; she was like an empty shell. Not long afterward, she caught flu, which turned into pneumonia, and this killed her. Kyoko would have been twenty-one. "She still had no idea where her father was, though she kept trying to reach him through the same post office. So she was the only one at her mother's funeral."

That's when Kyoko happened to see a want-ad placed by an inn down here in Ise that was looking for live-in help. Eventually, not six months after she'd moved to Ise, her father phoned. Whether he had escaped or simply was no use to anyone any more, he was free. But he was a broken man. He wheezed and barely managed to answer her questions. Kyoko urged him to come to Ise, but he wouldn't listen. " 'I'm finished,' he told her. 'I haven't got the energy to start over. Men aren't as tough as women. I should know.' Finally he just hung up. He probably couldn't afford the long-distance charges."

Kurata wiped his mouth with the back of his hand. "Kyoko never found out where he was." He rummaged around for his cigarettes. "Mind if I smoke?"

Honma nodded for him to go ahead. He noticed that Kurata's hand was shaking as he raised his lighter.

"I knew the family who owned the inn where Kyoko worked. The son was a friend of mine and he introduced us. He said she was good-looking, sharp, a hard worker. And she was."

A live-in maid and the son of a prominent local businessman. For Kurata, it was probably just a lark at first. Honma knew he was being nosy, but he asked anyway.

Kurata smiled nervously. "In the beginning, yes, all I wanted was a bit of fun and games. But as things went on, I began to realize I was in over my head. I was really hooked."

"Because she was beautiful and intelligent?"

"Yes, that, but not only that. There's plenty of beautiful women out there. It's just that, when I was with Kyoko, I … how can I describe it, I felt like a real man. I was solid, confident. I knew Kyoko depended on me and I was there to protect her. That's all."

Honma was listening to Kurata's words but seeing his nephew's face. It was almost the same story. All the time they were together, it was Jun who had made the decisions. Going ahead with the engagement despite his parents' opposition had only made him more determined. When he first learned of her bankruptcy, he hadn't bothered to inform Kyoko, but instead went, on her behalf, straight after the source of this "misinformation."

Kyoko Shinjo's delicate but animated looks attracted the men around her, and the hard time she'd had aroused their protective instincts. Her pathos was seductive. Men *had* to come to her rescue, to shield this flower in their hands.

Come to think of it, Jun and this Kurata had a lot in common. The products of good homes, top of their class in school, sons who did their parents credit. Self-assured, with above-average ability, but, somewhere deep inside, the boy-next-door's need to rebel against his upbringing. Not by anything so obvious as delinquency or openly taking on his parents. After all, he could never hope to better them. To him they remained his good, strong, upright parents, the people who had provided him with a happy childhood, who'd laid down the rules for a good life, who'd done nothing to deserve to be wronged. So he curbed his own rebellious impulses by becoming a bit "parental" himself—and a woman like Kyoko allowed him to do this. Jun and Kurata knew that, however high they rose in the world, they could never treat their parents as equals. They knew, even as they walked the path their parents had marked out for them, that they needed some path of their own where they could "test their mettle," just as they needed some prize to defend. Kyoko was made to order.

She was clever, though. She must have seen straight through that male psychology when she let them come to her defense. As long as she had willing "knights" at her command, she could let them go charging off into battle for her, then shake them down when they came back with the spoils.

Still, if either Jun or Kurata had been the least bit devious, Kyoko might have found herself just being kept on as a mistress, whiling away her youth in the shadow of a real wife. But both of them had turned out to be nice boys—both very young, both needing her in the most honest, traditional way.

Who knows? Maybe that's the way Kyoko wanted things. Although she was barely twenty at the time, she had shown greater resourcefulness than the more pampered Kurata was ever likely to develop.

When Kurata first talked about introducing her to his folks, Kyoko had been flatly against the idea. And they, on their side, were dead set against her. This she'd been smart enough to anticipate, which was why she'd made a show of holding back. Kurata then had no choice but to rally to her defense. *Kyoko has told me everything about her family background. We've discussed it all. She has nothing to be ashamed of ... and I want to marry her.* The words he used must have been practically identical to what Jun had said a few years later.

Kurata's passionate pleading eventually won out, though he and his parents went on arguing right up to the wedding, in June 1987.

"My mother opposed it to the very end, but my father helped bring her around. I can't be sure, but sometimes I'd get the feeling there'd been someone in my father's past, a Kyoko of his own. Only he'd given up on her. It was a distant memory that I'd stirred up

234

again. He never said it in so many words, but twice when my mother wasn't around he got pretty emotional, saying how it was my life, my one shot at the real thing, and I should stick to my guns so as not to regret it later." Kurata was twenty-six when he married her. He could still afford to have romantic notions.

"Kyoko didn't want a big ceremony. There would have been no one from her side. No parents, no relatives. For our honeymoon we spent four days in Kyushu ..." Kurata trailed off. He ran a hand across his face and started again. "We went to the Ward Office and set up a new family register as a couple—the little piece of paper that showed she was my lawfully wedded wife. We were so confident, so proud that we were building a new life."

"There's just one thing I'm still not clear about," Honma said. Kurata stubbed out his cigarette and looked up. "Kyoko wasn't in debt herself. It was her parents who had incurred the debts—her father, for the most part, right? So, legally, no bill collector should have been able to threaten her about repayment. Couldn't you have got an injunction ordering them to stop?" Under Japanese law, parents and children, husbands and wives share liability only for debts on which their joint signatures appear.

"Sure, that's the law," Kurata said with a smile. "But these guys, they know their way around it. They never told Kyoko she was liable; they just let her read between the lines."

*It's money your parents borrowed. You benefited from having it. Now it's time to pay up. Hey you, you tell this young bride of yours that she's got responsibilities.*

"They'd hang around saying, 'Your father's bound to call, just tell us where to find him when he does.' We'd say we didn't know and that the whole thing had nothing to do with us, but they were impossible to shake. They'd turn up at our clients' offices, going on about how tough things were for them because of the debts young Mrs. Kurata's family had run up. One bank even went so far as to cancel its contracts with us." That alone would be enough to make him touchy on the subject of his first wife.

"What about bankruptcy?" Honma asked. "Not Kyoko, I mean— her father. Couldn't she have found him and had him file for personal bankruptcy? With four years' interest thrown in, the debt must have run into the tens of millions, which was obviously too much for any ordinary working man to pay off. There's an open-and-shut case if I ever heard one." Or even earlier. Why hadn't he filed for bankruptcy back in Mureyama, before the family went into hiding? Had he just not known? Something the attorney, Mizoguchi, said flashed into his mind. *Surely there's no need to sacrifice tens of thousands of people every year.*

"By that time, her father was nowhere to be found," Kurata said, his voice becoming a mumble by the end of the sentence.

"You look for him?"

"Of course we looked, don't worry."

"And Kyoko couldn't file for bankruptcy on his behalf?"

Kurata grinned. "If you could pull off a trick like that, no one would ever have any problems. Kyoko suffered precisely because that *isn't* possible. We talked to a lawyer, who told us all about how the law in this country considers debt strictly the business of the person who enters into it, and how no member of a family can declare bankruptcy on another's behalf. Of course since Kyoko had no legal liability, she shouldn't have been inconvenienced in any way by her father's debts. She should never have been threatened by bill collectors. So, logically speaking—and legally, too, as it happens—she had no basis for filing. Even getting a court order issued to protect her wouldn't have done any good, with a business like ours. Customers walk in and out all the time, you couldn't stop them and check their credentials. Since her father's debts were a simple fact, you couldn't even sue for defamation of character." So long as the yakuza refrained from actual violence, the police couldn't do a thing. Non-intervention in private affairs is one of their first rules.

"When they put the squeeze on you they're careful not to leave any marks, so there's not much you can do on that count. Kyoko and me, my parents, we were all going out of our minds. We had staff quitting …

"At the time, the lawyer said there was only one course of action we could take. First of all, Kyoko should officially declare her father missing—declare that she had no way of knowing if he were alive or dead. If the court accepted that, her father would be struck off the parents' family register. After that, Kyoko could go to Family Court and relinquish any claims to her father's estate—in this case, his negative estate." The problem was that in order to declare someone missing, seven years had to have passed since the person was last seen or heard from.

"In Kyoko's situation, nobody could have held out that long. So the lawyer said we should look into one other possibility, that Kyoko's father had already died. He'd been working as a day laborer, so he might just have dropped dead one day in the street. Without our knowing. If we could prove he was dead, she could start disinheritance procedures immediately. Or she could inherit his debts and use them as a basis for filing bankruptcy papers. The result would be the same. So Kyoko and I went up to Tokyo, and after going to see those distant cousins of hers, we hit the libraries."

"To skim through the *Gazette*?" The *City Government Monthly Gazette* regularly runs lists of unidentified bodies. It has a "Deceased Itinerant" column, deliberately named to avoid labels like "vagrant" or "homeless." In his line of work, Honma himself had sometimes resorted to the *Gazette*. It was a depressing and time-consuming task, scanning the endless roster of anonymous people posted by date and place of death: "Male, name and address unknown; age 60–65; height 5' 4"; underweight; wearing khaki overalls and workboots." Like prowling around a graveyard full of unmarked stones.

"I'll never forget it," said Kurata, staring outside at the rain. "Kyoko sitting there at the library table, poring over those *Gazettes*, looking for any description that might fit her father ... No, it was worse than that." His voice was small and strained. "She was flipping through the pages for what seemed like hours and hours. There were so many entries. She must have forgotten about me and everything else in the room because I heard her chanting to herself—a whisper, almost—'Please be dead, Dad, please be dead.' Her own father! It shocked me to the core ... That's when I saw what sort of person she really was. And something burst inside me."

No matter how much he told himself he loved her, it was more than this man—this product of a comfortable and loving home—could stomach: the sight of the real Kyoko rooting through the lists of unidentified dead in search of a likely corpse. And who could blame him?

At one stroke, she'd wiped out the life they'd tried to claim for themselves. Smashed it into little bits. "I told her, 'Take a good look in the mirror,'" Kurata said in a shaky voice. "'You're evil.'"

Honma's hunch had been right. Kyoko Shinjo was completely on her own. The ghosts that haunted her eventually drove everyone else away.

Kurata's voice was now barely above a whisper. "The formal divorce was a couple of weeks later." September 1987, after a mere three months. This was what she had meant by *Got married too young and it didn't work out*, the phrase Wada had used. "After we split up, I believe she went back to Nagoya to look for work."

Her records would have moved back, then, to her original family register in Mureyama. That could be checked easily enough. A year later, apparently, she found a job in Osaka, which suggested she had begun to get nervous again.

"After that, I've no idea what became of her," Kurata said dismissively. "But you know, when we were getting married, there was a friend she said she just had to tell. I remember she sent her a postcard. Some older girl who had helped her out when she was working part-time in Nagoya. I should have the address at home, though she may have moved."

The soft, steady rain emptied the streets and gave their taxi a clear ride to a villa whose grounds could easily have held the entire housing complex where Honma lived. The plain cypress fence shone wet and clean, the gate looked private and imposing. Up under the gray rooftiles hung a hand-drawn plaque: So Mon—the Gate of Smiles. Also a short length of rope, used as a Shinto blessing. Very impressive.

Honma thought he should wait outside. After five minutes, Kurata reemerged, a sheet from a memo pad in one hand, a plastic umbrella

238

in the other. As the gate opened and closed, Honma caught a glimpse of a small red tricycle abandoned on the white pebbled path. Belonging to Kurata's little daughter, presumably.

"Here." Kurata held out first the piece of paper and then the umbrella. "I didn't know if you had an umbrella. If you don't think you'll need it in Tokyo, just ditch it at the station."

Honma thanked him, then remembered to ask about the piece of rope.

"Oh, that. It's a custom around here," he replied.

"Something to do with Ise Shrine, I suppose?"

"That's right," said Kurata. "That was about the first thing Kyoko mentioned, too. A superstitious soul, that one. If she had to drive a nail into a wall, she'd say a prayer, just in case she'd picked an unlucky direction."

It was about the first thing he'd said with any affection for the woman who used to be his wife, however briefly.

"But prayers didn't keep the bill collectors away," he added. Nothing, it seemed, had been able to do that.

## ✧ 24 ✧

Kurata had said the girl's name was Kaoru Sudo. The address he had for her was in the Moriyama district of Nagoya. But directory assistance was unable to come up with a phone number, so Honma had to go and look for himself. He got the bullet train first thing in the morning and spent the better part of the next day poking around the neighborhood, till finally a newspaper boy told him that Ms. Sudo had moved two years ago. This left him no choice but to ask Funaki for another favor—her new address. He headed back to Tokyo, arriving home after midnight.

The light was on in the kitchen. Tamotsu was sitting at the table, unaware of Honma's return. He'd stayed on to talk to the people Shoko had worked with at Kasai Trading and at the bars Gold and Lahaina. He'd done some asking around too in the neighborhoods of her old apartment buildings, Kawaguchi Co-op and Castle Mansion Kinshicho.

"I'm back!" Honma said loudly. Tamotsu gave a start, his knees jerking up against the underside of the table. He laughed and just managed to keep a book from sliding to the floor.

Honma made it a habit to call home once a day whenever he was away. This time, Isaka had picked up the phone and kept on about what a good houseguest Tamotsu was. Decent, hard-working. He even washed the dishes. "He's especially good with Makoto. After that thing with Blockhead, the boy was real depressed. But since Tamotsu's been here, he's been a lot more lively."

Honma was happy to hear it. Ever since the Blockhead incident, he hadn't quite known how to deal with his son.

All Honma said now to Tamotsu was, "You seem pretty engrossed. What's that you're looking at?"

"This." Tamotsu flattened the pages a bit for him to see.

"A high school yearbook, it looks like," Honma said.

He nodded. "Shoko's and mine. I've got all of them: kindergarten, elementary school, middle school, high school." Four books of various colors and sizes, with the high school one open on top.

"You've had them all this time?" Honma's eyes wandered over the sea of adolescent faces.

"No," Tamotsu replied matter-of-factly. "These are Shoko's."

Honma looked up sharply and met his eyes.

"Here on the last page, these are all her friends' signatures, and Shoko wrote her name in the middle." There it was, "Shoko Sekine" in an uncertain, slightly feeble hand, surrounded by a wreath of messages and names.

"Where did you get them?" There had been no sign of them at her Kawaguchi Co-op apartment. Like the landlady Nobuko Konno had said—with a knowing air, now that he thought about it—yearbooks and photos were the kind of thing you'd grab if you were running off in the middle of the night. And Kyoko would have known the danger of leaving something like that lying around. Anyway, no yearbooks had turned up when he and Jun searched the Honancho apartment where she'd lived as Shoko.

"Actually, they turned up in the darnedest place," Tamotsu said. "An old classmate of Shoko's had them. This girl we used to hang out with, named Yumi. See, when I started asking our old friends about her, word must have gotten around because Yumi got in touch to let me know that she'd been keeping Shoko's yearbooks. She brought them over to my place, and my mother sent them along here."

"Shoko actually handed them over to this girl?"

"No, that's the thing." Tamotsu pulled out a thin envelope. Dusty from long neglect, the envelope had been snipped open at one end. Inside was a note, word-processed on a sheet of stationery.

Dear Yumi:
Sorry to spring this on you. I'm sure you're surprised to be get-

ting such a big package, but I have a big favor to ask. Would you mind holding onto my yearbooks for a while?

I guess you've heard that things haven't been going so well for me here in Tokyo. I've been so unhappy here, I don't even know why I'm unhappy.

Now that my mom's gone and I'm on my own, I know I should try to get my life together a bit. But every time I see these yearbooks, I remember what a mess I've made of everything. I don't have the heart to stash them away in the back of the closet. Could you hold onto them for me, since you were my best friend back then?

Someday when I can look through them and feel good about myself, I'll come get them. But till then, could you hang onto them?

Thanks.

Best,
Shoko

Honma read through the note twice, then picked up the high school yearbook and flipped back to the autograph page.

Let's stay best friends forever and ever! —Yumi Nomura

Beneath the cheerfully rounded characters a trail of teardrops fell away: a last tribute to girlish sentiment.

"It was Kyoko Shinjo that sent them to Yumi," Tamotsu said, narrowing his eyes.

How could he be so sure? The letter mentioned that her mother was "gone," which put it after November 1989. "When did Yumi say that she received this?"

Tamotsu took out the dog-eared notepad he had been using. "She threw away the wrapping paper, so she couldn't check the postmark, but she figures it was the spring after Shoko's mother died." The spring of 1990. Shoko disappeared from the Kawaguchi Co-op apartment on March 17. If the package had been mailed before that, Shoko had probably done it herself; any later meant Kyoko. Hard to call.

"Yumi says she was just taking out her clothes for spring and summer. She knows because she had room to put the yearbooks away in the back of her closet. That's how I know it wasn't Shoko who sent them."

"But it's hard to say just when people put their winter clothes away. Could have been March, or even April."

"Utsunomiya is colder than Tokyo. Nobody does that in March, I guarantee you."

Tamotsu spoke confidently, but Honma didn't see how he could be so certain, when households had such different habits. "Was there anything else, something she might have said that would help nail down the date for us?"

He thumbed through his notes some more. "Like how she forgot to bring any ID showing her address, so at first they wouldn't hand it over?"

"Wait a minute. You mean nobody was home when they first delivered it, so Yumi had to go to the post office to pick it up?"

Tamotsu fumbled for words. "Yeah, I guess. I didn't explain it so good, did I? When she got the notice saying that a package from Shoko Sekine had been brought around, she didn't have the vaguest idea what to expect. So she hurried down the next morning, but when she opened it up and saw the yearbooks, she said she felt a bit put out."

"I take it Yumi's family isn't around the house much?"

"It's a shop, so there's always somebody there. Only that time, they all happened to be away or something."

"And why was that?"

"Let's see, did I ask?" Tamotsu looked over his notes. After a few moments, he scratched his head and apologized. "Nope. I wasn't thinking."

Honma thought for a second, then asked, "Mind if I take a look at that little book you've been carrying around everywhere?"

He looked embarrassed. "Yeah, okay. The handwriting's a bit messy but ..."

It wasn't the most legible handwriting Honma had seen. Tamotsu had marked the date at the top of each page, along with the heading "Yumi's Comments." The questions and answers started off in an orderly way, but, as the conversation progressed, lines began to jump here and there, the writing drifting free of gravity. Still, it was a proper record. In one spot was the isolated phrase "Yumi annoyed." Right above that, curiously enough, were the words "sweet hydrangea tea."

"What's this?" Honma pointed at the page.

Tamotsu chuckled. "On the way home from the post office, she saw they were giving out sweet tea at the local temple. Yumi is a bit chubby but still—anything sweet, she can't resist it. That's all she talks about—today I had this, yesterday I had that. What's so funny?"

"There's a clue right there," Honma grinned. "She stopped at a temple on the way back from the post office and had some hydrangea tea—that's what this means?"

"Yeah, so?"

"Well, there's only one day each year when they do that at temples—Hana Matsuri, the Buddha's Birthday. April 8."

Tamotsu's jaw fell open. "That means—"

"The package would have been delivered the day before, April 7. So it wasn't Shoko who mailed it."

"Hey!" He let out a little cheer. "I'm doing all right, huh!"

The index at the back of the yearbook and the class roll both listed Shoko Sekine and Yumi Nomura in the same "Third Year, Group B." That plus the "best friends" message on the autograph page—wasn't that why Kyoko-as-Shoko had decided to send the books to Yumi?

Judging from her note, Kyoko knew that people back in Shoko's hometown had heard about her problems. Perhaps Shoko herself had told Kyoko as much on the cemetery tour. People sometimes feel comfortable telling a perfect stranger—a taxi driver, or the person sitting on the next barstool—things they would never reveal to an actual friend. *I don't know you and you don't know me*: that's what's nice about it. Especially in a cemetery, what else is there to talk about except the sad turns your life has taken? Kyoko must have been fishing around for just that sort of story, coaxing her to open up.

But then, why hadn't the bankruptcy been mentioned? Was it too soon, or was the topic too serious for light conversation? The irony was that if Shoko *had* talked about it, she'd probably still be alive, living at Kawaguchi Co-op and working at Lahaina.

"When Yumi got these, did she notice the sender's address? Did you ask?"

Again Tamotsu shook his head. "I did ask, but she didn't remember. Somewhere in Saitama, she said."

Then it might have been Kawaguchi Co-op. "Did Yumi say anything about how she felt, suddenly being sent these things? Besides feeling put out at having to go pick them up?"

"Well, she was surprised." Tamotsu pointed at the message "Let's stay best friends forever and ever!" "Actually, this line's a bit of an exaggeration."

"You mean they weren't best friends?"

"It's not like they weren't on good terms, but they weren't all that close either," he said with a shrug. "They just got a little carried away with the excitement of graduation. So anyway, when she read the letter, Yumi thought, 'This Sekine girl's got a lot of nerve ...'" He lowered his eyes. "And then when everything got forwarded here, even before I knew anything about the date and all, my first thought was—hey, Shoko never sent Yumi this stuff." He spoke quietly, with conviction. "When I read that letter too, I thought, no, Shoko didn't write this."

"Why not?"

"Shoko isn't hung up on the past like that. She's not the kind of girl to look at some old yearbooks and moan about how her life now doesn't measure up. Shoko used to say there wasn't anything happy at all about her schooldays."

That made sense, thought Honma. A none-too-happy childhood would explain why she was so anxious to make *something* of her life. Unfortunately, she chose the wrong way to go after that dream. Instead of actively making herself *somebody*, she just bought a mirror that showed an image of herself as somebody. A reflective ID photo on a plastic card.

"Shoko's dead, I've finally got to admit it. Shoko would never have done this." Tamotsu's tone was heavy, resigned. "The minute I saw these yearbooks, I knew it. She's gone." He let his hands fall from the table and clenched them into fists, not so much in anger or sorrow, but as if gripping his memories of her.

Tamotsu then asked Honma to tell him everything he knew about Kyoko Shinjo. He listened without saying a word. When Honma at last fell silent, all he could say was, "Strange woman."

"Yeah?"

"As if everything else she'd done weren't enough, going and sending the yearbooks to an old friend. Why didn't she just toss them out? Just toss them. Why did she have to pretend to feel sorry for Shoko?"

Tamotsu pushed his chair back abruptly, stood up in one swift motion, and cut across the living room to the dark veranda. He stood out there leaning against the window, the clothesline strung taut above him, his white sweater flat up against the glass. His back was turned to Honma, looking too solid to be a ghost, but still hollow inside. Lonely.

Shoko's Nagoya friend wasn't easy to track down. Funaki got in touch with the local Utsunomiya force, but they said they were too busy to help. Actually, Funaki himself had no time to be playing middleman. Honma knew he was racking up one debt after another, but Funaki was good-natured about the whole thing. After all, Honma *had* cracked that armed robbery–murder he'd been working on. The case had unfolded almost exactly the way Honma had predicted. They'd arrested the wife of the murdered businessman and a former co-worker from her secretarial days. Their motive was simple: they wanted his property and his business.

"You're a genius," Funaki had told him. Honma could practically see his beaming face, even over the phone.

"What clinched it?"

"Patience. We kept them under constant surveillance. And obviously too, so that they'd be sure to notice. In the end, it's the guy's widow who cracks. We call her in for questioning and, just like that, *snap*! She starts crying her head off. Sometimes this psychological warfare stuff is a bitch." After griping about all the paperwork they now had to do, he said: "But you sure gave me a lot to think about, about the way people's minds work."

"You say that every time."

"This time it's true. By the way, take a guess. Where do you think the young wife was when she first approached her friend about offing her husband?"

Funaki wouldn't be too happy if he got this one right, Honma could see, but before he could answer, Funaki was telling him: "A funeral."

"Whose?"

"Their former boss's. The department head. A woman, no less. Cancer at thirty-eight. The whole time the priest was chanting the sutras, the two of them were sitting there plotting how to do in her husband."

"I'd say that's taking the Buddhist impermanence thing a little *too* literally."

Funaki changed the subject. "Hey, so how's it going with you? Any progress?"

Honma gave him a quick rundown. Funaki said grimly, "Nailing this Kyoko Shinjo's the main thing, but at some point you really ought to get yourself a corpse, too."

"Hm."

"You put in a request with the Yamanashi police for information on that dismembered body?"

"Not yet. I'm pretty sure about it, but it's just a hunch. And I'm operating as a free agent." He needed some hard evidence before he could ask for formal procedures like fingerprinting. 'Listen, woman A has disappeared. Woman B, who's posing as her, seems to have killed her, but now she's also vanished without a trace'—who's going to rush off to ask the local force for their cooperation with a story like that?

"If only you had something to identify her with. You say this Shoko Sekine had crooked teeth? That's distinctive." The head, he was thinking. "But we're clutching at straws here. There's no way to search for that."

"Oh yeah? Actually, you'd be surprised what might turn up."

"Why? What have you got?"

Honma quoted Tamotsu. "Kyoko Shinjo is a strange woman. She's got this—what would you call it?—moral streak? Sentimental side? Like with those yearbooks, she could have just thrown them away. But no, she goes to the trouble of sending them to an old classmate. Not only was it a lot of extra trouble, who knows?—it could have blown her cover."

"... Yeah, I'm with you."

"It's not logical. It's like she's got these principles. In everything else, her moves are planned and precise, then all of a sudden with the yearbooks she becomes human. She's not consistent." What Kyoko's ex-husband said about her being *a superstitious soul* had stuck in his mind. "So, just for the sake of argument, let's say she goes ahead and chops up the corpse to get rid of it, but feels she has to give the head a decent burial."

"It sort of follows."

"Mm ..."

Both men were silent for a moment, then Funaki suddenly said, "If it was me, I'd check out Shoko's parents' grave."

Honma smirked. "Good idea. Problem is, there isn't one." Her parents had died destitute, and their remains were in urns in a temple.

"Okay, scratch that. I keep forgetting that we're searching thin air." And with a click of his tongue and a sigh, Funaki hung up.

During the period that Isaka dubbed "the holding pattern," Honma slept on his own futon for the first time in what felt like ages. He was able to pay more attention to Makoto and to get his full dose of therapy sessions with Dr. Machiko. Meanwhile, Tamotsu would head out every morning and return in the evening with the information he'd dug up that day. Not that he was finding anything that would help pinpoint where Kyoko Shinjo was right then. He concentrated instead on Shoko's life in Tokyo. There were some small details that linked Shoko to Kyoko, although at this stage their usefulness was limited. Tamotsu knew that but insisted on continuing. He was nothing if not determined.

"There's just one thing I want to ask," he said one evening.

"What's that?"

He scowled. "We're gonna find Kyoko Shinjo, right?"

"I'd like to think so."

"I mean *we're* gonna find her, right? We're not turning this over to the police."

"Not if we can help it."

"When we do—when we meet her—what I want to ask you is, to let me be the one to talk to her first. I want to hear what she has to say."

On his third day back from Ise, Honma got a call from Wada, the young manager at Roseline. He said he'd been talking to the people who had worked with Kyoko and who were still there, but he hadn't come up with anything worth reporting. Still, he had wanted to call to let Honma know he hadn't forgotten his promise. By now his earnestness was starting to sound fishy. Honma was pretty sure it was through him that Kyoko had broken into the Roseline data.

"Did you talk to her roommate yet? What was her name?—oh yes, Orie Chino," Wada asked.

Honma had marked Orie Chino's return from her overseas trip on his calendar. It was tomorrow. "Not yet. She's probably still in Sydney or Canberra, isn't she?"

"Ah, yes, that's right," he said, stumbling a bit over the words. It almost sounded as if he didn't really want Honma talking to her. But he hadn't set up any obvious obstacles, nor did he seem particularly devious. Strange man.

"I'll give her a call tomorrow. Anyway, thanks for checking in. I may need to get in touch again later, if anything crops up."

Wada sounded worried, judging from the timid way he said okay and quietly hung up.

Thinking he'd better talk to her as soon as she came back, before Wada could get to her, he decided to try first thing the next morning. On second thoughts, though, he felt it would be more polite—and perhaps more effective—to let her have a day to herself first. So he figured out roughly when she'd be getting home from work on her second day back, and dialed her then. The first time he got her answering machine; the second time the woman herself answered. She was guarded at first, but relaxed a little at the mention of Wada's name.

Before long, she was chattering away. "You know, Mr. Wada just can't seem to get over Kyoko," she teased.

Uh-huh, here it comes. "Oh? So it was like that?"

"I mean, when Kyoko was rooming with me, I don't know how many times he drove her home. Kyoko never talked like she was interested in him or anything, but he seemed to have his own ideas." Which would help explain why he was so edgy now. Maybe he was hoping Honma's search would turn up something that would improve his chances with her.

"Since we were living so close together, Kyoko and I were careful not to step on each other's toes. So I really don't know all that much about her. And then, whenever either of us got any time off, we'd generally go away."

Honma's eyebrows rose. "She went away on her holidays?"

"Yeah. I don't know where exactly, but they seemed to be pretty long trips."

"Did she have a—"

"Driver's license? Uh-huh, but the cars were always rentals."

"And did she go with somebody?"

"Hmm … mostly she went alone, I think."

It could have been reconnaissance work, getting ready for the switch. "So you're with Roseline as well?"

"Yeah, I'm in the computer room. I handle company data," she said.

Honma's surprise must have been clear from his silence, because the next moment Orie was saying anxiously, "Hello? You still there?"

"Just a second. You're in the computer room?" But Wada had said she'd been a clerk. So that had been a lie—if a relatively small and harmless one.

"That's right. I process data from Roseline, Minami Green Garden and a couple of the other companies."

"Where do you actually work, then?"

"The computer room is in the Mitomo Group's headquarters. I only got to know Kyoko through the bulletin."

"Bulletin?"

"The roommate-wanted column in the company newsletter. I ran an ad. Neither of us could afford a condo by ourselves." Enter Kyoko Shinjo, thought Honma.

"My job is specialized," Orie continued. "So the pay's not too bad. Whereas she was just a trainee, so I had my doubts about whether she could swing it. But she seemed serious enough, so I said okay."

"Ms. Chino, I'm afraid I'm going to have to ask a rather tough question."

"Ask away."

"Did Ms. Shinjo ever ask you to steal customer data for her?"

There was a stunned silence, and then she burst out laughing. "No, why would anybody do something like that?"

"But if someone did ask, could you do it?"

"Sure I could," she said, still laughing. "But if word got out, I'd be out on the street. Probably never work on computers in this town again, either." Honma didn't really imagine Kyoko would have let the key element in her plan depend on a roommate she'd only just met. But he had better be sure ...

"Okay, what about Mr. Wada? Do you think he'd do it if Ms. Shinjo asked?"

She answered immediately. "That's an easy one. Definitely." Bingo, thought Honma.

Then she slipped in a disclaimer. "But it wouldn't happen."

"Why not? He knows his way around computers, doesn't he?"

Orie laughed. "Oh, he talks big around clients. But actually he hasn't got clearance for the computer room. He doesn't have an ID badge." It was obvious that, from her point of view, Wada was just an amateur.

"Sorry to keep harping on this, but how was Ms. Shinjo with computers herself? Could she have messed around with the Roseline system and extracted customer data on her own?"

"Are you saying that that's what happened?"

"No, I'm just testing a theory. While she was living with you, did she have the kind of know-how a person would need to pull off something like that?"

Her response was immediate. "Kyoko, she couldn't tell a 'mouse' from a moose."

"A mouse?"

"Oh dear," she said. "Listen. Kyoko? If she knew how to steal data from the computers, let's see, when I get married someday, instead of wearing a wedding dress I'll come as Rambo."

Honma gave a quick laugh. But how *had* she pulled Shoko's data?

"What was she like as a roommate?" he said, trying a different tack.

"As a roommate?"

"Was she neat? Messy? She keep the place clean?"

Orie's tone brightened. "Oh, I see. She was great to have around. Plus she was careful with money and a good cook, too. She could whip up the best fried rice just from the leftovers in the fridge."

Honma remembered the shiny fan blades in the Honancho apartment. "Did she ever use gasoline to cut the grease on the oven fan?"

Orie was astonished. "How did you know that?"

"I heard about it from somebody who knew her."

"Well, of all things ... Yeah, I didn't like it, the way it would stink up the place. Besides it's scary, having gasoline sitting around like that. Use detergent, I told her. But no, she had to keep her little bottle of it out on the veranda. No real danger, I suppose, but you never know, what with the stacks of newpapers out there." This reminded her of something. "Hey, now that I think of it, Kyoko used to take a Tokyo paper."

"Which one?"

"The *Asahi*, was it?... The *Yomiuri*?" she muttered to herself. "That's right, the *Yomiuri*. I remember telling her the Osaka *Yomiuri* was a lot more interesting, hands down. Why would she want the Tokyo edition?"

"What did she say to that?"

"Um ... I forget. What *did* she say?"

It figured that Kyoko would need to know all she could about

Tokyo if she was going to be living there as Shoko Sekine. Maybe the city had also had an emotional pull on her, and the paper was her way of telling herself that a new life was on its way. So every evening she'd scan the events of the day in Tokyo.

"When did she first start subcribing to the *Yomiuri*?"

Orie had to think about that one. "Pretty soon after she moved in, I guess. She used to clip articles for her scrapbook sometimes too."

This was the first he'd heard of a scrapbook. "What sort of articles? Do you remember?"

Orie just laughed. "I don't know, maybe recipes. I didn't pay much attention."

Well, if something came to mind later, he told her, she should call him, collect. They hung up. So the mystery remained a mystery, even to the roommate who had sat across the table from her at meals for months. Kyoko's image, though, was coming clearer step by step: taking the job at Roseline, finding the condo with Orie from the computer room, playing the manager Wada along, fitting everything into her scheme. But how did she finally get the information on Shoko? Should he forget about this Wada altogether?

"I give up," he said, without realizing he'd spoken out loud.

"Give up what?" asked Makoto, who was sitting at the table right behind him, doing an assignment. "Is this a game?"

"Hey, you're in a good mood." The boy was actually smiling. Ever since Blockhead had been killed, he'd done almost nothing but cry, and Honma hadn't known how to help. In the end Makoto had gone to Aunt Hisae for sympathy, which let Honma off the hook. "No more tears, then?"

"Only sometimes. I can handle it. Anyway, Auntie Hisae says if I cry too much I'll get an earache." Trust Hisae to get around the usual boys-don't-cry formula.

"Hey, you know what?" he went on. "Me and Kazzy were talking. We decided to make a grave for Blockhead."

Honma was puzzled. Hadn't Isaka said they had looked everywhere but failed to turn up the dog's body? Makoto seemed to sense his father's confusion, because he added, "We're gonna bury his collar."

"His collar?"

"Uh-huh. Blockhead had two collars, you know. The one he was wearing when he disappeared was just a flea collar. We still got the leather one. The real nice one, with his name on it."

"So where are you going to bury it?"

"I don't know yet. Kazzy's looking for a good spot now. If we just buried it secretly out front in Minamoto Park, you think the caretaker would be mad?"

"Mm, that may not be such a good idea. It is a grave, after all."

He frowned, propping his chin on one hand. "Yeah, we kind of figured that... Tamotsu says he'll make us a marker for it." He seemed to have taken a real shine to Tamotsu. "Uncle Tsuneo said from now on Blockhead's gonna help look after Mom. That's gonna be Blockhead's main job."

Honma just smiled. Good for Isaka.

"And he'll have lots of space to run around in." Makoto looked at his mother's photograph on the Buddhist altar. "Dad?"

"Yeah?"

"That creep Tazaki, why'd he have to kill Blockhead?"

"I don't know, son. What do you think? Try to put yourself in his place."

Makoto swung his legs back and forth and gave it some thought. "Maybe he was bored."

"Bored?"

"Yeah, see, in his house they won't let him have a dog."

This was the same boy who'd said that dogs weren't allowed in the apartment complex, and that if Makoto didn't like that he should get his folks to buy him a real house.

"Everybody was talking about it at school. Uncle Tsuneo, he said he heard from the neighbors too that the Tazakis had thought about getting a dog but decided not to. His mother said they'd had enough trouble getting the money together to build the house, and she didn't want a dog messing it up."

Honma looked at Makoto. "So maybe this Tazaki didn't really want to kill Blockhead?"

"What do you mean?'"

"Maybe he would rather have kept him. But his folks wouldn't let him. So he didn't want Kazzy to have a dog if *he* couldn't."

"So he killed him?"

"Seems like it."

"Why would he do that? He could have gone over to Kazzy's and played with Blockhead anytime."

"Maybe he didn't think of that. Or maybe he was too upset about not getting a dog of his own."

Makoto twirled his pencil between his fingers. "You know what Uncle Tsuneo said?"

"What?"

The boy frowned with the effort of repeating something that had been hard for him to understand when he'd heard it. "He said there are people in this world who can never be happy with what other people do."

"Yes?"

"And when they see something they don't like, they just go and smash it. Then, later, they come up with a reason. So if Tazaki gives some excuse about why he killed Blockhead, we don't have to listen. It doesn't matter what he says, only what he did."

Hm. It seemed surprisingly cynical, coming from someone as mellow as Isaka. Had Honma misread him?

"Uncle Tsuneo's a housekeeper, right? And him and Aunt Hisae, they got enough money, but don't want to move, he says. Well, if people say bad things about them, he doesn't care. Let them say whatever they want as long as they keep out of his way, he says. 'Just let them make trouble for me, they'll wish they hadn't.'"

Makoto had run all this together in one breath, and paused for a minute. "He says people who do terrible things don't really think about what they're doing. Same with Tazaki."

"So you shouldn't forgive Tazaki, is that the idea?"

Makoto shook his head. "No, wait. He said if Tazaki came and said he's sorry, then we should forgive him."

That was a relief. "Good. I think so too."

Makoto looked relieved as well, and turned back to his home-work. Honma snapped the newspaper open again. But Makoto hadn't quite finished.

"Dad?"

"Yeah?" Peering over the top of the paper, Honma saw that he looked worried again.

"The woman you're looking for, you haven't found her yet?"

"That's right. We're still looking."

"Did she kill somebody?"

"I don't know yet what she did."

"When you find her, you gonna take her to the police station?"

"Well, we've got a lot of questions to ask her."

"Why? Is that your job, asking people questions?" Up to now, Makoto had never probed much into what his father did; his dad was just a detective who caught the bad guys, and that was it. He had never pressed him for details. Honma felt like telling him there was a little more to it. He wanted to tell him about how he sympathized with Kyoko Shinjo. How he almost wished he could just let her go. But all he said was, "Right, that's my job." Then, as an afterthought: "This woman, she had reasons. She didn't do terrible things to other people just because bad things had happened to her. She *wanted* to do the bad things."

Makoto took a moment to absorb that. "You waiting for a call now?"

"That's right."

"And when this call comes, where you gonna go?"

"Nagoya or Osaka, probably."

Just then the phone at Honma's elbow began to ring. Makoto rolled his eyes and sighed. "Bring me back some presents, okay?"

# ✧ 25 ✧

"It's been two years since I heard from Kyoko. I haven't a clue what she's up to nowadays."

Kyoko's friend in Nagoya, Kaoru Sudo, had gotten married and changed her name just the year before. She was now living in the suburbs of Nagoya with her husband's parents, so meeting her at her house wouldn't be a good idea; but they could easily talk somewhere outside, she suggested, since she still went to work.

Honma asked if they could meet near where she'd lived back when she knew Kyoko. This was fine with her. "There's a nice little lunch place near my old apartment. Even after Kyoko moved to Osaka, she used to come up and stay overnight, and the next day we'd have lunch there."

Coty was strictly a neighborhood coffee shop, the kind of place where all the customers were regulars who lived in the area. The minute Kaoru walked in, the proprietor smiled broadly and asked how she'd been. Kaoru was tall and slim with a small face—the model type. She looked about thirty-two or thirty-three. As soon as they had settled in at the table, she came to the point. "The police officer who called—Mr. Funaki, was it?—said Kyoko was missing."

Honma explained the circumstances, keeping back only the part about suspected murder, as usual. Kaoru took a long sip of coffee. Her composure was spoiled only by a slight crease between her penciled eyebrows. "What *can* she be doing?" she muttered into her cup.

Kaoru had known Kyoko since the girl had fled to Nagoya with her mother at the age of seventeen and started working part-time there. "I know all about the family skipping out on their debts. She told me everything." For the most part, her information overlapped with what Kyoko's ex-husband had already said, but some new facts did emerge.

"After she and Kurata split up, the bill collectors caught up with her once." Since they knew where the couple had lived in Ise, that wasn't surprising. "The first time I saw her after her divorce was—" Kaoru cocked her head to one side—"the following year, around February, maybe. That's right, it was snowing."

The divorce was in September, which left almost six months unaccounted for.

"Do you remember anything much about that visit?"

Kaoru nodded emphatically. "I sure do. It was quite upsetting, actually."

She had shown up in a taxi in the middle of the night and Kaoru had paid the fare. "All she had on was a slip under her raincoat. Her skin was completely gray, her lips all cracked. I knew right away what kind of work they had her doing."

When Kaoru asked where she'd been, Kyoko didn't say much. "It wasn't any big place like Tokyo or Osaka, even Nagoya. Probably more like some resort town out in the sticks."

"They were getting her to work off the debt?"

"No. They'd *sold* her."

Kyoko stayed with her for about a month. "She asked if I could lend her some money, so I gave her five hundred thousand yen. She said she was putting me in danger by sticking around Nagoya, because the next time they'd come for me too. She said she was going to Osaka to look for work."

In April Kyoko landed the job with Roseline.

"At first she was living in some hole-in-the-wall place, but later I heard she settled into a nice condo with someone from the office."

"That must have been Ms. Chino."

"Could be ..." Kaoru rubbed her temple with her finger. "Well, when I heard that, I felt better. Her salary at Roseline wasn't too bad, either. It was around then that Kyoko started driving up once in a while to visit."

"She'd always drive? Never take a train?"

Kaoru nodded. "She said she was scared of trains. And not just trains—she avoided crowds in general. She never knew who she might run into." Her meaning was clear enough. "But driving a car, even if she did suddenly get into some kind of trouble, she could get away. Of course, it was always a rental car." Kyoko was obviously scared out of her wits. The odds of her bumping into a collector in a huge city like Osaka or Nagoya were close to zero, but even so she wasn't taking any risks.

"Were they still after her then?"

Kaoru shook her head. "Not that I could see. And I told her, don't you think it's safe by now? But she wouldn't listen. She said she was going to have to keep an eye out for them for the rest of her life." Kaoru had tried to find out what happened during the six months when she'd lost contact. Kyoko never really opened up, but it seemed there was one guy in particular—one of the mob, a yakuza—who fancied her. And he was going to look all over hell for her—not just because of the debts, but for reasons of his own. "'A regular monster' was all she would say."

Kaoru's expression was bitter. "I had a pretty good idea what went on. One thing still puzzles me, though. Kyoko suddenly couldn't stand the sight of anything uncooked … You know, sashimi or anything raw. Said the smell of it made her sick. She was never that way before." Kaoru folded her arms across her chest.

"Did Kyoko ever talk to you about any concrete plans?" Honma was thinking of things like an ordinary, happy marriage, a life of her own.

Kaoru shook her head again. No, it wasn't likely—not without a father, a mother, anything to protect her—even the law. Even her Mr. Wada, whom she'd thought she could depend on—his big, rich family had dropped her like a hot cinder. Men just let you down. From that point on, she couldn't rely on anyone. She'd have to fend for herself, crawl her way back up.

"Did Kyoko ever show you a photo of a house?"

"What house?"

"Here." He pulled out the Polaroid of the chocolate-brown model home and slid it across the table.

"Oh, this …"

"Then you've seen it before?"

Kaoru smiled and nodded. "Sure, it's from her training session, right?"

"Oh?" he said, as if he didn't know.

"A friend had a Polaroid camera and she borrowed it. Kyoko liked going around model homes. I used to tease her about it, seemed like a funny habit to me."

*Liked going around model homes.* "Even though a housing loan was the cause of all her troubles?"

Kaoru put the photo down on the table. "Yes, when you think about it like that, I guess it does seem odd. But you know, I think it's probably the other way around. She practically said as much—someday she'd have a family and live in a place like this. That was her dream, and all the things she'd been through only made it all the more important for her. She was pretty determined." And that's why she had hung on to the picture.

"She liked this house best of all the ones she'd ever seen, apparently. She showed it to me when she first came to visit. 'Kaoru,' she said, 'someday when I get my life together, I'm going to live in a house like this.'" Kaoru was trying to imitate the cheerful tone she'd used.

"She didn't say she'd like to show you the house, invite you there sometime?"

Kaoru drew back a bit in surprise. "Come to think of it, no, she didn't." She couldn't have, he thought, because the home would belong to someone with another name. Kyoko's plans were already in place by then.

Honma looked up from the photo and said, "You haven't heard from Kyoko lately?"

Kaoru looked a little irritated, crossing her legs and pouting slightly. "She's been completely out of touch. It's the truth."

"You haven't had any phone calls where the caller hangs up when you answer?"

"No, none that I'm aware of."

The effort involved in taking over another woman's identity must have left Kyoko shaken and insecure, yet she hadn't tried to contact the one friend she had, the one person she'd shared her dreams with. What could that mean? Where was she?

"When Kyoko and I knew each other, I was going out with my husband and we'd decided to get married in another year or two. So maybe she thinks I'm well and truly married now and she can't just come visit like she would have in the old days." Then again, Honma thought darkly, maybe she's just decided not to trust Kaoru and to keep running on her own.

"Were you living around here at the time?"

"Right over there, see?" She pointed out the window to the building diagonally across the street, saying that hers had been the corner room on the second floor. A row of colorful potted flowers now lined the window and a pair of red socks hung on the clothesline above an air conditioner. Honma could almost see Kyoko helping Kaoru hang out the wash.

In all the places she'd lived in—the cheap rooming house with her mother; the apartment in Nagoya; the inn where she worked in Ise; the sprawling Kurata family home; that unknown hell when she'd been caught and sold for sex; the condo down in Osaka; then that neat little Honancho apartment—wherever she lived, Kyoko had fended for herself: cleaning and washing clothes and doing the shopping and the cooking. Her life had been by turns frightening, sad, dirt-poor, occasionally even fairly happy. But one thing never changed —she was always a fugitive. She had run to get away from the yakuza, and kept on running. Then, when she thought she'd found a way to leave her past behind for good, she'd had to start running again. Nothing had changed.

Honma wanted to call out, "You must be tired. I know I am. Let's call off this chase, stop for a minute."

"The last time Kyoko came to see me, she'd just quit Roseline."

Honma took out his notes and nodded. "She left at the end of December 1989."

"That's right. She came up here just after New Year's ... or no, in late January. She took me out to dinner, I remember. She'd just gotten paid." And she was well on her way to becoming Shoko.

"She said she'd moved out of the condo she'd been living in in

Osaka. So I asked her, where now? And she said she was thinking about Kobe."

"Oh …?"

"But the funny thing was, in the course of the conversation she mentioned something about the Keihin Tohoku Line. That's a Tokyo-area train; runs between Yokohama and Tokyo and then north to Saitama, right?" So naturally Kaoru had asked what Kyoko was doing up there. "And, boy, if looks could kill … She said there was some stuff she had to take care of in Saitama—Kawaguchi, actually, of all places. She was renting a room by the week, but she couldn't give me the phone number …"

*Shoko was all paranoid, she said somebody had been opening her mail.* That was what the older girl at Gold had said. So that would be how Kyoko found out about the cemetery tour. Shoko's schedule at the time had her getting up around noon, working nights, coming home in the small hours of the morning. Plenty of opportunity to go looking through her mailbox.

One little link—and the fuzzy outline of the image came sharp and clear. A single unbroken line now joined Shoko Sekine and Kyoko Shinjo. No mistake.

"One thing," Honma said, shifting in his seat. "When Kyoko came to visit, or when she called, was there any time when she seemed strange, different somehow from her usual self? Over the last few years, say?"

Kaoru gave him a quizzical look. "Strange?"

"Yeah. Irritable, nervous, crying for no reason?" The question was vague, but what he was getting at was how Kyoko might have been acting on or around November 25, 1989, when Shoko Sekine's mother fell to her death. If Honma's suspicions of murder were correct and Kyoko Shinjo had had a hand in the old woman's fall—admittedly hard to prove—then the first order of business was to place her in Utsunomiya that day. The nine-day period before and afterward, from the eighteenth through the twenty-sixth, she'd taken off from Rose-line. That much he'd learned from Wada. But what he wanted to know now was, had Kyoko contacted Kaoru on the day or, more likely, the night of the twenty-fifth?

Kaoru sat propping her chin on a fist. She looked as if she were thinking, not trying to hide something. More than likely, Kyoko had been working entirely alone, even then. Certainly the following March when she killed—yes, killed—the daughter, she had already lost touch with her old friend.

"I don't know about strange, but that last time, the end of January, she seemed different." Kaoru spoke slowly, choosing her words with care. "Whenever she left at the end of a visit, it was always 'See you!' Then, outside the door, she'd wave and say, 'Later.' But that one time she actually bowed and said 'Goodbye.'" And it was goodbye: "Kyoko" was finished. Kaoru would never see her again, nor of course would she ever meet "Shoko Sekine."

"Yes … now that I think about it, she talked about her mother's death too," Kaoru went on. "In fact, death was a big topic that evening. She said, 'Kaoru, when you die, where do you want to be buried?' She wanted to be buried as far from Mureyama as possible. She said, 'I wouldn't let them bury me in my old hometown if it killed me.'" But when Kaoru asked if anything was wrong, Kyoko just laughed. "I could see *something* was going on, even if I had no idea just what. When she dropped out of sight and no word came, I thought, well, that's it—I should have made her tell me. A lot of good it does to say all this now."

Kaoru had talked herself straight into a black mood. Her tone reminded Honma of how he'd felt when he'd suggested to Kurata that Kyoko might be dead.

"Was there anything else?" Honma asked.

Her shoulders drooped. "I can't think of anything," she said with a sigh.

"Well, then, how about if I pick a day? November 25, 1989. Anything come to mind?"

"Something in particular happen that day?" she asked, narrowing her eyes.

Honma smiled. "No, it's just that according to the Roseline time sheet, Kyoko was absent for a total of nine days before and after the twenty-fifth, which was a payday. Did she by any chance come and visit you?"

Kaoru's eyes wandered away. She reached clumsily for her coffee cup and brought it to her mouth. She took a sip, then set it firmly down and asked, "While she was at Roseline, did Kyoko ever take any other long leaves?"

Honma checked his notes. Wada had run a search for just that information, so it was easy to tell right away. "No. She had other absences as long as three days. But nine days, just the once. November 18 through 26."

Kaoru looked relieved. "In that case, I do know. My memory's full of holes, but if Kyoko never took off any other long stretches, then it has to be then."

Honma edged forward. "Did she contact you?"

"She did. She came up. It was the second day of her leave—that would make it the night of the nineteenth. It was real strange. She had hurt herself."

"Hurt herself how?"

"Burns. Not too serious, luckily," said Kaoru. "But she did have to go into the hospital. She was running a high fever."

For a moment Honma thought he'd misheard. "Say that again."

"She was hospitalized. Emergency," she explained, "At City General, near here. She was admitted and stayed through the morning of the twenty-sixth, that's why the nine-day leave."

Kyoko Shinjo was in a Nagoya hospital when Shoko Sekine's mother fell down the stairs …

"She ended up with pneumonia," Kaoru told him. "On the eighteenth, she went for a drive with a friend. They stayed at an inn one night, then on the way back they had an accident. That's why she showed up at my place after midnight on the nineteenth. When I asked who she'd been with, she wouldn't say. Clammed up. Her right arm was covered with burns, not third-degree, but covering most of her arm. Even though it was cold, she was wearing just a blouse and a skirt and a thin raincoat. Said that when they had the accident, the engine caught fire and her sweater got burned. She got on the train and just came up here, without stopping to put on any other clothes. She was shivering, running a fever."

The first thing Kaoru did was put her to bed, keeping a close eye on her. "But it was more than I could handle. One minute she's going to the toilet and the next thing she's in the bath, banging her head against the wall. She was all hyper, like she didn't know if I was there with her or not. Eventually I had to call an ambulance. She never did tell Roseline the truth. Said she'd caught a bad cold and was resting up at her aunt's place—and they never questioned it, as far as I know. Anyway, she was in the hospital for seven days altogether. Even later, when she got well, she refused to tell me whose car it was. Must have been quite a date, is all I can say."

Kaoru wasn't one to keep a diary, but she did keep track of her accounts, and they were as good a record as any. "I lent her the deposit for the hospital room, so if I go back over my books I can probably tell you in more detail. Shall I check it?"

"That would be great," Honma said, jotting down his number for her.

He had just arrived back at the hotel room when she called to say there was no mistake about the dates. She could even fax a copy of the hospital receipt to his hotel. The front desk clerk seemed a little surprised at the way Honma lunged at the sheet as it rolled out of the machine.

*Kobata City General Hospital*

Received in full for Ms. Kyoko Shinjo, inpatient care and room charges, November 19–26, 1989, inclusive. Six-bed ward. Showed National Health card. Room deposit: ¥70,000.

## ✧ 26 ✧

"Well, if that doesn't beat all," Funaki said. He grinned and slurped at his *kombu* tea.

Honma had been back for two days. They were sitting at the kitchen table talking things over. Isaka was half listening as he got dinner ready. The unexpected twist had so overwhelmed Honma that he had completely forgotten to buy Makoto the promised presents.

"Looks like there might have been an accomplice after all," ventured Isaka. Tonight, at Makoto's request, they were having *oden* hotpot for supper. Isaka was stewing up an extra-large batch so he could take some home for himself. The broth simmered, filling the house with a warm, cozy aroma.

"But why wouldn't the accomplice have surfaced till now?" Honma said.

"What about that Wada character?" Funaki suggested.

"He was in Osaka. The night Mrs. Sekine died, he was working at the office till nine. If the guy had sprouted wings and flown there, maybe he'd be in Utsunomiya by eleven."

"An accident, then?" Funaki said, looking unconvinced. "Stranger things have happened."

Honma laughed. "Then Shoko Sekine's mother sure chose to have her accident at a very convenient time for Kyoko Shinjo."

"You know what they say about truth being stranger than fiction."

"Her companion, then," Isaka struggled on, "—the person with her in the car when she had the accident on the nineteenth. Couldn't that be the killer?"

This did give Honma pause.

Funaki muttered, "What if the companion had been her fiancé, Jun Kurisaka?"

"Both of you have been reading too many detective novels."

"Yeah, well."

"Hey, what's happened to him, anyway? He hasn't called once," Isaka said, suddenly concerned. "It was Jun who dragged you into this in the first place. He can't be that uninterested."

"You'd think a man of his 'caliber' wouldn't need us to do his dirty work for him," Funaki said. Ever since he'd heard about the way Jun had flung that money at Honma, he'd had little use for the junior banker.

Isaka went over to the stove to check on the *oden*. As he removed the lid, a delicious cloud of steam curled out. Funaki, who'd been slouched over, chin practically resting on the tabletop, perked up enough to say, "Sure smells good!"

"You're staying for supper, aren't you?"

"Not if you want sparkling company," he said sourly, and chuckled. "I wonder if she's having dinner now too," he added.

"Who?" Honma asked.

"Kyoko Shinjo."

Honma looked at him. "Yeah, probably."

"And why not? She's got to eat and bathe and get all dolled up to go make some man's life miserable. She's probably out there having a good time." He gave a gloomy laugh. "Here we are racking our brains like this, and she's at a Shiseido cosmetics counter trying out the new spring lipstick colors."

"Where'd you get all the detail?"

Holding a pair of cooking chopsticks in one hand, Isaka looked past Funaki to offer Honma a bit of insight. "I believe somebody just had himself an arranged meeting with a prospective bride. I wonder if she might have been—let's see—a Shiseido beautician."

Funaki smiled, despite himself. "Of all the slanderous ... Bull's-eye."

But where *was* Kyoko Shinjo now? Honma hadn't given it that much thought. Did they go back to the starting line, then? Back before they'd discovered that "Shoko Sekine" was someone else?

Should they do what the attorney Mizoguchi had recommended and put an ad in the paper? "Kyoko, let's talk it over. Come back, please." But whose name to sign? Jun's? It was ridiculous.

The most ridiculous part was thinking that Kyoko might actually respond, when called by her own name. *Yes, Shoko Sekine sold me her family register... Shoko? Oh, she's working down in Kyushu now. Talked to her on the phone the other day. Sorry to cause all this concern.* Jun hears her out with tears in his eyes. The two of them get back together and marry. I'm hospitalized with an ulcer. Make that a bleeding ulcer.

Come on, get serious. Kyoko was out there somewhere, holding her breath. Probably as far from Tokyo as possible.

Honma abruptly stood up.

"What gives?" Funaki asked, startled.

"I was just thinking," Honma said. "What do you suppose Kyoko is really doing these days?"

"Crying her eyes out, probably," Funaki said, grinning. "Or else consulting a Shiseido beautician."

"I'd say she's working," Isaka suggested. "I doubt she left here with enough to get by on, let alone settle into somewhere nice."

"Doesn't seem like she's kept in touch with Kaoru Sudo, either," added Funaki.

Honma let his mind wander, his eyes half shut. "Don't you think she might try the same scam all over again? I bet the reason she hasn't contacted her old friend Kaoru is because she's scared to."

"Scared?" Funaki prompted.

"Yes. She dumped Jun when things started to come unstuck. Once she was on her own, she must have gotten to thinking—what would Jun do now? He'd search for her, that's what. And who knows? Jun found out about the bankruptcy easily enough, maybe by now he would have pieced it all together, that 'Shoko Sekine' was really Kyoko Shinjo ..."

"Nah. She wouldn't think that far ahead."

"She wouldn't have any way to be sure, but it must have crossed her mind. All the more reason not to contact her friend Kaoru. Cut off all ties that might identify her. She couldn't go back to being Kyoko, could she, so she had to find someone else to be."

Funaki and Isaka exchanged looks. "She'd need to get a job at another mail-order place," said Funaki.

"Start all over again from the beginning," echoed Isaka.

Honma let out a deep breath. Whatever glint of insight he thought he'd had, this talk had driven it away.

"Uh-oh, got to run," said Isaka, glancing at the kitchen clock. Five minutes to three. Makoto and Kazzy had insisted they come to Blockhead's funeral that day. In the end, the boys had asked the Isakas if they could use part of their ground-floor garden plot, a patch of earth that technically belonged to the housing project—not that the Isakas minded. Tamotsu had banged together a cross out of scraps of wood, proving himself both handy and respectful of the dead.

The boys had done their digging with a trowel, and had barely gone deep enough to cover the poor dog's collar. The collar was practically brand-new. Before burying it, Makoto showed everyone the inscription he'd made inside. Tamotsu planted the cross on top of the grave and Hisae covered it with a wreath. Each person there lit a stick of incense, then pressed their hands together in prayer.

"Think Blockhead will like this ceremony?" Makoto asked.

"I think he'll love it."

"I bet he's real pleased to have his new collar," Funaki said, patting him on the shoulder.

"When summer comes, we're gonna plant morning glories right here and let them grow up big," Makoto said with a smile, pointing at the veranda railings.

"I already got the seeds," said Kazzy.

"We can plant different flowers in the right seasons, so there'll be something all year round," Hisae promised. "Anyway, why don't you put the trowel away and get yourselves washed up. There's cake, if anybody's interested." And they all started drifting back inside.

Honma noticed that Tamotsu was acting strange. He'd hardly said a word the whole time. At first Honma thought he was simply trying to keep his own sadness to himself. But that wasn't it. Something seemed to be bothering him deep inside; he kept his shoulders hunched, and cocked his head to one side every so often.

"What's wrong?"

269

"I don't know, my neck is acting up." He brushed the dirt from his trousers. "Digging that hole and putting up the cross got me thinking about something that happened a long time ago."

"You had a pet that died when you were a kid?"

Tamotsu shook his head. "No, nothing like that. Actually, my dad hated animals. I'd cry my eyes out, but he still never let me have one," he grumbled. "It's something I ought to ask Ikumi about. She knows me better than anyone, even better than I know myself."

"She's a good wife."

"Too good. I just *think* about stepping out of line, she knows about it."

That evening, while Honma was going over his notes, Tamotsu called Ikumi. Honma encouraged him to phone home once a day. Regular as clockwork, almost the first words out of his mouth were, "How's Taro? How's the baby?"

Today, however, his "Hello, it's me" seemed to meet with some resistance, because his next words were, "What do you mean, 'Who's that?'"

Honma smiled to himself. Pretty soon it would be time for Tamotsu to head back to Utsunomiya, whether the investigation was properly wound up or not. Sure, it was Tamotsu's life, but anyone could see that he belonged back home with her.

"Don't say it like that!" Tamotsu protested. "Of course I do. Sure, I'm worried about … You know I—how can you say that?" Tamotsu got up from his chair, stumbling a bit. "Don't be an idiot, okay? I don't want to hear it!" he yelled into the phone. "Come on, give me a break. I called you because there was something I wanted to ask. Are you sitting down?"

Fortunately the conversation now settled down, as Tamotsu began to explain the events of the day. "The thing is, I seem to remember, a long time ago, digging with a trowel, making some kind of grave for a pet or something. But Dad, you know how he is. He would never let me have a pet. So what is this, then—you got any idea?"

Tamotsu listened. "What? Elementary school, huh? How come you know all this, anyway? I told you? Hey, I wet my bed till fifth grade—but I suppose I told you that too."

Their discussion seemed to be going nowhere in particular. Honma had turned away when Tamotsu suddenly pounded the telephone stand with his fist and let out a whoop. "That's right! I remember now! Shoko was with me!"

Honma looked at him.

Tamotsu nodded energetically. "That's right, that's what it was ..." Talking to her had jogged his memory. "Ikumi, you're a genius! I'm a lucky man," he exclaimed. He hung up and rejoined the others at the table.

"Shoko and I did an animal project together, in grade school," he said, still a bit out of breath. "We had to take care of a lovebird that flew into our classroom." When the bird died, they buried it in a corner of the schoolyard.

"So that's what it was," Honma chuckled.

"But listen," Tamotsu said eagerly, leaning across the table. "There's something I remembered from talking to Ikumi."

Honma was a bit overwhelmed by all this energy. "What's that?"

"Shoko was pretty attached to that bird." No doubt her family's budget had been too tight to allow her to have a pet. "So when it died it broke her up. She cried her head off, just like Makoto did the other day. 'Poor thing, all on its own,' she said." There were red spots in Tamotsu's cheeks.

Honma stared blankly at him. All at once the young man's meaning became clear. "You're not saying—"

Tamotsu was shaking his head. "No, it's true. Shoko never forgot it. Back in grade school, she said to me once, 'Tamo, if I die first, bury me out here with Pippi.'"

A bird. Buried in a corner of the schoolyard.

"You get it?" he continued. "Two things Ikumi heard Shoko muttering to herself at her mother's funeral. How ashamed she was, not being able to afford a regular grave. And how she herself wanted to be buried with Pippi. Ikumi said she heard her. So somebody else could have heard her too."

"Slow down," Honma said, reining in his own thoughts. "That alone doesn't ..."

Tamotsu wasn't listening. "The way I see it, Kyoko Shinjo went on that cemetery tour to spend some time around Shoko. And it was, after all, a grave-shopping tour, right? So what if Shoko got all sentimental and started talking about where she wanted to be buried someday? Once they got on that subject, she probably told her all about Pippi. Even if Kyoko didn't know the exact spot, she could sure as hell have given our school a visit."

It was a long shot. Still, Honma remembered what Funaki had said. When people are faced with death—its rituals and emblems—they confide in people. Like that young wife who murdered her businessman husband.

Would the subject have come up naturally? Or did Kyoko steer the conversation in that direction? Though why would she want to do that? She didn't need to know, unless …

Of course. There *was* a reason. Kyoko hadn't been able even to throw away Shoko Sekine's yearbooks, and had gone to all the trouble of mailing them to her "best friend." Wasn't it because she somehow had a guilty conscience? And if she went that far just for the yearbooks, then what about the body? She may have had to cut it up to dispose of it, but Honma was beginning to think that, with the *head* at least, she'd had other plans—which Shoko had inadvertently given her.

Tamotsu's confidence was contagious. Honma forced himself to cool down. "Well, maybe it did happen like that. Thinking it doesn't prove it."

But Tamotsu was all fired up. "That's why we've got to dig! I've got lots of friends from school back in Utsunomiya. We'll plow up the entire schoolyard if we have to."

Amazingly enough for a Sunday morning, it was the slug-a-bed Makoto who managed to get up in time to give Tamotsu a hero's send-off. Tamotsu was catching an early bullet train back to Utsunomiya. His face was clear and relaxed; he looked like he was ready to set to work.

Honma, on the other hand, woke in a mental haze. The day before, while sitting at the kitchen table talking with the others, something had formed just below the surface of his consciousness, then evaporated. Now, as he lay in bed still half asleep, that same something whispered in his ear, teasing him, giving him no rest.

All right, all right. Time to get on with more practical matters, Honma said sternly to himself, lumbering out of bed. Nothing, though, would go right. He broke a plate clearing up after breakfast and had to pay Makoto the household penalty fee.

"You seem weird," the boy told him as he helped dry the dishes. "Like you're not really here."

"Mm, maybe I'm not."

"But your knee's better, right? Are you going back to work soon?"

He guessed he should; he couldn't stay on this case forever.

"What's Dr. Machiko going to say?" teased Makoto. "You been skipping all your appointments, so you're heading for trouble."

"But I'm walking perfectly normally now."

"That's what you think. I think you still walk stiff."

"That so?" said Honma, turning off the faucet.

Makoto went out to play and Honma returned to reviewing what he knew about Kyoko Shinjo and Shoko Sekine. Papers covered the table. He focused on the gaps in what he knew. One: how Kyoko had managed to get her hands on the Roseline customer data, and whether Wada was involved. Two: how Kyoko had killed—if that's what she'd done—Shoko's mother. Two major snags. He'd been struggling with them for about two weeks, but still had precious little to go on.

He kept imagining Kyoko catching sight of the short personal ad—"Kyoko, let's talk it over. Come back, please"—and appearing out of nowhere, running into Jun's open arms.

"Beats me," he groaned.

He sat down and stood up, sat down and stood up. Meanwhile, the morning came and went. It was one o'clock when Makoto popped back in to ask what was for lunch. Usually, on Isaka's day off, Honma would putter around the kitchen, throwing something together, but he didn't feel like it today.

"How about eating out?" he said. He didn't have to ask twice.

The two of them set out for a family restaurant near the apartment complex. Getting out into the open air felt good. Honma decided he wouldn't go straight back after lunch.

"Got any plans this afternoon?" he asked as they were strolling out of the restaurant.

"I gotta be at Kazzy's at three. Right now he's out buying a new computer game."

"What's the game this time?"

Honma got lost not far into Makoto's explanation. The boy started again at the beginning three times, but never managed to reach the end. Something about bonus points in each player's scorecard. "It's really neat."

"Yeah, right."

"Nice day, huh?" Makoto said, lazily stretching out one arm.

"Sure is."

"Dad, you know what? You're walking okay."

"What did I tell you?"

"But if you get really better, Dr. Machiko's going to be lonely."

They headed for Minamoto Park. The calendar said it was spring, but the trees in the park didn't know it yet. The rows of poplars pointed their barren branches skyward, stretching their knobby fingers into the cold wind like hands raised in protest. Through a stand of rust-red zelkova trees, birds flew almost low enough to touch.

The iris garden was still a mudhole. A group of amateur artists had set up their easels and were gazing at a patch of narcissus, brushing the wintry scene onto their canvases in paintings that cried out for greener colors.

Honma thought about Kyoko Shinjo. Would she be off on an outing on a day like this? Or just airing her bed linen and squinting up at the sun? Tamotsu came to mind as well. Was he planning to turn up the entire schoolyard? Not that it was possible. Honma should have tried to stop him.

Maybe it had all been an elaborate mistake. Maybe he should knock down the house of cards he'd been building and get back to work, real work.

"Gee, it's been a long time since we done this," said Makoto, running ahead a few steps. "I'm glad you feel better."

"You're the best doctor I've got, Makoto."

For a while they watched the people fishing along the moat. Then

Makoto sneezed twice, so they started to head back, promising each other they'd do this again soon. The clock by the park gate read a quarter to three.

Makoto paused at the entrance to the apartment complex, looking this way and that. "Might see Kazzy coming," he said.

"What if the game's sold out and he comes back empty-handed?" Honma prodded.

"Kazzy called ahead to check. So there!" He stuck out his tongue.

Today's kids have got things pretty well mapped out, Honma thought. A huge, almost untapped market. He and Makoto kept on walking till their building came into view.

Makoto stopped in his tracks. "Hey, what's going on?"

Acrid smoke blew at them suddenly from the side. Honma peered in the direction of the garbage incinerators. "I'll just go have a look."

"I'm coming with you." Makoto ran after him.

A man in overalls was crouched alongside a small incinerator, fanning the smoke away with one hand and holding down a pile of garbage with the other. He blinked up at Honma, then bobbed his head, apparently expecting him to complain. "Sorry. It's just papers. The stuff got a little damp, so it sends up smoke." Hot clouds spilled out from under the metal furnace flap. Makoto coughed.

"No problem," Honma said. He had started to lead Makoto away by the hand when he happened to look down. At the base of the incinerator were stacks of old ledgers, bound together with black cords.

"You burning those?" asked Honma.

The maintenance man wiped his forehead with a gloved hand. "Yessir. Guy moved out this past Sunday was an accountant. Had all these records going back ten years."

"Lot of work there."

"You're telling me. But we can't just leave them. Somebody's got to get rid of it all. Sure did use a lot of ink, that guy. Ought to give it to a museum. Nobody does accounting like this any more. Nowadays they all got home computers. Input the stuff once, you don't need any paper."

*Input once, you don't need*—Honma echoed the man's words to himself.

"That's not true," Makoto piped up.

"Oh no?" grinned the maintenance man.

"That's what my teacher says. She bought one of those electronic diaries, but you know what? In the instructions it said that if the batteries run out all of a sudden, everything goes blank, so any important stuff, you've got to keep a record of someplace else, just to be safe. That's what it said."

The man laughed. "That's with the cheap machines."

"No, they're all like that, she says. That's why you're supposed to keep it all on paper too."

"But that means twice the work."

"Yeah, but that's what it said."

The caretaker opened the lid of the incinerator and heaved in a fresh bundle. Makoto looked up at his father, who was standing there, strangely quiet. "What's the matter, Dad?"

Honma placed a hand on the boy's head. "Thank you very much, young man."

"Huh? For what?"

Honma tousled his hair and smiled. "Except now, you know what? Thanks to you, I've got to go to Osaka tomorrow."

# ✧ 27 ✧

"Printouts?"

They were standing in the Roseline waiting room, Wada scowling as Honma repeated his request. Honma had taken the bullet train first thing in the morning, gone straight to the Mitomo Group's headquarters, and asked for Wada. This time the receptionist showed him in. This time Wada shut the door behind him.

"You came all the way down here to ask me that?"

"Well, actually, that isn't the only thing." Honma leaned forward and spoke a little more forcefully. "Those questionnaires and order forms. After you input the information into the computer, what happens to them? Do you get rid of them right away?"

"Of course. Otherwise they'd take up too much room. We shred them in one-month batches."

"Really?"

"That's right. Every last scrap." Wada's voice was confident, almost overconfident.

"Oh, yes?" said Honma, stretching out each word for emphasis. "And who, may I ask, is in charge of these disposal procedures?"

Wada lowered his eyes and glanced this way and that.

Honma asked again, "Who does the shredding?"

Wada shifted his weight from one leg to the other, brought a hand up in front of his nose as if to hide his face, and looked down.

"It's not such a difficult question. Is there some reason why you can't tell me?"

"Administration, the General Affairs Section," the answer finally came. He added hurriedly, "But Ms. Shinjo wasn't in General Affairs."

"So how do you deal with the papers that are going to be shredded?"

"Once a month, we send them out to a special data security company."

"And till then?"

"They're kept in a storeroom in the basement."

"And this storeroom is unlocked? Anybody can get in?"

This time the pause was even longer.

"Mr. Wada."

"Yes, sir." It was the lifeless tone of a student responding to a teacher.

"Anybody can get in?"

Wada coughed. "Any of the women staffers can, yes."

Honma heaved a sigh of relief. Papers. Handwritten forms from customers. Kyoko didn't need to know the first thing about computers to pull it off. But would there be any evidence left now?

"I assume you have a confidentiality agreement with this data security company."

"Of course. Our questionnaires and order forms contain personal information."

"So when you send a truckload out, does anybody count the boxes and keep an eye on what's going where? Who's in charge of that?"

"Administration, I think."

"Can you check? Go back to—oh, when Kyoko Shinjo was here—from April 1988 to December 1989. See if there were any irregularities—box numbers not matching up, papers short."

Wada looked stunned. "Check all that?"

"If you could."

"I'm afraid I don't have time to—"

"Fine, then, I'll just take the matter a little higher up. Could you give me the name of your boss?" Actually, things would get bogged down in all sorts of complications if Wada refused to play along. But there was no harm in seeing what happened when a little leverage was applied.

"My boss?" he said.

"Of course, I'd rather not involve anyone else if it isn't necessary.

This *is* rather a sensitive case," said Honma cagily. A second later, he was convinced: there was no need for checking—*the man knew.* "Mr. Wada. Did Ms. Shinjo ever ask you to show her or make copies of customer data?"

Wada suddenly wilted completely. He hung his head and confessed. "She asked, okay? I showed her. I helped her. I told her how."

Honma gave another sigh.

"I can't remember exactly when it would have been, though."

"Oh no? No idea?"

He shook his head.

"Never mind," Honma continued, "just tell me what you did."

"It's dead easy. All you have to do is pinch a few papers from the outbound boxes. The company only comes to collect once a month."

"So what was in the boxes you opened?"

"Just some questionnaires."

"Your ordinary, standard questionnaires?"

Wada shrugged. "Like I said, I don't remember. Honest to—"

"Nothing?" How long was he going to keep up this pretense? His eyes were still roaming around.

"First time was in May."

*The first time?* "This happened often, then?"

Another nod. No wonder he was so uncomfortable.

"May," Honma repeated. "May *when*?"

"The year she came to work here." In 1988.

"And how many times altogether would you say you walked off with this confidential data?"

"Four times."

"Was that four times running? Through August?"

"That's right, every month." Then he volunteered, quietly, "All from the Tokyo-Kanto-Kofu-Nagano area. Funny taste in reading material this girl's got, I said to myself. Guess that's why I still remember."

"Kyoko didn't say why she wanted them?"

"Well, sort of ...," Wada hedged. "She said she was practicing her computer skills, how to run programs and that sort of thing, so she needed some data to work with."

"That was the reason she gave?"

Wada was silent.

"You couldn't have believed that."

He smirked. "Actually, I figured she was selling them to some direct-mail company." Whatever Kyoko's reasons, he'd been there to help, no questions asked.

"Mr. Wada."

"Yes?"

"Do you have any way of knowing whether Shoko Sekine's questionnaire might have been included in those papers?"

"Not offhand. But when I get some time, I'll check on it." He spoke faster as he explained. "The information taken from the questionnaires is all tagged by date, so we can run a search program and collect data that was input over a particular period."

"Could you print out the lot—all four months, starting from April? I don't care how long it takes. I'll wait."

Wada sighed. He had seen this coming. "Is this really necessary?"

"Well, I'd be curious to know whether your boss thinks it is."

"Okay, okay." He scratched his head with both hands. "But let's just keep this to ourselves, if you don't mind." As Honma had suspected, he didn't want it getting out of hand.

Wada closed the conversation with a vague promise to "see what I can do." Give him two hours, he said. Honma was told to wait in that same coffee shop, Kanteki, and could see himself sitting over cup after cup.

Fifteen minutes ahead of time, Wada showed up with a computer printout two inches thick. "One hundred and sixty entries," he announced, depositing the load on the table.

Kyoko had been here, too, before him, thought Honma. He started flipping through it. "And Shoko Sekine?" he asked.

"She's in there," answered Wada, pointing two-thirds of the way down the stack. "Back there in the July data."

Shoko was logged into the Roseline customer database on July 15.

How exactly had Kyoko targeted her? What were her priorities when she sifted through all these names, ages, addresses, workplaces and passport numbers?

Age first. Women too far off the mark—either too old or too

young—wouldn't do. The occupation should be nothing too remarkable; nobody with a "good job." Someone unemployed or freelancing, whose absence wouldn't set up any waves. Somebody with few or no attachments. Women who hadn't made themselves very necessary to anyone.

May, then June and July, with finally more data for August. Kyoko must have sorted through each batch, picking out possible "sisters," coming up with maybe five women, certainly no more. Once she had what she needed, she'd put the brakes on. Narrow things down, keep things simple.

"So you've got your Shoko Sekine," Wada said. "Well, I'd better be off. The work's piling up on my desk and …"

"No, hold on just a second. Another five minutes." Honma looked up from Shoko's data. Suddenly, he'd seen something. It was as if all the energy he'd used up looking for her all this time had ignited, rising in a thin but steady flame.

"What is it?" Wada asked.

*Shoko Sekine hadn't been Kyoko's first choice.*

Honma could have kicked himself. Shoko was in the July printout. But Kyoko had had Wada go and get her the August data too. That would suggest there were other candidates, someone closer to her requirements, maybe.

Suppose Shoko were running a close second, but then Kyoko happened to find out about her mother's death? By sheer coincidence. After all, she used to take a Tokyo newspaper. Wasn't it possible that she'd run across a little filler piece about "faulty architectural design" resulting in Mrs. Sekine's death? Not murder, but an accident or possibly suicide. Wouldn't the discovery that Shoko was now alone have been enough to make Kyoko shift her attention to her? In his mind's eye, Honma could see the crosshairs being realigned.

"I don't know what you're thinking, but how serious is this, anyway?" Behind his blank expression, Wada was getting scared.

"Could be very serious."

"But, look … I never …"

"Mr. Wada, try to remember. Did Ms. Shinjo ever go up into the mountains? Yamanashi prefecture?"

"Yamanashi?"

"That's right. Nirazaki. It's near Kofu on the Chuo Line. There's a big statue of the Goddess of Mercy there. She ever mention it to you?"

Wada's voice was thin and uncertain. "I, I believe she did."

"Yeah? How exactly do you happen to know about it?"

"Because we ... I mean I, I went there with her."

"Together?"

"For a drive, yes. Actually, that was our second trip together." He swallowed hard. "My sister's married and lives in Kofu. So I thought I'd take Kyoko to meet her. We went to Nirazaki, for the grapes."

Putting a finger to his forehead, Honma repeated, "You two went on drives together?"

"Yes."

"You were in love with Ms. Shinjo, right?"

No comment.

"If she'd had another man at the time, you would have known about it, wouldn't you? There was no sign of anyone else?"

Wada shook his head.

"You sure about that?"

"I'm sure, okay? I mean, we were ..."

"You were lovers."

Wada nodded miserably.

Kyoko had had this guy eating out of her hand. But who was the man Kaoru Sudo had mentioned? The one in the car with Kyoko when she had her accident. The one whose name she wouldn't reveal.

*Her right arm was covered with burns.*

*She was shivering.*

*The next thing she's in the bath, banging her head against the wall.*

"I was quite serious about Kyoko," said Wada, out of nowhere. "I'm sure she knew that. There couldn't have been anybody else."

Honma looked him straight in the face. "All right. I believe you." There *was* nobody else, and that was why Kyoko never came up with a name. There had been no accident on a drive in the country.

As Honma glanced over the printouts again, a shiver ran down the length of his back. On the day in question, November 19, 1989, Kyoko Shinjo had been up in Tokyo or Yokohama or Kawasaki, stalking a particular woman. The prime target hidden in these pages. Or perhaps someone close—a little too close—to her.

*Not third-degree, but covering most of her arm.*

*Her sweater got burned.*

The bottle of gasoline in the Honancho apartment. That strong smell when he picked it up. Those gleaming fan blades.

Arson.

Back in Tokyo, the next step was to talk to all the women Kyoko might once have approached. Funaki took a day off from work, and the Isakas joined in as well, searching the printout for women in their twenties.

"Say 'police' if you have to," Funaki instructed. "Ask the women listed if two years back some close relation might have met with an accident or been badly injured somehow. Get them talking, no matter what it takes."

Some had moved. Some had answering machines. Few came directly to the phone. It was nerve-racking. When it got dark, Funaki and Honma sent the Isakas home. Their voices were hoarse.

It was past eleven, time to call it a day, when they got a break.

Funaki cupped his hand over the receiver. "We're in business!" he called to Honma, who was over by the window tentatively stretching his legs. Then, speaking into the phone again, he said, "Hold on, I'll turn you over to the officer in charge."

Emi Kimura was twenty-four years old. The printout gave her occupation as "freelancer." At first she spoke in a sweet, almost child-like voice. She interrupted Honma to ask, "Is this for real? This isn't Candid Camera or something?"

"No. Look, I'm sorry to bother you like this. I don't know if you'll be able to help us or not, but let me explain. We traced you through some customer data provided by a company called Roseline. I believe you know the name?" Honma paused. "Ms. Kimura, I'm sorry, but these questions are important for an investigation we're working on.

You don't come from a large family, and you live by yourself, is that correct? And both your parents have passed on."

Emi's voice trembled. "How do you know all that?"

So far so good, Honma nodded to Funaki. "My colleague, the person you spoke to a minute ago, asked if you had any close relatives who might have had an accident or some kind of personal tragedy in the last two years. You said you had. Could you tell me more about that?"

It took a moment for Emi to answer. "It was my sister."

"Your sister."

"Ye-e-es."

Honma quietly repeated, "Yes?"

Emi was clearly getting upset. "Listen, I'm going to hang up. I mean, how do I know this isn't some kind of crank call? How do I know you're actually detectives?"

Honma hesitated. Funaki grabbed the phone away from him and rattled off the number of the direct line to Investigation. "Got that? Here's what I want you to do. Ring up and say our names. Ask if there are any detectives by those names on the force. Tell whoever answers that you need to get in touch with Inspector Honma immediately. Ask them to have him call you back as soon as he can. Only give a totally made-up name and phone number. Don't give your real ones. The officer will contact us to say you called. Then we'll call you back at your real number and give you the false name and number he tells us. Just to make sure there's no mistake, that we are who we say we are. Fair enough?"

Emi agreed and hung up.

"When you're in a hurry, take a side road," Funaki said. He reached for a cigarette and lit up. "Okay, so what we do next? If this Emi's story doesn't pan out."

Honma shook his head. "You know, I wonder. Why would she go back to square one when she had all that data? Knowing Kyoko, she would have kept detailed records. Just in case."

Funaki grunted. "Makes sense."

"Well, her most obvious choice at this point would be the person she'd opted for before and dropped. Her former number one candi-

284

date. And when we find her, we should find Kyoko as well. We're closing in on her."

"So you think Emi could actually lead us to Kyoko?"

The phone rang. It was the precinct officer on duty. "Hon? You had a call from an Akiko Sato. Said she had to get in touch with you. Urgent. I told her you were on leave, but she insisted."

It was ages since he'd heard his Division nickname—"Hon." Like something an old married couple would say.

"The phone number?"

"That's the funny thing. 5555-4444, is what she tells me. Think it's a prank?"

"It's okay. Thanks for calling." He pressed the dial tone button with his finger and redialed.

Emi picked up on the first ring. Honma kept his voice as neutral as possible. "Hello? Is that Akiko Sato? At 5555-4444?"

"You've got to wonder about that girl's powers of imagination," Funaki whispered.

But Emi Kimura was in no mood for flip remarks. She burst into tears.


"Three years ago, so that would have been 1989, sometime in late November. The nineteenth or twentieth … it was a Sunday. My sister had a terrible accident."

"Yes?…"

"It was a fire. She was badly burned. She had brain damage from all the smoke she inhaled. For a long time she was in a coma. Then last summer she finally died."

So that had been Kyoko Shinjo's big mistake. Her first choice had been Emi, and the only member of her family she'd needed to eliminate had failed to die. Sure, Kyoko could have gone ahead according to plan and taken her chances with the sister later, but the whole situation was risky. What if the sister woke up? And if Kyoko were to try again, it would be obvious that it was no accident. So she switched to someone else, someone recently orphaned.

There were still some points that needed clearing up. "Ms. Kimura, about this fire," Honma prompted.

Emi responded on cue. "We don't know how it got started, but the fire department and the police both suspected arson. There were other fires in the area around the same time. Like somebody was terrorizing the neighborhood. The story got into the news and, once that happened, the pace picked up. Everybody was getting nervous."

Honma closed his eyes. Kyoko's newspaper again, the Tokyo one. Maybe she'd read about the string of fires there and decided to take advantage of it.

"That day I had dance lessons. I just happened to be out because I was late getting home from class. My sister was in bed already and she couldn't get out in time."

Honma suspected it hadn't actually been like that; he thought the fire had achieved precisely its intended purpose, in due course. "Ms. Kimura ..." He glanced at Funaki and swallowed hard. "Around the time of the fire, or a little before, did either you or your sister make any new acquaintances?"

"You mean women friends?"

"That's right. Was there anybody?"

Emi was silent for moment. "I don't know, I forget. The whole period's kind of a blank, it was such a shock."

"I'm sure it was," Honma sympathized. "How about more recently? Have you made any new acquaintances recently?"

"New acquaintances?"

"That's right. Someone who was, say, an old friend of your sister's, or just someone asking directions who stopped to talk, or ..."

"Actually, I did."

"You met someone?" His throat tightened. "Who? Do you know the name?"

"Her name is Shinjo. Kyoko Shinjo."

"Kyoko Shinjo."

When he heard Honma repeat the name, Funaki slapped the flat of his hand against his forehead, then slowly waved one fist back and forth overhead in a silent cheer.

"Who is she? How do you know her?"

"She's a friend of my sister's. She just got in touch a few days ago."

His breathing stopped. "How's that again? 'She got in touch a few days ago'?"

"Yahoo!" Funaki was on his feet now and had actually let out a yell.

Honma lifted his good leg and mimed a swift kick at him across the room. "Sorry for all the noise. My colleague's just really pleased to have found you."

Emi sounded a bit surprised, but gave a little laugh.

"What did this Kyoko Shinjo have to say?"

"She said she hadn't heard from my sister in so long that she decided to call. When I told her my sister had died, she said she was really sorry. She wanted to pay her respects and asked me to take her to see the grave. We made an appointment to meet this Saturday afternoon, in Ginza."

Honma made the arrangements for Saturday. His next move was to go back to Utsunomiya.

On the way up there, his thoughts rocked and swayed in motion with the train. There'd been no word from Tamotsu. When he'd left Tokyo he had seemed so confident, but did he really think he could dig up every inch of the old schoolyard? Honma had even thought about putting his earthworks on hold. If they could just nab Kyoko Shinjo, the search for the corpse could wait. But there was always a slim chance …

Honma had only left a message, but as soon as he stepped through the turnstile he heard someone call his name. There across the station lobby were those familiar square shoulders, that craggy grin.

Outside, the north wind swept down over the Great Kanto Plain—piercing cold, enough to make your sinuses hurt. It was a relief to climb into the passenger seat of the Honda Motors van. For the first few minutes, Honma had to rub his knees to get his circulation going.

"I've got a few things to report—" Tamotsu began.

"Great. But let me start," Honma broke in. "We're going to meet Kyoko Shinjo this coming Saturday."

Tamotsu blinked back his amazement as Honma told him about the latest developments. Twice, Tamotsu had to tell him to slow down. Finally he pulled the van over to the shoulder and cut the engine. He was feeling jittery, he said. It was a full ten minutes before he touched the ignition again.

"Saturday, did you say? That's the day after tomorrow. Can I come along?"

"Of course."

"You remember what you said? About me talking to her first."

"I remember."

Tamotsu swung the van out across an intersection just as the light turned red. "Before we head home, I'd just like you to see the school," he said, staring straight ahead, his hands gripping the wheel. "It's over near Hachiman Yama Park."

They sped down streets that Honma remembered from his last visit there and soon came to a rise looking out over green hills in the distance. This was a city with open spaces, a luxury unheard of in Tokyo. The playground at the school Tamotsu and Shoko had gone to wasn't just some stingy little basketball hardtop, but big enough to hold a rugby match and a baseball game at the same time. The four-story gray concrete building looked far away. Rows of cherry trees reached around either wing of classrooms to circle the entire playground. The place must have looked magnificent in April.

"You could never dig up all this dirt."

A squadron of kids in maroon-colored tracksuits was out there jumping rope. Twenty or thirty of them, high school students, probably. Their instructor blew sharply on his whistle from time to time.

"I asked all my friends and we tried to recontruct how the school and the yard were when we were here," Tamotsu said, grabbing the chain-link fence with both hands.

Honma looked at him. "What d'you mean 'reconstruct'?"

"They rebuilt the whole place five years ago."

"Oh." Then anything was possible.

Tamotsu scratched his head. "They shifted the school building around, so now I can't really tell where the damn bird's grave was." He laughed out loud.

Honma looked at the young man again. What was he so happy about?

"I was thinking about giving you a call," Tamotsu said. "It's not like I came up empty-handed, I just thought I should check out a few more things first."

He went on to say that two years earlier—in the spring of 1990, at the peak of the cherry blossom season—a woman who must have been Kyoko Shinjo came to visit the schoolyard.

"Oh, really?"

Tamotsu leaned into the fence, nodding slowly. "That's right. One of the older teachers, Mrs. Kina, she was here even back when we were. She's over fifty now but she's got a card index in her head better than any librarian. She's the one who told me." She had positively ID'd Kyoko's photo, too. "Said she remembered because the girl was so beautiful."

"Where did this teacher actually see her? Did she ask what she was doing?"

"It was a Saturday afternoon. Kyoko came straight into the school-yard and walked right over there," Tamotsu said, waving one arm toward a line of cherry trees. "She hung around like she was looking at the cherry blossoms, which isn't so unusual. Lots of folks from around here, even some tourists, come for that. At first Mrs. Kina didn't think much about it. But the girl stood out there so long that she started getting worried and went over. She was wearing a black skirt and jacket, almost no makeup. Like for a funeral or something."

When the teacher approached, the young woman told her she'd lost all track of time gazing at the cherry blossoms. But there was something that didn't seem quite right, so Mrs. Kina asked what had brought her here. "And you know what she said? She was making the trip in place of a friend."

Honma looked up at the leafless tops of the cherry trees. *A trip in place of a friend.*

"Then Mrs. Kina asks if this friend is from around here. And the young woman nods, see? And—you ready for this?" Tamotsu took a deep breath. "She says that the friend had attended this exact same school, and had really loved it. The friend had mentioned something about burying a pet bird out on the playground. But this woman, of course, has no idea just where." Kyoko had come, in Shoko's place, to retrace the past.

"So Mrs. Kina starts to get suspicious and asks a few more questions. Where is this friend, why didn't she come herself?" The young woman didn't answer at first, but finally admitted that her friend was dead.

Honma stood right next to Tamotsu, their shoulders practically touching. Kids were dashing about, doing some athletic drill. Honma could almost feel the smell of the earth seep inside him.

"I guess I didn't do too bad, huh?" said Tamotsu, pushing himself away from the fence. "I was thinking about talking to the principal and the PTA, to get permission to dig up the yard. It's worth a try. I bet this Kyoko woman did come here to bury Shoko. If we searched, we might just find her."

The ground at their feet was beaten down, hard and dry. Honma leaned into the fence, gripping the steel mesh with the tips of his fingers. "All right, so Kyoko Shinjo did come here," he said, choosing his words carefully. "But still, I don't think your Shoko is anywhere hereabouts."

Tamotsu looked him full in the face. "Why not? But I thought, since you bothered to come all the way up here—"

"She *couldn't* bury her here. What I mean is, maybe she *intended* to, but there was no way—it would have been too risky. This is a schoolyard, after all. Somebody would have seen something. My guess is she came and looked it over, and saw it wouldn't work."

"But hey …"

Honma went on, keeping his voice quite calm. "Kyoko Shinjo, as near as I can figure, must have gotten rid of Shoko's head in the safest location she could find, somewhere else. It just stands to reason. Of course she never expected the Nirazaki remains to come to light. She probably thought they'd just get hauled off to some garbage dump."

Tamotsu stood stock still. A whistle sounded and the tracksuits scrambled up to a starting line.

"She wanted to get rid of the head someplace where it wouldn't be discovered. Once she'd done that, she came here to bury Shoko's memory. She couldn't rest till she'd been where Shoko as good as asked to be buried." The same way that Makoto and Kazzy had buried Blockhead's memory.

Springtime, petals clinging to her hair, Kyoko had come and stood beneath these cherry trees. Was it her way of begging Shoko's forgiveness? Was it so important to see, just once, the bed where Shoko's childhood slept?

*Her friend was dead.*

"Okay, then, where *is* Shoko's head buried? Where *did* she put it?" Tamotsu said plaintively.

There was only one person who could tell them for certain.

The whistle blew again. Its sound froze in the cold, clear air as the runners set off, straining slightly against the wind.

"Let's get back to Tokyo," Honma said. "We've got a date to keep."

## ✧ 29 ✧

The Italian restaurant where Emi Kimura had agreed to meet Kyoko Shinjo was technically in Ginza, but well away from the heart of the shopping district. Maybe that was why it could afford to be so spacious. It had a high ceiling, a mezzanine level, and a round sunken area right in the center of the room. The meeting was set for 1:00 P.M. It was now 12:45.

"You don't have to hang around if you don't want to," Honma had told Emi. "We'll know her when we see her."

But she wouldn't hear of it. "I'm a little scared, I admit, but if she's the one you think may have killed my sister, I want to see her for myself."

"Just act normal," Honma had coached her. Emi was sitting at a table near the middle of the sunken floor area. The wait was making her nervous. She pressed a hand to her chest as if to keep her heart still. She hardly touched her cappuccino.

Honma and Tamotsu had stationed themselves at a side table on the main level right next to the stairs, overlooking the lower area. They hadn't touched their coffee either, although Tamotsu was on his second glass of water.

"I get to talk to her, right?" Tamotsu said for the umpteenth time.

"Yes," said Honma. "So what are you going to say?"

Tamotsu lowered his eyes. "I don't know."

Funaki was sitting on the far side of the main floor, holding up a newspaper spread wide open and wearing a dark suit that stood out in the bright interior. He was on his second cup of coffee.

The restaurant had two entrances. Whichever one she used, they'd spot her. They'd also be watching to see if she tried to bolt back out of either of those doors.

Honma hadn't slept much the night before. He had stayed up going over every detail with Funaki. There was no tangible proof yet, no body, just one woman missing and another posing as her. Possible motives for murder, but method and weapon still unknown. Circumstantial evidence was all well and good, but speculation had its limits.

As Funaki had said, "No judge is going to buy this. Where's our case?"

"Well, you never know."

"Without so much as a fingerprint? How far can we stretch eyewitness testimony?"

"We could rough up our witnesses a bit. 'Out with it. And only the things we want to hear, now!'"

Funaki smirked. "It doesn't seem to bother you. You're just happy to have found her."

Sunlight slanted across the parquet floor. Sitting here now, Honma had to admit Funaki was probably right. Never once during any of his previous cases had he felt so relaxed. He felt no bitterness, no grim determination. The fact was, Honma wasn't at all sure what he would say if he were the one to meet her first. All he could think of were questions.

*Are you planning to keep doing this over and over? Just because you blew it with Shoko Sekine, are you really going to backtrack to Emi Kimura? What then? A quick exit from Tokyo, where there's always a chance you might run into Jun?*

Or should he ask what she'd done with Shoko Sekine's head? Or how she felt when Jun first told her about Shoko's bankruptcy? Mitchie at Imai Office Machines was anxious to see her again, Mr. Imai was worried too, should he tell her that? Should he mention the way that Jun's teeth had chattered that first night when he came by and explained the situation?

*The only thing I know for sure is you'll never have another crack at turning yourself into anyone else. You're Kyoko Shinjo, period. The same way that Shoko Sekine never became anyone else, no matter how much she longed to.*

This off-white and Naples-yellow place wasn't somewhere people like Funaki, Tamotsu and himself belonged in. The waiters passing by, the young couples seated at the other tables, all said so with their eyes. *Will you think so, too?* Honma searched out Kyoko's face in his mind. *Will you set one foot in the door and sense that something's out of place? Will you catch on immediately and start running again?*

*It would almost be easier for us if you did run. Then we'd know for sure it was all true.*

"There she is," Tamotsu said quietly. He straightened up, his back tense.

Across the room Honma saw Funaki lower his newspaper slightly as a sky-blue hooded coat swung by him. There could be no mistake. It was her.

Her hairstyle was different. Earrings flashed beneath shoulder-length waves of hair. She rode forward on long legs, brushing between the tables, neither avoiding the waiters' looks nor trying to play down her own height.

She stopped and looked around. Even from this distance, Honma could appreciate her looks: the delicate nose, the slightly pursed lips, the hint of rose blush on her pale cheeks. Not a trace of suffering, not a shadow of loneliness showed in her face. She was beautiful.

Her gaze settled on Emi Kimura and she raised a hand in greeting. Emi responded, half rising from her seat and waving back. Not a glance at Honma or Funaki.

Kyoko approached: down the steps, skirting the next table, coat hem swaying. Emi smiled.

Kyoko took off her coat and draped it over an empty chair. She put her bag down and took the seat across from Emi. She was wearing a white sweater. A brooch sparkled at her throat. As she settled in, making herself more comfortable, the brooch nestled into the folds of the sweater.

Kyoko had her back to Honma and Tamotsu. She was wearing rings on both hands, but there was no sign of Jun's sapphire.

The waiter brought menus. She and Emi flipped them open simultaneously and laughed. Emi's smile was a bit forced, perhaps.

"You were going to talk to her, right?" Honma said.

Tamotsu rose, keeping his eyes fixed on the young woman's back. He moved forward automatically, as if drawn by an invisible pulley. He walked stiffly down the stairs. The other customers paused, holding their forks in the air. Conversations stopped, glasses of wine caught the light and grew still, and the eyes of everyone in the room seemed to rest on Tamotsu's broad shoulders.

On the far side of the room, Funaki started moving slowly toward the opposite stairs. Honma stood up and hovered beside his own table. He could only see Kyoko from the back but stared intently at her as she talked with Emi. This was her, all right; she was as charming as everyone had said.

Tamotsu reached the bottom step and started toward her table. Emi remained remarkably poised, never once looking at him. Her eyes were filled with the stars in Kyoko's earrings, the line of her shoulders.

*My questions don't matter. I want to hear your story. The parts you've never told anyone, the lives you carry everywhere with you. The months in hiding, the interest you've been quietly compounding.*

*There will be plenty of time, Kyoko.*

*Starting from now, as Tamotsu's hand comes to rest on your shoulder.*